Copyright © B. Baskerville 2018

All rights reserved. No part of this publication may be reproduced or transmitted without the written permission of the author.

This is a work of fiction. Any resemblance to actual persons is coincidental.

Cover design copyright © B. Baskerville 2018

ISBN: 9781729405574

CW01212955

□●○⊙╳■▲✗■●●✖□○○╳■□△✗✗△◉╳■▲✖■

□○▲╳╳▲⊙⊙⊙✖○✖○△✗✗○╳╳▩◉▩✖▲✖◉◉

◉✖□△◯◯◯╳△✗■□

- CHAPTER 1 -

Kris Kava massaged his face. He'd broken up eight fights that evening and had received a punch in the teeth for his efforts. Kris was rapidly concluding that working as a doorman at a crappy pub in the Meadow Well estate was not worth its minimum wage rewards.

It was three in the morning when Kris left his post to walk the short distance home. As always, he made sure no one was following him. In this estate, chucking the wrong person out of the wrong pub could land you in the bad books of some powerful people.

It was a windy, balmy night and the streets of North Tyneside's Meadow Well were deserted. The only sound Kris could make out was the distance tyre screeches of a car being taken for a joyride.

'Scumbags,' he muttered to himself. Kris's accent gave away nothing of his Polish birth. It was instead, the unusual mix of a Londoner who'd spent years living in the north.

Ahead, a wheelie bin toppled in the wind and vomited its contents into the road. An empty can of lager rolled the length of Padstow Road and came to rest at

Kris's foot. He kicked it into the kerb and checked behind him once more. The coast was still clear, no one was following him, but ahead, someone was waiting.

Kris squinted towards his house. A shadowy figure crouched by his door. *Great.* It was either someone with a grudge, or cousin Vinny had gotten himself into trouble again and had fled the capital for the anonymity of the north-east.

You can't pick your family, Kris thought to himself. He slowed his steps and hugged the shadows, using parked cars for cover. But as he neared his house the shiver that ran down his spine subsided and it became apparent that the figure huddled in Kris's doorway wasn't a man at all. A short, scantily-clad girl stared up at him from his doorstep.

'Hey, Kris.'

Athena Fox was a petite powerhouse. A flimsy, silvery dress clung to muscular thighs and shimmered in the orange glow of a street lamp. Athena pulled herself to her feet and staggered on ridiculously high heels. Her short, blonde hair billowed about in the breeze and she had a nose that was so squashed it was easy to tell she'd broken it at least twice.

Kris blinked at her. He took in her grazed knees, the bruising forming on her biceps and a trail of dried blood that ran from her hairline down to her jawbone. She reeked of wine and menthol cigarettes.

'Foxy, you're bleeding,' said Kris, 'and drunk. What the hell happened?'

He systematically opened the many locks to his door and ushered Athena inside. It had been twenty-five years since the Meadow Well riots but the estate was still a no-go area for many. Whilst some residents were ashamed to see their estate burn on national television, torched by its own inhabitants, others saw it as a status symbol. To be from the Meadows meant you were hard. No one messed with Meadows folk. And here was Athena, roaming the streets after dark, wearing next to nothing and with enough alcohol in her system to make a pirate proud. Could Athena be the only woman in the north who hadn't noticed the spate of unsolved sexual assaults that were all over the news?

'I'm not drunk,' said Athena, with an upperclass inflection. 'You're just blurry.'

Kris locked his door, slotted two bolts into place and secured the chain. He turned back to the blonde and watched a trickle of blood flow from her knee to her ankle.

'Don't bleed on my carpet.'

Athena rolled her eyes. 'You must be the only bouncer on Tyneside with haemophobia.'

She bent over to remove her heels, allowing Kris a quick glimpse of a silk covered crotch. Then she made her way to the living room and searched for a place to sit between piles of junk mail and dirty laundry.

'What happened, Foxy?' repeated Kris. 'Why are you on my doorstep at three in the effin' morning?'

She was no more than five-foot-three and a half and she stood with her arms outstretched as if to say, *isn't it obvious*. 'I got into a fight. D'uh.'

Kris shrugged and abandoned Athena in favour of putting the kettle on. Athena Fox getting into a drunken fight wasn't exactly out of character. The woman was a walking time bomb.

From the kitchen, Kris could hear hiccoughing and muttered complaints that he hadn't tidied up.

'I would have if I'd known your drunken, beat-up arse was going to turn up at this hour,' he grumbled to himself.

'There was this awful woman,' started Athena, over the noise of the kettle. 'You know the sort. Wearing a top two sizes too small. Going on and on about how I must totally love myself because I'm like famous or something.'

'But you do totally love yourself,' laughed Kris.

'I know that. You know that. Daft chavs in badly fitting clothes don't know that. Anyway, words were exchanged,' she paused to inspect a fingernail, 'and things just got a little out of hand.'

A little? Sure. Kris finished making the tea and returned to the living room where he also handed Athena a couple of antiseptic wipes and some plasters.

'Thanks,' said Athena, opening the wipes.

Kris watched her wince as the alcohol stung her wounds. 'Looks like she gave you a run for your money.'

Athena narrowed her beautiful, pale-green eyes at him. Even in this state, with wine breath and grazed knees, he thought she was captivating.

'Er, no. She did not give me a run for my money and neither did her fat mate. Or her fat mate's fatter mate for that matter. Anyway, that creepy bouncer, the one with the missing tooth and the watery eyes? He picked me up like I weighed half a kilo and dumped me outside the club. My key must have fallen out. I didn't realise until I got back to mine.'

Once Athena had finished dressing her wounds, Kris cupped her chin in his hands.

'You're not going to try and kiss me, are you?' she asked. 'Because you know my rule about Polish boys.'

'Yeah, yeah,' said Kris with a yawn. 'Sit still while I check your pupils.'

Athena squirmed free. 'Fret not, Florence Nightingale. I don't have a concussion.'

Unconvinced, Kris took a sip of tea. 'So, you lost your key? That still doesn't explain why you're on *my* doorstep.'

Athena looked away and there was a slight pause before she answered bluntly. 'Where else would I go?' She shrugged and turned her attention to the blank television screen.

Kris felt his heart tear in two. She was right. Where would she go? Who else could she turn to?

Athena yawned. Her blinks were becoming longer and her eyes were glossy. Kris sat in silence for a moment, allowing Athena to be alone with her thoughts until one of her blinks was so long her cup of tea almost slipped out of her hands.

'Bedtime,' said Kris, getting to his feet. He took Athena's hand and led her upstairs, listening to the sound of her beaded bag bouncing on each step as she dragged it behind her. He laid her in his bed, knelt beside it and tucked the duvet around her.

Athena looked at Kris out of one eye and reached out to stroke a scar above his right eyebrow.

'You're very handsome.'

'You're very drunk.'

'I could kiss you,' she said with a giggle.

'And I'd let you if you weren't suffering from a head injury.'

'But we can't...'

'I know. No Polish boys.'

Then, with a violent twitch of her leg, Athena fell asleep.

Kris pushed himself back to standing and looked down at his bedroom floor. The contents of Athena's bag had spilt out. Amongst her makeup and loose change, a shabby grey notepad had fallen open. Kris picked it up and scowled at the writing. It was utter gobbledegook. Complete nonsense. Page after page was filled with squares, circles, triangles, and crosses. Kris flicked through the pages hoping to find a key or some other explanation but there were no words, only shapes.

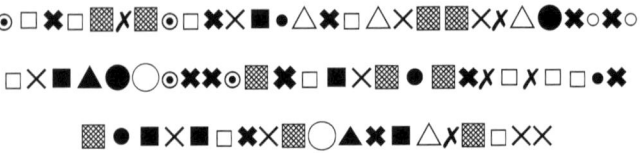

⊙□✖□▩✗▩⊙□✖✕■•△✖□△✕▩▩✕✗△●✖○✖○

□✕■▲●◯⊙✖✖⊙▩✖□■✕▩●▩✖✗□✗□□•✖

▩●■✕■□✖✕▩◯▲✖■△✗▩□✕✕

'Foxy,' he whispered, nudging her shoulder. 'Foxy, what is this?'

Athena opened one eye and shut it again. 'It's Molly's suicide note.'

- CHAPTER 2 -

Athena Fox awoke in the darkness with a tightness in her chest. She couldn't breathe, it was as if a giant snake had coiled around her ribs. *Calm down*, she told herself, *it was just a dream*. But it wasn't *just* a dream. It was a recurring nightmare. A morgue. Three bodies. Sheets being pulled back. And a man in a white coat nodding as two young women identified the bodies.

Calm down, she told herself again. She took a deep breath and then the mother of all hangovers kicked in.

Athena's mouth was arid and her tongue clung to her palette like a limpid to a rock. The taste of cigarettes and greasy pizza lingered at the back of her throat and it felt as if someone was hammering her eye sockets with a pneumatic drill. Burying her face in the pillow, she inhaled but something didn't smell right. This was not her bedroom.

What loser was it this time? He was probably making her breakfast and drumming up the courage to ask if he could see her again. Athena was not in the mood for awkward morning-after conversation, not with this hangover. *If your mother could see you now... Oh please, my mother would be a fine one to talk.*

Athena never used to make a habit of waking up in stranger's beds. She'd had the same steady boyfriend through year eleven, sixth form and university, She'd been a devoted and adoring girlfriend to a pathetic, unfaithful, waste of space called Owen. But these days, the thought of returning to her empty house had led her to make some questionable decisions. The memory of a narcissistic nineteen-year-old Newcastle United prodigy came to mind.

Pushing herself up to seated, Athena became aware that it wasn't only her head that was aching. Her torso was tender and her shins throbbed. Trying not to aggravate the contents of her stomach - which could come back up at any moment - she reached across the bed and flicked on the bedside lamp. The room was littered with cans of Lynx deodorant and copies of Men's Health magazine, and beneath a pile of laundry, Athena could spy a set of heavy dumbbells.

Why was she so sore? She could remember sipping basil and plum caiprinihas in The Botanist and there was a vague memory of standing outside Perdu bar and laughing at a stag party who were dressed as Oompa Loompas. She had definitely downed tequila slammers whilst dancing to Pharell. Sadly, the rest was a drunken blur.

Athena bent over the side of the bed to retrieve her bag and pop today's contraceptive pill. Her heart began to race once she realised there was no sign of the little grey notepad. *No, no, no, no, NO!* Where was it? She tore the bed sheets from her and jumped out of bed. Her bruised shins caught the bed frame and she cursed in an affluent accent that seemed at odds with her appearance. On her hands and knees, Athena searched under the bed as a feeling of hopelessness overcame her. Under the bed was as cluttered as the rest of the room. Athena tossed t-shirts and pairs of socks about but the notepad was nowhere to be seen. Something about one of the t-shirts caught her eye. Athena uncrumpled it and frowned at the logo.

'The Pit?' she asked herself. The Pit was a gym, one Athena knew like the back of her hand. She practically lived there.

Kris? Krzysztof Kava? The relief that she hadn't hooked up with one of the Oompa Loompas caused Athena to vomit a tiny amount of partially digested pizza and pinot into her mouth. She swallowed it back down and grimaced.

Athena opened a drawer and helped herself to one of Kris's t-shirts. She pushed her dress into her bag and pulled the t-shirt down low enough to cover her behind. She peered into the hallway. *Well, this is going to make training awkward,* she told herself. *You're an idiot. You'll have no friends left at this rate.* Athena edged her way down the staircase. She could hear the radio, and Kris singing - badly - along to it.

Naked, other than his black Calvin Kleins and a pair of Marigold rubber gloves, Kris stood at the kitchen sink. He sang along to the radio as he washed dishes, oblivious to Athena's watchful eye. Krzysztof Kava was, though she hated to admit it, unquestionably attractive. Not sexy in a boy band way. If you could even call that sexy. There was no fake tan or waxed chest here and the tall Pole wouldn't be seen dead in skinny jeans or a v-neck. Kris was a primitive sort of sexy. At six-foot-three his frame was almost as impressive as the inkwork that went into his elaborate leg tattoos. His muscles weren't formed from a cocktail of steroids and a few bench presses. They were formed from a lifetime of intense training, running sprints and eating clean. His hair was auburn, scruffy, and just asking to have Athena's fingers run through it.

'Love me, love me,' sang Kris to himself.

'Morning,' smirked Athena.

Kris jumped and came close to smacking his head off the ceiling. 'Jesus, Foxy. You scared me half to death.'

'Sorry,' laughed Athena. She pulled at the hem of his t-shirt. 'So, last night... Did we...?' She shifted her weight as colour flooded her cheeks. 'You know... Oh, don't make me say it for Christ's sake, Kris.'

Kris put down his scourer. 'No,' he answered. 'But you wanted to.' Kris pointed at Athena with a Marigold clad finger, a proud glint in his eye.

'Liar.'

'I'm not lying. You were all *ooh Krzysztof I want to kiss you, you are so handsome*, and I was like *no Foxy, you are drunk* —'

'OK, OK, I don't need to hear any more.' It was a relief. It was a stupid rule of Athena's that she never dated Polish boys. She knew the odds of Kris - or any random pole - turning out to be her half-brother were minuscule, but she wasn't going to take the chance.

Athena was not going to be the sort of woman you read about in trashy magazines who unwittingly married her brother and ended up with a bunch of cross-eyed offspring. Of course, her no Polish boys rule could be an extension of her commitment-phobic attitude after the whole Owen thing, but who wanted to analyse that with a hangover?

Athena opened Kris's fridge, picked up a carton of orange juice, peered at the expiry date and thought better of it. 'Anyway, moving on,' said Athena, giving her temples a rub. 'Have you seen a notepad? It's important. It's grey and kind of old—'

'This one?' Kris held it up in his soap covered gloves.

'Don't get it wet,' snapped Athena, tearing it from his hands. She flicked through the pages and then held it to her chest. 'What happened last night?' she asked. 'And why am I bruised?'

'You don't remember?'

Athena shook her head.

Kris removed his rubber gloves and handed Athena a cup of tea. 'All I know is you turned up here at three in the morning, having walked through Meadow Well dressed like a short-supermodel. Not your brightest idea. And you were talking about getting into a fight with a couple of fat chavs, your words, not mine, because they dared to question the humbleness of the famous Athena Fox.' He took a sip of his tea. 'And apparently, you lost your key during the scuffle, didn't realise until you got back to yours so you walked here in your ridiculous heels.'

'Hey! Don't diss the heels.'

'And,' continued Kris with caution, 'before you fell asleep you told me that...' he nodded at Athena's hands, 'was Molly's suicide note.'

'I did?'

'Yeah.'

'Well, yeah, I think it is. It's some kind of code. I found it not long after I found...' She stopped herself. 'After she died.'

Athena slumped on to the sofa. A huge hole in her heart opened up when she thought of Molly, her sister. She remembered her gorgeous face, glowing beige skin, cute freckles, and bee-stung lips. She thought of Molly's thick brown curls and doe-like eyes. She was slender and graceful. The opposite of Athena. If Molly were a feather floating effortlessly on the breeze, Athena was a cannonball.

She tucked her feet up under herself and felt her hands begin to tremble. Her mind was going someplace dark.

'Hey,' said Kris nudging her on the knee and bringing her focus back to the present. 'Don't go there.'

Athena shook her head and gathered herself. 'I can't read it though,' she said, handing Kris the notepad. 'It's consumed me. But look,' she turned to one of the last pages and pointed to small watermarks. 'Tear stains. She was crying when she wrote these last few pages. And look how shaky her handwriting it. Whatever she wrote in here, it might tell me why she killed herself.'

△⊙⊙⊙×△×▪⊙▪× ×○× ×□ ▫ ×▲⊙◯⊙×⊙▪×

▲×△⊙× ×▪▪×□△×▪△× ×

Kris looked intently at the notepad, then back at Athena. 'Do we need to call a locksmith?'

'I've got a spare key at The Pit. Don't suppose you'd give me a lift?'

'What?' asked Kris, his voice laced with irony. 'You don't want to walk there in your perfectly, practical shoes?'

- CHAPTER 3 -

Kris's V reg Golf contained at least three empty Costa Coffee cups and five empty bottles of water. They rolled around Athena's feet as Kris set off east, slightly above the speed limit and left Meadow Well for the neighbouring area of North Shields. They passed shoppers, dog walkers, and churchgoers before turning left as the mouth of the Tyne came into view. Housed in an old industrial unit halfway up the bank from the mouth of the river was The Pit, the north-east's premier mixed martial arts gym. Established in 1998, The Pit, named after its former life as a garage, was ahead of its time and churned out some of the country's top talent. Kris parked his car and grinned at Athena.

'Good luck.'

'Why do I need luck?'

'Luke opened up today.'

Athena groaned at looked to the heavens. She loved Luke, he was the big brother she never had, but it wouldn't be an understatement to say that he could be too much when you had a hangover. It was time to employ some serious ninja skills. Could she get in and get out without Luke spotting her?

'OI, OI,' boomed Luke when Athena closed the door to The Pit behind her.

Damn it.

'Do my eyes deceive me? Or, did young Athena Fox just get out of Krzysztof Kava's car wearing one of his t-shirts?'

Luke Mar was a giant of a man, tanned from head to toe with short curly black hair that had the chemical smell of Just For Men hair dye. Today, like most days, he was topless, showing off his huge upper body to no one other than his own reflection. He wore turquoise shorts that were too short for this decade and a matching sweatband sat lopsided around his head. He bounced across the gym, jumping on a swivel chair from the main desk and gliding the rest of the way. 'I smell gossip,' He beamed as the chair came to a stop in front of Athena. 'Do tell.'

Athena sighed, shook her head and manoeuvred her way around Luke. 'I know how it looks, but there's nothing to tell.'

Rubbing her temples, Athena moved to a white, box-style shelving unit at the far end of the gym. She pulled a wicker basket from one of the dockets and fished through old socks and emergency tampons until she found her spare key. Charlie Fisher, the club's owner, had got so sick of his fighters leaving their crap all over the gym that he'd invested in the shelving unit. If your belongings weren't in your docket by locking up time they were as good as in the bin.

It took Athena over ten minutes to escape from Luke Mar's interrogation about everything that did or did not happen last night. She'd even suffered the indignity of having to twirl for him in Kris's oversized t-shirt because evidently, she could, 'Work it, sister.'

'Was that as brutal as I imagine?' asked Kris when Athena returned to the car.

'Worse,' she replied, tugging at her seatbelt. 'Apparently, we'd have the cutest babies.'

'We would.'

Athena shot him a look before burying her face in her hands.

Kris started the engine. 'Where to m'lady?'

'Camp Terrace,' she muttered through her palms. 'Head towards the Gunner and turn left before the crossroads.'

Five minutes later and Kris had turned through the ornate wooden gates that marked the entrance to the quiet Georgian serenity of Camp Terrace. He got out of his car and stood in the glaring sun, staring up at the impressive terraced house, his mouth hanging open.

'Jeez Foxy, Charlie said you had a big house but…'

Stone steps and iron railings led up to a shiny black door that was flanked by thick stone pillars. Athena turned her keys through various locks and walked into the double fronted, six bedroom house only to be almost bowled over by a huge ball of white fur.

'Argh! Down, Simba!' yelled Athena, as a sixty-kilogram Akita stood on its hind legs and licked her face. 'Outside Simba. Wee wee!'

The dog bounded past her to the garden, found his favourite tree and relieved himself. Athena wiped a trail of glistening dog saliva from her face and looked at Kris. He was still stood on the street in awe, looking back and forth between the remarkable building and her red Audi TT convertible that was parked by the door. Athena had often witnessed the look of wonder that passed over people's faces when they entered the Camp Terrace property but it still agitated her. Their looks of envy made her feel like a fraud, after all, she hadn't earned this, she wasn't the one who had paid off the mortgage.

'Stop gawping and come in,' she snapped. 'I'm going to make us some breakfast.' Athena turned and walked to her kitchen, closely followed by Kris and the hungry dog.

Kris busied himself exploring the ground floor. His feet tapped on the hardwood flooring, the occasional board of which would creek under his weight. He looked up at the ceiling roses and coving, ran his hands over the marble fireplaces, and played with the latches on the old sash windows. Meanwhile, the mammoth Akita sat at Athena's heels awaiting his scrambled eggs.

When Athena emerged from her kitchen carrying two omelettes and two cups of tea she found Kris staring at an old family photograph that sat in a display cabinet.

He pointed at a slender girl with dark curly hair and caramel skin. 'Is this Molly?'

Athena placed the plates and cutlery on her twelve seater dining table and joined Kris at the display cabinet.

'Yeah, that's Molly,' she answered. 'And that's Mum, Nana, and that's Gramps,' she added, pointing to her family members in turn. Her mother had the same poker straight golden hair as Athena, only much, much longer. 'And the short fatty,' said Athena, pointing to the last family member, 'the one refusing to smile for the photograph, is me.'

Kris took the china cup from Athena and sipped his tea. 'Wow, talk about chalk and cheese.' His eye's flicked from the stubborn looking blonde to the elegant dark girl. 'Tell me to mind my own business, Foxy, but Molly was adopted, right?'

The sound of the Akita burping echoed through from the kitchen.

'No, she's my sister,' answered Athena. 'Sorry, she *was* my sister, my half-sister. My dad's Polish, her dad was black.'

A haunting image of Molly's cold waxy skin and lifeless eyes forced its way back into Athena's mind and she turned to the window to try and shake it.

Sitting down to eat, Athena and Kris took turns flicking through the pages of Molly's notepad, munching on their mushroom and ham omelettes without saying a word until Kris piped up. 'Do you think the little crosses are vowels? There are loads of them. Maybe an A or an E?'

'Maybe,' replied Athena, finishing the last mouthful of her breakfast. The omelette had done wonders for her sore head and fragile stomach and she felt a lot more prepared to face another day of grief. 'There's loads of the little circles with dots in them too. I thought they were As or Es. But look here,' she pointed to the third line on the page, 'it goes circle with a dot, little cross, circle with a dot. That would be A, E, A or E, A, E. I already used a Scrabble app online and there aren't many words using those letters, unless she was saying "Simba has been defleaed."'

Kris itched himself behind his ear and pulled the notepad back towards him. 'And here, it would be E, E, E.' He pointed to three circles with dots inside. 'Unless it was one word ending in two Es and the next word starting with an E?'

Athena's head fell back and she breathed out forcefully. 'This is impossible!' she growled up at the chandelier. 'There's no spaces, no punctuation.'

Kris inclined his head to one side so that the light from the window highlighted the little scar above his eyebrow. 'Well, if I was going to go to the effort of creating a secret code, I wouldn't want to make it too easy to crack.'

Athena forced herself to tear her eyes away from Kris's handsome face. 'True.' she concurred, wiping her palm over her forehead and feeling the slime of stubborn, day-old makeup mixed with sweat on her cheeks. 'Listen,' she continued, 'I need a shower. I need to scrub away about ten layers of skin and check out all of these bruises. Feel free to keep looking at that damn code,' she said, 'if you don't have to rush off that is.'

'I'm due at The Pit at one. Said I'd train with Big Ahmed. I can stay until then if you like,' he said. 'I'll do some googling, see if there's anything online about weird circle-square-triangle codes.'

Athena gave a slight nod with her lips pressed tightly together, and without saying a word she turned and made her way up the stairs to her bathroom. As a teenager, she always had to adjust the settings upon getting in the shower. There used to be five people over three generations living here and each of them liked the shower set to a different temperature. Now there was only Athena and the shower was always set to cold.

Alone and naked, as the icy water poured over her, Athena allowed herself to cry. Pictures of Molly fleeted in and out of Athena's mind. Molly laughing on her sixteenth birthday. Molly, aged seven, climbing a tree. Molly's ballet recital, aged twelve. Molly dead. The shock of it. Time standing still and the feeling that it wasn't real. The smell. That God awful smell. Athena squeezed her eyes closed and hit the heel of her palm into the side of her head over and over. She sank down and sat on the floor of the shower cubicle, wrapped her arms around her legs and sobbed into her knees.

- CHAPTER 4 -

A stooped man in a dirty camouflage jacket and scuffed jeans sat upon a toppled gravestone from 1812. Sunbeams penetrated the tall oaks and cast a glowing spotlight on the destitute man. He looked to be in his late sixties but it could be down to his matted grey hair and weathered face. The man avoided looking up from his laceless boots as he sipped the last dregs of a can of lager. The dog walkers and weeping visitors of Preston Cemetery gave the man a wide birth, avoiding eye contact and trying not to take in the strong smell of body odour and Special Brew.

'Eugh, he stinks,' said a greasy-haired teenager. She pinched her nose. 'You stink, you know that?'

The girl's friends giggled, egging on their queen bee. The man shuffled around, turning his back on the tormentors.

'You're supposed to look at people when they talk to you.'

The giggles escalated into cackles.

'Are you autistic or something? On the spectrum? Imagine that Megan, imagine being a stinky, homeless, spaz— HEY!'

Athena - who had seen quite enough - grabbed the doughy girl, lifted her a few inches, and threw her into her friends. 'Get out of here,' she spat. 'Clear off.'

The teens assessed Athena and decided not to chance it. They sauntered away shouting insults over their shoulders.

'Tramp lover!'

'Watch your back, blondie.'

'Yeah, we'll be back.'

Athena approached the man and placed a hand on his shoulder. 'You all right, Harry?' she asked.

Simba, the sixty-kilo white Akita, bounded over to lick the man's face and hands.

His eyes sparkled when he saw Simba. 'Good boy, good boy,' he mumbled, scratching Simba behind the ears and under his fluffy chin.

They made an odd pair: the muscular blonde in designer jeans and the vagabond in his stained combat gear.

'I brought you something,' said Athena, rummaging in an Armani messenger bag that hung across her chest.

'Good boy - oh you shouldn't have darlin', you really shouldn't have - good boy.'

Harry was the only man Athena could ever tolerate calling her darling.

'Here, I picked these up yesterday but you'd gone when I left the co-op.'

'You're an angel, you know that darling?' murmured Harry as he examined a pack of wet wipes, a tuna sandwich, a pack of apple slices and a plastic tub of multivitamins. He opened the wet wipes and cleaned his neck and brow. 'Oh, that feels wonderful. Absolute angel.'

Simba defecated on the pathway.

'I'm not an angel,' said Athena, curtsying with a poop bag over her hand. 'I'm a goddess.'

Harry winked and leaned in. 'Well, I am eternally indebted to you, my goddess.'

'Urgh! Simba, what *have* you been eating?' asked Athena as she tidied up after the Akita, wincing at the stench. 'No Harry,' she continued, 'I'm the one who's eternally indebted. Remember?'

Harry joined Athena and the pair looked down and paid their respects to the Fox family grave. 'I remember,' he said solemnly, placing his hand on her shoulder. 'You take care of yourself, girl. Promise me.'

Athena's eyes turned glassy. She placed her hand on Harry's arm and smiled at him. 'I promise. You stay safe, you hear me?'

'I always do.'

Athena strolled away through the sunny cemetery with Simba by her side. His fur bounced with each step as if he had no idea of the sorrow this place emitted. They continued out the back of the cemetery and followed Beach Road all the way to the coast, occasionally checking behind for vengeful teenage girls.

The sun sparkled cheerfully on the water. Children skipped hand in hand holding ice creams and seagulls lurked in the hope of stealing chips from unsuspecting tourists. Athena's mind was too busy to involve herself in the merriment of the hot summer day. Her brain was awash with small circles, large circles, triangles, and squares.

In the week since she had awoken in Kris's bed they had met up twice to solve the mystery of Molly's code and twice they had drawn blanks. There were five varieties of squares, three types of crosses, three sorts of triangles, and four types of circles. That meant there were only fifteen symbols altogether. Even when Kris had suggested over a pint on Wednesday evening that they could discount some lesser used letters like Q, X, and Z, it still meant that there were too few symbols for the code to be English.

Athena and Simba continued walking south along the coast, enjoying the sea breeze until they reached the ruins of the Benedictine Priory and Tynemouth Castle. Sitting dramatically atop of Pen Bal Crag, and overlooking both the North Sea and the Tyne, the remnants of the priory looked magnificent against the cloudless sky.

Simba jerked against his leash, trying to chase four seagulls that were feasting on an abandoned battered cod. Athena almost toppled over as she struggled to restrain his might.

'Looks like your dog's taking you for a walk,' chortled a squat man with three chins and pink wobbling jowls. Beside him sat a perfectly obedient miniature poodle. Athena repressed the urge to let Simba swallow the little dog whole and instead gave a sarcastic laugh. No time for idiots today.

If the code wasn't English, thought Athena as she turned into wealthy Tynemouth Village, it could be code for another language. Molly had studied Japanese and Korean at school but as far as Athena could remember, they were only short courses, she hadn't sat exams in either language.

Athena tied Simba to a lamppost and popped into The Wine Chambers to pick up a bottle of Chilean white. While waiting to pay she pulled out her phone and googled *Japanese alphabet.* There were forty-six characters in each of the two Japanese writing systems and several thousand kanji.

By the time they made it home, Athena and Simba had walked almost five miles. This was no big deal for Athena who could run the route in under forty minutes but Simba was in need of a bucket full of water and a lie down on the cold kitchen tiles.

Athena busied herself for the next few hours. She did not like to be idle at home as the silence of the big empty house could quickly overwhelm her. She synced her phone to the house speakers and filled the building with the sounds of Chopin and Debussy. The notepad was sat on the grandiose dining table where she had left it. Scraps of crumpled paper were strewn across the table, each piece covered in Athena's neat and looping handwriting where she'd tried to decipher the meaning of the coded shapes. Athena scooped up the papers and tidied them into a neat pile. Next, she dusted the vast building from top to bottom and mopped the wooden floors. She had done the very same tasks the day before last, but lately, Athena had never been able to get the floors clean enough.

Simba peeled himself from the kitchen floor, the fur around his mouth still wet from where he had gulped water from his bowl. He curled himself into a ball on an old Chesterfield in the lounge. Here he would sleep for the rest of the day.

Once Athena had cleaned the already clean house, she sat next to Simba, opened her laptop and searched for languages with fifteen letters. An island in Papa New Guinea had a language consisting of only twelve letters and the Samoan language used fourteen letters, but she wasn't having any luck finding a language with an alphabet of fifteen. Athena gazed up at a family portrait that hung from the north wall. Molly's warm skin and cute freckles stood out amongst the rest of the pale Fox family. Athena frowned, stroking Simba gently along his back, and typed *African languages* into the search box. Molly had often joked about how she was the long-lost princess of some isolated Tanzanian tribe. It had driven their mother crazy.

'You are NOT an African princess! You are Molly Fox of Camp Terrace, North Shields and if you don't do your homework, so help me, I'll pull you out of Church High and send you to that bloomin' comprehensive down the road.'

Athena opened a Wikipedia entry. It informed her that there were up to three thousand languages spoken in Africa. She slammed her laptop shut and set about polishing the silver picture frames in a bedroom that hadn't been used in over a year.

×××

'It's fookin' roastin',' barked Charlie Fisher later that afternoon. He was shouting commands at his professional fighters whilst they hit the heavy bags in time with one another. With one hand Charlie fanned himself with a pile of flyers advertising The Pit's ladies only kickboxing class and with the other he held a cold can of energy drink against his neck. To say Charlie was a hairy man was an understatement. Half of his face was hidden behind a thick unkempt beard of black and grey. It grew down his neck making it impossible to tell where the beard ended and his chest hair began. His arms and legs were covered in the same bushy rug of salt and pepper, meaning the only part of Charlie Fisher's body that wasn't covered in hair was his big dome of a head, which was as bald as a Sphinx cat, and as wrinkly too. The boxer - who had once been known as *Pretty Boy* - had retired from the ring ten years ago and kept his promise to himself that he'd spend his retirement doing far less exercising and far more eating. He fondly referred to the layer of visceral fat that had accumulated over his belly and hips as his fuel tank or, when he really wanted to gross Athena out, a fuel tank for his sex machine.

'Ya right there, Charlie,' boomed Luke Mar between punches. 'When ya gonna invest in some air con?'

'Air con?' scoffed Charlie, putting the pile of flyers down and wiping his brow on the sleeve of his Pit t-shirt. 'I'm not spending a fookin' fortune on air con for the two weeks of the year we actually get some sunshine.'

'Well, we need something to deal with all the heat coming from Kris and Foxy.'

Athena had been under a constant barrage of innuendo and taunting from her teammates ever since Luke had witnessed her retrieving her house key after spending the night at Kris's. The fact that she and Kris hadn't had sex was inconsequential to Luke and his tormenting was showing no signs of slowing. Athena had had all she could stand of Luke's rumour mongering so she responded to his latest joke by stopping mid boxing combination to punch him in the nuts.

While Luke writhed around on the floor, holding his groin in his day-glow green boxing gloves, Athena stood over him and promptly kicked her shin into his thigh. Luke's thigh was thicker than Athena's waist but it flashed red when her bony shin made contact with it.

'Argh! Here man, Foxy. Leave it out. I tap. I tap,' begged Luke, his chocolate coloured eyes scrunched up into tight wrinkles.

'Foxy!' bellowed Charlie over the belly laughs of the other fighters. 'Switch bags with Jimmy if you can't work next to Luke. Honestly, you lot are worse than the juniors.'

Athena kicked her shin into Luke's thigh once more and stalked off to the last punching bag in the line to resume her combination training.

'Ignore him,' whispered Kris as she passed his bag.

Jimmy, a ginger, five-foot-eight stick of a man with stalk thin legs and skin like tracing paper, vacated his post and tiptoed around Athena, avoiding eye contact.

The strong winds had dropped since the previous weekend and without the help of the North Sea breeze, temperatures had soared to the likes no northerner was used up. Athena was working out in lycra shorts and a pink vest. Sweat had caused her blonde hair to stick to the side of her face and beads of perspiration flew from her skin with every explosive movement. Little pools of sweaty water formed beneath each of the fighters, who grunted and groaned in time with their punches.

The heavy canvas bag swung violently from its chain when Athena punched it. The teasing had brought out an extra venom to her jabs and crosses. Luke's stories had changed daily from Athena and Kris having had a drunken one night stand, to having been secretly dating for months, to being on the verge of announcing their engagement so they could settle down and have a bunch of adorable ninja babies. Kris had taken the whole thing in his stride, politely correcting every jibe with composure and a smile. Athena, as evidenced by Luke still massaging his balls, had not handled things quite so diplomatically.

When Charlie finally called time on their training Athena picked up her kit bag, removed a towel to wipe herself down and headed to the tiny cubicle that was the so-called ladies changing room. Kris, Jimmy and the other men headed to their much roomier changing area. There were no showers at The Pit so Athena washed in the cracked sink and peeled the sweaty vest from her body. It stank. Most of the bruises from her tequila-fuelled fight had faded but the ones on her ribs had developed into a vibrant shade of pistachio. Athena pulled out her mobile and typed a brief message.

Pint?

She stripped off her soaking sports bra and knickers, washed her underarms and waited for Kris's reply.

Low Lights in 10.

Bollocks, thought Athena when she realised she'd failed to pack a change of underwear. She pulled her jeans up over her naked behind and wiggled into her clean t-shirt. It was tight fitting and her nipples poked at the material. Sighing, she pulled her hooded Pit sweatshirt on top. Not ideal in this weather.

As she left the changing room she passed Luke, who would be hanging around to help coach the amateur fighters. He cowered in the corner as she approached and protected his groin with his hands.

'Bye Foxy, please don't hurt me, Foxy.'

The little bell above The Pit's door chimed and the first of the amateurs walked in and immediately complained about the stench of body odour.

Luke draped his heavy arm around Athena's shoulder and pulled her freshly washed face into his glistening torso. Athena could smell tanning oil.

'This new bunch are a load of fairies,' Luke whispered. 'Scared of sweat. What they gonna dee when they get in a brawl and all they can smell is blood?'

'Oh I love that smell,' replied Athena, closing her eyes. 'It's so metallic and intoxicating.' She paused. 'When it's someone else's blood, obviously.'

Luke gripped Athena's hand and span her around in a tight pirouette, releasing her in the direction of the door. 'You're a little psycho, Foxy. You know that, right?'

'That's what makes me a winner,' she called back over her shoulder.

'Later, Foxy.'

'Later, Superstar. 'Watch your back, blondie.'

'Yeah, we'll be back.'

XXX

The Low Lights Tavern prided itself on being the oldest pub in North Shields. Although records dated it as far back as 1832 it was rumoured to be much older, maybe even four hundred years old. It was named after the now defunct low lights lighthouse which sits next to the river. The high lights and low lights lighthouses were commissioned by Henry VIII after the black middens reef in the mouth of the Tyne claimed five boats over three stormy nights. There had once been over one hundred pubs lining the fish quay of North Shields, catering to sailors, merchants and fishermen alike, but now only a handful remained, the others replaced with brasseries, cheap Italians, and swanky apartments.

Athena trotted down Brewhouse Bank with her kit bag thrown over her shoulder. She entered the inviting, white painted building, bought two pints of Tyneside Blonde and took a seat at a table in the corner.

Kris arrived a few minutes later. His eyes immediately caught sight of the pint of ale awaiting him and he forgot to lower his six-foot-three frame to allow for the tiny doorway. 'Bastard' he cursed, rubbing his forehead.

The eyes of the pub turned to the tall Pole and he gave an apologetic shrug and took a seat next to Athena.

'Every time,' she said with a giggle.

'That damn doorway gets lower, I swear it does.'

Athena passed him his pint. 'Here, have a nice cool pint of Man Up Juice.'

Kris raised his glass and clinked it against hers. 'To manning up,' he toasted, before wincing at his sore head and pulling a notepad and pen out of his kit bag. 'Right, let's crack this damn thing.'

'I had an idea earlier. I thought maybe Molly had coded a foreign language. She'd studied Japanese and Korean a little bit at school. French and German too.' She took a sip. 'But with the number of symbols only being fifteen I just don't think it could be any normal language you'd do at GCSE.'

Kris scratched at his shin. 'Hmm, what about Egyptian? They use pictures and stuff don't they?'

'Hieroglyphs,' confirmed Athena. She took out her phone and did a quick Google search. 'I wondered about African languages. Molly's father was African or Caribbean. Nope, not hieroglyphs. There's like seven hundred of them.' She put her phone back in her hoody pocket and squirmed uncomfortably from the humidity. 'That only leaves another two thousand nine hundred and ninety-nine African languages to rule out.'

Kris drained his pint - it hadn't touched the sides - and went to purchase another. 'Was she a Trekkie?' he asked upon his return. 'Like, into Star Trek? Could be Klingon.'

Athena snorted and almost spat out her ale. 'I doubt it. Good idea though, thinking outside the box.'

Kris reclined back in his chair, interlocked his fingers and put his hands behind his head. Athena caught herself staring absentmindedly at his biceps. She shook her head and pulled the diary toward her. *Concentrate.*

Athena finished her pint, got herself a second and Kris a third. On an empty stomach and after a sweaty training session the alcohol was quick to take hold. For the next twenty minutes, Kris would suggest languages and Athena would look them up on her phone only to sigh, frown and rule them out one by one. They looked up shorthand, Esperanto, languages from Tolkien and even a language from the hit TV show Game of Thrones.

Once Athena had confirmed Swahili had too many letters she placed her phone - rather forcefully - screen side down on Molly's open diary and excused herself to use the bathroom. The toilets were tucked away behind an awkward corner. Athena staggered as she rounded the tight bend and slid herself into a cramped cubicle with an unreliable lock and a dodgy flush. When she returned, Kris's eyes were wide and excitable, the whites showing all around his gull grey irises.

'Look, Foxy!' He pointed to the back of the diary. 'Did you know a page had been ripped out here?' Look it's been ripped out carefully, near the binding. But you can see, right?'

Athena snatched Molly's diary from him and peered where the pages met. There was the very faintest edge of a torn out page.

'Your phone was still lit up when you left for the bog,' said Kris. 'I saw this weird shadow. Look.' He lit up the screen on his own phone and scanned it back and forth across the next page. 'The indents.'

Athena looked closer. Kris was right. Something had been written on the page before it had been ripped out. She took a picture of the page on her phone in case she damaged the code on it beyond repair and stopped a member of the bar staff as he walked past. 'Do you have a pencil?'

A barely pubescent looking glass collector balanced a tower of pint glasses in his arms. 'Erm, they have some for when they do the quiz.'

'Get me one,' snapped Athena. 'Please,' she added, pulling the diary to her face again and squinting.

'Here,' said the young man, handing Athena a stubby pencil a few moments later.

Athena pushed her hair behind her ear. She could feel the sweat that caked the strands on her fingertips.

'Thanks,' she said examining the pencil. 'Oh, this is an H, do you have something softer like a 4B or a… Oh never mind.'

The glass collector made a quick escape as Athena held the pencil on its side and gently shaded over the page, her hand trembling as little white letters appeared. She took Kris's notepad and started to scratch down the results.

Alan Sherwood

Ali Montgomery

Alexander Franklin - Ashleigh Grove, Benton.

'Mean anything to you?' asked Kris.

'Not a thing,' said Athena. 'But this is the best we've managed so far.' Beaming, she leant over and kissed Kris gently on the cheek. His dark stubble tickled her lips. 'Well spotted, Kris!'

- CHAPTER 5 -

Athena sat under the majestic sycamore tree at the end of her garden and savoured the last few draws on her cigarette. The recent sunshine had turned her shoulders and cheekbones a warm pink and a few extra freckles had formed across the bridge of her squashed nose. The sycamore provided a shady haven from the relentless summer sun and the cigarette provided a reassuring calm after Athena had berated herself for kissing Kris yesterday afternoon. He was a single, red-blooded man with an abundance of testosterone and here was Athena, showing up at his house in the middle of the night, drunk and wearing next to nothing, buying him pints and kissing him on the cheek. She did not need a man in anything other than a platonic capacity right now. Hanging around with Kris as often as she was wasn't fair on him and Athena knew it. And yet she couldn't stay away.

Examining the cigarette between her fingers and checking out her nail polish at the same time, Athena took a deep breath and roughly stubbed the cigarette out on a large, grey stone at the base of the tree. Charlie wouldn't be happy that she was smoking again, not after she'd acted like such a moody brat when he'd helped her quit the last time. Athena would be in for a world of push-ups if he caught her with another fag in her hand. Athena had always hated push-ups. She'd been unable to do a single one without putting her knees on the floor when she'd first walked into The Pit. Charlie had said she had arms like marshmallows. These days she could knock out sixty chest to floor push-ups without breaking a sweat, but that didn't mean she had to like them.

Athena walked to the bus stop just beyond the wooden gates that marked the entrance to Camp Terrace and deposited her cigarette butt in the litter bin. She tried to avoid eye contact with an elderly lady on a mobility scooter who was looking back and forth between Athena and a two-metre high poster that adorned the bus stop. The poster - advertising a night of cage fighting - featured Athena in a tiny sports bra and hand wraps. Behind her stood Luke Mar with his championship belt slung over his shoulder. Athena slid into the driver's seat of her red Audi and lowered the top. She was headed to the local Tesco to stock up on groceries, a drive which had it not been for extensive roadworks on the main commuter route from North Shields to Newcastle would have taken Athena less than four minutes. As it was, she'd be stuck bumper to bumper for up to twenty minutes. *Bloody council.*

The previous evening, after having kissed Kris for his keen eyesight at discovering Alan, Ali, and Alexander - the three Als as Athena was referring to them - she had returned home to drink half the bottle of Chilean white she'd purchased earlier that day. After extensive searches on Facebook and Twitter Athena had found over sixty Alan Sherwoods, none of whom lived in the north-east, let alone in Benton. She'd discovered hundreds of Ali Montgomerys - including a B list actor and an elite level swimmer - and a handful of Alexander Franklins. The tipsy blonde had wasted no time in copying and pasting hundreds of messages to any Alan Sherwood, Ali Montgomery or Alexander Franklin she could find who lived in the UK.

Athena Fox

Hello, I hope you don't mind me messaging you. My name is Athena Fox, we haven't met but I wondered if you knew my sister, Molly Fox. Molly lived in North Shields, near Newcastle. She took her own life earlier this year and I was hoping to get in touch with anyone who may have had contact with her in the months before her death. I guess I am hoping to piece together what she was going through and why she felt that there was no alternative to suicide. I found the names Alan Sherwood, Ali Montgomery and Alexander Franklin in a notepad of hers and am contacting as many of them as I can find. Please let me know if you knew Molly.

Yours, Athena.

Athena joined the queue of traffic waiting to join the Coast Road. *It would be quicker to walk*, she thought to herself as the lights changed and the traffic crawled through the junction. A temporary 30 mph limit had been in place for months, much to the annoyance of North Tyneside residents who were used to flooring it on the usual 70 mph road. Sticking the car into cruise control Athena thought back to the handful of responses that had come through to her Facebook Messenger account overnight:

Alan Sherwood

So sorry to hear about your sister but I can't help you. I've never met a Molly from the north-east. Good luck with your search. Al.

Alicia Montgomery

Hello Athena, I didn't know Molly. Sorry I can't be of assistance.

Alan Sherwood

Hi Athena, I don't know a Molly but I'd like to get to know you. Hot profile pic.

Alexander Franklin

Such awful news Athena, I wish you luck but I didn't know Molly. Alex.

Al Montgomery

You are Fit! (Note the capital F!) DM me back.

Alex Franklin

Hi Athena, sorry about your sister. I wish I could help but I'm based in Belfast. I never knew Molly. Sorry for your loss.

Alison Montgomery

Are you that fighter chick? I'm a huge fan! Sorry about your sis.

Al Sherwood

Sorry, you have the wrong Alan. Good luck.

Alexander Franklin

Hey Athena, Molly sounds familiar. I think I know who U mean. Sorry 2 hear about her dying. I'm based in Glasgow. I could come meet U n talk about Molly? I'm a bit low on funds coz the factory I worked in got closed down. Maybe you could send me the coin 4 the train? About £150 should dee it. My PayPal is AlFranklthelegend@gmail.co.uk.

Athena had read that final message whilst downing a pint of water in an attempt to counter her wine induced dehydration. She'd spluttered water all over her kitchen counter and had typed a barrage of foul-mouthed insults at Al Franklin *the legend.* He didn't bother to message back. The thought of that money grabbing dickhead trying to exploit money out of her grief was enough to make Athena clench her jaw and pull out of the next junction with dangerously little space to do so. The car behind blared its horn and Athena glanced in her rearview mirror to see a two-fingered salute from the trailing driver.

Turning into Tesco's car park, Athena took a parent and child bay near the entrance. A black Ford Focus took the bay next to her and a tall, thin, childless man in a smart suit exited his vehicle. The pair exchanged approving glances at their flagrant flouting of the rules. The Baby Boomers had managed to raise their offspring without the need for specialist parking bays. What made Gen X and the Millennials so incapable? Earlier in the week, Luke had been moaning at length about the junior team. He was right, the next generation - with their trigger warnings, micro-aggressions, safe spaces, political correctness and bloody parent and child parking bays - they were well and truly screwed.

'Looking lovely today, Angel.'

Athena almost didn't see Harry huddled in the covered entranceway to the supermarket with a blanket wrapped around his shoulders. Even on this summer's day, without a cloud in the sky, he still looked cold.

'Thank you, Harry,' smiled Athena. She curtsied and her mood lifted due to Harry's presence. He had trimmed his beard since Athena had seen him yesterday and the result made his face seem kinder than usual. 'You hungry, Harry?'

'Oh don't you worry about me, Angel. Couldn't spare me a smoke though could you?'

Athena reached in her bag and handed Harry the rest of her packet. 'I'll get you lunch. You fancy chicken or a tuna?'

'I'm fine, Angel. Don't you worry—'

'Chicken or tuna?'

Harry put his palms together and bowed his head in gratitude. 'Chicken.'

'That wasn't so difficult, was it?'

Harry lit one of the cigarettes - it smelled fantastic - and hid it behind his back as a Tesco security guard walked past. 'Angel, you need to stop acting like you owe me.'

'You need to stop acting like I don't.'

Athena headed straight for the sandwiches aisle. Passing the newsstands she perused the headlines: *NUFC in Transfer Shocker; Fire at Black Bull, New Owners Devastated; Tyneside Prowler Strikes Again, Two Assaults This Week; Duchess Dazzles on Royal Tour; and Road Works Delayed until 2020.*

2020? You've got to be kidding me? Athena picked up two copies of the local rag, one for herself and one for Harry. Tesco was busy but the chilled and frozen aisles were a welcome sanctuary of cool air. Athena, who rarely dawdled anywhere because she considered it a grotesque waste of time, sauntered through the chilled sections. She had to resist the temptation to grab a bag of frozen peas out of the chest freezer and hold it across her neck. She stocked up on meats and vegetables, treated herself to a little alcohol, grabbed her favourite shampoo, conditioner and face mask and picked up a meal deal for

Harry. She chose a chicken sandwich, a bottle of Fanta and a tub of prepared fruit for him.

As she forced the final items into her carrier bag, Athena heard a voice that made her skin crawl. The voice belonged to Owen Daley Phelps, the pathetic, waste of space that Athena had dumped five years ago after she was finally shrewd enough to realise that there was no future with a man who declared he had no intention of ever getting married or having children, ever. Yet here he stood in the middle of Tesco with what looked suspiciously like a dowdy wife and a chubby baby.

'Fox—' he stopped himself from addressing her as *Foxy*. 'Athena, good to see you. How long has it been?'

Owen leaned forward in a clumsy attempt at a hug.

Athena stepped out of the way. 'It's been a long time, Owen.'

Her speech was low and slow but it took effort to prevent her voice from quivering. Owen's round, electric blue eyes and full lips were as captivating as they had always been. *Damn him. Damn him and his kissable lips*. Five years. Five bloody years and he still made her heart flutter and break all at once. He was wearing a white V-neck t-shirt that clung to a newly acquired paunch, a pair of low slung jeans and some garish yellow flip-flops. The supermarket's strip lighting reflected off a forehead that reached far further back than it had five years ago. Athena tried not to smile too much as she remembered Owen's obsessiveness over what used to be a full head of long, hippy hair.

'Athena and I used to date in high school, sweetheart,' he explained to the plain looking woman next to him. *Dating in high school* made it sound like he and Athena had been to the cinema a handful of times and shared a few inexperienced embraces. It did not quite convey that they had gotten together after a spin the bottle dare at aged sixteen and had stayed together through GCSEs, two years of A levels and three years of university education. Owen's sweetheart looked Athena up and down through her thick-rimmed glasses and Athena noticed her gaze pause on her biceps. Two could play that game. Athena returned the favour, scanning her up and down in a deliberate move to make her feel uncomfortable. She wore bootcut jeans and an unflattering floral t-shirt. In her arms, she held a gurgling little baby with snot streaming from its nostrils, and on the ring finger of her left hand Athena spotted a simple silver wedding band.

'Claire,' said the woman, introducing herself as she adjusted her t-shirt self-consciously. 'And this is Daley.' She bounced the baby on her hip and asked, 'Have we met before?'

'I doubt it,' replied Athena, not even attempting to disguise the contempt in her voice. She wanted to get out of there. Almost six years she'd wasted on Owen. Six years of worshipping a false idol. Six years squandered on a relationship that he had put no effort into whatsoever. She hated him and hated herself more for having been so damn naive. For five years she'd managed to avoid bumping into him and then Tesco, bloody Tesco…

Claire looked Athena up and down once more. 'I'm sure I recognise you.'

Athena resisted the urge to rip Claire's glasses from her face and snap them in half. That would stop her incessant gawping.

'Oh sweetheart, you'll have seen her picture on all the phone boxes,' suggested Owen.

'You make me sound like a whore,' said Athena.

Claire covered Daley's ears and a woman in hair curlers who was pulling a shopping trolly paused to rubberneck.

Owen twitched. 'Athena's a fighter, sweetheart. She's on all those big fight night posters that are plastered all over the phone boxes and bus stops in town.' He turned to Athena. 'Yeah, you're fighting some bird called Sissy, right? Imagine that? Imagine being a fighter with a name like *Sissy*!' He snorted like a mangy jackass.

Athena pursed her lips and took a deep breath. 'Sissy Clark,' she stated. 'She's the UK's pound-for-pound number one and she'd put her fist through your skull if she heard you calling her *a bird*.'

'The number one? So it's for the title?' asked Owen, tickling his son's feet, sounding impressed and completely oblivious to Athena's disdain.

Athena was distracted by Claire, who was taking a long hard look at the contents of her shopping bags and silently judging her on the amount of Absolut Citron vodka she had bought. 'Erm… yeah. It's for the title.'

'That's awesome, Fox— Athena. Isn't that awesome, sweetheart?'

Athena felt like she'd be the one to put her fist through Owen's skull if she had to hear him call Claire sweetheart one more time. Claire, who obviously couldn't stand the awkwardness any further, picked up her shopping in her free hand and said she'd wait in the car. Athena watched her and Daley leave and the moment she was out of sight she rounded on her ex.

'Congratulations Owen, you got everything you *never* wanted! That takes a lot of skill,' she spat at him.

Owen lowered his eyes and swallowed. He had the pathetic look of a man who so desperately wanted to be Peter Pan - to never grow up - but somehow woke up one day with a wife, a snotty nosed kid, and mortgage payments.

'I, look Foxy, when I said that I'd never marry you or have kids I didn't mean *never* never, just not for the foreseeable future.'

'Don't call me Foxy. You lost the right to call me Foxy when you got off with that Estonian stripper.'

'Don't be like that.' He looked feeble.

Athena would be able to walk away if only his eyes weren't so sparkly and full of memories. She thought about how this asshole had had a hold over her for so long, she'd have done anything for him. She'd have robbed a bank for him had he asked. But now, well now it was Athena who had what looked like the carefree existence that he'd craved so hard for: no spouse, no ugly kid, no boring job, no receding hairline and premature middle-aged spread. She should feel jubilant. She had won.

'The truth is,' continued Owen, meeting Athena's eyes and taking a step towards her. 'I still think about you a lot, I still…' His voice trailed off for a second as he moved even closer. 'I drive the long way home from work sometimes. If I take Albion Road I know that I'll get caught at the lights and be able to look at that poster of you. You look incredible in it, well not just in the poster, in real life too. You're ripped! You were always strong, your legs were anyway, I always loved how your body felt. I still have the same number, you can text me if you want to meet up or—'

'I deleted your number five years ago you cowardly piece of CRAP!'

Owen winced and looked nervously around at his fellow shoppers who had stopped to stare.

'Excuse me,' continued Athena, pushing past Owen, her firm shoulder colliding with his soft chest. 'I have steak to eat, vodka to drink, and big muscly fighters to hang out with.'

That last part was a lie. She was heading home to walk Simba, drink vodka and watch Netflix until she fell asleep.

'Enjoy the wife you didn't want and the kid you said you'd never have. I don't want your number! I don't want to hear from you! Trust me, the only time you'll hear my voice,' she prodded her finger into his chest, 'is in your head when you're doing your wife and wishing it was me!' And with that, Athena marched out of Tesco and unceremoniously dumped Harry's meal deal in his lap.

- CHAPTER 6 -

Undefeated Sissy Clark on UK title defence; 'expect quick and violent finish.'

Don't let the name fool you, Sissy Clark is far from cowardly. On September 17th, Clark, AKA The Little Lioness, (6-0) will make the third defence of her strawweight Demons Fighting Championship belt when she steps into the cage for the seventh time. The London born Thai boxing specialist amassed a number of impressive European and World gold medals before making the shift to mixed martial arts four years ago.

“My record is better than any girl in my weight class. I hit harder and kick faster than half the men in my gym. The girls I fight, they don't stand a chance. Their coaches should be locked up for letting these girls get in the cage with me. They're supposed to look after their fighters, not feed them to the lions. That's what I am. I'm a lioness and I destroy any prey that's in my way.”

Clark is the first UK born woman to be featured in the unified MMA rankings and despite her small frame, she is ranked as the UK's pound-for-pound champion. She has wins over Holt, Spear, and Pryor and is rumoured to be of interest to the big US-based organisations.

"I'd love to fight for the UFC, they have the best fighters in the world so maybe if I sign for them I'll finally get to fight a worthy opponent."

Clark's next opponent is the largely unknown Athena 'The Goddess' Fox, (4-1). Fox hails from Newcastle, a working-class city in the north-east of England, which is the venue for Demons FC 16. It has been argued by Clark's camp that Fox is only getting a title opportunity because the event is being held in her hometown.

"She's a local favourite, the crowd will be behind her when she walks to the cage but they're going to see a vicious beat down. I'm going to expose her as an unworthy challenger. I expect a quick and violent finish and the crowd will turn against her, mark my words."

Only time will tell. On September 17th we will find out if Athena Fox is capable of doing what no other woman before her has managed, to last more than two rounds against The Little Lioness.

For more on **Demons FC 16** see the **European MMA** section of the site.

Athena shut her laptop with a little too much gusto, startling Simba, who had been snoring at the end of Athena's bed. *Unworthy challenger? I'll show you who's unworthy.*

It was quarter to six in the morning and Charlie Fisher had made it quite clear that the team was to meet at the gym by 6 a.m. Athena begrudgingly dragged herself out of her restored antique four-poster bed and dressed in a green vest and black shorts. She scraped a hairbrush through her messy bed-head hair and stifled a yawn whilst brushing her teeth. *And since when do I 'hail from Newcastle?' I'm from Shields. Everyone knows that.*

'Simba! Simba come!' The giant ball of white fluff bounded down the stairs after Athena. 'Outside.'

Athena let the Akita out to take care of his toilet duties whilst she filled water bottles and made snack packs of sunflower seeds, mixed nuts, and cubes of feta. She locked the front door after herself, lowered the top on the Audi and slid into the driver's seat. It was the sort of morning that smelled of clover and rose petals, the sort of morning that made you take deep inhalations through the nose and be thankful for simply existing. The sun had been up for almost two hours but the early morning still had a slight chill in the air. There was a solitary cloud hovering overhead and Athena relished the gentle breeze that tickled her cheeks and made Simba's fur ripple. Her phone synched automatically to her car's sound system and the soft melody of Clair De Lune began to play.

'Get a move on, boy.'

The dog looked up from whatever tantalising smell lay at the foot of the sycamore and bounded over to jump into the passenger seat.

Every month or so Charlie would take the pro team off-roading. He liked to switch up their cardio training and instead of having them pound the paved streets of North Shields he'd get the gang out into the countryside. Today, Charlie wanted his team to head fifty minutes south to the North York Moors.

Athena pulled up at The Pit as the clock ticked over to 6 a.m. Charlie and the other members of the pro team were huddled by the doorway. The men ranged from tiny flyweights like Stevie Kelly, who could turn on a sixpence and make you dizzy just by watching him, through to heavyweight behemoths like Luke Mar, who's arms alone probably weighed more than Athena. Athena was the lone female fighter from The Pit to manage to turn pro. There was another girl who was close to going pro, Erin Summers. She had skills. The raven-haired beanpole was a sponge for information and a technical wizard, but she lacked killer instinct. It was unfortunate for Erin Summers, therefore, that the ability to switch off empathy and let the darkest parts of your soul run rampant was part of the job description.

'Cutting it fine, Foxy,' tutted Charlie.

Athena chewed the inside of her cheek. Snapping at Charlie that he should be grateful she was here at all at this ungodly hour would only earn her extra push-ups.

'Good morning to you too, Charlie,' she mumbled under her breath as she caught sight of Kris who was dressed all in black, sipping from a Costa Coffee cup. The summer weather had brought out the auburn tones in his scruffy hair and his face and arms were bronzed and inviting. He caught Athena's eye and waved good morning to her, earning him a playful elbow in the ribs from Luke.

'Morning,' smiled Athena, ignoring Luke.

'You read MMA Junkie this morning?' asked Kris.

'Yep.'

'Want to talk about it?'

'Nope.'

Tiny Stevie and Jimmy the day-walker were eyeing the Audi. Luke followed their gaze and barged the pair of them out of the way with his titanic arms. 'Shotgun!'

Luke ran his hand along the bonnet of Athena's car and clumsily manoeuvred a space for himself under Simba's sixty kilos of muscle and fur. 'Losers weepers.'

Stevie and Jimmy exchanged a look and the remaining guys dispersed between Kris's Golf, Charlie's Ford and Ahmed's old Mazda.

'Why yes, Luke, of course you can have a lift.' Athena's voice dripped with sarcasm.

Luke tussled his fingers through Athena's hair. 'Oh shush. You love my company. Admit it.' He flashed a bright white, Hollywood smile at her.

Athena swept his hand away and pursed her lips. 'If I beat you today you're riding back with Big Ahmed.'

'No deal. Ahmed doesn't have air con, that car will stink to high heaven on the way back and… Oh holy Mary mother of God!'

Simba - with perfect timing - took the opportunity to turn around on Luke's lap, and with his furry behind facing the massive tanned man, he let out a fart of deadly proportions.

'What do you feed this thing?'

Athena started the engine and headed west towards the Tyne Tunnel. 'Organic meat,' she replied. Her short hair blew about wildly behind her as the car gained speed. 'But I've smelt far worse from you lot.'

'Yeah, yeah. Let's not pretend like you don't fart in the gym, Missy. Everyone sneaks out a cheeky one while they're grappling. I let one rip on Smithy last night when I had him in an armbar,' laughed Luke, referencing a brutal grappling technique for hyperextending your opponent's elbow. It was a technique Athena knew only too well, she'd dramatically ended her last fight with an armbar and she could still remember the loud popping noise of the woman's elbow when she'd stubbornly refused to quit.

'And to think I could have stuck with ballet…'

'Ballet?' scoffed Luke, scratching Simba's head. 'A nutter like you would be wasted in ballet, you'd be… What's this classical shite we're listening to?'

Athena smoothly exited the Coast Road and joined the A19 south. 'It's not shite,' she pouted. 'It's Adagio for Strings.'

'Adagio *borings* more like it.' Luke took over the Bluetooth connection. 'Nineties dance,' he announced. 'That's what we need,' and within seconds the sounds of Fat Boy Slim were booming from the speakers with Luke's head bouncing violently back and forth to the beat.

Despite his overabundance of energy and his locker room talk, Athena had to admit that driving with Luke was fun. It was near impossible to be moody about Owen, conflicted about Kris, or worried about her upcoming fight with Sissy, when Luke was choosing classic dance tune after classic dance tune. He was singing along to each song, one arm wrapped tightly around Simba and one fist pumping up and down in the air as the Audi slinked in and out of the traffic.

As the sun rose higher into the sky Athena donned a pair of polarised Burberry shades while Luke wore a pair of garish green counterfeit Ray-Bans. Athena slowed the car and lowered the volume of the music as they left the main roads and headed on to the quiet country road that would lead them to the little village of Newton Under Roseberry. The narrow road was lined on either side by tidy hedgerows and beyond them lay fields of jade and gold. Cows and sheep grazed in the meadows, taking shade under grand oaks and elms, while tiny blue tits danced amongst the branches.

Luke squirmed under Simba. 'My legs are starting to go numb.'

'There's only room for one heavyweight in this car,' smiled Athena, breaking for a rabbit that was bounding across the road. Simba growled, his eyes locked on his prey.

Luke tightened his grip on the dog. 'Why'd you get a dog that's bigger than you, anyway?' he asked. 'I had you pegged as a yappy little Chihuahua kind of girl.'

'A Chihuahua? Really, Luke? You insult me. I inherited the beast. He was my sister's ball of fluff. Couldn't believe it when she brought the bugger home.'

'What? How could you not love this gorgeous animal?' Luke patted Simba on his side and the dog returned the favour by enthusiastically licking all over Luke's face.

'I do love him… but it's complicated,' started Athena. 'Molly bought him a few days after Mum, Nana and Gramps died. He was an adorable puppy. Cute as a button. He looked like a little teddy bear, all white with a big pink tongue and a curly tail. She said she bought him off some guy she met on the internet and then I went and accused her of stealing him.'

'Stealing him?'

Athena hit the breaks again. 'Damn rabbits! Yeah, she used to shoplift when she was a teenager and I thought the stress of everything that had happened had set her off again. She used to do it for attention. It started with magazines and sweets from the corner shop and ended up with designer handbags. She got in a tonne of trouble. Anyway, she went in a foul mood when I accused her of stealing him and she didn't speak to me for a week.'

'I'm not surprised.'

Athena pursed her lips, changed gears and ruffled Simba's fur with her left hand. 'And then I didn't exactly help matters by telling her that buying new family members wasn't a healthy way to cope with losing the other ones. That she was ignoring her grief and separation distress and distracting herself with a creature that relied entirely on her to look after it when she couldn't even look after herself.'

Luke looked sideways at Athena with one dark eyebrow raised high above his green framed sunglasses.

'I know. Not helpful. Not one bit. But I was right… As much as I wish I hadn't been.' Athena swallowed and took a long slow breath, her eyes fixed on the road ahead. Luke continued to sit in silence and a lonely cloud passed in front of the sun, momentarily casting the country lane into shadow. 'And now,' she continued. 'I have a dog that's bigger than me and who eats more than I do and who reminds me of Molly every single time I look at him. He's a good guard dog though and it's definitely nice to have him in the house, it can be a bit creepy when the house is empty but…' her voice trailed off for a second as she swallowed down the lump that had appeared in her throat. 'But he's not Molly.'

Luke turned to face Athena. His eyebrow was still stuck halfway up his forehead and like a goldfish, he opened and closed his mouth repeatedly, trying to find the right thing to say to his grieving teammate. In the end, he settled on, 'Want me to change the subject?'

'Please,' answered Athena, grateful that her sunglasses were hiding the undoubted redness of her eyes.

'That Sissy Clark sounds like a right arrogant cow. Did you read MMA Junkie this morning? Saying she hits harder than the men in her gym! Mind you, I've sparred some of the blokes from her gym and she might have a point about a few of them. And Sissy? What kind of a name is Sissy?'

Athena couldn't help but let out a belly laugh. 'I don't think I'm in any position to mock someone's name. What was my mother thinking?'

'Aye, you've got a point there, Foxy.'

'And you're a fine one to talk, Luke Matthew Peter James Mar.'

'Could be worse. Those bible bashing parents of mine could've gone the whole hog and squeezed in all twelve of the disciples.'

Athena and Luke pulled up in the public car park at the end of Roseberry Lane and waited for the rest of The Pit convoy. Within ten minutes the rest of the squad had arrived. Charlie emerged from his Ford Focus and began rummaging around in his boot. He pulled out a flask of coffee, a bottle of water, a bottle of sunscreen, a stopwatch, a newspaper and a deckchair. The team followed Charlie to the end of Roseberry Lane, where he set up his deckchair and made himself comfortable in the sunshine. After squeezing a small amount of sunscreen into his hand and rubbing it vigorously on to his bald head, he looked up at the imposing hill of Roseberry Topping.

At over a thousand foot high, Roseberry Topping dominated the North York Moors. Its distinctive half dome summit was formed in 1912 when a huge chunk of the sugarloaf hill fell from the south-west slope and left a jagged peak that many thought of as a miniature Matterhorn.

'Right, you lot. Six sets,' grunted Charlie.

'Six?' gasped Kris, putting his head in his hands.

Charlie tilted his head. 'Yeah, you're right, Kris. Best make it eight.'

Athena grunted and punched Kris in the gut. 'Thanks, Kris.' She took a big gulp of her water, poured some into her hand for Simba to lap and left the bottle next to Charlie's deck chair.

Charlie opened his newspaper and lay it across his legs, he took the stopwatch in his right hand and looked up at the team. 'Three, two, one, go.'

Fourteen men, one woman, and a dog set off at a quick pace along Roseberry Lane. The team ran uphill in the shade, through ferns and birch and over uneven steps until they reached the zigzagging stony ascent. The steep, uneven terrain managed to fatigue every part of the legs and by the time the team made their first visit to the trig point at the summit they were already heaving, sweating and sore.

Athena had large sweat patches under her arms and Luke had discarded his t-shirt, much to the amusement of a group of middle-aged ladies out on a morning hike.

Kris stood on the rocky crag at the summit, bent over with his hands on his knees, taking in the vast views of the Cleveland plains. One by one, Stevie, Jimmy, and the other men made it to the top where the standard display of empathy was to slap each other on the back of the shoulders, nod, and head back down the hill again for Charlie to clock their lap times.

The first two climbs to the summit were filled with the sound of chit-chat and banter. Stevie would talk tactics, Luke would describe in bloodthirsty detail what he planned on doing to his next opponent and Kris would moan about not being included on the next fight card. Some of the men discussed their women troubles, including Jimmy who complained at length about his unfair custody arrangements and used some highly inappropriate terms to describe his soon to be ex-wife. Athena saved her breath. She kept her mouth shut and her mind focused.

By the third ascent the talking had died down and was replaced by the sounds of running shoes on rock and deep, exhausted breaths. Running behind Kris as she approached the summit for the third time, Athena's face was level with the tattooed lions on his calves. The lions reminded her of Sissy 'The Lioness' and her condescending, pompous, drivel about needing a worthy opponent. With Simba at her heels and a determined look in her eyes, she accelerated and overtook Kris, almost rolling an ankle on a wobbly rock.

'Easy, Foxy,' puffed Kris, catching Athena in the safety of his athletic arms. 'You can't fight with a sprained ankle.'

'I know,' she puffed back. 'But I can't win if I'm not in shape.'

'You're beating half the men, look.' Kris motioned down the trail behind them. The team's tight running pack had dispersed into a stretched out crocodile line.

'I'll be careful,' reassured Athena, taking a deep inhalation before finishing her push to the trig point.

Each climb to the top was slower and more painful than the last. By the time Athena returned to Charlie for the fourth time Simba was ready to give up. He curled into a ball in the shade of Charlie's deckchair and let out a long sigh. Charlie gave him some water and patted him on the back. 'Good boy,' he said, before looking at Athena. 'Tick tock.'

Athena held her tongue and set off for her fifth set. Halfway.

Once the team entered into the final few climbs the lighter members of the group had stretched further and further into the lead. The heavier men struggled more, not only with their size but also with the heat. Once you were beyond the tree line there was no shade, nowhere to hide from the sun and the heat was reflecting harshly from the exposed rock. On her final stop at the summit Athena took a second to stretch her thighs and take in the full panoramic vista. To the south-east, she could see the fifty-foot monument to explorer and navigator James Cook who had grown up in these parts. Athena's grandfather had taken the family for a hike up to the monument one windy afternoon when she and Molly were still young and their little legs could barely handle the climb. *Look at me now, Gramps*, she thought, taking one last deep breath before heading back down, on wobbly legs, to Charlie and Simba.

Athena finished third out of fifteen - sixteen if you counted Simba - and she sat at the end of Roseberry Lane, rehydrating, cuddling Simba and congratulating her teammates as one by one they returned to Charlie, panting, cursing and begging him to never make them do eight sets of the Topping again.

When the last of the team had made it back they hobbled the short walk to the picture-perfect Kings Head Inn where they collapsed on the outdoor seating. Charlie set a tray of soft drinks in front of the thirsty group.

'Why do we do this to ourselves?' asked Jimmy. His usual milk bottle white skin was flushed puce with a mixture of exhaustion and sunburn.

'It beats working the doors,' replied Kris, slouching forward and resting his chest on the wooden table.

'I'll drink to that!' Ahmed lifted his glass and clinked it against each of his teammates' in turn. 'To the dream job,' he toasted.

'To the dream job,' they replied in unison.

With time, the sun began to dry the sweat patches under Athena's vest. She sipped at her diet coke and wished that there was a shot of Bacardi in it. Charlie handed his bottle of sunscreen around the group but Luke waved it away like it was an annoying fly.

'I'm fighting next month, Charlie. I need my tan in tip-top condition for the weigh-ins.'

'And I thought Foxy was the poser in the group,' he laughed.

Athena playfully stuck her tongue out him. 'I'm not a patch on Luke and you know it,' she said, feeling the soft vibrate of her phone in the back pocket of her shorts. The men continued arguing over who was the biggest poser at The Pit whilst she fished it out and looked at her notifications: one text and one Facebook message.

Hey gorgeous, haven't stopped thinking about you since yesterday. Still a fan of Opihr? I know a sweet place in Tynemouth that serves a mean cocktail.

Owen x

Bloody nerve. Athena deleted the text and then jumped to her feet, eyes wide and mouth agape. She practically barged one poor fighter out of the way and forced a space for herself next to Kris.

'Ahh how cute,' cooed Luke, making kissing noises at her.

Athena picked up a bar mat and threw it at Luke. The bar mat bounced off his hideous sunglasses and landed corner first in his drink.

'Foxy!'

'Shut up, Luke,' she snapped, thrusting her phone into Kris's hand. 'Look!'

Alan Sherwood

Hello Athena, I'm sorry for your loss. My wife and I met with Molly back in the autumn. She was a charming girl and I am deeply saddened to hear of her passing. I think I can shed some light on why she had those names in her diary, though I feel it might be best to discuss it in person. I am available at the weekend if you would like to meet for a coffee?
Alan

- CHAPTER 7 -

The air in Athena's bathroom was heavy with the smell of disinfectant and indignation. Last night, Athena had dreamt about Owen Daley Phelps and she was taking her annoyance out on the mop. It banged back and forth between the decorative feet of the bathtub and the skirting boards. Bloody Owen Daley Phelps. How could he worm his way back into her mind after all these years? The dream had started pleasantly enough, he'd been stood behind her, his arms wrapped protectively around her waist while he delicately kissed her neck and whispered sweet memories to her.

'Remember Switzerland, Foxy? Remember the hot tub and the Champagne? Do you remember Paris?'

But then his grip had tightened. Owen's forearms pressed against her ribs and Athena struggled to breathe. The more she wiggled and tried to escape the tighter he held her. 'You'll never forget me,' he hissed. 'Never.'

'Yes, I remember Paris,' grunted Athena through gritted teeth as she swung the mop across the tiles. 'I remember finding the text messages on your phone from that French tart you cheated on me with!'

The mop head ricocheted off the skirting board and knocked over the bucket of disinfectant. Athena growled and viciously threw the mop to the floor. She stomped her foot petulantly and punched her fist into the wall.

'Damn it.'

Athena shook her hand and examined her bloody knuckles. On the wall, two circles of blood stood out on the ivory coloured tiles. She needed to calm down. Athena was meeting Alan Sherwood later and she knew she would make for a less than welcome guest if she turned up in this ghastly mood. What she wouldn't give for a cigarette right now.

Athena used an old towel to soak up the spilt cleaning fluid and took ten slow deliberate breaths. She brewed a pot of green tea and meditated whilst she waited for her drink to cool. It helped, but did not completely clear Athena's mind from all that was troubling her. The nightmare was not the only consequence of reading Owen's text message three days ago. Training had not gone well since the Roseberry Topping cardio session. As well as losing focus during a round of sparring with Jimmy (and now sporting a faint black eye as a result) she had struggled over and over with a basic triangle choke. Charlie had got so frustrated with her ineptitude at such an easy technique that the whole team had been punished with extra conditioning training.

Athena disposed of the remnants of her green tea, washed and dried the mug and put it back in its correct place in the kitchen cupboard. She dressed in skinny jeans, ballerina slippers, and a fitted white t-shirt. She tried to cover her black eye with makeup but gave up after it became clear that she was fighting a losing battle.

The best she could manage was making the discolouration appear less green and more yellow.

Athena removed a panel in the wooden headboard of her four-poster bed and retrieved Molly's diary from the secret location. A decade before Athena was born, her grandfather had received the heirloom as a gift from the Baron of Ravensworth. The bed was a show of gratitude to Athena's grandfather for performing the pioneering surgery that saved the man's heart. As a teenager, Athena had used the secret compartment to store anything she didn't want her mother or the cleaning lady to find: condoms, vodka, and novels of a certain nature. Now it held her more prized possessions. Molly's diary was tucked away with her grandmother's jewellery, a family photo album, her Christening shawl and her grandfather's collection of newspapers from the days his granddaughters had been born.

Alan Sherwood lived in High West Jesmond, an affluent, middle-class area of Newcastle that Athena knew well from her days at Jesmond's most prestigious private school. She knew very little of Alan Sherwood from his online presence: his Facebook page was private, he was listed as married, had attended Kenton High School and his profile picture was a photo of a ginger cat.

Athena parked her car opposite Little Moor Allotments and threw her bag over her shoulder. The smell of compost filled her nostrils and the sound of two chickens fighting over a worm punctuated the otherwise quiet neighbourhood. Athena stared up at house number twelve as she approached. It was an old three-story red brick terrace with attractive wrought iron decor over the porch and bay windows. The neat front yard was filled with well-tendered plant pots of rosemary and lavender. The beautiful aroma overpowered any trace of the compost smell from across the road. Athena raised her hand to an old brass door knocker but before she could grasp it the door swung open and an overweight ginger tom cat sprinted out.

'Athena Fox?' asked a gentle northern voice.

Athena looked up at the man in the doorway, but she didn't have to arch her neck too far, the man was no more than three inches taller than she was. His face was dark and devoid of wrinkles, his friendly eyes were small, set wide apart and framed by round John Lennon glasses. He had a precision trimmed beard of black with flecks of grey. Charlie Fisher's untamed beard should take notes.

'Alan Sherwood,' he said, introducing himself with a big neighbourly smile that revealed large front teeth.

Athena shook his hand and felt Alan's eyes dart around her face, getting a good look at her.

'Invite the poor girl in already,' called an American accent from indoors.

'My wife,' explained Alan. 'Please,' he added, stepping aside and motioning for her to come in.

Alan's home was bright and warm and loved. Framed photographs of his family covered every windowsill and mantlepiece. The soft orange armchairs were draped in handwoven blankets and rows and rows of books on veterinary medicine lined a floor to ceiling bookcase.

Athena took a seat on one of the armchairs, it felt so spongy compared to the Chesterfield back home. She cleared her throat and put her bag on the floor as Alan's wife entered the room. She was as vertically challenged as Athena but with an hourglass figure that could stop traffic. She had warm skin and thick bouncy curls of deep brown.

'Elizabeth Wainwright,' she said with a friendly Floridian twang that didn't match the look she gave Athena.

Athena shuffled uncomfortably as Elizabeth continued, 'I'm so sorry for your loss, when did Molly pass?'

'January,' answered Athena. Alan and Elizabeth looked to be in their early to mid-forties and Athena wondered how they would have known her little sister.

'It's so tragic.' Elizabeth tilted her head to the left. 'I do hope she has found peace. Could I get you a drink, Athena? Tea? Coffee?'

'Tea, please. Milk, no sugar.'

Elizabeth left the room and Athena heard the clinking of crockery. Alan who had been leaning against the mantlepiece pushed himself upright and sat down on one of the armchairs.

'So,' started Athena, not knowing where to begin. 'How did you know Molly? She never mentioned an Alan or an Elizabeth.'

Alan took a seat on the sofa. 'She didn't mention me? Well, that makes sense, we only met her the once, you see. We didn't really know her at all, but she gave us quite a start, showing up on our doorstep the way she did, asking if I was her father.'

'Her father?' Athena was incredulous. 'Why did Molly think you were her father? You don't look anything like her, well I mean, apart from that you're—'

'Black?' finished Alan.

'I mean… How did she even find you? Was she just going door to door or—'

Alan chuckled into his palms. 'No, no, nothing like that. She'd hired a private investigator and—'

'She WHAT?' interrupted Athena. Molly hadn't told her any of this and that made Athena ache inside.

Elizabeth returned and handed her a brightly decorated mug of hot tea.

'Oh she knew all the statistics,' said Elizabeth. 'Could tell you the population of Tyne and Wear when she was born, the percentage of Africans and Caribbeans, how many of those were men—'

Alan crossed his legs. 'Did you know there were only two hundred Caribbean men aged sixteen to sixty-five living in Newcastle when Molly was conceived?'

'Erm… No,' answered Athena, distracted by a family portrait on the side table. Three handsome young men and a cheeky looking girl in identical Catholic school uniforms smiled out of the picture. The youngest of the boys was the absolute double of Alan. 'Only two hundred? That doesn't seem like a lot.'

'Well, that's just the city of Newcastle, it doesn't count Gateshead or North Tyneside.' Elizabeth took a seat next to her husband and laid her hand on top of his. 'But Molly knew all the stats for those boroughs as well. Smart girl, your sister.'

'Very smart,' added Alan, taking his glasses off for a moment to clean them on his shirt. 'She said she didn't know much about her father other than he was called Al. That meant he could be an Alan, an Alexander, an Alfred, an Alistair… The PI got her three names from Newcastle to get started with and was working on North Tyneside—'

Athena's head was a mess. 'How long had she been searching?'

The ginger tomcat sprinted past the living room window at high velocity, emitting a loud meow. Alan's head swivelled to follow it until the ginger blur was out of sight.

'I was the first she contacted. She said she started looking after your mother passed. Apparently, your mother didn't want you girls to know your fathers?'

'It wasn't that she didn't want us to know them,' explained Athena. 'She didn't know them either. Mum was… a… a party girl, shall we say? I was the product of a one night stand with a Polish saxophonist at a gin festival in Brighton. He doesn't know I exist. And Molly, she was conceived after a long night of high-rolling at an underground casino.'

Elizabeth's face spread into a big, open-mouthed smile. 'Your mother sounds like she was quite a character.'

'Vivian Fox was that all right,' said Athena. 'Mother by day, international party girl and professional gambler by night.'

'Professional gambler? I get the impression a quiet church mouse like my Alan wouldn't be her type,' said Elizabeth. 'No offence, darling,' she added.

Alan bowed his head and laughed silently, his eyes creasing into thin lines. 'I'm not what you'd call a party animal, Athena. My idea of a great night is a glass of port and the Antiques Roadshow.'

Athena laughed too, feeling strangely at home with Alan Sherwood and Elizabeth Wainwright.

Alan unfolded his legs. 'I offered to take a paternity test. To put her mind at rest. But she could tell just by looking at me that I wasn't her father and I'd been married to Elizabeth for over a year when Molly would have been conceived. Our eldest would have been on the way by then, this is him…' Alan handed Athena a framed photograph. 'John, he's 20 now, in the army like his grandfather was.'

Athena studied the handsome face in the photograph. 'He looks like he could break a few hearts.'

'John?' said Elizabeth. 'He's a handsome boy but he's painfully shy. I hope the military brings him out of his shell. He was bullied at school, left him terribly withdrawn. Molly reminded me of him in many ways.'

Athena raised her eyes from John's picture. 'What do you mean?'

'Molly told us about the schools the pair of you had attended,' started Alan. 'Very good reputation apparently, but she said she didn't fit in at all. For the first four years she was the only nonwhite in the school, then some Indian and Chinese students joined but she was the only black girl.'

'Oh the teasing she said she got for her hair,' added Elizabeth. 'Children can be so cruel.'

'Her hair?' Athena put her cup on a side table and blinked several times, her lips were pulled into her mouth as she thought for a moment. 'Molly must have been one of the most beautiful creatures on the planet. She could have been a model. Bullied? She never said a word about being bullied.'

'A lot of people don't seek help when they need it,' said Alan. He looked at Elizabeth, who nodded for him to continue. 'We're heavily involved in the church, Athena, and I hope you don't mind me saying this… We have contacts, at shelters. You'd be safe. I hope I'm not overstepping my bounds here, but if you need help, we can help you.'

I'd be safe? Athena looked back and forth between Alan and Elizabeth feeling completely bewildered until the penny dropped.

'Ohhh! The black eye!' she gasped, putting her hand to her face. 'No, no, no, it's nothing like that. This…' she pointed at her eye, 'is what happens when you don't pay attention at boxing training. I wasn't hit by my boyfriend or anything. I don't even have a boyfriend.' Her words echoed in her brain several times whilst Owen's smug face darted in and out of her mind.

Alan and Elizabeth looked relieved.

'Boxing? Well that sounds adventurous,' said Alan, sipping from his mug of tea.'

'MUM, DAD, I'M HOME,' chirped a voice from the hallway, followed by the sound of fast footsteps running up the stairs and a bedroom door slamming.

'Our youngest,' explained Elizabeth, 'the future veterinarian.' She handed Athena another photo frame, this time featuring the cheeky looking girl with the mischievous smile. 'She'll be wanting feeding. Bottomless stomach that one, no idea how she stays so slim. Must be taking after Alan in more ways than one.'

Elizabeth gracefully got to her feet and made her way back into the kitchen.

'What else did Molly say?' pressed Athena.

Alan sighed. 'She told me about how she was a summer baby and that she was always behind academically. The other girls would mock her and say that she was bringing the school average down, it only got worse when she was suspended for that business with the head teacher. She spent most of her childhood thinking she was dumb because she didn't get straight A's. It just didn't sound like she enjoyed that place at all. I think she held on to those insecurities into adulthood.'

Athena stared out the window. 'I had no idea,' she sighed.

Athena and Molly had been close. Sure they had argued, like all sisters do, but they'd always been there for each other, or at least Athena thought they had been. Perhaps she didn't know Molly as well as she thought she did. She seemed to have been more open with Alan and Elizabeth in their one meeting last year than she had been with Athena in her entire life. A pang of jealousy ripped through Athena, quickly followed by anger.

'If she'd have just said,' she grumbled. 'I'd have choked those stupid girls with their own ponytails.'

Athena sat back in the chair and folded her arms against her chest. Unsure where to look, she settled on a photograph of the attractive, happy family and felt another wave of jealousy threaten to drown her. She sat in silence, her leg bouncing up and down while she conjured up memories from her own childhood until Alan asked:

'Is there any more I can help you with Athena?'

Jolted back to the present, Athena relaxed her leg and unfolded her arms. She could feel the start of a stress headache in her temples.

'Did Molly show you this book?' she asked. Handing Alan the grey notepad from her bag.

'Sorry,' answered Alan, turning the book over in his hands and frowning at the odd assortment of crosses, squares, circles, and triangles.

'She didn't mention the code or what she was writing about?'

Alan shook his head from side to side. 'I'm afraid not.' He passed the notepad back to Athena. 'You can't read it?'

'No,' Athena shook her head as well, feeling her heart sinking. 'I'm sure whatever was troubling her was in here, but… but it's too confusing for me to work out. Thanks for your time, Alan,' she said, looping the shoulder strap of the bag over her arm. 'You and Elizabeth have been very sweet. I think…' she hesitated. 'I think Molly would have really liked it if you were her dad.'

Alan and Athena stood and walked to the front door.

'She was a wonderful girl. I am very sorry for your loss, Athena.' He shook Athena's hand and slid two cards into her palm: one for the local church and one for the women's refuge.

Everything felt muted on the journey home. The blue sky seemed grey, shadows seemed darker and the breeze gave Athena goosebumps. Her jaw remained tight for the entire journey, her teeth grinding together with guilt and frustration. *She* should have known those things about Molly. Not two strangers. *She* should have known that Molly would want to find her father after losing her mother. *She* should have known Molly had been bullied at school. *She* should have helped.

Athena unlocked the heavy door to Camp Terrace and peered down the long empty hallway. There was a feint smell of green chilli, okra and lemongrass that permeated the home. The Rowes next-door must be making a curry. Simba poked his great furry head around the doorway to the kitchen and blinked sleepily at her. After the warmth of Alan Sherwood's family home, Camp Terrace felt cold and soulless. Her mother should be in the kitchen, cooking something tasty with one hand and winning an online poker game with the other. Gramps should be reclined on the old Chesterfield with his head in a book. Nana would be tutting over the newspaper and morbidly checking the obituaries for people she knew. Molly would be sprawled on her bed reading Cosmo and listening to some boyband Athena would have no doubt despised.

Athena took one step into the dark silent house but the sight of the stairwell was too much. She couldn't go in there, not sober anyway. She turned around, walked straight back out and pulled her phone out of her pocket.

Hey Kris, going to Low Lights with Simba if you fancy a pint.

- CHAPTER 8 -

When Athena's alarm thundered to life the next morning she visualised throwing it across the room and watching it smash into a thousand fragments. Golden sunshine streamed through the sash windows to her bedroom. Evidently, she'd neglected to draw the curtains after sinking three pints with Kris and returning home to finish a bottle of Malbec. Molly's notepad lay open on the floor next to Athena's four-poster, it was joined by an empty chocolate bar wrapper and an open packet of menthol cigarettes.

She dragged herself out of bed, picked up the packet of cigarettes and emptied the remains into the toilet. Shaking her head she pushed aside the thought of what Charlie would say. Athena recalled spending most of the previous evening filling Kris in on the details of her meeting with Alan Sherwood and his wife. She'd eaten a Low Lights pie and pea supper - a North Shields institution - and had been immensely grateful that Kris hadn't reminded her that she should be cutting sugars and starches ahead of the Sissy Clark fight.

Kris had walked Athena and Simba home, kissed Athena on the forehead and looked at her with pity.

'Molly loved you, Athena. You know she did. Now get to bed, get some rest. You're sparring tomorrow.'

Athena replayed the previous evening in her mind as she brushed her teeth. She despised pity. Pity was worse than hatred. She swallowed two paracetamol and showered under icy water. She opened a tub of exfoliator and scrubbed herself until she felt energised, but no amount of scrubbing would wash away the guilt of not being the good sister she thought she'd been.

Wrapped in a white towel, Athena sat on the edge of her bed and checked her emails and social media. It was a habit and a distraction more than a genuine interest in who was going where tonight and what Celebrity A thought about Celebrity B, but a Twitter post caught her attention.

> **Sissy Clark @LittleLionessMMA**
> Who's excited to watch me make the goddess bleed on the 17th? #southernersdoitbetter #sexysissy

Accompanying the post was a photograph of Sissy. Her long, lean body reclined on a red bedspread. Sissy's face was thin with sunken cheeks. She had a strong, almost masculine jaw and cat-like gunmetal grey eyes. She wore a pair of silver Thai boxing shorts and her long black hair - with dip-dyed blue tips - fell over her bare torso and covered her diminutive breasts.

Athena rolled her eyes dramatically. 'Attention seeker,' she huffed. But as she read down the long list of comments: fans baying for blood, men lusting after her, women envying her, Athena's self-aggrandising ways couldn't help but surface. With water still dripping from the tips of her short blonde hair, Athena pulled on black booty shorts and a pair of Louboutin heels. She applied a thick layer of mascara to frame her pale green eyes and set the camera on her phone to timer mode. Athena folded her arms over her chest, which had the dual function of covering her breasts and showing off her upper arm muscles. She engaged her core muscles and gave a wry smile.

> **Athena Fox @GoddessMMA**
> #AnythingYouCanDoICanDoBetter
> #TeamGoddess #Worthy

That ought to shut her up. Athena's plans for the rest of the day were simple. First, try not to get another black eye at training. Second, go to Ashleigh Grove, Benton and track down Alexander Franklin, and third, try to stay sober. Athena swapped her Louboutin heels and booty shorts for running shoes, lycra shorts, and a baggy Pit t-shirt. On her way out she stopped to look through the door to Molly's bedroom.

Athena had kept the bedroom as Molly had left it, other than changing the bedding if Simba had chosen to sleep in there. Molly's room was bright and feminine, filled with pastel shades and seashells. Dotted around the room were postcard-sized watercolours that Athena had never paid much heed to before. The one on Molly's dresser was of colourful fishing boats, resting in the shade of palm trees on a white sand beach. One pinned to her mirror by a small magnet featured a sea turtle in turquoise waters, and another resting on her desk was of the distinctive peaks of the St. Lucian mountains. On Molly's bedside table, a set of coasters were decorated with sepia maps of Africa.

Athena bowed her head, her hand resting on the doorframe. 'I'm sorry, Molly.'

×××

Charlie Fisher sat on the edge of his desk and folded his hairy arms over the shelf of his stomach. 'Right ya wee shites,' he said, referring affectionately to the lighter fighters, 'to the end of the pier and back. And as for you biggins, get ya gloves on and pair up.'

The larger fighters scattered in search of their sparring gear while Athena checked her shoelaces and adjusted her sports bra. Jimmy rubbed a stick of sunblock over his cheekbones and held the door open for Athena and the other wee shites. The run to north pier was one of Athena's favourites. It was as beautiful as the Roseberry Topping run, but nowhere near as demanding. Stevie, being the cardio machine that he was, led the pack down Brewhouse Bank towards the Low Lights Tavern.

The aroma of North Shields fish quay was something that most locals appreciated. It was the strong reassuring smell of fresh seafood and salty air. The smell of local history, industry, and tradition. It was the smell of jobs. Yet on days like today, when the mercury hit twenty-eight, the stench from the crab shacks could test even the hardiest of Shields folk. Athena held her breath as she ran across the main road and towards Low Lights beach. Starved of oxygen, her muscles burned and her vision began to grey around the edges. It was only when her feet reached the promenade that lined the mouth of the Tyne that she felt it was safe to take deep gulps of salty air.

'Fat chance,' laughed Stevie, pointing to one of the old smokehouses.

Some ne'er-do-well had spray painted the words *Go Vegan* in large, fluorescent green letters. The corner of Athena's mouth curled up as she considered the irony. This town was built on fishing and Lord help any man or woman who tried to come between a local and their fish supper. The graffiti artist, she considered, had more chance of converting the Pope to paganism than convincing the people of North Shields to a vegan diet.

Athena quickened her pace as she continued along the promenade. Erin Summers and her lamppost-like legs kept pace with the professionals, she even jostled for first place with Athena. Athena may have the shortest legs, but she was damned if she was going to come second to another woman. The hierarchy of the gym was clear. They may all love each other but everyone knew Luke was the top dog and Athena was the alpha female.

'Watch out,' called Erin as she side steeped a pile of dog mess halfway up the final hill.

With Luke still sparring away in The Pit there was a distinct lack of banter. Jimmy had panted as he complained to the group about his divorce and how he wished he could spend more time with his son. Erin had hinted that her parents deeply disapproved of her learning martial arts and a wiry old timer called Cliff moaned about his damn neighbour stealing his damn milk. Athena shook her head as she ran, Luke would not approve. If he were here he would have clipped the lot of them around the backs of their heads and told them to stop looking like someone had pissed on their chips.

Built to protect the Tyne from the stormiest of tides, North Pier jutted almost a kilometre into the North Sea. As Athena ran towards the end of the pier, not even out of breath, she had the sensation of running out to sea, there was nothing but dark indigo water in all directions. Setting the pace, she rounded the lighthouse at the end of the pier and began the dash back the gym. A lone porpoise swam parallel to her as she ran. He was stalked by dark clouds that cast a welcome shadow over the runners. A couple of men cast fishing lines over the wall of the pier and looked sceptically at the encroaching clouds.

The run had been a nice warm-up for sparring practice and by the time Athena ran back through the doors to The Pit the cloud cover had darkened considerably and the air was charged with electricity. She removed her running shoes and lay down on the matted floor to stretch out her hamstrings while the heavier men finished their last round of sparring. Luke, in his day-glow green boxing gloves and matching shin pads, landed a hard body shot to Kris's ribs. Kris let out a grunt and returned the favour with a stunning kick to Luke's face. Luke's head recoiled but he showed no sign of pain.

'Good shot.'

Charlie stood next to the sparring cage - stopwatch in hand - and called time on the match. His bald head was shiny with sweat but there was little chance exercising had anything to do with it. Luke and Kris gave each other a high five and began peeling away their protective clothing as they exited the cage.

'Right, yee lot,' called Charlie to the heavier fighters over the din. 'End of the pier. Yee kna the drill. Everyone else, get ya run times on the board.'

A booming clap of thunder caught the attention of everyone in the gym, their bodies froze instinctively and their eyes darted to the large front window in time to see the deluge. Huge droplets of water bounced off the pavement like ping pong balls, instantly saturating the road and pavement with water.

Big Ahmed picked up his running trainers. 'Ah Charlie, it's pissing down!'

'Ya skin's waterproof, big boy. Quit moanin' and get oot there.'

Ahmed, tall with balloon-like muscles, stomped his feet and threw his arms to his sides like a spoiled child. Luke laughed and peeled off his t-shirt before following

Ahmed, Kris and the others out the front door. They bowed their heads and took off towards Low Lights. Athena picked up a pen and scrawled her run time on the whiteboard that was mounted behind Charlie's desk only to spot a print out of her almost naked Twitter photo pinned to the side of his computer monitor.

'Charlie! Really?' The man had been a surrogate father to her these past few years and the thought of him looking at her half naked pictures felt seedy. She tore the print out from the monitor, scrunched it into a ball and threw it at Charlie. The ball of paper bounced off his man boobs and he caught it in his free hand.

'You're the one who posted it on the damn internet for the world to see. Now get ya gloves on.'

Athena opened her kit bag to retrieve her boxing gloves and conceded that the hairy bastard had a point. Once you put something online you can't control who looks at it. Athena pulled her mobile from the side pocket of her bag and checked her notifications.

'You always say I should do more to promote the fights,' she grumbled, staring at the phone screen and putting a positive spin on things. 'And in the time it took me to run to the end of the pier and back I gained six hundred new followers, two offers of sponsorship and one marriage proposal.'

Charlie shrugged. 'Fair enough.' He threw the scrunched up picture of Athena into the bin. 'Now get ya bloody gloves on.'

- CHAPTER 9 -

Athena and Kris stared down the length of Ashleigh Grove. The street was a mixture of bay-windowed Tyneside terraces and semi-detached council houses. St. Bartholomew's Church overlooked the long street that served as a thoroughfare between the North Tyneside districts of Longbenton and Forest Hall.

Kris shut the passenger door to Athena's Audi with a bang. 'And you couldn't find any Alexander Franklins online?'

'None from around here,' said Athena, locking her car. She and Kris had washed and changed after training and were now back in their civilian clothes, which for Athena meant skinny jeans, ballet pumps and a designer vest, and for Kris meant black jeans and a dark grey t-shirt. 'I don't even know if we're looking for an Alexander who lives here now or one who lived here back when Mum would have sha—' Athena shuddered. 'Back when Mum would have met him.'

The storm from earlier in the day had cut the humidity considerably. The blue sky and sunshine had returned since the rains but the heat was no longer as stifling. To Athena, it was a welcome change to be able to go more than two minutes without getting sweat patches. Kris extended his arm towards the first house.

'After you.'

Athena marched up to the first house on the street, her chin raised and shoulders pulled back. She knocked on the door and waited with her sweetest smile forced across her face. After twenty seconds of silence, she knocked again.

Kris shrugged. 'No one's home. Should we split up? I'll take the odd numbers, you take the even.'

Athena nodded and knocked on the door to the next house. She could hear loud cartoons playing on a television, a dog barking and a lot of commotion. A woman no older than Athena opened the door. She had limp copper hair, bags under her eyes and two giggling toddlers clinging to her legs.

'Yes, I'm happy with my broadband provider. No, I don't want to hear about our lord and saviour Jesus Christ and no, I don't want to donate three quid a month to whatever famine is going on this week.'

The woman pointed to a sticker in her window that read salesmen will be fed to the dog and tried to shut her front door in Athena's face. Athena threw out her arm and stopped the slamming door in its tracks.

'I'm not selling anything,' she said more aggressively than she intended. 'I promise, and I'm sorry, I know you must be busy.' Athena pulled a photograph of Molly from her bag. 'Have you ever seen this girl hanging around here? Her name was Molly.'

'Was?' The tired looking woman scanned the photograph.

'She died in January. She was my sister. I think she met a man called Alexander Franklin who lived on this street. Does the name mean anything to you?'

One of the toddlers pulled at Athena's jeans. 'You're funny looking.'

So are you, thought Athena, he was far too old to still be sucking on a dummy.

'He may have been known as Al Franklin or Alex Franklin, maybe Xander,' she pleaded, pushing the photo further through the doorframe.

The woman shook her head. 'Never heard of him.'

'Okay.' Athena lowered her eyes. 'Thanks for your time.'

Athena walked down the driveway and watched someone close their door in Kris's face. He turned to Athena and shook his head before moving on to the next house. Athena had no luck at the next house, or the one after. No one was home. When she knocked on a black door with a pair of garden gnomes sat on the doorstep she fully expected the same result.

'Sophie? Is that you?' The voice was croaky.

'No, no I'm not Sophie,' answered Athena.

The door opened a crack - still on the chain - and a hunchbacked lady with a tight white perm looked through the gap.

'Who are you then?'

'I'm... My name's Athena.' Athena held up the photograph of Molly. 'I'm sorry to bother you. I just wondered if you'd ever seen my sister around here. It would have been late last year.'

The woman looked back and forth between Athena and the photograph. 'Your sister?' she questioned.

'Half-sister. Did you ever see her around here? Or do you know anyone called Alexander Franklin?'

The elderly lady squinted and surveyed the photograph again. 'No luv,' she squeaked. 'I'd remember if I had, you don't see many darkies roond here, pet, and I've lived here since 1929.'

'Oh…right.' Athena was taken aback. She'd only heard such language on television shows set in the seventies, never in real life, and certainly never directed towards her sister. If the woman hadn't been so old and so desperately frail Athena might have reeducated her with a punch in the teeth, but old dogs, new tricks…

'Erm… Thanks for your time.'

Athena tried a few more doors without luck and whistled to get Kris's attention as he left the last house on the street. 'Get anywhere?'

'Nothing whatsoever. No-one's heard of Alexander Franklin or seen anyone who looks like Molly. I think we need to come back on a weekend when more people might be home.'

'I don't know if that will help,' said Athena, catching up with Kris. She sighed and held her hand over her eyes to protect them from the sunlight. 'I just spoke to a woman who's lived here since 1929. She said you never see... minorities around here.'

Kris placed his hands on his hips, scanned up and down the street and sighed. 'You don't think…'

Athena followed his eyes as they moved over St. Bartholomew's and settled in its cemetery. She put her head in her hands. 'Oh, you've got to be kidding me?'

As Kris and Athena crossed the road, Athena took in the size of the cemetery, it was huge. This could take forever, she thought as her phone vibrated.

Very alluring photo! Take it for me?
Owen xxxxxxxxx

'Who's Owen?'

Athena hastily clicked the lock button and stored her phone back into the back pocket of her jeans. 'No one.'

'Well, no one signed his name with a lot of kisses.'

Athena chewed on her lower lip and stomped her way past the older graves and headed for an area filled with modern black granite headstones.

'Just some loser who can't take no for an answer.'

Kris halted mid-stride. 'Someone hassling you, Foxy? Coz I can have a word if you—'

'I can fight my own battles, Kris,' she spat, folding her arms across her chest.

Kris turned his back and silently skulked away to begin scanning the names engraved into a row of gravestones.

Men. Athena flapped her arms to her side and shook her head. She walked quietly up and down the rows of graves, occasionally stopping and finding herself sorrowful for the number of children's graves decorated with teddy bears and brightly coloured toys. The rains from earlier in the day had waterlogged the grounds. The sun had yet to dry the grassy areas and Athena's ballet pumps squelched and stuck in the mud as she walked.

A muddy cemetery. It was a scene that triggered distressing memories and made Athena's skin prickle. For twenty minutes she forced herself to read name after name of deceased men, women, and children until at last, she heard Kris call, 'FOUND HIM!'

Athena scanned the grounds of St. Bartholomew's and spotted Kris in the shade of a large beech tree. She pulled her hands out of her pockets and ran full speed to Kris, only to skid through a puddle and leave her left shoe behind in the mud.

'Goddammit!'

Athena angrily shoved her short hair out of her eyes and pulled her bare foot out of the mud with a squelch. She retrieved her shoe, slipped it back over her dirty foot and wiped her mucky hands over the thighs of the jeans.

Alexander Franklin

14th September 1953 - 23rd March 2008

Loving husband to Glenda.

Devoted father to Helen, William, and Natalie.

Always in our thoughts.

'Just coz he's dead, doesn't mean he's not Molly's father,' said Kris. 'Born in fifty-three. He would've been in his forties when Molly was born.'

Athena folded her arms and looked down at the white marble headstone. 'I spent all that time checking social media for Alexander Franklins. I should have been checking the obituaries.'

Kris's phone beeped. 'We could look up his kids? See if they know anything.' He looked at the screen. 'It's Luke. Telling me to check out MMA Junkie.'

Athena pulled out her phone and stepped into the shade of the beech tree. She was greeted by the semi-naked photographs of Sissy and herself, posted side by side for comparison.

'Oh, that's just great.'

Things Heat Up At Demons FC

The co-main event at Demons Fighting Championship 16 is sure to set pulses racing for more than one reason. Strawweights Sissy 'The Little Lioness' Clark (6-0) and Athena 'The Goddess' Fox (4-1) are due to square off on September 17th when Demons FC returns to Newcastle Upon Tyne, England. Whilst the strawweights might be playing second fiddle to the main event - a heavyweight showdown between Luke 'Superstar' Mar (9-2) and 'Dangerous' Danny Davison (7-3) - the ladies are dominating the pre-fight hype since the pair posted revealing photographs on Twitter only a few hours ago.

Clark is heavily touted to defeat the lesser known Fox on September 17th but her opponent appears to be winning the battle for hearts and minds with #TeamGoddess trending throughout the UK.

What do you think? Will Clark be rattled by the attention coming Fox's way? How will this play out in the cage? Leave your comments below.

For more on **Demons FC 16** see the **European MMA** section of the site.

- CHAPTER 10 -

A sea fret rolled in from the North Sea and engulfed Longsands beach in a haze of white. It was an unusual occurrence this late in the summer but every northerner knew that Mother Nature was a hormonal beast and if she wanted snow in May or heatwaves in October then by goodness she'd have them.

Athena watched the view from Crusoe's cafe blur from majestic seascape to opaque coastal fog. Within a moment children were shrieking with wonder, 'Mum! Look, I'm in the clouds!' and mothers shrieked with fear, lest their little ones wander too far and fade into the fog.

Athena sipped strong black coffee and tucked into a double chocolate chip muffin on the wooden deck of Crusoe's castaway themed cafe. She was trying not to think about how she should be cutting sugars from her diet and trying even harder not to ask the group of heavily pierced young men on the next table to spare her a cigarette. She'd brought herself to the cafe on the beach to calm down after yet another frustrating training session. Salty air and a sea view usually did the trick, but today, even the weather was against her.

Athena was still messing up the damn triangle choke and Charlie was not letting her forget it. For two hours they'd run through the same bloody drill over and over. She'd been pitted against every guy on the pro team and not once did she submit any of them on the first attempt. This was a basic exercise. Jiu-jitsu 101.

Kicking off her sandals, Athena admired a rainbow of bruises across the insteps of her feet. Her right thigh had also taken some punishment and was throbbing rhythmically due to the heavy leg kicks that Jimmy had landed on her during their sparring match. Still, she'd gotten her own back by wrestling his milk bottle body to the ground and landing an elbow to his temple. He'd make her pay for that, Athena was certain.

Pulling a chocolate chip from the muffin and holding it in her mouth until it melted away to nothing, Athena stared at the list of names she'd gotten from Molly's notepad. The trail had appeared to run cold. Yes, Alan Sherwood had met Molly, but he wasn't her father and he had no clue how to read the diary. Alexander Franklin was dead, so he was no use, and none of the Facebook messages to the Ali Montgomerys of the world had bared fruit.

Athena pulled out her phone and began Google searches for *Alexander Franklin 23 March 2008* and found a brief but intriguing obituary from a local newspaper.

> Alexander James Franklin died yesterday at the age of 54 from pneumonia. Mr Franklin is survived by his wife, Glenda, their three children, Helen, William and Natalie, and two grandchildren.

Mr Franklin moved from Trinidad to the United Kingdom at the age of six where he soon found his legendary entrepreneurial spirit. By seven he had founded a mobile sweet shop that operated from a basket attached to his bicycle and provided the children of his estate with their daily sugar fix. It was fitting, that after meeting and marrying the love of his life, Glenda, at age 20, he founded a European-wide chain of bicycle rental franchises. The success of Franklin Rent-a-bike in the UK went on to fund notable charitable works including a scheme that provides second-hand bicycles to children in care and a project that takes children from disadvantaged parts of British cities to the countryside for cycling adventures.

Mr Franklin remained a keen cyclist and philanthropist into his fifties until complications arising from influenza resulted in hospitalisation. His wife and children were by his side until the end.

Services will be held this Friday at St. Bartholomew C of E at 2 p.m. The family has asked for donations to their charity, the Franklin Cycle Fund, instead of flowers.

Alexander Franklin sounded like another man Molly would be proud to call Dad, but as a charitable businessman, Athena doubted he would be the sort to risk his riches in casinos with the likes of her mother. The obituary was accompanied by a photograph of Franklin. Dressed in a navy suit and striped tie he looked every bit the businessman. He had a round face with deep nasolabial folds and marionette lines. A thin grey moustache adorned his upper lip and he had a shaved head. Athena stared at the photograph, her eyebrows drawing together as she tried to see Molly in his face. He didn't look much like her sister, she concluded as her eyes scanned back and forth. His eyes though, there was something familiar there.

She looked up the Franklin Cycle Fund, taking long sips of her coffee and slowly making her way through the rich chocolatey muffin. Athena found a contact form on the fund's website and penned a carefully worded message along with an attachment of Molly's photograph. It was worth a try.

Next, she tried Ali Montgomery again. The first page of results were Wikipedia and IMDB entries for the B list actor of the same name. This Ali had quite the resume, having starred in hospital dramas, daytime soaps, and cheesy sitcoms to name but a few. He'd also made appearances on almost every reality television show going from Dancing With The Stars to celebrity Fear Factor. Athena had to scroll through eighteen pages of entries to even get to Alison Montgomery the swimming star.

Athena closed her internet browser and logged into Twitter and saw that retweets for her racy photograph were still coming thick and fast. Between the good luck messages and the perverted requests were the trolls advising her to pull out of the Clark fight, telling her how much pain she'd be in once Clark was through with her. Then there were the body shamers, who let Athena know exactly what was wrong with her. She was too short, too muscular, and positively boy-like.

> **Anthony Trent @AntTrent81**
> Can't decide what's flatter… Fox's nose or Clark's chest?

Athena clicked on Anthony Trent's profile, took a long hard look at his media feed and decided to fire back.

> **Athena Fox @GoddessMMA**
> Can't decide what's smaller… Your brain or your dick?

A middle-aged couple and their lurcher took a seat outside Crusoe's. They made no attempt to lower their voices as they complained about the lack of sea view that TripAdvisor had promised them. Athena imagined them leaving a one-star review on the travel website. *The staff made no attempt to control the weather!* Athena drained her coffee and looked around into the fret. She had hours to kill until training. Simba had been walked, the house was clean, the groceries were bought, she'd completed enough Molly related research for one day and she didn't want to spend the rest of her free time trolling trolls. Though it did feel mighty satisfying.

What challenged Athena most about being a professional fighter wasn't the amount of training she was subjected to, it was the amount of rest time forced upon her. In the months following the deaths of her family members Athena practically lived at The Pit. If it wasn't time for her usual training sessions she would join in with the ladies only class, the junior class, the kettlebell class, the yoga class. Sometimes she'd jump on the treadmill or cross trainer and while away the hours until her body was so tired that a single glass of wine would send her to sleep when she begrudgingly returned to her empty house. The chronic overtraining made a mess of Athena's body. First, her joints would ache and little niggling injuries would never heal. When Athena's periods stopped and her hair began to fall out Charlie demanded Athena cut it out and start to rest between training sessions.

The row that followed was an explosive, red-eyed argument with items thrown and doors slammed in faces. It wasn't until Charlie threatened to kick Athena out of The Pit for good that Athena lamented and agreed to cut back on her gym time. The recuperation over the next few months helped Athena's body return to its usual powerful self. Her hair grew back thicker and colour returned to her cheeks. The same could not be said for Athena's mind. Rest and her mindset did not make good bedfellows. She despaired at being alone with her thoughts and if the devil made work for idle hands, imagine what he could conjure up for idle bodies.

Athena flicked back to her messages and reread her latest text from Owen. She twirled the phone between her fingers, focusing her eyes on the long string of kisses he'd added after his name. It would be so easy. One text was all it would take. One text and he'd be at her door. It was the technological equivalent of clicking her fingers so he'd come running. *Don't do it, girl.* Owen, she vividly remembered, was a magnificent kisser. Perfect full lips that could be so gentle and yet so passionate. He knew exactly how to hold her, how to touch her, how to—*Don't be an idiot.* Athena could invite him over to Camp Terrace, enjoy his body and send him on his way. He could give her exactly what she needed. *Except for love. He'll go back to his wife and brat. He'll break your heart. Again. And it will be your own stupid fault.*

Athena glowered into the white haze, she could make out the faintest outline of a tanker making its way towards the docks. Her eyes flickered to the young men on the next table. University-aged with boyband charm, slim builds, and shaggy hair. They were good looking enough - apart from the piercings - and the one with the cigarettes was positively—

'Hi.' He'd noticed her staring.

Athena blushed and looked away. 'Sorry… I'm… I'm trying to quit smoking,' she said truthfully. 'The smell is very tempting.'

He held the cigarette out towards her and Athena summoned all her strength to hold up her hand, shake her head and decline.

The young man sat back in his chair, took a long drag on the cigarette and slowly blew smoke from pursed lips. 'You sure there's nothing else tempting you, sweetheart?'

Sweetheart? The pierced stranger ruined his chances with one word. 'Quite sure. I'm just leaving.'

Athena stored her phone back in the pocket of her denim cut-offs and slid the notepad into her bag. She slipped her sandals back on to her aching feet and made the tiresome walk back up the ramp to the parade.

'Your loss, beautiful.'

'I doubt it.'

Athena made her way from the beach to Tynemouth village. Visibility was still terrible and she was almost run over by a car whose driver didn't think sea frets required headlights. Athena cursed instinctively as she jumped out of the way. She hated how it sounded. Her voice was posh and delicate, any attempts to convey anger only ever resulted in her sounding like a sulky toddler. Sticking to the path, she took a slow stroll through the village. She needed a distraction and there were few viable options. There was the narcissistic nineteen-year-old footballer. He could certainly keep her busy for a few hours, but Athena had no energy for dodging paparazzi. The city centre chef who liked to do unspeakable things with his melon baller? The surgeon with the swanky quayside apartment and foot fetish?

Kris? Why not Kris? He was tall, strong and lean. A handsome face, beautiful auburn hair and that cute, little scar above his eyebrow. It was true what they said, chicks dig scars. At least Athena did. He was bound to have superhuman levels of stamina, and those eyes, those steel grey Slavic eyes that could bore into your soul. *He could be your brother*, an internal voice teased. *He is NOT my brother. You're being ridiculous. His family hadn't even moved to this country when I was born. You're just putting up obstacles because Kris wouldn't be a one-night thing, he'd be a relationship and you're scared of relationships because the longest one you've had was based on lies.*

Athena dragged her fingernails over her scalp and thought of Kris. He was fond of her, that much was obvious. Single men don't hang around single women for no reason. It was true they were friends, they liked to spend time together and had a shared hobby. If that wasn't friendship then Athena didn't know what was. He was protective of her, he'd offered to warn Owen off, but Athena wasn't so sure that was a good thing. She despised people trying to fight her battles for her or acting like she couldn't handle herself. She was strong and independent and she was a professional cage fighter for goodness sake. Then there was that pitying look he'd given her the other night. Being thought pitiful was worse than being thought weak. But, if he was so fond of her why hadn't he hit on her when he had the chance? When she was drunk and locked out of her home? Or when she kissed him on the cheek in the pub? *Because*

some men are actually decent human beings, not every guy is like O
—

Athena ducked behind a muddy Land Rover, attracting a curious stare from a young mother pushing a buggy. His receding hairline was hidden under an Adidas baseball cap and his electric eyes were concealed behind a pair of aviators, but there was no mistaking Owen Daley Phelps as he sauntered out of The Wine Chambers. Athena peered at him from behind the corner of the Land Rover's bonnet.

'Damn it,' whispered Athena to herself, wiping mud off her denim shorts and getting it all over the palms of her hands. Only Owen would keep his shades on during a massive sea fret. When Athena and he had first started dating he'd insisted that she always stand on his right. Athena thought it was just a quirk of his until one day she overheard him saying that his left was his best side. Trust that vain bastard to present his best side to the rest of the world instead of to his girlfriend. Then there was the time he'd kept his shades on the entire time they made love because he'd been convinced he'd seen a wrinkle in the mirror that morning. Athena could remember every dirty detail of that particular encounter. She could recall every bit of bare skin that those tender lips had caressed. Athena could feel her face flushing and chest heaving as she snuck around the car and stayed out of Owen's line of sight as he made his way along Front Street.

Once Owen rounded the corner and disappeared from view, Athena caught sight of herself in the wing mirror of the Land Rover. *Crouching to avoid your ex-boyfriend? Strong, independent woman my ass!* Athena threw her head back and chastised herself. It was unbelievable that mere minutes ago she was contemplating returning his text message. How desperate could she be? Athena dusted her hands and continued on her walk home. She stopped outside The Wine Chambers herself and peered through the glass like a child outside a toy store. Charlie would deliver quite the sermon if he found out how many units of alcohol she could get through weekly. The fight was only a few weeks away and it should be Athena's sole train of thought, not distractions like getting laid and solving mysterious codes. But the closer she got to home, the more she knew she wanted someone to keep her company. Someone who would make her feel feminine and beautiful and make her forget about how empty the house was. Athena stared up at her home once she reached the wooden gates to Camp Terrace. She tapped her foot impatiently and looked at her phone one final time. Throwing her arms to her sides, she marched to her front door. This dilemma was one itch she could scratch herself. *Make it quick*, she told herself, unlocking the door and heading straight upstairs to get undressed. *And for God's sake don't think about Owen.*

- CHAPTER 11 -

The evenings were cooler now that the fever of August had passed. September had rolled in with refreshing sea breezes and fragile cloud cover. Athena was curled on the old Chesterfield in her living room, enveloped in a thick, white woollen throw. Simba had curled up in the crook of her leg and it was hard to tell where the Akita ended and the throw began. Light from the old, cast-iron streetlamp outside was reflecting off the living room's chandelier, creating the effect of a burnt orange disco ball as beams of warm light hit off the walls.

Athena was doing her homework. Charlie had assigned her the duty of watching YouTube videos of Sissy Clark as research for the upcoming fight. The process was a necessary evil. It allowed fighters to analyse their opponents' strengths and weakness. Strengths could be avoided and weaknesses could be exploited. Problems arose when fighters spent too much time looking at an opponent's strengths. Seeing the opposition knock opponent after opponent to the ground could play hazardous mind games with a combatant.

Training had gone well today, which felt like a rare occurrence these days. Athena had arrived at the gym to be greeted by the reassuring smell of disinfectant.

'You deserve a raise,' joked Luke. 'You've cleaned... What? Twice this year?'

Charlie had glowered and informed the pro-team of a rampant outbreak of ringworm in the junior fighters. This led to most of the team subconsciously scratching and itching at their arms and backs.

'Dirty little bastards,' moaned Kris, scratching so hard that he left red claw marks down his arm.

To Athena's relief, Charlie hadn't focused on grappling and triangle chokes again. Instead, the team practiced kicking drills. Following a childhood of ballet lessons, Athena had incredible balance and flexibility. She could excel in any kicking exercise Charlie threw at her. Athena loved kicking. There was something wonderful about feeling her instep connect at full force with the heavy kick bags.

Athena adjusted her laptop and clicked to the next Sissy Clark video on her playlist and watched with a stern face and stiff body as Sissy picked her opponent apart before elbowing her into submission. She watched the eight-minute video over and over, looking for patterns in Sissy's behaviour or movement. Athena opened a spiral bound notepad and clicked the top on a pen. She divided the page in two and titled the two columns, *What To Watch Out For* and *How To Kick Her Ass.* Under the first column, she noted Sissy's hard leg kicks, knee strikes and elbows. Sissy was a former Muay Thai specialist and it showed in her fighting. She wasn't afraid to stand and trade blows with anyone. She was powerful and she knew it.

Athena moved on to the next video. She watched - stroking Simba with her free hand - as Sissy stalked her opponent down and landed punches over and over. Her opponent's nose began to bleed, it hindered her breathing and slowed her considerably. Before the bell, Sissy landed a hard stomach kick, winding her platinum-haired foe. As she gasped for breath, Sissy kicked high. The head kick sent her unconscious body flying across the canvas, followed by a trail of scarlet blood. The kick felt painfully familiar to Athena, who's jaw clenched reflexively. She watched the short video on loop, trying to find the weak chink in Sissy's armour. Under *What To Watch Out For*, Athena noted Sissy's ability to switch from low kicks to high kicks with ease.

Athena gave herself a quick break from the fight analysis and made herself a mug of low-calorie hot chocolate. It tasted like dirt. Athena opened her Facebook account and checked to see if any more of the Ali Montgomerys that she'd contacted had got back in touch, but her inbox was empty. A little red circle appeared over her email icon indicating that she'd received an email. It was from Helen Franklin. Hope rose through Athena's body and she held her breath in anticipation. *Please say you met Molly, please say she told you about her diary.*

> Dear Athena,
> Thank you for contacting the Franklin Cycle Fund. We are sorry to hear about your loss. Bereavement can often put a financial strain on

young families. Our aim is to help all young persons in need of transport. If you are struggling financially and would like us to assist you please complete the attached form and a representative will be in touch shortly.

Yours sincerely,

H. Franklin

'Struggling financially?' Athena's eyes darted from the chandelier to the antique table. She had no mortgage to pay and a sizeable inheritance. She had no need for a charitable bicycle when there was a bespoke TT parked on the drive.

'I don't know about you, Simba, but I get the impression Helen Franklin didn't read our email properly at all.'

She began to type a short-tempered reply, capitalising certain words and formatting entire sentences bold. Feeling her pulse drum in her temples and realising that she was pursing her lips into tight wrinkles, Athena took a deep breath, deleted the reply and vowed to return to the task when she wasn't so edgy. Athena tucked her feet under herself and turned her attention back to the fight videos, still shaking her head at Helen Franklin's woeful response.

Sissy was the champion for a reason. She was fast, furious and she put her kicking and punching combinations together with flawless accuracy. Every one of her opponents left the cage looking like they had been in a car crash and not a single one of them could last longer than ten minutes with Sissy. The latest girl in the videos fared better than most but after only seven minutes of back and forth fighting, Sissy pounced like the lioness she claimed to be. Elbows rained down from all angles, then Sissy grabbed her head and pulled it down sharply, raising her knee at the same time so that skull and femur could crash together at maximum speed.

Don't stand and trade, thought Athena. *Take the bitch down and keep her down*. The camera zoomed into the poor woman's face, or what was left of it. Athena wasn't a squeamish person, she'd been the sort of child to pull her wobbly teeth out to tempt the tooth fairy into paying up early. But the sight of this poor woman, with blood teeming from at least three parts of her face and eyes wide with befuddlement, it was enough to make even Athena look away. *Poor cow*.

Athena closed her eyes and held her breath for a few seconds. The violent images flashed over and over in her mind. Athena concentrated and froze the moving images to still mental photographs. She drained the colours to black and white and shrank the pictures in her mind, making them smaller and smaller until they faded away. It was a technique she had learned after the deaths of her mother and grandparents. It had worked wonders in situations such as this but there was one memory it still failed to work on, the memory of discovering Molly's body.

Athena gripped her pen between her tanned fingers, she gripped so hard that the pads of her fingertips turned white. Under the *How To Kick Her Ass* heading, she wrote, *Nobody knows.*

Athena got up from the comfortable Chesterfield and emerged from the cocoon of the warm white throw. She laid the throw back over Simba, who's legs were twitching as he dreamed. Athena's breathing was erratic and her arm hair stood on end. Athena was usually calm before fights, but she'd never faced anyone quite like Sissy Clark before. Could Sissy be right? Was she unworthy of a title shot?

Athena made herself another mug of hot chocolate and wished she could top it up with a shot of whiskey. She wondered what Kris would make of her uncharacteristic insecurity, and then she wondered why she was wondering about Kris. *Have those videos taught you nothing? You need to focus or this psychopath is going to put you in the hospital.*

- CHAPTER 12 -

Athena awoke screaming and tearing at her bedsheets in a blind panic. She screamed so loudly that Simba bounded up the stairs, slammed her door open and pounced into her bedroom. The sixty-kilo Akita snarled and growled, his teeth snapped at the air and foam formed around his exposed gums.

'Shh,' purred Athena. 'It's OK, Simba. Shh. I didn't mean to scare you.'

Athena's heart was still pounding in her chest and she gasped for air as if she'd escaped from being drowned. The huge dog stalked around the bedroom, his hackles raised. When he was satisfied no one was harming his owner he jumped on the bed and licked Athena's face, leaving drool in her ear.

Athena scrunched up her face. 'Thanks, Simba.'

A seagull cawed outside the bedroom window, causing the dog to growl through bared teeth.

'It's a bloody seagull, Simba. Calm down,' she told herself almost as much as she told the dog.

Athena rested her face in her cold clammy hands. She'd had the same dream about Owen trying to crush her while he whispered reminders of all his infidelities in her ear. Then Owen had faded away and it was Sissy

Clark who had hold of her. Sissy's long, strong legs wrapped around her waist and her tattooed arms folded around her neck.

'Triangle, circle, circle, circle, cross,' Molly had called to her from outside the wire fencing of the cage. Athena had tried to call back, pleaded with her to make sense, but Sissy was choking her harder and harder and the more Athena tried to talk to Molly the less she could breathe. Then her mother had appeared with Gramps and Nana. They were translucent and ghostlike. They floated to the edge of the cage and peered through the wire fencing. Athena reached out her hand, trying to get her fingers to the cage to touch her sister, but with her hands reaching for the cage she couldn't defend the choke and as Sissy strangled Athena into darkness her mother and grandparents grabbed Molly, surrounded her and turned her ghostly white too.

With no family or boyfriend to rouse her from her nightmare, Athena had no choice but to follow it to the end, only stirring when her screams had been loud enough to wake herself. Athena engulfed Simba in a tight hug and pulled him close. His fur tickled Athena's skin but she didn't let go for several minutes. It might be time to consider a lodger. Someone who could be there to knock on her door in the early hours to disturb nightmares. There was plenty of room after all. She'd need someone who was obsessively clean, who didn't mind her 6 a.m. gym starts and who liked giant dogs. Making a mental note to look into it later, Athena released Simba from her grip and checked down the side of her bed. It was a relief to see no empty wine bottles or cigarette packets. The fight would be over soon and then she could sip wine and smoke cigarettes to her heart's delight.

Athena took a cool shower and dressed for the day. She was planning on heading to Tesco to grab her protein and vegetable supplies for the next few days. Then she would meet Kris at Low Lights Tavern to drink diet coke, take another crack at Molly's diary and come up with ideas to chase down the final Al. Athena wasn't due to start training at The Pit until mid-afternoon so she'd take Simba out on a run before hitting the gym. Hopefully, no one else had contracted ringworm.

Athena chose black running leggings and a yellow vest that clung to her muscular curves. She checked her phone and opened Facebook messenger. She squealed with excitement when she saw a message from an Alistair Montgomery.

Alistair Montgomery

Hi, just saw this. Sorry for the late reply. Never met Molly. Hope you find answers soon.

Athena grunted and sat down on the end of her bed feeling deflated and dejected. Was this was all a waste of time? Maybe Athena would never know why Molly left her. It felt pointless checking Twitter but logging into all of her social media applications each morning had become as automatic as brushing her teeth. She had one hundred and three notifications all pointing back to a tweet from Sissy Clark that had been posted at 4:57 a.m.

Athena pursed her lips and considered the merits of looking, but curiosity got the better of her, as it often did.

> **Sissy Clark @LionessMMA**
>
> Up early and training while the so-called goddess sleeps. Who thinks I can put her to sleep like Smith did? #5amclub #NotWorthy #TeamSissy

The tweet was accompanied by an animated gif. It was a clip Athena knew all too well. She watched as Michelle Smith (the only woman to beat Athena in a professional cage fight) kicked her in the jaw and knocked her out over and over in a continuous cycle of animation.

Athena's brow furrowed and her shoulders hunched as she seethed and primed her thumbs ready for retaliation. *No*, she thought. *Revenge will be had in the cage. Let her talk the talk. You just make sure you walk the damn walk.*

Athena sucked her cheeks in and let her teeth sink down into the delicate flesh while she drummed up the strength to turn her phone off and ignore Sissy's drama, for an hour or two at least. Picking up an Armani messenger bag she filled it with Molly's diary, a pen, some plastic carrier bags and a litre bottle of water.

The drive to Tesco involved the usual roadworks and temporary traffic lights at the junction to the Coast Road. Athena (along with most of North Tyneside's residents) felt her tempter being tested by the overnight installation of average speed cameras. It was going to take another three years to finish the works and yet the money making cameras could be installed in an instant. *Typical council*, she thought.

Athena parked in her usual parent and child parking bay and caught sight of Harry. The homeless man was dressed in his old combat jacket and there looked to be a long tear down the right sleeve. He was sat on the hard concrete floor, his back resting against the brick wall, as shoppers walked past and pretended not to notice him.

Athena turned the engine off and looked across the parking lot at Harry. She took a deep, silent breath. She had first met Harry in the bleak cold of January when three unrelenting days of rain had caused the Tyne to burst its banks and battleship grey clouds had kept the north-east under a constant cover of darkness.

The deluge had saturated the grounds of Preston cemetery into a muddy quagmire, and in the mud and the torrential downpour had sat Athena. Her mother, her grandparents, and her sister had all left her, so with nowhere else to be, Athena had kept vigil over the family grave. The panic attack induced by her sudden loneliness had so consumed her that she had failed to notice that her clothes had long since soaked through, that she had been shivering and on the verge of hypothermia for hours, and that the blackness of night was quickly approaching.

Through her tear-filled eyes, she hadn't seen the homeless man in the flimsy raincoat advancing. He pushed a Morrison's shopping trolly - its contents protected from the wet by bin liners - and carried an umbrella which was missing a spoke. When Athena looked up and stared into his gaunt face and sunken eyes, she didn't feel afraid. She felt too empty. His appearance should have been terrifying. His hair and beard were matted and his grizzly outline was rapidly silhouetting against the darkening sky. If he were a psychopath hell bent on killing her, Athena would not have tried to stop him that night.

Harry, as it turned out, was no psychopath. He pulled a space blanket from his trolly of possessions, wrapped it around the grieving girl's shoulders and handed her his last can of Fosters. He stood over Athena for an hour, using his lopsided umbrella to shield her from the rain. When Athena had slowed her breathing enough to speak, she told Harry about how her mother and grandparents had died last year in a car crash. Her mother, Vivian, had been driving her grandparents home along the A19 after visiting a sick friend in Morpeth. A speeding motorcyclist lost control of his bike and skidded across their path. Vivian had slammed the brakes to avoid hitting him but the articulated lorry that had been behind the Fox family car couldn't stop in time. Vivian's chest was crushed and her broken ribs punctured her lungs. A shard of glass from the passenger side window cut into Gramps's leg, the glass sliced through the femoral vein and he bled out in seconds. Nana managed to fight her way free from her seatbelt. She tore fabric from her dress and tried to stop her husband's bleeding, only to suffer a heart attack before the ambulance could arrive. All three died at the scene. The motorcyclist lived.

Survivor's guilt had crushed Athena. She had offered to drive her grandparents to Morpeth that day but had asked her mother to take them instead because an offer of shopping and afternoon tea with an old friend had made for a more enticing afternoon.

Then, precisely one year later, Athena had walked into their home carrying a large bunch of lilies. She and her sister had planned to go to the cemetery to pay their respects to their mother and grandparents. Only, Athena had walked through the door to find Molly hanging by her neck in the stairwell.

Athena had dropped the lilies and fallen to her knees. She tried to scream but no sound escaped her lips. Athena scrambled to her feet and ran on unsteady legs to her sister. She wrapped her arms around Molly's legs. They felt swollen and had turned purple from the pooling of blood. She tried to lift Molly, to reduce the pressure on her neck from the rope, but Athena's five-foot-three frame was too short to create enough lift. Athena's feet slipped in a pool of saliva and urine and she fell to her knees again. Scrambling back to her feet, with the smell of death and urine in her nostrils, Athena readied herself and climbed the stairs to cut Molly down. On the sixth step, Athena saw her sister's face. Her usually warm tawny skin was pale and ashen, all the blood had drained away. Her tongue, swollen and black, protruded between blue lips. A trail of saliva glistened on Molly's chin and ligature marks blotched her neck. Her once beautiful face looked monstrous. Cutting her down was pointless. Molly was gone.

When Athena had finished recounting the horrific events of her recent past she'd looked up at the homeless man.

'Got a light?' was all he had said.

Athena rummaged in her pockets and retrieved a plastic lighter, she handed it to Harry, her hands shaking uncontrollably.

There was a pause. 'Got a fag?'

Athena blinked. 'Yeah, but they're all wet.'

'Ah. Nee bother, pet,' he replied. 'Can I keep the lighter?'

Athena fixed her eyes on the muddy grave. 'Why not?' she shrugged. 'I won't need it.'

'You quitting?'

'Quitting life.'

'Ah pet, divint say things like that.'

Harry crouched down and sat in the mud next to Athena. He made sure his umbrella covered Athena's shivering body, exposing the left side of his own body to the icy rain.

'Ya said ya have a dog? A Japanese sumit?'

'Akita.' Athena lifted her head. Her eyes were raw. 'And he's not mine, he's Molly's.'

'He *was* Molly's,' said Harry. 'He's yours now. What ya gonna dee? Leave him in ya hoose to starve to death while ya gan kill ya'sel? And if they find him in time they'll just stick him in a shelter. Like jails for dogs, those places. It's nee life that, locked in a cage all day, getting twenty minutes of exercise.' He paused. 'I should know.' He paused again. 'Or he'll wind up on the streets like me, begging for handouts. Ya can't dee that to him.'

Athena nodded but said nothing.

'Ya sure those fags are nee use?'

Athena pulled them out of her pocket. The damp box almost fell apart in her hands. 'I'm sure,' she said with a gentle sigh.

'Where you from anyways?'

'Shields,' said Athena in barely more than a whisper.

Harry looked her up and down. 'Ya divint soond like ya from Shields, pet.'

Athena's soft, polished voice had meant she'd heard that many times before. The lack of strong accent, cultivated in the private schools of Newcastle's affluent suburbs put her at odds with the majority of locals who preferred *toon* to town and *doon* to down.

'Ya got kids?'

Athena shook her head.

'Ya want kids?' he pressed.

'I used to. I'm not sure I want anything now.'

'Yee'd make a good mother. Not that I knaa ya from Adam, like. But ya seem like a sweet lass.' He nodded towards the can of Fosters. 'Drink up, luv. It's medicinal.'

Athena snorted and took a long drink from the cold can. It had been chilled, not from a refrigerator, but from the freezing conditions of that awful January night.

'When the time's right ya can start ya own family. Ya obviously have a lot of love to give.'

Athena's plans for that evening had been to walk from Preston Cemetery to Low Lights beach and to walk into the freezing waters of the overflowing Tyne until its currents swept her past the piers and out to sea.

As Athena sat in her Audi, gazing across Tesco's carpark and remembering the lowest days of her life, she knew she would be forever grateful to Harry for sheltering her from the rain, and more importantly, for rescuing her from the storm that resided inside her mind. Athena dabbed her watery eyes with the back of her hand, took a deep, forceful breath in, lifted her chin and exited her vehicle. She forced a smile and strode confidently across the tarmac.

'Morning, Harry.'

Harry looked up and squinted in the sunlight. 'Morning, angel.' His skin was dry and flaking around the edges of his beard.

'You look dehydrated.'

'I'm fine, angel. Divint worry about old Ha—'

'Have some water,' interrupted Athena, unclasping the expensive messenger bag that hung across her chest. 'I'll get you a snack as well, do you fancy some fruit?'

'I fancy a gin and tonic.'

'Yeah?' laughed Athena, still trying to hold back a tear. 'You and me both.' She pulled the bottle of water from her bag and sent Molly's diary tumbling on to the pavement. The little scrap of paper that listed the three Als slipped out of the back cover and flittered around in the breeze.

'Shit.'

Athena grabbed at the air while the piece of paper bobbed around her, each time evading her grasp by millimetres. Harry's eyes followed the torn page as it twirled in the air. He reached up, plucked it from its dance and examined the writing. Harry's eyes narrowed intently and then he looked up at Athena to meet her gaze.

'Ali Montgomery?' he asked, enunciating each syllable with a deliberate slowness. He handed the paper back to Athena. 'Now why's a nice girl like you interested in a cheesy bastard like L'il Monty?'

- CHAPTER 13 -

Athena paid little heed to the highway code as she tore through the Meadow Well estate. After all, red lights were merely a suggestion. Having been unable to wait until lunchtime, Athena brought her car to a screeching halt on Padstow Road. She thundered her fist against Kris's door and hopped from foot to foot with excitement and a bladder full of coffee that was supposed to be decaf. There was no answer. Stamping her right foot, Athena scanned up and down the street but there was no sign of the blue Golf.

At your place. Where are you?

Athena took a seat on Kris's doorstep and fidgeted, throwing her phone back and forth between her hands. The gravel step felt uncomfortable through the thin lycra of her running tights but the little garden was sheltered from the breeze, making it quite the sun trap. She leaned back and rested her head against Kris's door until she felt her mobile vibrate in her hand.

Thought we were meeting at the boozer? I'm at the library.

Athena did a double take. It was easier to picture haemophobic Kris giving blood than it was to picture him in the library. As far as she knew, the only things Kris read were MMA blogs, Men's Health magazine, and the Sunday tabloids.

The library?

Yeah. It's a big building with lots of books in it.

Athena smacked her palm off of her forehead and crossed her legs, squeezing her thighs together. She watched as a group of five boys in sportswear sauntered along Padstow Road with a bull terrier leashed on a heavy chain. They swore with abundance, using the f-word and the c-word as liberally as they would use sugar on their cereal. The youngest of the boys, who couldn't have been more than eleven years old, was dressed head to toe in navy Adidas. He eyed Athena's Audi, let out a long, low whistle and ran his hand along the bonnet. Athena sprang to her feet and coughed loudly. The group turned and the youngster promptly removed his hand from the car and placed it back into his tracksuit pocket. The boys continued to the end of the street, where they formed a circle and shared a bottle of cheap cider.

I know what a library is, cheeky bugger! What are you doing there?

A police car rolled by at no more than ten miles per hour. The tallest boy hid the bottle of cider behind a garden wall whilst the youngest, the one who couldn't keep his hands off Athena's car, yelled 'PIGS' at the top of his lungs.

'Ha! Classic Shauny,' laughed the one with the bull terrier. That was until the police car's brake lights illumined and it screeched through a U-turn. The youths scattered like bowling pins, running off in five different directions. Athena could barely contain her chuckling.

I'm checking out some books on Cryptography. Thought they'd be useful.

The corner of Athena's lips curled upwards into a tiny smile as she sat back down on the uncomfortable doorstep and pulled her knees into her chest. Kris must really like her if he was giving up his time to go to the library. What would the guys from The Pit think? She could picture Luke Mar's disgust at the thought of his favourite sparring partner with his nose in a book. Athena tilted her face to the sun and broke into a beaming smile until a pang from her bladder made her squirm.

Awesome Kris… But unless you want me to pee in your rosemary bush please hurry up.

The front gate to the house next door opened. A woman with extremely long, extremely platinum hair eyed Athena with suspicion. She wore a pink Juicy Couture tracksuit with Ugg slipper boots. She pushed a double stroller, containing twin boys in matching Nike gear, and shepherded three young Staffordshire bull terriers towards her front door.

'Do I know you?'

Athena's eyes flicked to a lamppost on Padstow Road that had a fight night poster stuck to it. 'I don't think so.'

'You look familiar,' said the neighbour as one of the infant twins began to whimper.

Athena shrugged and the second twin followed his sibling's example. It was the sort of high pitched whine that made mothers come running and made the childless cock their heads away and wince.

'You waiting for Kris?'

Athena began to bounce her legs up and down as she sat on the doorstep, trying to relieve the pressure on her bladder. 'Yes,' she answered, still wincing from the noise coming from the stroller.

'You his girlfriend?'

Athena snapped her head around and glared back at the nosey neighbour. 'No,' she replied abruptly, 'and I think your babies need you.'

The platinum young mum glanced briefly at her wailing offspring and turned back to Athena. 'Ya won't last long roond here with that attitude, luv,' she snarled.

'Good job I'm not from *roond* here,' said Athena, who made a habit of never taking advice from anyone in velour.

'Posh cow. Think ya can come roond The Meadows and talk to folk like that? I should set me dogs on ya.'

Athena looked at the Staffies. They had long canines, wagging tails and that big silly grin that terriers often wear. She slapped her palms on her firm thighs and called 'Come.'

The dogs cleared the fence in a single bound and trotted up Athena for scratches and cuddles. She played with them, rubbing under their chins and scratching their bellies.

'I'm terrified,' said Athena, her voice full of sarcasm. 'And just so you know, my dog could eat the three of yours in a single sitting.' She neglected to add that Simba would likely vomit them up and eat them again!

Kris's car pulled up behind Athena's. There was a low thud of dance music pumping from the stereo until Kris switched the engine off and jumped out of his car. He had three books under his arm and a pleased-to-see-you smile across his handsome face. The neighbour gave an angry snort and pointed her finger at Athena. A point that implied she'd be watching her. Athena bit her nails with mock fear.

'Bruno! Lennox! Gazza! Come!'

The dogs whimpered but grudgingly jumped back over the fence to follow their owner into the house.

'Should I ask?' inquired Kris. He was in his usual monochrome ensemble of fitted black t-shirt and baggy black shorts.

Athena allowed herself a sly glance at his deltoids. 'Just making friends with your neighbour,' she laughed. 'Lovely woman.'

Kris shook his head and opened his front door. Athena pushed past him and sprinted up the stairs to Kris's bathroom. 'Get the kettle on,' she called as she locked the bathroom door.

'So what was so urgent it couldn't wait until lunch?' asked Kris, when Athena had returned.

'I've found Ali Montgomery,' she beamed, leaning her back against the kitchen countertop. 'Well, I haven't found him. Harry found him.'

Kris stirred some milk into two mugs of tea and handed one to Athena. It had a picture of Lionel Richie on one side of it and *Hello, is it tea you're looking for?* printed on the other. 'Who's Harry?' he asked.

'Homeless Harry,' replied Athena. 'Well, he hasn't found him yet but he knows him.'

'And who the heck is Homeless Harry?'

'He's a homeless guy,' Athena paused, 'called Harry.' She giggled and took a tentative sip of the hot tea and giggled again, this time because of the Lionel Richie pun on her mug.

'I gathered that,' sighed Kris with a shake of his head. 'And, how do you know a homeless guy?'

Kris gestured for Athena to follow him to the living room. He moved a pile of ironing from one end of the sofa and took a seat.

'That's not important,' said Athena kicking off her trainers, taking a seat at the opposite end of the sofa and tucking her feet up under herself. 'They met at the YMCA. Apparently, he gives these uber cheesy motivational speeches.'

Kris knitted his brows. 'Who does? This Harry bloke?'

Athena couldn't help but notice that Kris smelled fantastic. He must have switched aftershaves.

'Homeless Harry attends the YMCA on Thursdays when they give out free tea and coffee. Once a month they have speakers come in to give talks on all sorts of subjects. Alistair Montgomery is one of those speakers.'

Athena took another sip of tea. 'He gets called L'il Monty but he's not so little according to Harry, he's about your height, maybe taller. Harry says he stinks of fish.'

'A homeless man is complaining about the smell of someone else?' snorted Kris.

Athena slapped Kris's leg. 'Don't be mean.'

'Sorry. So, when do we meet him?'

'We can't,' pouted Athena. 'I don't know where he lives or where he works. I called the YMCA but they refused to give me any details and googling him just gets me a million pages about that actor from New Jersey. Harry's going to ask around his mates from the soup kitchen, see if anyone knows where he's based.'

'So, Harry will call you?'

'Call me? Kris, homeless people don't have phones. I'll see him about. He's usually in the cemetery.'

Kris sat open-mouthed and turned his empty palm up to face the ceiling.

'If the wind changes you'll stay like that.'

'Meeting homeless men in cemeteries? Tracking down people who messaged you on the internet? Foxy, you need to be more careful. Tell me when you want to meet this guy and I'll go with you.'

Athena's lips thinned. 'That's hardly necessary.'

'I think it is,' huffed Kris. 'You're not invincible, and besides, they still haven't caught that bastard serial rapist.'

Athena took a long slow breath through clenched teeth. As sweet as it was that Kris wanted to protect her it was insulting that he didn't trust her judgement, or her ability to defend herself. She was a modern-day gladiator for Christ's sake.

'Promise me, Foxy,' he pressed again.

'OK fine,' snapped Athena, holding up three fingers. 'Scout's honour.'

Kris lay back and his shoulders visibly relaxed. 'Good,' he said. 'I worry about you.' He put his mug of tea on the floor. 'Want to see the books I checked out?'

Athena, still seething slightly at being told what to do, shrugged. 'Sure,' she said. Then she caught sight of Kris's beautiful pleading eyes and she softened. 'OK. Let's see what you've got.'

Kris picked three books off of his kitchen counter and sat back down on the sofa, this time sitting a little closer to Athena.

'I got *Cracking Codes and Cryptograms For Dummies*,' he said, handing the book to Athena.

Athena lightly punched Kris on the arm, causing him to spill some of his tea on his lap. 'Who you calling *dummy*?'

Athena was immediately engrossed in the book, flicking through the entire book before she started to scan read the first chapter. Kris chatted away about the other two books he was holding: a biography of Alan Turing and a GCHQ puzzle book. He figured if they could solve puzzles set by Britain's most secretive intelligence organisation then they could crack a code made up by Athena's little sister. Athena was barely listening though, she had curled herself up with her face buried in the book and the tips of her toes poking into Kris's thigh.

Athena had lost track of how long she'd been curled up on Kris's old sofa but she had plowed through to chapter four and somehow her feet had come to rest on Kris's lap. He held his puzzle book in one hand and rubbed her aching arches with the other.

'Lines,' he said.

'Lines?' asked Athena, noticing her feet and fighting the urge to yank her feet back under herself. His hand felt oh so good after all.

'A circle has one line, a cross has two lines. Triangles three lines and squares four lines.'

Athena pulled herself upright and released her feet from Kris's heavenly hand. 'Are you on to something?'

'I'm not sure. Let's have a look at the diary.'

Athena pulled the tatty grey notepad from her bag and opened it to a random page. 'Triangle, circle, cross, square, square, circle, cross, circle.'

'Three, one, two, four, four, one, two, one,' said Kris, noting it down in the margin of the book. 'That doesn't really help, that would be… Hmm… C, A, B, D, D, A, B, A? That makes no sense either.'

'What if we pair them up?' asked Athena. Closing the yellow and black *For Dummies* book and placing it on her lap. 'Let's see. Thirty-one, twenty-four, forty-one, twenty-one.'

Kris frowned. His scarred brow bone reflecting the soft light from the living room window. 'How many letters did you say were in the Japanese alphabet?'

'Forty-six,' answered Athena, 'If you don't count the kanji.'

Kris pulled out his phone and did a web search for the Japanese alphabet of hiragana. 'Hmm, I'm not sure what order these would be in,' he said looking at the chart with his mouth pulled into a perplexed grimace. 'Maybe, Ma, Ne, Ru, Na? Maneruna? Is that a word?'

Athena punched the word into Google translate. 'Hey! We might be on to something here. It means *do not imitate*.'

'Ha! Do not imitate?' Kris's grey eyes were enlivened. 'Brilliant! Let's plod on. What's next?'

Athena's heart was racing. 'Erm, it's... let's see,' she said with a high pitched and quivering voice. 'It's eleven, twenty-four, twelve, twenty-four, and forty-two.'

'Sa, Ne, Shi, Ne, Re,' said Kris, reading out the corresponding hiragana characters in turn.

Athena turned back to Google Translate. '*I imitate it, dead body?* What on Earth?'

Kris took the phone from Athena's hands and studied the screen for a moment before Athena snatched it back. She shook her head. 'I don't understand, Kris. *Imitate? Dead body?* What does that mean? Was the body I found not real, or did it belong to someone else? Could Molly be alive?'

Kris shrugged and placed a hand on Athena's knee. 'I don't know what it means, but... I don't think Molly's alive, Foxy. I mean, you buried her.'

'I buried someone.'

Athena's mind raced. Was the body she found really Molly? It must have been. Mustn't it? She'd recognise her sister anywhere. *You didn't recognise that she was suicidal. You didn't recognise she needed help.* Athena jumped to her feet and stared out of the window. She stretched her arms above her head and told herself to breathe.

'Should we keep going, Foxy?'

'Yes,' she replied, faking a smile. 'What's next?'

Kris squinted at his hiragana chart. 'Ka, Sa, Na, Re, Ru, Re.'

Athena sat on the windowsill and embraced the warmth of the sun on her back. 'Hmm. OK. This makes even less sense. Apparently, it says *Pretend yourself dead and get an umbrella*. I think we've gone wrong somewhere.'

Kris exhaled. 'It could be the translator? I used one to try and buy sage in a market in Romania and ended up with a bag of cannabis.'

Athena looked quizzical.

'But,' continued Kris. 'I agree, I think we're on the wrong track, Foxy. With this method, we can't use the full alphabet. There's only one, two, three and four. So we could never make seventeen or thirty-five or…'

'Oh,' said Athena. She folded her arms across her chest, feeling deflated. 'And we couldn't have anything under eleven or anything over forty-four. Man. I thought we had it there.'

All the excitement that she had felt only seconds ago had faded and a familiar empty feeling crept up inside Athena's stomach. Kris nudged her and smiled. 'We're closer though. We must be.'

Athena didn't know if Kris meant they were closer to cracking the code or if the two of them were closer to each other. She didn't ask. The mention of dead bodies had made her think of fighting, and fighting made her think of Sissy Clark. What was Sissy doing now? Was she training while Athena was sat on her backside reading books and playing with iPhone apps? If she was going to read she could at least do it on a treadmill or sat on an exercise bike. Maybe she could get the audio version and listen while walking Simba. That stupid little gif of Michelle Smith knocking her out played over and over inside Athena's mind. Being knocked unconscious could have serious repercussions on a person's health and whilst Athena knew this and accepted it as part and parcel of the life of a professional fighter - a workplace hazard if you like - it still played on her mind. Could it happen again? Sissy was more than capable of landing a devastating head kick. Athena could land catastrophic head kicks of her own, but Sissy's head was a good four to five inches higher in the air than hers. And whilst Athena's legs may be strong and flexible they were also short. There was no way around it, she couldn't waste another second curled up on a sofa reading a book when she could be hitting pads or lifting weights or doing something, anything, to move her closer to victory in the cage. It was time to put handsome training partners, code-breaking and men who smelled of fish to the back of her mind. It was time to focus.

'So, is that a yes?' asked Kris.

Athena had been a million miles away. 'Sorry, what?'

'Dinner, Foxy?' he said. 'You'll come to dinner on Friday?'

- CHAPTER 14 -

'Me?' asked Athena. Had she heard Kris correctly?

'No, the girl sat behind you,' said Kris. 'Were you listening to me?'

'No,' she replied sheepishly. 'Sorry Kris, I was thinking about Sissy Clark's shin.'

Kris raised his scarred brow. 'Her shin?'

'Colliding with the side of my head,' finished Athena. She stood, picked up the two empty mugs from the floor, wandered through to Kris's kitchen and flicked the switch on his kettle. Away from Kris's eyes she slowly counted to ten. Her mind was awash with nervous thoughts of broken orbitals and bloody noses. Was Kris asking her out? Now? Now, when she was days away from the biggest and most dangerous fight of her career? His timing really was excellent.

As the kettle began to gargle and hiss Athena started to chew on the inside of her cheek, when her raw flesh started to taste of blood she bit her lip instead. There was a part of her, a large part, that would welcome a date with Krzysztof Kava, despite her utterly childish rule about Polish boys. Besides, she'd only made that up in the first place to stop Tomasz Leppek from pestering her in year eleven. But, alas, Athena was certain that now was not the right time. Surely he could wait a couple of weeks. The kettle boiled and Athena brewed up two cups of tea, making them stronger than usual while her stubborn heart refused to slow down and her cheeks refused to stop glowing.

Looking down at her lycra-clad legs Athena couldn't help but wish she was dressed better. Head to toe lycra and trainer socks may have been her standard wardrobe but they did not make a great potential girlfriend outfit. *Oh, woman up for goodness sake!* thought Athena. *You're acting like a damn teenager.*

Athena composed herself and fanned her face with a tea towel. 'So…' she said, a grin on her face as she returned and handed Kris his mug. 'You were asking me out?'

'Thanks. Erm, yes. Well, sort of,' said Kris, fidgeting with a frayed hem on his shorts. 'But if you want to talk about Sissy, we can talk about—'

'Sort of?'

Kris batted his dreamy eyelashes and patted the sofa with his free hand. Athena moved the copy of *Cracking Codes and Cryptograms For Dummies* and took a seat.

'My parents are up from London and they want to take me and my girlfriend out to dinner.'

Athena gave a tiny cough. 'You have a girlfriend?'

'No,' said Kris. 'You know I don't. But my parents worry about me and they keep going on about having more grandkids. So, to get them off my back I told them I had a girlfriend… And now they're visiting and they want to meet her.'

Athena was still. Her brow was low and her mouth had twisted into a deformed and wrinkly pout. Kris didn't want a girlfriend, he just wanted someone to play the part. Part of her was relieved, but moreover, she was embarrassed and annoyed and though she didn't want to say it out loud, disappointed.

'I know,' said Kris with a heavy sigh. 'I dug myself into a right hole and I should dig myself out of it. But, it's this Friday and they didn't give me much notice so I either need to come clean and deal with a world of questions from my mother, or I can tell them Emily is sick and can't make it.'

Athena flared her nostrils. 'Your fake girlfriend is called *Emily?'*

Kris blushed (he never seemed to blush) and gave a shrug. 'Emily's a nice name.'

'And what does *Emily* do?'

Kris tipped his head back and puffed his cheeks out. 'Emily,' he paused, 'is a primary school teacher.'

Athena twirled a section of her short hair between her fingertips, her lips still contorted in a twisted pout. She said nothing while Kris squirmed, shifting his weight from one butt cheek to the other.

'I'm sorry,' he blurted after an awkward twenty seconds of silence. 'It was a stupid idea. Of course you don't want to be Emily. I'll do the right thing, I'll tell them the tr—'

Athena held up a finger, shushed him, and sat in silence for another painfully long moment.

'Fine,' said Athena. 'I'll come to dinner.'

Kris beamed and clapped his hands together.

'But,' she continued, her voice hard and resolute. 'My name is Athena Fox and I'm a professional cage fighter. I'm not being Emily-the-bloody-primary-school-teacher. You and Emily broke up. You dumped her for me.'

Kris said something in Polish, dived across the sofa, hugged Athena and sent boiling tea flying on to the already stained carpet.

'And…' Athena pushed Kris off of her, 'you'll owe me.'

'Anything,' said Kris.

'I'll need help with the weight cut. Someone to ferry me around while I'm dehydrated and to make sure I don't collapse in the sauna or drown in the bathtub.'

'Deal,' said Kris, 'but I'd have done that anyway.'

Athena was still put out and embarrassed. She absentmindedly tapped the book she was holding on her thigh until she finally said, 'You'd better tell me some stuff about yourself. Your mother's going to expect me to know more about you than how you never do your ironing and that you have the best spin kick at The Pit.'

'*You* have the best spin kick at The Pit,' said Kris. 'But you're right.'

A smug look passed over Athena's face. 'That was a test.'

'Let's see, I was born in Wroclaw on Valentines Day in '85. Apparently, I was born within an hour of my mother going into labour. She called for my father, but by the time he got home I'd already been born on our bathroom floor.'

'Blimey,' said Athena, crossing her legs.

'And she's never let me forget it. What else? My mother is Danika, my father is Piotr but gets called Pete. My brothers are Ulryk, Marcin, Felip, and Sylwester. We moved to London when I was ten. My father was offered work in my uncle's construction business. I know, I know, Polish builders, right? We're walking stereotypes. But there was plenty of work and the business is still going strong. Dad and Uncle Pawel still work but it's my brothers who do most of the heavy lifting now.'

Athena tucked her feet back under herself. 'And you're the youngest?' she asked.

'Yeah, which means I'm the baby, even at thirty-one. My mother still calls me *Little Krzysztof*.'

Athena snorted. 'Little? I doubt there's anything *little* about you.' Athena's cheeks turned beetroot and she wished she could pull the words back into her mouth. 'I meant, well, you're tall and broad and… Oh, you know what I mean, stop grinning!'

Athena slapped Kris with Alan Turning's biography and Kris adjusted himself on the sofa, sitting with his knees much further apart than they had been a few seconds ago.

'Anyway,' he continued, his face flushed, 'in Wroclaw, we lived in the suburbs and my brothers and I would always be out in the forests or hiking along the Oder. People ask me what I remember about Poland and the main thing I remember was the colour green. I was always surrounded by nature. Then we moved to the *Big Smoke*. And it was just that: too big, too smokey. I hated the crowds and the pollution, and everything was grey. The sky was grey, the concrete was grey, my school uniform was grey. I spent less and less time outdoors and more and more time playing indoor sports. I got hooked on basketball and taekwondo, and boy do I mean hooked. Every day I played basketball or went to taekwondo. Every. Single. Day.'

Kris took a long sip of tea and to Athena's relief he adjusted his knees and sat normally again. 'I was supposed to join the family business. I was never asked outright, but it was always assumed. I helped during the school holidays but by sixteen I'd ditched basketball for boxing and I was so obsessed with martial arts that they'd taken up almost all of my free time. I started MMA at eighteen and had my first amateur fight at nineteen. When I told everyone I was going pro it was like,' he took another sip, 'it was like I'd dumped them for a new family or something. They took it so personally. Not Dad so much but my brothers definitely. It was like *we have to mix cement and put up the scaffold, how come you get out of it?* Anyway, in my second pro fight - I was twenty-one - I got my arse well and truly handed to me by Brian Herbertson. Remember Brian?'

'Sure,' nodded Athena, 'he coached at The Pit a while back.'

'Well, he wasn't just a coach. Back in the day, he was a fighter, a damn good one. Brian *The Barbarian*. He battered me back and forth across the cage until I didn't know what year it was. He gave me this scar.' Kris rubbed the right side of his forehead. 'After that, I made a decision. I figured I was never going to beat the best if I didn't train with the best, so I swallowed my pride, gave Brian a call and asked to come train with him. Within three weeks I'd moved up north. Best decision I ever made.'

×××

A bead of sweat trickled down Athena's nose and she shook her head like a wet dog, sending it, and a hundred other beads of sweat flying off in all directions. Her early afternoon run through Jesmond Dene, a beautiful and tranquil valley of trees and lawns in central Newcastle, was flying by. The sun was still high in the sky and heat radiated from the paved tracks. Thankfully, the canopy of lush green sheltered Athena and Simba from the harshest of the sun's rays. Athena, her feet rhythmically tip-tapping on the road as she followed the burn through the dene, wasn't sure she'd made the right decision in agreeing to pose as Kris's girlfriend. She should have told him to get lost, she thought, as she dodged a young mother who was attempting to push a pram and text at the same time.

Simba plodded along beside Athena, his white fur billowing around with each light step. No matter how fast Athena pushed through the landscaped woodland, Simba never seemed to have to move faster than a brisk trot. It was infuriating.

Ahead, a pair of swans floated gracefully along the shallow burn. As white as Simba, their feathers gleamed against the backdrop of jade and emerald greens. The swans disappeared with the burn, under an old stone footbridge covered in ivy. Athena took a deep breath and quickened her pace. She targeted the swans and caught up with them just as a black Labrador ran across her path and jumped into the burn to cool off. The swans lost their aloof facade and took to the air, hooting with indignation. Simba eyed the Labrador with envy and made to jump in after him. A firm 'No' from Athena was enough to stop the obedient beast in his tracks. She had no intention of letting sixty kilograms of soaking wet Akita back in her car.

While Simba caught up, Athena pulled her MP3 player from her pocket and switched playlists. She ditched metal music and selected some fast-paced dance music from ten years ago. Luke would approve. With Simba back at her heels Athena's pace increased to match the music. She felt light as air. Her lungs were powerful and her muscles responded to everything she asked of them: jumping over logs, zigzagging through trees and steaming up hills. Physically, she felt unstoppable. Mentally, she felt frustrated. She should have told Kris that if he wanted to ask her out he should have done it properly and not have their first date under the watchful eye of his parents like damn twelve-year-olds. Better still, Athena could have asked him out herself. It wasn't as if she was shy when it came to men, the bondage-loving chef knew that all too well. His thick, hairy arms had been tied to the handles of his kitchen cupboards with black silk scarves while Athena had teased him - in a most unhygienic manner - with his fish slicer. Athena squeezed her eyelids shut and shook the image from her mind. Kris was was different though. She actually liked him, and instead of asking him out or demanding that he do it properly she had sold herself for a weight cut buddy.

The small car park at the edge of the dene came into view in the distance. Athena sped up again, determined to record a good time and keep Charlie off her back. He would want to know her distance and split times later. She did *need* a weight cut assistant though, thought Athena as she pushed hard through her thighs on the final uphill. Weight cuts were bad enough as they were but having to go through them alone was not only torture but dangerous. Last time, she'd been so light headed in the sauna that when she stood up she'd lost her footing and smacked her head on the wooden steps. Knowing she'd be pulled from the fight with even the slightest sign of head trauma she'd kept the entire incident to herself. It wasn't the wisest choice she'd made in her martial arts career.

Athena slowed to a walk and stopped her exercise tracker. Forty-five minutes and seventeen seconds. Charlie would be happy with that. Athena removed her car key from her sports bra and unlocked the convertible. She lowered the top and pulled a towel from the boot to pat herself dry.

'Here you go, Simba,' she said, pouring water into a large plastic tub.

The Akita eagerly lapped at the water, his tail wagging happily behind him. A black Vauxhall Corsa pulled into the space next to Athena and the sound of an infant in the throes of an epic temper tantrum perforated the sounds of the dene. Athena tucked her headphones into the glovebox and signalled for Simba to take his seat. He jumped over the door and made himself comfortable. A quick check of the mirrors and she started the engine. As Athena reversed out of the parking space she felt her stomach drop.

'Sweetheart, he needs changing.'

'So change him.'

'But sweetheart, you do it so much better than I do.'

'No, you just say that to get out of doing it. You're worse than a teenager who always does a crappy job of the dishes so his parents won't ask him to do them again.'

'That's not fair.'

'Then change him, Owen.'

Well isn't this peachy? thought Athena as Owen Daley Phelps laid his caterwauling child on the back seat and looked at the changing bag in his hand as if it were an alien life form. Claire, Owen's wife, looked like she needed to sleep for a week. She craned her neck as the Audi roared into action, shielding her eyes from the sun with her hand.

'Owen, wasn't that your fighter friend? The one with the weird name?'

XXX

The drive back to North Shields was a crabby one. Athena ran the red light at the junction to join the Coast Road and sped through the first section of dual carriageway until she had to slam her breaks in time for the speed camera on the North Tyneside border.

'*Weird* name?' she yelled into the wind. 'Who does she think she is? I don't have a weird name?'

Simba barked.

'OK, you're right as usual, you daft dog. So, I have a weird name. Better to have a weird name than a weird face.'

Simba barked again.

Athena ran her fingers over her squashed nose and shrugged. 'Fine! I have a weird name and a weird face, but so do you.'

Simba huffed, curled into a ball on the passenger seat, pressed his nose into his rear and smelled his own fart.

- CHAPTER 15 -

Athena took out her bad mood on the door to The Pit. The glass panel shuddered as it slammed behind her, causing poor Simba to jump. An encouraging smell of disinfectant hung in the air, a sign that Charlie Fisher was staying on top of his cleaning regime in the wake of the ringworm outbreak. He was sat behind his desk fidgeting with his fingernails and repeatedly crossing and uncrossing his legs. The closer it got to fight week the more anxious Charlie became. He wanted his fighters to win as much as they did.

'Get that bag of fleas out of here,' he said, pointing a chewed fingernail in Simba's direction.

'I'm not your messenger,' said Athena, 'tell him yourself.'

Charlie, his finger still pointed at Simba, muttered a deep, 'Outside.'

The dog curled his lips, bared his teeth and let out a low rumble of a growl. Charlie stared at the dog for a moment before lowering his hand and admitting defeat.

The Pit's ladies kickboxing class was coming to an end. Luke was leading the group (whose members ranged from mid-teens to mid-fifties) through a stretching routine. He lowered himself into a hurdler stretch and leaned forward to take hold of his toes. He looked darker than usual, his deep tan making the bright yellow of his shorts and the Barbie pink of his vest even more eye-catching than usual.

Athena threw her kit bag to the side and began to rummage around for her gum shield and hand wraps. She was still simmering over the appearance of Owen at the end of her run. Running was a sacred time, a time to purge the body of negative emotions and fill it with endorphins. She should have been a zen-like ball of calm on her drive home, not a raging, bitching ball of fury. *The one with the weird name indeed.* Owen Daley Phelps would not worm his way back into Athena's life, she wouldn't allow it. She was going to focus on Sissy and once all this fighting business was out of the way she'd ask Kris on a real date.

At the thought of his name, Athena turned to see Kris arrive at the gym.

'Hey,' he said.

'Hey, yourself,' replied Athena. He smelled of muscle rub and Athena had to restrain herself from leaning in and taking a deep inhalation of eucalyptus.

'The table's booked for seven on Friday. That all right?' asked Kris.

'Seven's great,' smiled Athena, desperately trying to shove Owen to the back of her mind. *He's a loser, you're better off without him and you know it.*

'Foxy,' called Charlie from his desk. 'Run time?'

'Erm… Forty-five, seventeen.'

Charlie made a note of her time but gave no indication as to whether he was pleased with it or not.

Luke got to his feet and bowed to his class. The women returned the courtesy and dispersed. Three of them made a bee-line for Simba, who was laying down in front of Charlie's desk.

'Oh my, have you ever seen anything so cute?' asked one as she ruffled Simba's fur.

The women of the class seemed to fall into two categories. There were the red-faced, sweaty backed, hard workers and the girls who still had pristine ponytails, perfect makeup and not even a hint of sweat. One such girl, with eyelashes as long as her legs, took a little longer than she should have to bend over and pick up her things.

'Bye, Luke,' she called with her pert bottom still bent over in his direction.

Athena let her head fall to the side and her eyes rolled back in their sockets. *Fans*. MC Hammer finished telling the room that they couldn't touch this and the girl power of the Spice Girls took over.

Athena began to wrap her hands in black cotton. 'I see Luke's in charge of the music again.'

'You can't beat a bit of Ginger and Posh,' boomed Luke, popping his hips back and forth to the beat. 'Bet you wanted to be Baby Spice.'

Athena laughed and flexed her biceps. 'Sporty,' she corrected, 'obviously.'

The long-lashed girl pouted and stomped her way out of the gym.

'You've got an admirer there,' said Kris as Luke danced his way into the fighting cage. He sidestepped around in circles, leaving a plume of tanning oil stench behind him.

'Who? Lisa?' he asked. 'Bah! She's barely old enough to drink. Besides, it's fighting season. Can't be having some young lass distracting me and costing me my belt. Teammates before dates! Ain't that right, Foxy?'

Athena sighed, she finished wrapping her fists and mentally superimposed Owen's face on to her left palm. She punched her right fist into it until his face disappeared. 'Right,' she replied. 'Fights before love bites.'

Luke began to moonwalk, humming the tune under his breath. 'Bicep curls before girls,' he said, pointing to Athena.

Athena climbed into the cage, appreciating the familiar feel of canvas under her bare feet. She popped her gum shield in her mouth and ran her tongue over its contours. It still had the residual taste of spearmint toothpaste.

'Kicks before dicks!' she proclaimed with a muffled voice.

Luke laughed and picked up a set of punching pads. 'Oh, I love a girl with a potty mouth.'

Charlie, stopwatch in hand, took his position at the side of the cage. Kris climbed the cage and sat on top of the fencing to get a birds-eye view of the action.

'Jab, cross, hook, cross, leg kick, head kick,' said Charlie, rattling off the desired striking combination.

Athena nodded. 'Yes, boss.'

The door to The Pit clicked open and Stevie and Jimmy rushed in.

'You're late,' said Charlie. 'Fifty push-ups.'

'Ah Charlie,' sighed Jimmy, his pink sunburnt skin clashing with his red hair. 'It wasn't our fault. My ex was late collecting the bairn and there're roadworks at the Coast Road—'

'Seventy push-ups,' snapped Charlie.

Stevie slapped Jimmy across the back of his head and the pair of scrawny but scrappy men dumped their bags and got down on the mats to begin their punishment.

'You waiting for a bus, Foxy? Hit the damn pads.'

Athena exchanged a look with Luke and began to hammer through the kicking and punching combination with ease. It was a simple combination and one Athena could execute with precision and power. It felt great as she slammed her strong legs into the pads. Her fists were fast, shoulders lose and her footwork was flawless. At the end of the round, Charlie didn't have a bad word to say about it, which made a refreshing change.

'One-minute active rest,' said Charlie, meaning Athena should get her breath back without merely standing still.

Kris handed Athena her water bottle and she took a quick sip.

'All right, ballet girl,' said Luke. 'A plié and a pirouette, if you please.'

Athena took deep breaths and recuperated while slowly executing a number of basic ballet movements.

The two arts: dance and combat, complemented each other. Slow and controlled, explosive and aggressive.

Charlie looked up at Kris and wiped a droplet of sweat from his brow. 'Never thought I'd see ballet in the cage?'

'She makes it look easy,' said Kris, his eyes fixed on Athena.

'Right, next combo,' said Charlie, before calling out the techniques.

Luke slammed the pads together to signal the start of the round and Athena got straight to work. Again, hitting the pads with speed and power. After the final kick Luke would swing one of the pads towards the side of her head and Athena would have to cover up and protect herself. She bit down hard on her gum shield, as Luke didn't hold back. The drill tested Athena's defensive skills but also forced her to stay calm under pressure. It wasn't easy to maintain correct technique when she was dazed or flustered. As the round wore on Athena's breathing became heavy, her heart rate began to rise and her shoulders began to stiffen. Each punch became gradually slower.

'Time,' called Charlie. 'Not bad, Foxy. Given Luke was trying to take your head off.'

Kris grabbed a set of pads and jumped down into the cage. Stevie Kelly, the little flyweight, slipped his hands into his boxing gloves and joined his teammates in the cage. Athena calmed her breathing and used the minute of rest to perform more ballet. She extended her leg above her head and held it vertically in the air. She was essentially standing in the splits. Noticing Kris's eyes on her, Athena gave him a smile, flashing the black plastic of her gum shield at him.

Kris nodded in admiration but Luke grasped his padded hands over his groin. 'Urgh! Freaks me out every time,' he moaned.

'Combo number six,' said Charlie. 'Make sure those elbows come in hard.'

'Yes boss,' said Athena and Stevie in unison.

Luke and Kris slammed their pads together and the two tiny fighters got to work. The sound of shins, elbows, fists, and knees hammering the pads echoed around The Pit and drowned out the sound of Britney Spears.

'Faster Stevie, Foxy's leaving you for dust.'

Athena could hear Stevie stepping it up a gear. She dug in deeper to maintain her lead without sacrificing technique. Sweat began to trickle down from Athena's armpits and hairline. She huffed and growled each time she reached up for Luke's neck and drove her knee into his stomach.

'Time,' called Charlie. 'Wrestle.'

Kris and Luke threw Athena and Stevie at each other. Stevie tossed his gloves to the floor and Athena grabbed him tightly around the torso. The pair battled to throw each other to the ground. It was exhausting but Athena was truly in the zone. There was no code, no diary, no Kris, Owen or Sissy. There was only Stevie, and Stevie needed to be slammed into the canvas. Athena turned into Stevie, pulling his left arm forcefully as she did so.

He catapulted over Athena's hip and came crashing down to the canvas with a thud.

Stevie scrambled and bucked Athena off of him. Now Stevie was in control. Back and forth they grappled, grunting with the exertion of it. When Charlie finally ended the round the pair fell side by side to the canvas. Athena stared up at the ceiling and took gasping mouthfuls of air until Kris leaned over her. 'Up,' he said, extending an arm. 'Active rest, ballet girl.'

Athena allowed Kris to pull her to her feet, Luke doing the same for Stevie. Stevie jogged on the spot and lightly shadow sparred but Athena resumed her old dance moves. She twirled - less gracefully than before - around on the tips of her toes until Luke scoffed, 'Is that all you've got?'

He dropped to the canvas and began to breakdance, spinning around on his back like an upturned turtle.

'Oh, I'll see your backspin and raise you a worm,' said Athena. She lay down on her belly and sent perfect ripples through her body from head to toe.

Luke clapped his hands together in glee and joined Athena. The two sweaty fighters, one a six-foot-four behemoth, the other a five-foot-three (and a half) powerhouse, wormed around the cage, giggling like children. Athena was lost in the moment. For the first time in a long time, she was truly enjoying training. She felt focused but relaxed and relishing the absurdness of it all.

'A right bunch of professionals yee lot are,' said Charlie. He looked down at Luke and Athena, shaking his head.

'We're the best team you ever had,' said Kris, lying on the floor of the cage and performing a quick worm of his own. 'Admit it.'

Athena caught the slightest smile creep across Charlie's bearded face. She smiled back at him until out of the corner of her eye she saw a black Vauxhall Corsa drive past The Pit.

- CHAPTER 16 -

There was a chill in the evening air. Athena's gym bag bounced up and down in time with her steps as she made her way back through North Shields. Her sweaty clothing was now cold and damp, her body shivered and the fair hairs on her forearms stood on end. Simba stayed at her heels, his fur occasionally brushing against Athena's lower legs. Stars sparkled in the clear sky overhead and the chimes from the church bell tower rang out ten times.

A familiar shadow huddled in the doorway of Christ Church. Harry was sat on the great stone step with his head resting against the heavy wooden doors. He pulled a blanket around his shoulders and dealt eight playing cards on to the ground in front of him. He took a sip of tea from a polystyrene cup and turned over the first card. As Athena approached she took in the beautiful herbal smell of freshly cut grass and let out a far from delicate sneeze.

'Angel!' said Harry, his eyes lighting up at the sight of Athena. 'Get yourself home and out of this cold. You shouldn't be gannin' roond in a vest at this time of night, ya'll catch ya death, pet.'

Athena closed her eyes for a second and listened to the gentle hum of traffic negotiating the crossroads.

'Harry, Harry, Harry,' she sighed as Simba ran up to his old buddy for a scratch. 'The irony of what you just s —'

Athena was cut off by the sound of two fire engines zooming through the crossroads with their sirens blaring. She watched them go in a blur of blue flashing lights and did a quick scan of the area for black Vauxhalls.

'I'd go home a lot happier,' started Athena, 'if you came with me and let me cook you a decent meal.'

Harry turned a card over. 'The three of clubs,' he said in a murmur. 'Ah pet, if you've asked once you've asked a thousand times. Thanks, but I'm fine here my angel.'

Athena clenched her teeth. The stubborn old fool was far from fine.

Harry patted the step next to him. 'If you're not going to get out of the cold you might as well take a pew.'

Athena sat down. The sharp cold of the stone seeped through her thin lycra clothing and chilled the bones of her behind.

'Blanket?' offered Harry.

Athena shook her head. 'No thanks, Harry.'

'I was hoping I'd see you,' said Harry. His breath had the faint smell of onion soup and strong coffee. He turned over another card and cursed at the six of hearts. 'I was askin' me mate Smithy 'bout ol' Ali Montgomery. He reckons he lives in Gateshead, but then Jenkins chimed in and he's adamant Mr. Motivator's based in the toon. Says when he's not giving his cheesy speeches he's flogging overpriced fish to overpaid lawyers and accountants. Said his restaurant's somewhere posh like Jesmond or Gosforth.'

Impressed, Athena's spirits lifted. 'That was fast work.'

'Aye, mind you, Jenkins loves the soond of his own voice so he might be talkin' oot his hairy arse.'

'But it's a start,' said Athena, trying not to think about arses, hairy or otherwise. She looked across the road to Oddfellows pub. Groups of merry drinkers were huddled in the doorway enjoying their between rounds cigarettes. The pub looked cozy, warm and welcoming and the soft strums of folk music carried in the breeze.

'Well Harry, if you're not going to let me cook you a meal, at least let me buy you a pint.'

'Ah, it's alreet, angel. Thanks but I'm...' His voice trailed off and he stroked the edge of the queen of diamonds. 'Oh, who am I kiddin'? Ah could use a pint.'

Harry collected in his playing cards and stashed them in his coat pocket. He folded up his blanket and tucked it under his arm, got to his feet and extended an arm to Athena.

'Where's your trolly?' asked Athena as Harry pulled her off the cold stone step.

'Roond the back, next to the bins, be safe as hooses there,' he replied.

Oddfellows was a squat, cream coloured public house on the main thoroughfare through North Shields. The smokers crowding the doorway parted to allow Athena and Harry through. The cloud of cigarette smoke was almost too much for Athena, who took a dizzying inhalation as she passed through the doorway. Heads turned as the pair entered the little pub, and questioning eyes moved between the older man in his tattered clothes and the sweaty girl in lycra. Simba performed a quick scan of the room, spied a labradoodle and ran over to sniff her behind. Harry shuffled uncomfortably into a seat in the corner. He looked up in time to see the lady on the adjacent table scoot her chair a foot to the left.

'On second thoughts, I'm not that thirsty angel. I should leave.'

'Don't you dare,' said Athena, shooting the woman on the next table a look. 'You're not standing me up.'

The pub smelled of furniture polish and cheese and onion crisps. In the far corner, two men played guitars and sang old folk songs. Next to them, a man and a woman in their fifties played darts. The woman, short with a pear-shaped body and mousy hair down to her waist, threw her first dart. It sailed straight into the triple twenty and was quickly joined by the second and third darts. The mousy woman turned to face her partner. He was only an inch taller, but probably a foot wider with a checkered shirt stretched over his beer belly. She placed her hands triumphantly on her hips while the man shook his head and looked at the floor in defeat. 'Best of three?' he asked.

'So what will it be?' asked Athena. 'Fosters?'

'Aye, yes please, pet,' answered Harry.

Athena caught the eye of a plump barmaid with an abundance of curly red hair. Her round, ivory face broke into a beautiful smile.

'What can I get you, luv?'

'A pint of Fosters please,' started Athena. She surveyed the rows of beer pumps and bottles in the fridge. She shouldn't be drinking alcohol this close to a fight but her brain ached for it. She was in good shape, one drink couldn't hurt. Besides, it would be rude to leave Harry drinking alone. 'And a vodka tonic please, with low-calorie tonic if you have it.'

The barmaid nodded and began to pour the Fosters. 'That's the old dear who hangs around Preston Cemetery, isn't it?' she said leaning in close so that she could keep her voice a whisper.

Athena bristled and stood as tall and assertive as her frame would allow. 'He's harmless.'

'Oh I know that,' said the barmaid, still whispering. 'Seen the local toe rags teasing him plenty of times. He never rises to it. Never snaps at the little shits, even when they threaten to set their dogs on him.'

Athena swallowed and looked back over her shoulder at Harry. His eyes were fixed on the table, trying to avoid eye contact with everyone and anyone. 'He's a nice guy in a bad situation,' said Athena.

'That's six sixty-five, luv,' said the barmaid, handing Athena the two glasses. Then she picked up two packets of crisps. 'He looks like a few extra calories wouldn't go amiss,' she added.

Athena smiled appreciatively. She bowed her head, took her change and returned to Harry.

'Thanks, angel,' he said, grasping the cold pint glass in both hands and taking a long, satisfying sip. 'Lovely.'

Athena opened the two packets of crisps and as if by magic, Simba reappeared at Athena's heels.

'Ya shouldn't have,' said Harry.

'I didn't,' replied Athena. 'You have the curvaceous redhead to thank for the crisps.'

Harry looked taken aback, his eyes widened and he coyly looked over at the bar. The barmaid smiled sweetly and mouthed, 'dig in.'

Harry nodded and turned back to the crisps. He picked up a salt and vinegar one and nibbled at it like a nervous mouse.

The couple who had been playing darts joined the woman on the adjacent table. She was a frail-looking lady with paper skin and tight black curls and was thoroughly engrossed in a crossword puzzle.

'She beat me again, Marge,' said the man as he huffed his body down on to a three-legged stool.

'Don't know why you still insist on trying,' replied the mousy woman, who sat down next to Marge and handed her a glass of port.

'How's ya puzzle going, Marge?' asked the man.

Marge perused her puzzle. 'Twelve down, Irish combat sensation? Five and eight letters.'

The couple looked blankly at each other and then the man suggested, 'Barry McGuigan?'

'Doesn't fit,' said Marge. 'Ends in an R.'

Athena leant into Harry and whispered in his ear. He coughed, catching the attention of his three neighbours.

'It's McGregor, C-Conor McGregor,' he stammered over the relaxing sound of folk singing.

'Oh,' replied the man. He spun the paper around and penciled in the letters. 'Thanks mate. Don't suppose you know a Korean composer famous for his works River Flows In You and Kiss The Rain?'

Harry shook his head and looked into his pint. 'No, sorry.'

'I do,' interrupted Athena. 'It's Yiruma. Y, I, R, U, M, A.'

The two women exchanged looks and the man once again looked impressed. 'Thanks.'

'I'm Athena, and this is my friend Harry.'

The three quizzers smiled uneasily and the man looked from Athena to Harry and back again. 'Ben,' he said, smoothing down his checkered shirt, 'and this is Marge and Leanne. So how do you two know each other?'

'Oh,' started Harry, taking a sip of his drink and nibbling on another crisp. 'Athena's a sweet girl, an angel actually. She helps me out, buys me snacks even though I've told her not to worry about ol' Har—'

'That's not how we know each other,' said Athena, cutting him off. 'Harry saved my life.'

Intrigued, Ben, Marge, and Leanne leant in closer.

'Yes you did Harry, don't give me that look. I was going through a tough time and I couldn't handle it,' said Athena. 'I was in a really bad place and I, I, well…' Athena wondered why it was so much easier to open up to complete strangers than it was to open up to her closest friends. 'I was going to commit suicide,' she continued, 'and then Harry turned up.'

Leanne, The mousy woman who had won the darts game, looked at Harry inquisitively.

'And I'm still here,' said Athena, a tiny tear in her eye. 'If it weren't for Harry I'd be a bloated corpse washed up on a beach somewhere. So yes, I buy him snacks and things. It's the least I can do.'

'Wow,' said Marge.

'Well,' said Ben, draining his glass. 'I'm buying Harry-the-Hero a pint. Anyone need anything from the bar? Leanne? Marge?'

- CHAPTER 17 -

Athena trudged half-heartedly through the streets of North Shields. Her feet were heavy and her bloodshot eyes blinked wearily in the harsh sunlight of an otherwise glorious morning. In her hand, she clutched a cup of extra strong Costa coffee. Athena was, at heart, a tea drinking sort of girl but there were some mornings when tea wouldn't cut it, and this morning was one of those mornings. The single vodka and tonic she'd enjoyed last night at Oddfellows had turned into a double vodka and tonic at the insistence of Ben. The double vodka had - at the insistence of Marge - been reborn as an ill-advised treble. Athena had continued her little party back home with a shot of brandy. She had chatted to Simba and fed him scraps of beef until the pair fell asleep on the old Chesterfield shortly after 2 a.m.

Athena had awoken at dawn with the rising of the sun and was appalled to find herself still in her sweaty gym gear. She'd dragged her shivering body upstairs and sat in the shower for several minutes before staggering back to bed. Once the ceiling had kindly stopped spinning, she managed to get herself another two hours of sleep. When 6:30 a.m. arrived, her body ached from the combination of training, drinking and sleeping on the sofa. Athena forced herself through a yoga routine and spent some time meditating. Meditation was part of her mental training in preparation for the Sissy Clark fight but it was an area she was neglecting. As she sat in the lotus position she quietly recited affirmations to herself.

'Winning feels natural to me. I strike with power and accuracy. I build my confidence daily. I have the drive and ability to beat any opponent.'

Athena wasn't too keen on mental training. Truth be told she would rather not spend too much time in her own head, but the likes of Luke Mar and Charlie Fisher swore by it. Luke had gone so far as to record his affirmations over his favourite dance tunes. When he was running or hitting the bags and he had his earphones in, chances were the beat of Fat Boy Slim would be overlaid with, 'Luke Mar is the fittest. Luke Mar is the strongest. Luke Mar is a warrior and he has massive balls.'

Athena balanced her cup of coffee on the low stone wall that surrounded the grounds of Christ Church. If mental training was good enough for Luke it should be good enough for her. He was a champion after all, and besides, it couldn't hurt. She bent over to adjust the velcro on her trainers and immediately regretted it. Blood rushed to her head and made her feel like a tiny wolverine was trying to claw its way out of her brain. *That's it*, she thought. *No more vodka. Ever.*

With a bitch of a hangover, it took Athena longer than it should have to finish the short walk from Costa to Camp Terrace. She waved hello and exchanged pleasantries with her elderly neighbours, Mr and Mrs Rowe. The Rowes were pottering in their garden, watering their roses and pulling out the occasional dandelion. Athena excused herself, lowered the top on the Audi, placed the coffee in the drinks holder and headed west towards the Coast Road and onwards to, 'somewhere posh like Jesmond or Gosforth.'

Jesmond was the obvious place to start. It filled the bill of being home to overpaid lawyers and accountants. Jesmond was a leafy and vibrant area populated by upper-middle-class professionals and well to do students. The popular suburb was close to the city centre but still retained a village-like feel, and as a result, the area had the best of all worlds: low crime rate, quality schools, bustling nightlife, designer shops and pretty public parks such as Jesmond Dene. Athena eventually found herself a parking space and looked up and down the surrounding streets. There was an air of excitement about the place. Students were beginning to return to the area after the long summer break. They were unpacking their cars, hugging their new flatmates and sharing stories of their steamy summers in faraway lands.

Athena knew the area well, the expensive private school she had attended was only a few streets away and on this very street, at number 47, was the flat she had shared during her second year at Newcastle University. Athena's mouth pinched to the left at the thought of her time on this street and she felt guilty at having lost touch with her former flatmates: There'd been Isabella, a bulimic Welsh sociopath whose life mission was to steal boyfriends and husbands; Mancunian Grace, a vegetarian coke addict who could snort powder at the same time as lecturing Athena on the evils of the meat industry; and local lass Louise, the cute as a button, quiet as a mouse, bookworm who seduced her lecturer, convinced him to leave his wife and three children, persuaded him to pay for her boob job and broke up with him two weeks after she graduated. Athena moved her pinched lips from left to right, shrugged her shoulders and concluded that maybe some friendships weren't worth maintaining.

Athena drained the last of her coffee, crumpled the cardboard cup and tossed it into the nearest rubbish bin. She threw her messenger bag over her shoulder and rubbed her temples as she wondered where to start. Jesmond was bursting at the seams with restaurants. Where in this busy little suburb of plum voices and trust funds would she find a motivational speaker who smelled of fish?

The green and white signage of Starbucks caught her eye and she smiled. Caffeine was always the best place to start.

The sun was out and it brought with it the beautiful people of Jesmond. All young and slim with perfectly straight hair and radiant skin. Athena joined a queue of perfect specimens at the counter of the coffee chain and admired a feminine cream coloured dress teamed with funky boots worn by a modelesque woman. It was the sort of outfit she should wear for dinner with Kris. Cute but edgy.

''scuse me,' said Athena. She pulled a photograph of Molly out of her messenger bag and showed it to the girl who stood in front of her in the queue. 'Don't suppose you know this girl or saw her hanging around Jesmond during the winter?'

The girl studied the photograph intently with her baby blue eyes and shook her head. 'No, sorry,' she said, before turning to the barista and ordering herself a cappuccino.

Athena ordered an Americano and checked that the hipster barista hadn't met Molly either.

He shook his head. 'She missing?'

'Something like that,' said Athena. 'Do you know an Alistair Montgomery? Sometimes called Ali Montgomery or L'il Monty? Apparently, he owns a restaurant around here.'

The man shook his head again and lifted a marker pen to the paper cup. 'Name?'

'Anna,' said Athena. She had no intention of having the inevitable conversation that came when strangers heard her name, not with this headache.

Athena continued to show Molly's photograph to everyone who passed her in the little coffee shop until her drink was ready. Then she headed out and continued her line of investigation in the tree-lined streets. She asked for Alistair Montgomery in the amusingly named Fat Hippo, then checked the Sushi bar. She stopped a parking enforcer and showed him Molly's photograph then popped into a little cafe but she had no luck. No one recognised Molly or had heard of Ali Montgomery.

Most of the students she spoke to had only just moved to the area. That was the problem with Jesmond, the younger population were so transient that anyone who did know Molly or Ali Montgomery could easily have moved out at the end of last semester.

Athena turned on to Osborne Road and stared into the party hub of Jesmond. Filled with hotels, bars, pubs, and restaurants, Osborne Road was to Jesmond what the strip was to Vegas. That is if Vegas had been shrunk to a millionth of its size. It was loud, busy, sparkly and the place to be seen. Even now, when they can't have been open for more than an hour, each bar was packed with trend monkeys and socialites keen to spend their daddies' fortune on half price cocktails and sliders. As she entered the first bar, the smell of alcohol made Athena's delicate stomach turn over. For a second she thought she'd have to make a dash to the ladies room to bring up what remained in her stomach. Instead, she took a deep breath and had a stern word to herself about womanning up.

Athena pulled her shoulders back and made her way to the bar to ask the staff if they could help. None of them could, nor could the customers. This pattern repeated itself in bar after bar.

'What can I get you, darling?' asked an older woman who was tending bar in a typical student venue. She had a thick brown bob and wore glasses that wouldn't be out of place in a 1950s library.

Athena pushed her shades up on to her head and let out a long, low sigh. 'Please tell me you know where Ali

Montgomery works, or where I can buy some overpriced fish.'

The bartender stared over the top of her glasses for a moment. 'Well, we've got Thai fish cakes and I think the chef has a sea bass pasta dish on the specials.'

Athena folded her arms on the bar and rested her head in the crook of her elbow. 'Is it overpriced?' she asked, her voice muffled by her arm.

'It's happy hour till one, pet. But if it's seafood you're after the Caribbean place round the corner does some decent prawn dishes and the red mullet's good too.'

Athena lifted her head. 'What Caribbean place around the corner?'

'Flamingo Cove. It's on Holly Avenue, next to the doctors. Took over the Italian's about a year ago. Has some student offers on at the weekends and the odd bit of live music. Now can I get you drink or— '

Athena was already out the door.

- CHAPTER 18 -

Flamingo Cove was a pastel paradise of beach hut charm and cool ambience. The sign above the door promised fresh food, live music, and good vibes. Real palm trees, housed in giant planters, bowed against the ceiling and murals of fishing boats in turquoise waters adorned the walls. Tables were fashioned from beer barrels, surfboards, and driftwood. Athena wasn't sure if she was imagining it but she was sure that the room even smelled of the sea. Making herself comfortable in a deck chair, Athena pulled Molly's notepad out of her messenger bag and absentmindedly scanned the pages in hope of some inspiration. When a tie-dye wearing waiter approached her, she ordered a diet coke and a salad and watched as a group of female students gathered around a surfboard table. They were probably first years, given that Athena thought they looked about twelve-years-old. They clinked Champagne flutes together and toasted to being best friends forever. Athena rolled her eyes. *Naive fools*.

Within minutes Athena's diet coke and exotic looking salad had arrived courtesy of a smartly dressed man with a bouffant hairdo and a hooped earring.

'Is Ali Montgomery in today?'

The gentleman placed some cutlery on a small table to Athena's right. 'The actor, the swimmer, or the owner?' he replied in a thick northern accent.

Athena's eyes bulged. 'The owner,' she gasped.

'I'm the manager, Morgan Shepherd. Is there something I can help you with?'

'It's a long story,' said Athena, thumbing the pages of the notepad and pulling Molly's photo from the inside of the back cover. 'Have seen this girl in here?'

Morgan's shook his head. 'I don't think so. Are you with the police?'

Athena took a sip of her diet coke. 'No, nothing like that,' she appeased. 'So, is he here? I really need to speak with him.'

The manager frowned and took a step back. 'He's not, I'm afraid. He doesn't come in every day. I can get a message to him if that helps.'

Athena took a slow look around the room. Disappointment coating her face. 'OK, yeah. I'll leave a note when I go.'

'Sorry I couldn't be of more assistance. Enjoy your meal, miss.'

Bloody hell, thought Athena. What a waste of a morning. She could have been in the gym sweating out her hangover. Instead, she was eavesdropping on a bunch of Millennials and wondering what to wear to meet the parents of a man who wasn't even her boyfriend. *Yet.* He wasn't her boyfriend, *yet.* She'd just about put together a suitable outfit in her mind when a tall man with doe-like eyes and freckles across his nose strode confidently into the restaurant and took a seat at the bar.

'Morgan, I need you to adjust my diary. I can't meet Yahia this afternoon. There's a reporter coming at three with a photographer. They want to take some shots of us presenting the cheque from last week's fundraiser to a lady from the hospice.'

'Yes, boss.'

The mystery man was a good foot taller than Athena and he was impeccably dressed in polished shoes, smart navy trousers, and a well-fitted shirt, Hugo Boss by the looks of it. His hair was styled into thin braids that reached his collar bones. The top layers were tied back into a short ponytail and the lower layers sashayed side to side as he adjusted himself on the bar stool.

'And while you're at it, can you add a note in my diary that the high school wants a second lecture, this time for the year nines. Check my email to see if they've sent some suggested dates over yet.'

'You got it, boss.'

'I got a good deal down the market this morning. Wilkinson will be over shortly with a crate of squid and mackerel. Call Lance, let him know so he can come up with some specials for tonight's service.'

Morgan, the manager of Flamingo Cove, bent over the bar and whispered to his boss and pointed in Athena's direction.

The man stood up and dusted the front of his trousers. 'Banana and berry smoothie when you get the chance, Morgan.' He was slender, with long graceful limbs that Athena couldn't help but compare to Molly's. She'd been so elegant. Molly could make Athena feel dumpy just by standing in the same room as her.

'Alistair Montgomery?' asked Athena.

'Please, call me Monty,' he replied. His voice was silky with mild Geordie undertones. 'Only my bank manager calls me by my full name, and between you and me, I can't stand my bank manager.' He extended his arm and shook Athena's hand.

'I'm Athena,' she answered, noticing that yes, Monty did have a vague whiff of the fish market. 'This is quite a place you've got here. Really impressive.'

'Thank you, it's not as big as the one we've got in the town or the one in Morpeth but this is definitely my favourite. So, what can I do for you? My manager said you wanted to speak to the owner.'

Athena took a bite of lettuce. 'Would you sit with me?' She motioned to a driftwood chair with embroidered cushions. 'I wanted to ask you about my sister, Molly. I found your name in the back of her diary.' She passed him the photograph.

A flicker of recognition passed over Monty's face. 'Wow,' he said with wide eyes and a crooked grin. 'This girl gave me the fright of my life.'

'Let me guess. She thought you were her father?'

Monty pointed at her. 'Bingo! Can't blame her. I definitely see the resemblance. I mean, look at those eyes.' He held the photograph up to the light. 'How's she doing anyway? We were going to get those home DNA kits and see what results we got but I never heard from her again.'

Athena puffed out her cheeks and put her glass back on the table. 'She's… Well, she's dead.'

Monty's head lowered and he ran a hand over his head. 'What? I mean, oh, Jesus. Is that why you're here? To tell me?'

'Sorry,' said Athena in a hushed voice. 'She took her own life.'

Monty looked up, his mouth was agape. 'What a waste,' he said. 'Poor soul.'

'When Molly came to see you did she show you this?' Athena handed Monty the diary and he frowned as he flicked through the pages.

'Do you recognise it?' asked Athena. 'I think this was her diary and all those symbols are some sort of code. I know Molly was sad and in a bad place but I just want to know if anything else was going on, you know? I miss her and I guess if I manage to understand what she was going through I'll feel closer to her and maybe, maybe I'll forgive myself for not being there.'

Monty folded his long legs so that his left ankle rested above his right knee. 'I'm sorry Athena, truly I am.' He shook his head again. 'Jeez, she was so young.'

Athena put down her fork. She didn't feel like eating anymore. 'Did Molly mention anything to you about being depressed?'

Monty's braids jiggled as he shook his head but he didn't look up from the diary. 'This is quite a doozy. Have you managed to translate any of it yet?'

Athena shrugged. 'Not a damn word. For all I know it could be utter gobbledegook. Molly's idea of a joke. But,' she paused and took a deep breath, 'something tells me that it isn't.'

'Well I was never the sharpest tool in the box when I was at school but I always enjoyed a good puzzle. Could I copy a few pages? One of the young glass collectors here is a genius. IQ of 153, or so he tells me, off to Cambridge next week. I'll ask him to take a look.'

A small smile crept over Athena's face. 'Sure, why not?'

Monty signalled for his manager and asked him to scan a few pages. Morgan disappeared into an office and returned a few minutes later carrying a tray laden with coffee and biscuits. He handed the diary back to Athena and placed the coffees on the table. 'Wilkinson is here,' he told Monty.

A stout man with shaggy, dirty blond hair and a matching beard sauntered out of the office. He wore a wife-beater vest and Bermuda shorts and sipped from a can of cider. 'Afternoon,' he said, tipping an imaginary hat to Athena. 'Boss, stats are good from the weekend. Lewis negotiated a nice price on the stuff you were after and asks if you need him to speak to the Pasternaks. Pete fed Rocky and I've got the fridge stocked for tomorrow's poker game.'

There was a quick spike in Athena's adrenaline levels. 'Poker?' she asked.

Wilkinson turned his shaggy head back to Athena and let his eyes pass over her chest. 'Wilkinson,' he said, introducing himself with an extended arm. 'But you can call me whatever you like.'

Athena shook his hand and tried not to shudder. 'Erm, Wilkinson is fine,' she said awkwardly, putting the diary and Molly's photograph back into her bag.

Wilkinson squinted. 'Hey, boss,' he gasped, jabbing a stubby finger at the photograph. 'Ain't that the lass who —'

'Thought I was her father? Yes, Wilkinson, it is.' He bowed his head again and let out a long sigh.

Wilkinson must have picked up on the sadness that polluted the air because he shoved his hands in his pockets and changed the subject back to poker. 'I've got a caterer delivering fancy whatnots at half seven but they've asked to be paid in cash. I told them it wouldn't be a problem but let me know if it is and I'll book someone else.'

'Cash is fine,' said Monty, his eyes still lowered. 'Go call the Whites, make sure they can still make it.'

Wilkinson dipped his imaginary hat at Athena once more and scuttled out the front door of the restaurant, making sure to let his eyes sweep over the pretty young things who were drinking Champagne.

'My mum played poker,' said Athena. 'She was talented by all accounts.'

'Talented?' said Monty, an eyebrow raised and a smile returning to his face. 'The woman was a trailblazer. Yes, yes,' he said looking at Athena, 'I knew Viv from the casino days, but you probably worked that out already.

Couldn't believe it when your sister told me about that crash. I always had Viv pipped as invincible.'

His eyes glazed over and he began to fidget with the shoelace on his left shoe.

'So,' said Athena, feeling cocky. 'Can I play?'

Monty narrowed his eyes and followed an ant as it crawled out from under an old wooden tea crate that had been refashioned into a table. 'Huh? What?' he asked, looking up.

'The poker game,' repeated Athena. 'What's the buy in?'

'Oh sorry, no.' He placed a hand on Athena's knee and left it there longer than she would have liked. 'I mean, you don't want to hang about with a bunch of sleazy blokes like Wilkinson, do you?'

'Come on, Monty,' pleaded Athena. 'We're practically family.'

Monty laughed. 'You might be right there. Or, we might never know. But, if you want to meet to talk about Molly or see what we can get out of that diary of hers it would be nicer to meet here over coffee.' His eyes scanned upwards from her mucky trainers to the gym clothes she wore. 'Our games are pricey. I don't want to offend, but I'm not sure you could afford—'

His words were like a red rag to a bull. 'Oh, really?' she asked. 'Try me.'

- CHAPTER 19 -

'A GRAND?' Kris sounded more southern than usual as his voice grunted out of Athena's mobile phone. 'A grand, Foxy?' he repeated. 'I ain't got a grand, I ain't got a damn lady.'

'I do,' said Athena, naked on her bed with her phone on speaker as she painted her toenails. Kris had just about drawn breath after lecturing Athena about disobeying his wishes and swanning off to find Monty on her own.

'Foxy, you can't waste your mon—'

'It's not *my* money,' interrupted Athena. 'It's my mother's. I didn't earn a penny of it and she'd be quite impressed that I plan on gambling it all away. Trust me.'

Athena could hear Kris huffing and squirming on the other end of the phone.

'Anyway,' she mused. 'What do you mean *you ain't got a damn lady*?'

'Lady Godiva. I ain't got a damn fiver,' said Kris. 'If Charlie doesn't get me a fight soon I'm going to have to bite the bullet and go back on the doors full time.'

'Don't you dare,' said Athena, screwing the lid back on to the bottle of nail polish. 'Bomber jackets and dusk till dawn shifts? Speak to Charlie, he must be able to get you on the Euro Fight Series card in Dublin.'

'Fingers crossed. There's two vacant spots left on the card and if I don't get one of them I'll have no choice but to stand in the cold and deal with drunken idiots five nights a week.'

'Or,' smiled Athena, pulling a wad of fifties out of the hidden compartment in the Baron of Ravensworth's bed, 'you could get a royal flush tomorrow night and pocket a fortune?'

A little snort came out of the phone. 'Yeah, and what are the odds of that?'

Athena replaced the wooden panel, checked that her toenails were dry and began rolling sheer stockings up her strong legs. 'About one in forty-three thousand.'

Kris didn't respond.

'Anyway,' she continued. 'I'm almost dressed. I'll pick you up in twenty.'

'You sure you want to drive, Foxy?'

'Yeah, best not to drink a load of wine and then struggle through training tomorrow. Besides, would you rather take my car or yours?'

'Your car. Without a doubt. See you in twenty, Foxy.'

'Later,' said Athena. She hung up, checked her makeup in the mirror and pulled on a Ted Baker skater dress. After a quick pirouette in front of the mirror, she grimaced and decided she looked like runner-up from The X-Factor. Hastily, she pulled the dress back over her head and replaced it with a Vivian Westwood number.

XXX

Athena knocked on Kris's front door and took a step back. She ran her hands over her dress, inspected its hem, examined her nail polish, pushed a few strands of hair behind her ear and told herself to *stop fidgeting, damn it*. The curtain of the neighbouring house flittered and the orange face of Kris's Ugg boot wearing neighbour squinted out at her. Athena blew her a kiss and the woman scrunched up her face in disgust before disappearing back behind the curtain. Athena's jaw dropped as Kris answered his door. The classic black suit he was wearing hugged his broad shoulders and accentuated his athletic torso. The perfect creases in the trouser legs made him look even taller than usual and the crisp black shirt with its top button undone looked to Athena like it needed to be torn from his body immediately. Kris's auburn hair had been trimmed and he'd shaved every hint of stubble from his jaw. Athena was utterly mesmerised.

'Kris! You look, well you look just, you, erm, you look very…'

'Same to you,' nodded Kris.

Athena looked down at her shoes and smoothed her dress before trying again. 'You look unquestionably magnificent, Krzysztof Kava.'

Kris stepped out of the doorway, closed the door and one by one turned his keys in the many locks. He moved back to Athena and offered her his arm to link into.

Athena's heart skipped a beat when her bare arm stroked against the fabric of Kris's suit.

'And you, Athena Fox, well I can see why I dumped Emily-the-primary-school-teacher for you.'

Athena snickered, teetered on her heels and almost rolled an ankle. Kris caught her weight and set her right again.

'Don't make me laugh,' she said. 'I can't walk and laugh at the same time.'

'And here I was thinking women were the experts on multitasking.'

It was a twenty-minute drive into the city centre from Kris's house, fifteen minutes if you drove like Athena. She pushed the pedal to the metal the second she found her way out of the average speed check zone and parked her car, typically, somewhere she shouldn't.

A tiny waitress with long chestnut hair greeted Athena and Kris and showed them to a table on the mezzanine level of Athena's favourite steakhouse. Her pristine ponytail had been pulled so tight that it stretched her eyes into cat-like almonds.

The restaurant was a vast open space of dark wood and red tartan. Impressive arched windows lined the front of the building, allowing the radiant light of the early evening to filter in and reflect off the many glass and mirrored surfaces. Perched above a broad wine display cabinet, a statue of a bull, head down, horns pointed and ready to charge, stood watch over the restaurant.

'Can I get you anything to drink?' asked the waitress through collagen-filled lips.

Athena took her seat and stroked the lacy material of her dress over her knees. She ordered a glass of soda water and sighed at the sight of a couple on the ground floor who were sipping Mojitos.

'And for you, handsome?'

Kris coughed and adjusted himself in his seat with a childish giggle. 'A pint of bitter, please.'

The waitress fluttered her eyelash extensions and trotted down the stairs to the ground floor with an enthusiastic bounce in her step. Athena took a moment to visualise grabbing her by her perfect ponytail and slingshotting her over the glass mezzanine balcony and on to the couple below.

A stiff silence fell over the pair as they sat opposite each other. Kris stroked his non-existent stubble and perused the menu. Athena drummed out a little rhythm of a concerto on the edge of her chair and took in the sounds of ambient music and the general hubbub of the kitchen. Kris began glancing around the room. He half pointed at one of the many bull inspired artworks, opened his mouth and shut it again. Urgh, how awkward. Athena would rather talk about anything than talk about nothing so she huffed out her cheeks, looking somewhat like a hamster for a moment, and chose the ever safe topic of conversation that was fighting.

'Do you know much about this guy Luke's fighting?'

Kris's eyes came alive and he pushed himself more upright in his chair. 'Danny Davison? Not a lot. He fights out of The KO Factory in Edinburgh. Has a decent record. His last three victories came by knock out but he's got a loss via armbar in there too. He's as big as Luke but he's struggled with cardio and gassed early on in his last few fights. He blamed the recent loss on his conditioning coach and rumour has it he's not getting on with his teammates.'

Athena nodded as a swishing chestnut ponytail bounced back into view. 'The KO Factory? You've faced one of their fighters before though, haven't you?'

'Yeah,' he answered, as the waitress returned with their drinks.

Athena's glass of water was deposited with a thump and a slight spillage. Kris's pint, on the other hand, was placed delicately, with a wide smile, eye contact and enough of a bend at the hips to allow Kris a look straight down her top had he chosen to turn his head. Kris, however, was still away with the fight fairies.

'Henry Wallace. I knocked him out. Great boxers up in Edinburgh,' he mused. 'Good technique, loads of heart. Those Jocks don't go down without a fight but they've got no ground game up there. If Luke can get him to the canvas he'll — Oh, they're here.'

Danika and Piotr Kava waved earnestly up from the ground floor. The tiny waitress's smile vanished and she stood upright. She glanced down at her own cleavage and shrugged before welcoming the Kavas to the table and pulling out a seat for each of them.

'KRZYSZTOF!' boomed Danika, enveloping her son in a hug a bear would be proud of. She was a tall and handsome woman with broad shoulders and a strong jaw. Her hair was auburn with flecks of silver, and it was styled into a loose and fashionable topknot. 'My handsome son,' she said, grabbing Kris by the chin and examining his face. 'You don't eat enough.'

'Leave the boy alone, Danika,' said Piotr, also tall and broad-shouldered with what would be a perfect head of black hair were it not for a handful of greys on either temple. His eyes were a striking steel grey and surrounded by crow's feet. He patted Kris on the back and turned to Athena, grasping her hands in his and planting a kiss on both of her cheeks. 'So nice to meet you, Athena.'

'Yes,' repeated Danika, 'So very nice to meet you, Emily.' Her hands shot to her ruby lips to cover a horrified gasp and her eyebrows folded apologetically. 'Athena, I'm so sorry. It's nice to meet you, *Athena*.'

Athena couldn't help but laugh. 'It's fine Mrs Kava. Honestly.'

'Danika, please. Call me Danika. And this is Pete,' she said extending an arm to her husband.

Athena nodded. 'I see where Kris gets his height from,' she observed.

'Yes,' said Kris as the four of them took their seats and the waitress noted down the drinks order for the Kavas. 'You'll notice that my father is *tall* with *dark* hair and *grey* eyes. He's not short and blond and green-eyed like you.'

'Duly noted,' said Athena, kicking Kris under the table with her stilettos while both of his parents shared confused glances.

'So, Athena,' began Danika without looking up from the menu. 'What do you do?'

Danika's eyes were still on the menu so Athena answered into her topknot. 'I'm a fighter, like Kris.'

Danika looked up with narrowed eyes and muttered something in Polish to Pete, who shook his head at her.

'That's not quite true,' said Kris. 'She's not a fighter *like me*. She's one of the most talented strawweights on the planet, on a three fight winning streak, and is about to fight for the Demons FC title.'

Athena looked coy at the compliment and was about to start gushing about how great a fighter Kris was when Danika said something else in Polish before asking. 'So, you don't have a real job?'

'Mother. Fighting is a real—'

'Nonsense Krzysztof, real jobs come with a monthly salary, sick pay, and pension schemes. Fighting comes with black eyes, brain damage, and no future.

This time Kris answered in low, hushed Polish words. Athena's belly rumbled and she glanced around hoping to order some damn food. Where was that bloody waitress when you needed her? A baby began crying from the other end of the restaurant and someone in the kitchen dropped a tray of cutlery loud enough to drown out the sound of Kris arguing with his mother. Eventually, Pete clasped his hands together and declared that he'd be ordering the t-bone.

'Good choice,' said Athena, glad of the change of topic.

'Now, where's our waitress?' he asked, glancing around.

'She's a little taken with Kris,' teased Athena.

'And who could blame her?' interrupted Danika between sips of a red wine that Athena could smell was full bodied and probably Argentinian.

'If Kris waves, she'll come running,' she continued.

Kris sighed and took a gulp of bitter. 'Don't be daft,' he said with foam across his top lip.

Athena spotted the waitress walking back to the kitchen with a tray full of empty glasses and tried to get her attention. It was no use. She turned back to Kris, raised her eyebrow and waited.

'OK, fine,' he pouted raising his hand, 'but I don't see what this will prove.'

The waitress stopped in her tracks, deposited her tray of glasses on an unoccupied table and came bouncing up the stairs.

Athena tried her best not to smile too much but Pete couldn't help himself. 'You're an observant one,' he nodded, raising his glass of lager to toast Athena.

'Are you ready to order?' panted the waitress, slightly out of breath from her little jog up the stairs.

'Erm, yes, I think so,' answered Kris.

The waitress looked at Kris expectantly with a little electronic tablet in her hand to record the order.

'Ladies first,' said Kris, looking between his mother and Athena.

'Oh yes,' said the waitress apologetically. 'What can I get you?' she asked Danika.

'Rump, medium well, regular fries, honey and mustard dressing, porcini sauce,' answered Danika without pausing.

The waitress nodded in time to each demand, typing the specifications into the tablet before turning to Athena.

'I'll have the T-bone,' started Athena.

Kris shook his head. 'It's too big, Foxy. Too many calories, go for an eight-ounce one.'

Athena pouted but knew he was right. 'OK, the fillet please,' she continued, 'with the beef dripping sauce and —'

'No sauce,' interrupted Kris.

'Oh, come on, you can't have steak without sauce.'

'Yes, you can.'

Pete turned his palms up to the ceiling. 'Let the young lady have some sauce, Kris.'

Kris scowled. 'No sauce,' he repeated.

Athena turned to the waitress and shrugged. 'Eight-ounce fillet, no sauce, no dressing on the salad, no fries and some more water please.'

The waitress took the remaining orders from the two gents. They both ordered T-bones with beef dripping sauce and extra fries. Athena consoled herself with the thought that she could at least smell the beef dripping, even if she couldn't taste it.

After a few minutes of sulking over only being able to eat an eight-ounce steak when she was capable of eating at least twice that amount, Athena forced a happy expression back on her face. The Kavas's were deep in conversation about Kris's older brothers. Pete and Kris spoke in English for Athena's benefit but Danika jumped back into Polish whenever she needed to say something in lower, angrier tones. The siren of a passing ambulance drowned out the noise of chit chat and ambient music. Once it had passed the shout of 'Service,' echoed out of the kitchen.

Moments later the previously bouncy little waitress thumped her way up the stairs to the mezzanine. She placed Athena's barren looking plate in front of her with apologetic eyes and half a smile. Mr and Mrs Kava's plates were delivered professionally but Kris's plate was plopped with a thump and a frown.

'What was that about?' asked Kris, shoving a handful of fries into his mouth before being chastised for not saying grace by his mother.

'I think she's gone off you,' giggled Athena. Must be the beer moustache you've been sporting for the last ten minutes.

Kris rubbed the back of his hand over his mouth.

'Use a napkin, Krzysztof,' said Danika as she licked her napkin and rubbed it over Kris's mouth.

'I'm not five-years-old, Mother,' he squirmed, swiping her hand away.

'Well I should treat you like a child,' she snapped back. 'You don't act like an adult. Adults have real jobs.'

The smells of steak sauces, salad dressing, and bone marrow were driving Athena crazy. Her steak was tender and delicious but it wasn't the same without her favourite sides. No one should ever be forced to eat steak without chips, she thought. And, eating one without red wine was basically criminal. It was the very definition of a first world problem.

'Your brothers are working all hours of the day, breaking their backs, earning as much as they can to give their families a good life…'

'I don't want to be a labourer, I want to be a fight—'

'How can you support a family on fight bonuses?'

'What if I don't want to start a family?'

'Nonsense, everybody wants a family, Krzysztof. All women want children, you think this girl will stick by you when you're broke and brain damaged and have given her no sons?'

Athena's steak knife plunged into her fillet with enough force to make the table vibrate. All eyes turned to her. 'Kris is going to be a star,' she spat. 'In a couple of years, he'll be a household name. And the pride of Poland.'

Danika folded her arms and sat back in her seat. She had salad leaves stuck in her teeth.

'And you don't get to speak for all women,' continued Athena. 'I might want children, I might not, and right now the crying coming from over there is thoroughly putting me off the idea.' Athena turned her head to glare at the family in question, wishing someone would shut that bloody baby up. She scowled across the room in the direction of the noise and her eyes came to rest on an exhausted-looking Claire Phelps bouncing snot-nosed

Daley on her lap. Owen - true to form as a good for nothing, waste of space - was busy texting on his phone and making eyes at a voluptuous bartender.

'Oh for crying out loud,' snapped Athena, crumpling up her napkin, throwing it down on the table and excusing herself. She stomped down the stairs in the same manner as the waitress and made a bee-line for the toilets in the basement. Her head swirled with hunger and frustration. Could she not even go on a simple fake date with her fake date's parents without bumping into her pathetic ex? Athena slammed her palms into the wooden door of the unisex bathroom and sent it into the wall with an echoing bang. Checking that all the mirrors and artwork had remained on the walls she selected a stall and was about to pull up her dress when she heard a delicate knock.

'Miss? Are you OK, Miss?'

It was the tiny waitress. Athena smoothed her dress back down and cursed under her breath. She opened the door and eyeballed the young woman.

'What?' hissed Athena.

'Sorry,' squeaked the waitress. She was playing with her pony-tail. 'I just wanted to check on you, you seemed upset.'

Athena softened, but only slightly. After all, this woman, despite her good intentions, was keeping her full bladder from the porcelain bowl.

'I'm fine,' she answered curtly, pulling the door closed once more.

The waitress slid her shiny shoe through the gap and winced as it became trapped between the door and its frame.

'You don't seem fine,' she whimpered through the pain. 'And I know it's none of my b—'

'You're right, it's not. And if you don't mind, I need to pee.' Athena pulled on the door once more, a little harder this time, but the woman wouldn't budge. 'Seriously? Please tell me you're not into watching the customers go to the toilet? That's gross. Do I need to check this place for cameras?'

'No!' gasped the waitress. 'I'm not like that. It's just…' she paused and swallowed hard. 'My last boyfriend used to do that to me too.'

Athena frowned. 'He used to watch you go to the—'

'No, no. You've got me wrong. He used to control me like that. It started out with food, telling me not to eat fatty foods, then not to eat sugary foods. In the end, he'd only let me eat salad.' She looked at the floor with glassy eyes. 'I got so thin, but because he wouldn't let me see my family or friends no one noticed.'

Athena's heart swelled with pity. 'Bloody hell.'

'It took a long time before I had the nerve to run away, and when I saw you being controlled like that, well, I knew how it would end up.'

Athena gave a gentle smile and relaxed her grip on the door handle. 'I'm sorry that happened to you, really I am. But you have the wrong idea. That's not what's going on here.'

'That's what I would say too, back in the first few months of our relationship, when I thought the sun shone out of his you know what.'

'You're really brave,' said Athena, placing a hand on her shoulder. 'But Kris isn't like that, I promise. I'm not being forced to diet. Believe it or not, I'm in a cage fight soon and I need to drop a few kilos for the weigh-in. That guy up there is keeping me on track. Without him, I'd have got through fourteen hundred calories by now and would be kissing the title fight goodbye.'

The waitress blinked several times and pressed her fingertips around her eyes to mop up the tiny tears that were forming in the corners. She glanced at Athena's dress and her pretty heels. 'You don't look like a cage fighter,' she sniffed.

'Most fighters don't.' Athena pulled a few tissues from the dispenser and handed them to the waitress. 'I meant what I said. You are brave. Not just for leaving him, but for this, for trying to help me too. I know I'm not the easiest of strangers to talk to.'

The waitress let out a small snort. 'Yeah, now I've chatted with you, you don't come across as being easy to control.'

A memory of Owen making up a bullshit excuse as to where he'd been all night when he'd come home stinking of cheap perfume and becoming aggressive when Athena didn't buy his crap floated into her mind.

'You'd be surprised,' was all Athena said.

'Well, I'll give you some privacy,' said the waitress, removing her foot from the door.

When Athena sat down on the toilet she wondered to herself how many more times that evening Danika would accidentally on purpose call her Emily and how many more times she would question Kris's choice of career. After she'd finished and had washed her hands, she emerged from the little cubicle. In the stall opposite the waitress was splashing water on her face and gently patting it dry with a tissue. Athena gave her a reassuring look, turned on her heels and walked straight into Owen.

'Foxy! We must stop meeting like this,' he grinned, positioning himself so that Athena was stuck between him and the wall. 'People will talk.'

He stood so close that Athena could feel his breath on her face. It smelled of peppercorn sauce. Her legs froze to the spot and as much as she wanted to look away she forced her eyes to bore back into his.

'I thought I made myself clear,' she spat, 'I'm not interested.'

'You say that,' he said, leaning in closer, 'but then you go and post half-naked pictures of yourself on the internet knowing it would drive me wild.'

'You're delusional.'

Athena moved to push past Owen but he pressed his hands on the wall either side of her, blocking her exit.

'Move,' she commanded.

'Only if you say the magic words,' he teased. He pushed his face into her hair and took in her scent. 'The magic words are: Kiss, Me, Owen.'

Athena saw red, not unlike the bull painted on the wall opposite her. She grabbed Owen by his collar and judo threw him to the floor. Athena stood over him and pushed her stiletto heel into his groin.

'Let me up, Foxy,' he growled. His face now contorted from perverted predator to rabid dog.

Athena pushed her heel down harder making him wince. 'Not without the magic words.'

To her right, Athena saw the tiny waitress's head peering around the edge of the cubicle. 'Wow,' she said. 'You need to teach me how to do that.'

- CHAPTER 20 -

'Why did it have to be Jesmond? I fuckin' hate Jesmond.'

Luke Mar was a vision of orange skin wrapped up in colourful clothing. A pair of salmon pink jeans stretched and strained around his hulking thighs. Over his ballooned chest he wore a neon green t-shirt that turned purple when you touched it. Athena knew this because the first thing Luke said to her when she picked him up was, 'Hey Foxy, squeeze my pecs.'

Kris and Athena jumped out of the front seats of the TT and watched as Luke squirmed his way out of the back. He looked like someone had taken an orang-utan to a fancy dress party and the theme was 80's pop stars. The three of them surveyed Glastonbury Grove, an opulent street set back a few metres from leafy Jesmond Dene. The street was lined on both sides by large houses, expansive driveways and expensive cars. Impressive trees of green and purple tunnelled the street, allowing the sun to filter through in narrow beams, speckling the tarmac with early evening light.

'Posh wankers,' sighed Luke, eyeing the wrought iron security gate of a nearby house. 'I swear to God, last time I was on Osborne Road I overheard one precious, privately educated snowflake complaining 'cause she'd have to get the train home that summer 'cause *Daddy won't send the helicopter*. Eight miles from Shields and you'd think it was another planet.'

'Hey!' Athena jabbed Luke in the ribs. He doubled over and a small patch of purple blossomed in the neon green. 'I'm one of those privately educated posh wankers.'

Luke straightened up and put an arm around her. It was heavy, as if someone had dropped a python over her shoulders. 'Aye, but then you met us reprobates and we dragged you to the dark side.'

'Yeah,' smiled Kris. 'The dark, dark world of cage fighting. A world of sweat stains, black eyes, and ringworm. You know it's not too late to switch back to ballet.'

Athena shrugged herself free of Luke's arm and switched her feet back and forth in what was referred to as the Ali Shuffle after boxer Muhammad Ali. 'I wouldn't swap it for the world.'

'As if we'd let you leave,' joked Luke. 'Now which of these bloody mansions belongs to Monty the Motivator?'

Athena scanned the street before pointing at a set of metal security gates. 'That one.'

She pressed the button next to the gate. A noise drew her attention upwards and she found herself staring into a camera. The camera whirred and turned its attention to Kris and then Luke. There was a brief buzzing before the gates slid silently back to reveal a pristine lawn and a silver Bentley.

'Nice,' said Luke with a whistle. 'This Monty's not short of a bob or two.'

'Not sure about his taste in garden ornaments, mind you,' said Kris. He picked up a garden gnome sporting a mankini. 'And how did this gnome get hold of your swimwear, Luke?'

Luke belly laughed and picked up two other gnomes and rearranged them to make it look like one was doing unmentionable things to the other.

'Will you two quit it?' snapped Athena as she approached the front door. 'We're here to play nice. Let's find out if Monty's genius glass collector has worked his magic with Molly's diary. We might sell some tickets to the fights while we're at it and if we're lucky maybe we win some money.'

'You don't believe in luck,' said Kris as the front door to the house swung open.

'Hello again,' cooed Wilkinson, grinning like a Cheshire Cat at Athena. His sandy hair and beard were still shaggy and unkempt, the skin on his cheeks was pink and flaking and his hands were fidgeting in his pockets as he took in Kris and Luke. Wilkinson had swapped his wife beater vest and Bermuda shorts for thin cotton trousers and a short-sleeved white shirt with yellowing armpits. He removed his hands from his pockets and lifted his arms to shoulder height in a crucifix posture. 'Boss's instructions,' he said, indicating for the three of them to mimic his stance.

'Don't take it personally,' said Wilkinson as he padded Luke down, leaving purple handprints in his wake. He moved on to Kris, padding his black jeans and t-shirt. 'Boss has me check everyone who comes through the gates, even the pizza delivery guy. Hell, especially the pizza delivery guy.'

He turned to Athena and motioned for her raise her arms.

'If you think for a second I'm going to let you grope me all over—'

'For goodness sake, Wilkinson,' came Monty's silky voice from somewhere inside the house. 'She probably weighs six stone soaking wet. Let our guests in already.'

'You wish,' muttered Kris.

Athena thought for a second of the measly salad she'd had for her so-called dinner and nodded in agreement.

Wilkinson expanded his arms and shepherded the three of them into the ruckus of the dining room where Monty was sat at a spacious marble dining table with his guests. He immediately got to his feet and greeted Athena with a dazzling smile. 'Ms Fox!'

He took Athena's hand in both of his. His hands were moisturised and felt like satin against the sandpaper that was Athena's skin. Her wrists and knuckles were calloused from years of velcro burns and hitting pads.

Monty turned to Luke and Kris. 'Welcome, welcome. It's an honour to have celebrities in our midst.'

Kris blushed and began to stammer about hardly being considered a celebrity.

'Speak for yourself,' said Luke. 'I'm the talk of the toon. Wait till the seventeenth. I'll be the talk of the world.'

Athena slipped her hand free from Monty's and placed it in the pocket of her jeans. Monty's dining room was a gleaming kaleidoscope of marble, gold, glass and mirrors. Light bounced and reflected off every polished surface. Crystal Champagne flutes and mosaicked ornaments glistened from the sunlight that streamed in through floor to ceiling windows. Monty summoned a pasty matchstick of a man whose face was adorned with acne and tattoos. A tribal tattoo covered the right side of his face and an assortment of skulls and pentagrams decorated his left ear and the side of his neck.

'Lewis, please fetch two beers and a glass of the Malbec for our guests.'

Lewis skulked away to the kitchen, dragging his feet and hunching his shoulders.

'So Monty, what's with the airport security?' asked Luke.

Monty answered with an awkward smile and rubbed his chin for a moment. 'There's a fair bit of cash on the table tonight. Money attracts criminals. It's sad but it's true. A long time ago someone I thought was a friend came to a game, brandished a knife and took off with the pot. Now we take precautions. Fool me once, shame on you. Fool me twice, shame on me.'

Monty patted Luke on the arm and excused himself.

'So,' started Athena to Kris, 'did your parents enjoy last night?'

'My dad thinks you're the bee's knees,' answered Kris.

'I am.'

'My mother thinks I should give Emily a call.'

Athena giggled. 'Bloody Emily. I bet she's a Sissy Clark fan as well.'

Wilkinson slid up to Athena and Kris and nodded towards an Asian man of average height and exceptional grooming who was stood by the window. 'That's Yahia Saleem, he owns six convenience stores and at least four restaurants. Stinking rich. Two sons who are both in Oxford. Wife is super religious, doesn't know he drinks, definitely doesn't know he gambles and absolutely definitely doesn't know he has a daughter with one of his restaurant managers.'

Lewis returned with the drinks and handed them to Athena, Kris and Luke without saying a word or making eye contact.

'Moody git,' commented Wilkinson. 'Anyway, those two are the Whites,' he continued, motioning towards a couple in their fifties who were dressed as if they were about to enjoy an evening vegging out on the sofa with a film and a Chinese takeaway. 'They own a string of bars and pubs in the city centre. Make the right impression and you'll be on the guest list and sipping free drinks for the rest of your days.'

Athena raised an eyebrow, perhaps Wilkinson wasn't as useless as he first appeared.

'That old guy with the thick-rimmed glasses and the pipe. That's Willy Armstrong, no idea what he did for a living but he retired with a small fortune that he seems intent on spending on drugs and hookers.'

'Good for him,' said Luke. 'That's how I plan on spending my retirement.'

'Aye, living the dream is Old Willy,' continued Wilkinson. 'Erm, you might want to casually mention that you have a boyfriend or a husband or something,' he said to Athena. 'He likes 'em young and blonde so he might get a bit handsy once the whiskey kicks in.'

Athena scrunched up her face and moved closer to Kris.

'Unless you're into rich, eighty-odd-year-olds. I mean whatever floats your boat.'

'I'm not,' said Athena bluntly, 'but thanks for the heads up.'

'Nee bother, pet. That leaves Lewis and Silent Pete. Lewis is the miserable bastard with the crappy tattoos. He's the boss's pet project. He did a spell in a youth detention centre for robbing old grannies at knifepoint. The boss did one of his speeches at the centre not long before Lewis was released, something about not letting your past mistakes define you. Anyway, Monty took him under his wing and is teaching him about the restaurant trade. You'd think he'd be grateful but the guy never smiles so don't bother trying to get him to. And Silent Pete's the tubster hiding in the kitchen. He doesn't talk so don't bother trying to get him to. He can talk, he's not dumb or out, he just doesn't like to. Chronic social anxiety or some such shit.'

'Right,' was all Athena couldn't muster. She took a sip of her Malbec and almost climaxed. After all the water she'd gone through a full-bodied Malbec was truly the drink of the gods.

Kris must have read her expression of total pleasure and wasted no time in bursting her bubble. 'Remember you can only have the one, Foxy.'

'Shh,' said Athena, holding a finger to Kris's lips. 'Don't spoil this beautiful moment.'

Across the room, Monty lifted a remote control, pressed a button and the house filled with the sound of Janet Jackson.

Luke bopped his salmon clad hips from side to side. 'Old school,' he said in approval. 'Think me and this Monty chap will get along.'

Old Willy shook out a green felt tablecloth and laid it on the table. Mr White hummed along to the music and began to sort the poker chips into neat little piles while Mrs White shuffled the cards. Lewis mooched back and forth between the kitchen and table, taking empty glasses away and bringing replenished drinks back out. In the kitchen, Silent Pete was plating up some snacks that smelled oh so appetising. Athena watched as he occasionally popped a sushi roll in his mouth and looked around to see if anyone saw him. Yahia Saleem and Monty were deep in conversation by the window, they nodded and laughed in an animated fashion until Yahia held out his hand and they shook on some sort of arrangement.

'Come on,' said Wilkinson, nudging Athena and Kris lightly in the arms. 'I'll give you three the tour while they set up.'

The shaggy-haired man guided the group out of the dining room, through the kitchen and into a conservatory. Athena felt the hairs on the back of her neck prickle and she put it down to a fan circulating air in the corner. The room appeared to serve as a grown-up version of a playroom. A full-size pool table, two pinball machines, a table tennis table and a foosball table filled the space.

'Cool,' said Kris. He and Luke immediately jumped to the foosball table and began spinning the spindles and sending the small white football back and forth across the table until Luke scored a goal and celebrated by twerking his pelvis at Kris.

'You've easily got the space at your house for one of these, Foxy,' said Kris.

'True,' she agreed. 'Or, I could get a new shoe closet. I know which I'd get more use out of.'

Wilkinson's tour continued upstairs. The house was similar in size to Athena's property on Camp Terrace but none of the original features remained. Wilkinson pointed out where ceiling roses had been ripped out, where old fireplaces had been blocked up and where layers of horrific floral wallpaper had been stripped away. Glass gleamed, mirrors sparkled and shards of quartz glittered in black floor tiles.

'Blimey,' said Luke as he poked his head in the bathroom. 'The fish business must be booming.'

Every surface looked like it was daring you to touch it and leave a fingerprint. Everything shimmered and twinkled and everything screamed expense.

'And now,' said Wilkinson, dragging everyone's attention away from the mesmerising countertops. 'My favourite room in the house…'

Athena imagined him opening the door to a bedroom and saying something cheesy and sickening like *this is where the magic happens*, but she never in a thousand years would have imagined him pushing open the bedroom door to reveal a room full of floor-to-ceiling reptile tanks.

- CHAPTER 21 -

Athena crouched and pressed her nose up against the glass door of a ginormous snake tank. A heat lamp cast a warm orange glow over the bark chips that lined the floor. Laying across an artificial tree branch was a colossal Indian rock python. The glass felt cold against Athena's nose as she took in the pale brown snake with giraffe-like patches of dark brown along his spine. Athena met his gaze and wondered who weighed more, the snake or her?

'That's a staring competition you'll never win,' said Wilkinson. 'They don't have eyelids. He could be eyeballing you, or he could be sound asleep. You can't tell if they're not moving.'

Athena turned to Kris. 'You should come look at this, he must be at least nine foot.'

Kris stood in the hallway. He peered around the edge of the door frame, his arms folded over his chest. 'No thanks,' he shuddered. 'I'm fine where I am.'

Luke moved from tank to tank like an excitable child on his first trip to the zoo. 'How many are there?' he asked in bewilderment.

'There're twenty-six snakes, eight lizards, a handful of frogs and a couple of spiders,' replied Wilkinson. He tapped the glass tank next to him. 'This little beauty's Claudia. She's a rainbow boa. See how her scales are iridescent? Gorgeous looking girl.'

Athena straightened up and peered into a few more tanks. 'He's got his very own petting zoo.'

'Pretty much,' said Wilkinson. 'Monty told me when he was a kid he wanted to run a pet shop. Think this room is him feeding his inner seven-year-old. I blame his mother for never buying him something fluffy like a hamster. Anyway, the big guy's named Rocky and the fat boa over there is Betty Boo. This corn snake's Arnie and the little chap next to Luke is Jake.'

Luke laughed. 'Jake? Jake the snake!'

Lewis stuck his head around the edge of the door. 'Again with the reptiles, Wilko?' he mumbled.

'Just doing the tour, Lewis.'

'Hey,' said Luke. 'Is this snake wrapped around a wad of twenties?'

'Aye,' answered Lewis, peering into the tank. 'Monty lets the mamba look after his cash.'

Athena glanced sideways and then joined Luke. There was indeed a slender, brown snake coiled around a pile of twenty-pound notes. 'Did you say *mamba*? Aren't they venomous?'

Wilkinson made an affirmative noise. 'Just a little. It can kill a mouse in four minutes. A human? Well, you'd collapse within the hour and without anti-venom, you'd be dead as a dodo in about eight hours.'

'OK, hang on a minute,' said Athena, feeling suddenly on edge. She scratched her head and pushed her hair back out of her eyes. She wasn't entirely sure she had heard Wilkinson correctly. 'First, how did you even get a mamba? It's not like you can just walk into Pets At Home and buy one. Don't you need a licence or something?'

Lewis laughed without smiling. 'Come on, luv,' he said. 'You can get anything on the internet. If you know where to look.'

'And second,' she continued, 'how far are we from the nearest anti-venom?'

Kris pulled out his mobile and frantically started googling.

'Dunno,' said Wilkinson. 'Never checked. Lewis?'

'Nee idea.'

'Well that's reassuring,' sighed Athena in a low voice. She turned away from the mamba tank and bent over to check out a Burmese python that was so thick she thought even Luke wouldn't be able to wrap his hands around its girth.

'There's money in this tank too,' she said, her fingertips spread out over the glass.

'Yeah, Monty doesn't do banks,' said Lewis. 'Has a grudge against them. When he started off his business none of them wanted to loan him a penny. Now he's doing well they're all clambering for his dosh. Plus, he says these days the interest rates are so crap they aren't worth the effort.'

'Word,' said Luke.

Athena's jaw tightened. Not putting cash in the bank sounded totally legit.

'So, a snake tank is better than a safe?'

'Course it bloody is,' said Wilkinson, mesmerised by Chloe the rainbow boa again. 'There was a spate of burglaries around these parts a couple of years ago. The thieving bastards were targeting all the wealthy houses and that's when Monty decided to move his spare cash into the tanks. Any run of the mill robber can crack a safe. You wanna reach in the mamba tank and take that dosh? Be my guest, but it'll be the last thing you do.'

Yeah, totally legit.

The Burmese python stretched out, its muscular body rippling with the tiniest of movements. Athena thought of her own hidey-hole back home. The secret panel in the back of her bed housed a decent chunk of Athena's inheritance. Perhaps the snake tanks weren't as odd a choice as she first thought.

'What do you even feed these things?' she asked.

'The little ones eat rats,' answered Wilkinson. 'We let the biggins out of their tanks and hoy in a few rabbits or Guinea pigs. The lads place bets on how long they'll last.'

Athena felt bile rise in her throat. 'That's barbaric,' she gasped.

'Nah it's not, luv,' said Lewis. He sounded annoyed at the suggestion. 'It's mother nature, innit. Ya think these two would be slitherin' roond Africa munchin' on grass and berries and being best buds with the meerkats? Life's not a Disney film.'

Athena opened her mouth to let Lewis know that neither a Burmese or Indian rock python would be slithering anywhere near Africa but thought better of it when Kris gave her the subtlest shake of his head.

'Anyway,' continued Lewis in a low mumble. 'The game's aboot to start. Boss says to take your seats and if you want some scran you'd best hurry 'cause Silent Pete's already working his way through that raw fish shite that the boss loves so much.'

Luke clapped his hands together. 'Oh boy to do I love sashimi,' he drooled, putting his arm around Athena's waist. 'You know the best thing about being a heavyweight, Foxy?'

'Not having to cut weight?' she asked, already knowing and hating the answer.

'Abso-friggin-lutely,' he beamed.

Athena's stomach grumbled. 'I hate you,' she glowered.

Moments later Athena took her seat between Kris and Luke and felt like she'd taken the shrinking potion from Alice in Wonderland. Her legs dangled from the chair, the tips of her toes barely grazing the floor as Kris and Luke towered either side of her. Wilkinson took a seat to Monty's left and Lewis removed his jacket and sat to Monty's right. Lewis's face wasn't the only tattooed part of him. His entire right arm had been inked with a hodgepodge of poorly drawn flowers, birds and tribal designs. When Athena thought of the lions on the backs of Kris's calves she compared them to works of art. They had the precision and delicate touches of the great realists of the nineteenth century. If Kris had told Athena he had travelled back in time to have the likes of

Manet or Courbet use his calves as canvas she wouldn't have been surprised. Lewis's arm, on the other hand, looked as if it had been used as a colouring-in book by a drunk primary school pupil. The name Chantelle was inked along his forearm, it had been crossed out and replaced with the name Kylie. *Wow*, thought Athena, hoping she never ended up as a crossed out name on someone's arm.

Silent Pete deposited some chilled bottles of beer on the table and distributed them amongst the players. Yahia Saleem loosened his tie and Old Willy finished his pipe and tucked it away in his jacket pocket. Monty adjusted his posture and gave a little cough.

'Well ladies and gentlemen,' he started, shuffling the deck as he spoke. 'As you know, it's a straight G per player. House takes its usual cut.'

Around the table, hands reached into pockets and bags. Monty took a few notes from each wad of cash he was handed and slipped them into his back pocket.

'Big blind's twenty, little blind's a tenner. After the first hour, the blinds go up to fifty and twenty,' continued Monty as Lewis slid neat piles of poker chips to each player.

It wasn't long into the game that chat turned to business. The Whites bragged about how well their newest bar was performing, a vertical drinking pen in Newcastle's notorious Bigg Market. Athena had been in there once and vowed to never again. Service was terrible, the barkeep didn't know how to make a mojito and three of the toilet cubicles were missing doors. The place was a shit hole but there were plenty of people out there who couldn't get enough of Jagerbombs, especially when they were two for a fiver. After a while, Mrs White, who turned out to be called Nancy, asked what the three newcomers did for a living.

'We're cage fighters,' answered Athena.

There was a collective chortle at the idea until Monty assured them all that Athena wasn't joking.

'Ms Fox is quite the martial arts star. Luke here is the heavyweight champion.'

'I knew I recognised you from somewhere,' said Wilkinson, wagging his finger as the cogs in his head whirled. 'You're the chick on the fight night posters! Silent Pete's has tickets to that, don't ya Pete?'

Pete nodded with enthusiasm.

Luke scanned the cards on the table, huffed and folded his hand. 'Always the way. No one's ever like *Luke Mar! You're that sexy chap from the fight night posters!* I'm the one with the belt slung over my shoulder but it's always Athena they recognise.'

'Oh put that pet lip away, champ,' said Athena as she nudged his huge shoulder.

'Nee offence, Luke buddy,' laughed Wilkinson. 'But the majority of men walking past one of those posters are going to notice the hot chick in a sports bra and hand wraps before they notice the muscle man who's stood next to her.'

'Can you please stop calling me *chick*,' glowered Athena.

'Sorry luv, sorry. Nee offence to you either.'

Monty let out a silky laugh. 'Three trained killers in our midst and Wilkinson manages to insult two of them before the clock's struck nine.' He picked up three blue poker chips. 'Raise to sixty.'

Wilkinson bobbed his head up and down. 'You know me, boss. Besides, I'll have offended the hat-trick by the end of the night.' He folded his cards and Monty scooped up his winnings.

'Which reminds me,' started Monty. 'How are you three for sponsorship? A big show like that, international viewers, the talk of the town. If you're willing to wear Flamingo Cove t-shirts when you walk out to the cage I could compensate you all handsomely for the publicity.'

Luke lifted his beer. 'I don't say no to money, Monty. It's a deal.'

'Thanks for the offer,' said Kris, 'but I'm not fighting on this card.'

'But you're in my corner. Jimmy's too,' pressed Athena, knowing he could use the money. 'You still walk out to the cage, you'll get plenty air time.'

Monty clapped his hands. 'Then it's settled. We'll talk numbers later in the week but I'm sure we'll come to an arrangement that suits us all.' He extended an arm and shook hands with the three fighters in turn. When Athena saw the look on Kris's face, a mix of happiness and relief, she wanted to run around the table and hug Monty.

Nancy White tapped her husband on the shoulder. 'Don't we have tickets to that show, Glen?'

Glen White collected in the cards and began to shuffle for his deal. 'Sure do,' he answered.

'Exciting,' replied Nancy, drumming her fingers on the table. 'I'll be cheering for you all.'

'Thanks,' replied Athena. She picked up her cards, a seven and a two, off-suit. *Useless.*

'You don't look like a fighter,' huffed Lewis. He slumped back in his chair and looked Athena up and down. His stare caused a little shiver to run up her spine as he added. 'You're tiny. I reckon I could beat you in a fight.'

Athena felt Kris and Luke bristle on either side of her. She placed a calming hand on each of them.

'Lewis,' warned Monty. 'We don't speak to guests like that.'

'It's OK, Monty,' said Athena. By now she was used to the fact that weak men hated strong women. 'I'm sure Lewis could indeed beat me a fight. Just like he could beat Serena Williams on the tennis court or outrun Paula Radcliffe.'

Monty smiled. 'Never seen him do an ounce of sport in his life and he thinks he can take on the experts.' He shook his head at Lewis. 'Do something useful. Like fetching me another drink.'

By half nine the Whites were out of the game. Without skipping a beat Nancy White handed over another two grand to Monty to buy her and her husband back in. Kris looked both disturbed and impressed at the sight. He could take every shift at every bar and he still wouldn't make enough to throw away two grand on a game of cards. Right now he was four hundred up and Athena had told him he could keep anything he won, so winning was what Kris planned on doing.

As the clock struck ten, Glen White played his last hundred pounds worth of chips and found himself bust once more. This time it was at the hands of Luke who had a beautiful full house of kings over jacks. Nancy tried to buy his way back in for a third time but Glen whispered in her ear and they decided to go home to watch Game of Thrones.

'And then there were nine,' said Old Willy as he lit his pipe once more, his face briefly glowing orange behind the lit match.

Yahia Saleem's phone rang. He looked at the screen and turned it to silent. 'The missus,' he told the group, putting it back in his pocket.

Wilkinson picked up the cards and expertly dealt each of them a new hand. The blinds were doubled and Athena figured that the time had come to move the conversation to the topic that was occupying her mind. She looked down at the ten and ace of clubs, added some poker chips to the pile and asked, 'Did your glass collector manage to make any sense of Molly's diary?'

Monty looked up from the bottom of his glass. 'I gave him the pages during his shift last night. He said he hadn't seen anything like it before. Promised to work on it over the weekend. He was fascinated. The boy's a clever lad, I'm sure he'll get to the bottom of it. Oh, before I forget, he asked if Molly was a gamer?'

'A gamer?'

'Yes. The first thing the code reminded him of was keystrokes from a PlayStation.'

Old Willy puffed out a huge plume of smoke. 'What in the damn world is a PlayStation?'

A chorus of laughter filled the room. Yahia put his head in his hands while he regained enough composure to explain the world's best selling games console to Old Willy. A vibration from his pocket indicated that his phone was ringing again. He looked at it, declined the call and put it away a second time.

'The missus?' asked Monty.

Yahia folded his hand. 'Isn't it always?'

Athena's ace and ten came up trumps and she added a few hundred to what had been a dwindling pile of poker chips. Poker skills were clearly not hereditary.

'She wasn't a gamer,' said Athena, thinking back to her childhood. Athena had never really been into computer games. The only device she played games on was her smartphone and even then it was only the occasional game of Candy Crush. What about Molly though? Had Molly had a PlayStation in her room? Or a handheld? Athena tried to remember.

It was quarter to eleven and Yahia Saleem's phone rang for the umpteenth time. 'Oh for the love of… Hello darling,' he cooed into his phone. 'Yes. Slow down, darling. Really?' Yahia was rolling his eyes and yawning as he listened to the high pitched, frantic voice of his wife. 'Must I deal with this now? Can't it wait until morning? OK. OK. I'll see you soon. Bye.'

Yahia hung up and looked at the cards in his hand and folded.

'Trouble in paradise?' asked Wilkinson, who was down to his last hundred.

Yahia counted up his chips and handed them to Monty who did a quick scan and handed close to two grand over to him. 'My damn kid was seen smoking a cigarette by the neighbours. The missus is acting like it's the worst shame he could possibly bring on the family. It's the end of the world as we know it. I need to go home and pretend to threaten to send him to Pakistan to live with his grandparents if he doesn't quit at once.'

'Pretend?' asked Monty without lifting his eyes from his cards.

'Where do you think he got the cigs in the first place? He knows where I keep my stash. Now I need to buy his silence by getting him a swanky watch or some other trinket that he can flaunt on Instagram.'

'Well it looks like you cashed out about a grand up,' said Luke. 'That should cover it.'

'It better had,' sighed Yahia, putting his cash in the inside pocket of his tailored jacket with his phone. 'Good luck with the fights you two,' he added, nodding goodbye to Athena and Luke and shaking Monty's hand. 'I'll get those figures to you next week.'

Monty patted him on the shoulder. 'Lewis will show you out, dear friend. Oh, and Lewis bring us all some more drinks when you've done that. Beers, gents? Wine, Ms Fox?'

'Not for me,' sighed Athena. She held up her original glass of red wine that she'd been nursing for far too long. 'I'm savouring every sip.'

The front door shut with a bang and Athena saw Lewis's shadowy figure skulk through to the kitchen and return with seven bottles of beer. They clinked off of each other as he dragged his feet.

'Raise to seventy,' said Athena after surveying her cards. 'So what else did you and Molly chat about when you met?'

Old Willy and Monty matched the bet and Wilkinson dealt the queen of diamonds and the three and four of hearts.

Monty placed his cards down and pinched his nose while he thought about his next bet. 'Hmm, let's see. We talked about the crash. She showed me pictures of her dog, pictures of her family. We talked about those DNA kits you can buy off the internet. Wilkinson, you were there. What else did we chat about?'

Wilkinson shook his head and his shaggy hair bounced side to side like a golden retriever that hadn't been brushed in a while. 'Can't recall much, boss. I remember she got in a bit of a strop when we made the shoplifting connection.'

'Ah yes,' said Monty. 'Turns out Molly and I have more in common than just a few freckles. I was a little toe rag when I was a youngster. Drove my mother crazy. I fell in with a bad crowd and got a couple of cautions for shoplifting. Molly didn't like hearing that at all. Not one bit. Not that I'd expect her to of course. She started to fret that criminality was hereditary. She told me it must be my fault she got caught stealing that designer dress and that it was my fault she got suspended. Did she really take her head teacher's car for a joyride?'

Athena swallowed and gave the tiniest nod.

'Wow. Hardcore,' said Wilkinson.

'Anyway, I gave her a warm drink to calm her down and gave her my *your past doesn't define you* speech. It seemed to help. I told her, regardless of the DNA tests, she'd be welcome at one of my seminars. Oh, and we talked about work. She asked if we had any openings at the restaurant for summer staff. She was going to drop her CV in.'

Betting continued and Athena lost the hand. Kris was playing with more and more caution now that his pile of chips was beginning to tower over his half pint glass. He had enough to pay a few months worth of rent if he continued with this strategy. Wilkinson was out, as was Lewis. That left Monty, Old Willy, Silent Pete and the trio of cage fighters battling over the remaining chips. Luke was beginning to slur a little from the number of beers he'd made his way through but he still somehow managed to cling on to his final few chips.

'Did she seem depressed? I know she struggled after Mum and our grandparents died. She came with me to identify the bodies. I should have made her stay home. I should have protected her. She was too young to see that.' Athena's voice trailed off. 'Did she say anything about being suicidal?'

Silent Pete and Wilkinson exchanged a look and let their eyes sink to the table. Kris placed a warm hand on her back and stroked her spine. It felt nice. Monty's shoulders sank and he held her gaze. 'She didn't say anything like that. I'm sorry.'

Athena held back a tear and bit her lip. 'I'm going to sit out this hand.'

Monty held her gaze a little longer then placed his hands together on the table. 'I know you're cutting calories but I'm pretty sure you could do with something stronger than sips of red wine. Lewis, bring Ms Fox a small measure of brandy. The good stuff.'

Lewis begrudgingly got to his feet and left the room.

'Ms Fox?' said Old Willy to himself. He tapped his cards on the table. 'Ms Fox,' he repeated before staring into Athena's face. 'You're Vivian's girl!'

Athena's eyes widened. 'Yes. Yes, I am.'

'I knew you looked familiar. You're the spitting double of her my love. She had longer hair and her nose wasn't quite like that,' he said pointing at Athena's nose.

Athena followed the tip of his finger and went cross-eyed for a second. 'Yeah, I've broken it a few times. Three times actually. You knew my mother?'

'Everyone knew Vivian,' smiled Old Willy, taking a long drag on his pipe. 'Beautiful woman, had the prettiest green eyes I ever did see. Just like yours. You have a boyfriend dear?'

Wilkinson laughed. 'I did warn you, Athena.'

Athena forced a polite smile - despite the fact that her skin felt as if a hundred cockroaches were crawling over it - and placed her palm on top of Kris's shoulder.

'Lucky man,' said Old Willy, raising a glass to Kris.

Kris paused for a second and raised his glass in return. 'Erm. Thanks,' he said.

'Yes, you're a lucky man. Ain't he a lucky man, Lewis?'

Athena gave Kris a pleading smile and tried to convey a look of, *play along, for the love of God don't let this old pervert think I'm single.*

Lewis placed the brandy on the table and lowered himself into his chair and glowered. 'I don't like muscly women. I like lasses who look like lasses.'

'Well luckily I'm not your lass,' spat Athena, turning back to Old Willy and taking a lingering sip of brandy that burned her throat. 'So,' she coughed a little, 'you played poker with my mother? Was she as good as people say?'

'Oh, she was the best,' said Old Willy. He reclined in his chair and steepled his fingers as he reminisced. 'She held her own with all the old timers but she was best when the out of towners turned up. She was quite the actress, your mother was. Played a fair few guys for fools. Old Willy here included.' He tapped his chest. 'I remember the first time she showed up at that casino that was owned by Mike Whatshisface, can't remember what it was called, it's shut down now. Anyway, she came in dressed up like a princess in some pink lacy thing, all legs and long blonde hair. She was a stunner. She played dumb, lost half her money, bet on stupid hands and when the perfect hand came along she'd draw us all down the river and go all in. Us daft sods were sat there, mouths open so wide we'd catch flies, wondering where the hell all our coin had gone. Vivian slid all her chips off the table into her pretty pink handbag, blew us all kisses and off she went.' He looked at his watch and jumped to his feet with the energy of a twenty-year-old. 'Oh bugger. Is that the time? I'd better be off before the nurses do their rounds and realise I'm gone again.'

'The nurses?' Athena still had a huge grin on her face at the thought of her mother waltzing into some dodgy casino, winning a load of money and waltzing out again.

'Oak View Care Home, luv. The nurses do a round at midnight. If they realise I've snuck off again I'll never hear the end of it. At least if I do get caught it's the pretty little nurse with bosoms like boulders who's on duty tonight. She's not as pretty as Vivian was though. Lord, she was a stunner. Wasn't she a stunner, Monty?'

Monty took a long sip of beer and handed Old Willy his winnings. 'She was,' he agreed.

'She played you beautifully that night at Phil Gregson's place. I'll never forget 'cause she was wearing this handkerchief of a dress, and you'll probably never forget 'cause she cost you a small fortune.'

'It was only a few grand. Nothing worth crying over,' laughed Monty, though his laugh never reached his eyes. 'But I can thank Viv for teaching me a valuable lesson. Never judge a book by its cover. I didn't make that mistake twice.'

'I'll see myself out,' said Old Willy. 'Don't get up, Lewis.'

Lewis tilted his head back and sunk the rest of his bottle of beer. He let every last drop drain into his mouth before wiping his face with the back of his hand. 'I'll be honest, boss. I divint think you're that lass's father. You don't look that much like her and from what I've heard on the grapevine that Vivian wasn't exactly Mother Teresa.'

'Careful, Lewis,' said Monty.

Athena rose to her feet. 'What are you saying?'

'I'm saying half the blokes within twenty miles of the Tyne bridge had probably had a ride on Viv. I know she's ya ma but you need to know she was... What's the politically correct term? Oh yes, a slut. I heard she was a massive slut.'

The air in the room changed as Athena slammed the sides of her fists on the table. Poker chips wheeled off in countless directions. She could feel the static all around her, could hear her heartbeat in her ears and her breath rushing from her nose. Her blood boiled, her jaw clenched and a vein pulsated in her temple. Athena took half a second to choose between excusing herself and making her way upstairs to the bathroom to calm down or doing what she actually did.

Athena's chair toppled loudly behind her as she vaulted over the marble table. She grabbed Lewis by the neck and pressed the arc of her hand upwards under his jaw until his chair balanced precariously on its back legs.

Tunnel vision clouded Athena as she stared him down. His choices were limited. Option one, he could fall back off his chair and crack his ugly tattooed head open on the polished floor. Option two, he could swipe Athena's hand away only for it to instinctively boomerang back to its target, this time with a closed fist. Or, option three, he could do nothing and let her choke him unconscious. Athena watched as Lewis's eyes started to glaze over, and the feeling of power intoxicated her. The muscles in his neck tensed against her palm and the hairs on the back of his neck stood on end. His face grew redder, his tattoo becoming less black on white and more black on rose. She could feel his pulse quicken as his heart worked harder to get blood to his brain.

'What's the matter, luv?' Lewis wheezed as Athena tightened her grip and the veins in her forearm began to protrude. 'Did I hit a nerve? You're the one who turned up with two men.' He coughed and Athena squeezed harder. 'Does the apple not fall far from Vivian's tree?'

'That's enough, young man.' Monty thudded his glass on to the table. 'I don't know what's gotten into you this evening but you should know never to talk to my guests like that. It's time for you to leave.'

Lactic acid filled Athena's forearm as her fingers refused to weaken. Despite her rage, a dangerous thought crossed her mind, she could kill him if she wanted too. She really could.

In her periphery, she could see the other men on their feet. Kris had jumped up ready to throttle Lewis himself, but Wilkinson and Pete had rushed to put themselves between Kris and his target.

'You lay one finger on him and...'

'And nothing,' finished Monty. 'He made his own bed. He can suffer the consequences.'

Kris, Wilkinson and Pete didn't budge. They were like cats ready to pounce.

It was Luke, one of the most dangerous men on the planet, who appealed for everyone to, 'Calm the fook down.'

It was worth noting, that had Athena made her excuses and headed to the bathroom to wash her face and try to quell her rage, she would still have been unlikely to hear - over the noise of Jay-Z's latest single - the sound of stubby-fingered hands setting a newspaper on fire and dropping it through the conservatory window.

- CHAPTER 22 -

It took a while but eventually everyone heeded Luke's plea for calm. Monty adjusted himself in his seat, his mouth was the thin line of a man holding back. Athena's breathing was still heavy. Her chest lifted and lowered in quick waves a she watched Lewis rub at his red neck. Four white, fingerprint sized marks were dotted down the right side of his neck where Athena's hand had clamped around him. He was eyeing the three fighters with caution as he slowly pulled his coat on.

Silent Pete and Wilkinson gradually returned to their seats and nodded at Kris as a form of apology.

Athena was the first to break the silence. 'We should leave too.'

'You think?' answered Lewis.

'You've said enough,' said Monty. 'I'll see you at work on Monday,' his voice softened as he turned back to his guests. 'Please, accept my apologies, Ms Fox. We're working on his impulse control but honestly, I don't know what gets in to him sometimes.' He extended a hand back towards Athena's seat. 'Petey, whisky and some shot glasses if you don't mind.'

Athena chewed the inside of her lip for a few seconds and glanced at Kris. He had a large pile of poker chips in front of him and if they left now, on bad terms, the sponsorship deal might never materialise. Kris didn't have his next fight scheduled yet and the pile of chips alone was enough to pay his rent and utilities until Christmas. Athena could see Kris eying them longingly.

Luke followed Athena's gaze and picking up on her dilemma he tried his best to appease the group. 'How about another few hands, Foxy? Cash out at one?'

'Please stay, Ms Fox,' said Monty, his hand still extended. 'I'd hate our evening to end like this.'

Athena relaxed her shoulders, moved around the table and picked her chair back off the floor. Silent Pete took some shot glasses from a glass cabinet and arranged them on the table.

'Now get some of this down you,' said Monty, pushing his swaying braids behind his ear and pouring out seven shots of Yamazaki Whisky.

'You know that stuff's about ninety quid a shot?' asked Athena.

'And about eighty calories a mouthful,' added Kris, who swallowed nervously and looked away when Athena fixed him with a Medusa-like glare.

Monty smiled again, this time with an impressed nod. 'My, my, you certainly know your liquor. The cost is no matter though. This particular bottle was a gift. An apology of sorts, it's only fitting that I share it now, as an apology to you.' He handed the shot glasses to everyone but Lewis and raised his up in the air. 'To…' he paused and bore his eyes back into the trainee, 'to treating guests correctly.'

Lewis zipped his coat up and raised an imaginary shot glass to Athena. 'To treating guests correctly,' he growled as a tinny smoke alarm blared into action.

Monty downed his shot as he stared around. 'You leave something in the oven, Pete?'

Pete shook his head but got to his feet to double check. When he opened the door to the kitchen a wave of heat passed over him with enough intensity to make his head recoil. Pete stared past the kitchen into the conservatory where a couch was engulfed in flames. It crackled and spat embers on to the foosball table. Pete slammed the door shut and turned to face the rest of the group, his eyes darting about in panic.

'F-fire,' he managed to stutter.

'What the actual fuck?' asked Wilkinson, getting to his feet and opening the door to see for himself. 'Shit. Shit. Holy shit. Extinguisher. Where's the extinguisher, Monty?'

Monty frowned and leant back in his chair to get a better view. His jaw dropped. 'In the kitchen, under the sink. Quickly.'

By this point everyone was on their feet. Wilkinson dove through the heat in the kitchen to grab the extinguisher. He edged his way to the conservatory and pulled the pin. The foam slowed the flames from the couch but the fire had already spread to an armchair and the foosball table.

'WATER,' yelled Monty, grabbing a bucket from under the sink and filling it.

He threw the water into the flames but it made no difference. The flames broke the leg from the foosball table and it toppled to the floor. When the floorboards began to smoke Monty ran back to the dining room. 'OUT, everyone out.'

Kris grabbed Athena's hand and moved towards the corridor.

'Not so fast,' said Athena. 'We need to cash out.'

'Foxy, it's fine,' pled Kris. 'We need to go.'

'You need your money.'

'It won't do me any good if I'm burned alive.'

Monty scanned the piles of chips and tossed two wads of fifties at Luke. 'That should cover it, big lad.'

The fire reached a set of shelves in the kitchen. One by one bottles of oil exploded with loud pops. Kris tightened his grip on Athena and tugged at her arm.

'Wait,' she said as Wilkinson pointlessly threw another bucket of water into the flames. 'Finish the hand. Turn over the next card.'

Kris coughed. Smoke was filling the room. 'You're kidding, right? Let's get out of here.'

'I'm not kidding,' she reached across the table and pulled the top card from the deck. 'A king,' she said as she threw the river card on the table. 'That's four of a kind for me. I win.'

Monty, despite himself, let out a purr of a laugh. 'Like mother, like daughter,' he said as he pulled several crisp twenty pound notes from his pocket and thrusted them into Luke's chest.

Another bottle of oil exploded and Monty's face changed again. 'OUT, you three. NOW. Lewis call the fire brigade. Pete, Wilkinson, follow me. Save the pets.'

Monty moved to the corridor and raced up the stairs. He returned with nine foot of Indian rock python over his shoulders, a pair of brown snakes in one hand a wad of fifties in the other. He dropped the lot on the corridor floor and ran back up the stairs, followed by Wilkinson and Pete.

Athena and Kris edged around the giant serpent, trying to make their way to the front door. Athena had never been especially bothered by creepy crawlies but she'd never been this close to a snake of this size without a glass panel between her and it. An instinct handed down over millennia, from the days before humans first left Africa, told her to beware. Her hand shook as she grabbed the handle to the door, her eyes never leaving the snake. She tugged and her stomach dropped.

'It's locked,' squeaked Athena. 'Monty, it's locked.'

'The keys, Monty! Where are the damn keys?' yelled Lewis as he finished his call to the fire brigade.'

Wilkinson ran down the stairs with a pillowcase full of squirming snakes.

Kris barged past Lewis and began to throw his body at the door, shoulder charging it, but to no avail. The door thumped and rattled but the thick locks held it in place.

As Monty returned once more from upstairs, this time with the Burmese python around his shoulders and who knows what squirming in a bag, Lewis pressed him again. 'The keys, Monty.'

Monty patted his trouser pockets and the blood drained from his face. 'They're in the kitchen.'

A little brown snake emerged from a pillowcase and slithered its way over Luke's right shoe. Luke jumped so high that the snake was catapulted across the hallway where it hit the radiator and fell down to the floor. It curled defensively into a ball. Another snake, much larger and darker in colour snapped at Silent Pete's knee. He grabbed it by the tail and caught a nasty bite on his hand as he tossed it back in the bag. 'That had better not be the f-fuckin' m-mamba,' he said.

'You'll soon know about it if it is,' said Monty, now also throwing his body at the door.

'Move it,' said Luke. He grabbed Kris and Monty by the shoulders and pulled them out of the way to try his own bulk against the door. His behemoth body slammed and banged the door but with its industrial locks, it wouldn't budge.

Athena stood watching the chaos, still paralysed with fear and acutely aware of the smell of smoke as it seeped into the corridor through the gap above the dining room door. Snapping back to life and fighting against all her instincts she used her foot to gently slide the little brown snake out of the way.

'We can't kick it down from the inside,' she said.

Athena dropped to the floor, lay on her back and positioned her heel against the bottom panel in the wood. A great hairy spider crawled over her stomach and she winced. 'Cover me,' she said before delivering kick after kick until the panel shattered.

'We can't fit through that, Foxy,' said Kris, gesturing to the small rectangle of space that little Athena was already halfway through. The humid night air hit her lungs and fragments of wood ripped at her clothing. She had to tilt sideways, suck in her stomach, and scratch her nails across the gravel drive, but eventually, she was free.

Athena got to her feet and dusted her hands over her top. A splinter of wood fell out of her hair and caught on her fingertip. 'Ouch,' she gasped, pulling it out and watching a droplet of blood form at the puncture point. She bent over and yelled through the missing panel, 'Stand back!'

'She can't be serious,' said Lewis. 'She thinks she can kick the door d—'

The door flew off its hinges and landed square in Lewis's face.

Kris was out of the door faster than a cheetah on amphetamines. He grabbed Athena and pulled her into his chest. He kissed the top of her head and pulled shards of splintered wood off her back. 'When the bloggers call you a little powerhouse they aren't kidding.'

'You can say that again,' panted Luke as he patted Athena on the shoulder. 'Nice one.'

Monty took one last run upstairs, coughing smoke as he did so, and returned with an armful of cash and lizards.

Wilkinson and Silent Pete fought their way out of the door frame, followed by a red-faced Lewis. A boa constrictor of about six-foot circled Wilkinson and slithered off in the direction of the dene.

Sirens could be heard in distance.

'Hmm,' mused Monty, watching the sand and umber coloured serpent disappear under some shrubs. 'There'll probably be something about this in the papers tomorrow.'

Luke nodded with wide, traumatised eyes. 'Yeah. I think you might be right there, Monty. Seriously though, next time get some hamsters, or a cat.'

Monty looked up and down the street then settled his eyes back on Athena. 'Your fight, Ms Fox. You're the favourite, right?'

Athena lifted her head from Kris's chest. 'I'm a six to one underdog.'

'That kick saved our lives. I'm betting at least a grand on you.'

'This has Maxim Pasternak written all over it,' growled Lewis. He grabbed a potted plant from Monty's driveway and hurled it on to the concrete. Its casing shattered into hundreds of tiny pieces.

Monty toed a piece of the shattered pot plant. 'Let's not get hasty. Pete, here's my phone, you can access the CCTV footage remotely, but do it quickly before the fire spreads to the office. Wilkinson, warn the neighbours, get them out of their houses then round up the pets, Rocky's in the shrubs over there, God knows where the Berm is. Call some of the staff if you need a hand. Lewis, make some calls. Get in touch with that sergeant, the one who helped us out when the waitress was stealing from the till and ask Morgan to email me the insurance documents.'

Wilkinson, Silent Pete and Lewis nodded and set off in different directions. Monty plunged his hands into his pockets. His shoulders hung forward and his head bowed. He looked a shadow of his slender, graceful self. 'Do you believe in ghosts, Ms Fox?'

- CHAPTER 23 -

Simba yawned and filled Athena's bedroom with the stench of dog breath. He uncurled himself at the end of her bed, had an earthquake of a shake and began furiously scratching himself behind his right ear. The bed vibrated enough to wake Athena, who eyeballed her beloved Akita and cursed quietly.

'You fluffy shit. You'd make a great fur coat, you know that?'

The hefty dog's ears pricked up and he launched himself on to her. His tail was a blur of excitement as he licked his owner's face.

'Urgh. Thanks for the wake-up call,' grumbled Athena between kisses, 'but seriously, I'm going to sit you down and make you watch 101 Dalmatians.' She pushed Simba off her and grabbed a glass of water from beside her bed and took a long drink. Today was the start of her water loading cycle. Water loading was an annoying but necessary part of the weight cutting process. Athena would trick her body into a flushing mode by over hydrating it for a few days.

Athena couldn't shift a feeling in the pit of her stomach. Something wasn't quite right and it was more than pre-fight nerves. Who were the ghosts Monty spoke of? She picked up her laptop, opened Google and typed in *Alistair Montgomery* for what must have been the hundredth time. She frowned and changed the search to, *Alistair Montgomery, Pasternak.* After reading for a few minutes she completed one further search, *Alistair Montgomery, Durham.*

Athena closed her laptop, went to the bathroom and got herself another glass of water. Then she curled back into her four-poster bed and picked up her phone to do her usual morning scroll through social media and a quick check of a few news sites. Athena blinked as her phone lit up with texts and missed calls.

'Oh this can't be good,' she sighed as her finger hovered over a text from Owen.

Nice video Foxy, but I preferred the photo of you in your panties.

Athena frowned and wondered what in the world her pathetic excuse of an ex-boyfriend was on about now. She puffed her cheeks out and deleted the message rather than text him back to find out. She'd never text that man again, especially not when she had two texts from the distractingly handsome Krzysztof Kava.

Have you seen the news?

Then, sent eight minutes later,

Have you been on Twitter?

'Oh, this really can't be good,' grumbled Athena as Simba did a pirouette and curled his sixty kilos on to Athena's stomach. She squirmed and took another huge drink of water as she tried to read her phone over the view of bushy white fur. She had three missed calls from an international number and a text from Luke.

What a numpty! Check this fool out!

Luke's text came with a link to the website of Newcastle's Evening Chronicle.

Man Arrested for Bringing Python to Pub

Alex Davidson, 43 of Mayfair Road, Jesmond was arrested shortly before 11 p.m. last night after he arrived at Spy Bar on Osborne Road with a six-foot boa constrictor hanging around his neck. Panicked patrons called police after the man, who was refused entry to the bar by bouncers, became violent and threatened the security staff with the snake. According to witnesses, Davidson claimed that the snake had been trained to kill on command and would strangle anyone Davidson pointed at. Reporters spoke to the arresting officer and can confirm that Davidson was taking a shortcut through Jesmond Dene last night when he stumbled across the boa. Davidson made the extraordinary claim that he'd first spotted a

> much bigger snake in the dene's petting zoo and had watched it kill one of the pygmy goats and begin to devour it. According to Davidson, he then saw the boa constrictor hanging from a low branch and removed it from the tree to hang it over his shoulders. Davidson protested his innocence to the staff at Newcastle's police station on Forth Banks, saying that he only wanted to find a karaoke bar so that he could do an impression of Britney Spears's iconic performance at the 2001 MTV Video Music Awards. The boa constrictor - who has been named Britney by police staff - is now being cared for at Kirkley Hall Zoological Gardens. Staff at Pet's Corner have reported one of their pygmy goats as missing.

Athena let out a chuckle. 'Absolute numpty,' she said as she pried Simba from her, rolled on to her belly and opened Twitter.

XXX

Less than seven minutes later, the door to The Pit slammed against the wall as Athena stormed into the gym with all the grace of a small, blonde gorilla. Luke and Kris glanced up from a set of push-ups they were performing. Erin Summers froze mid kick and a group of youngsters paused their sparring drills to take a look.

Simba scurried across the gym and hid his face under one of his paws.

Athena scanned the room with laser-like vision and zoned in on Charlie Fisher who was lazing at his desk. He was sat in the swivel chair with his feet on the desk and a can of energy drink balanced on his beer belly. In one hand he held a phone up to his ear and the index finger of his other hand was exploring one of his nostrils. Athena wrinkled her nose at the sight of him and barged across the gym. She grabbed Charlie's feet and threw them off of his desk with enough force to send him spinning wildly on the swivel chair. His mobile phone flew from his hand and landed in the bin while the energy drink fell to the small patch of carpet around the desk, spilling red colouring and glucose syrup into the fibres.

'Foxy! What in blue blazes do you thi—'

'Who did you show the CCTV footage to, Charlie?'

Athena's eyes burned fury into him. She tossed her belongings into her docket in the shelving unit on the far wall and turned back to The Pit's boss. 'Well?'

Charlie fished his phone out of the bin and raised it back to his ear. 'Jennifer, I'll have to call you back.' He hung up and placed his phone on the cluttered desk. 'Right, Foxy. I take it you've been on Twitter?'

'Of course I've been on BLOODY Twitter.' Athena was yelling now. 'I had over six hundred notifications waiting for me and MMA Junkie want a statement.' She held her face in her hands for a second then released it to stare at the ceiling. Tiny crescent moon indents from her fingernails peppered her forehead. 'Christ, Charlie. Sissy Clark is posting footage of her kicking the shit out of a bunch of men. Meanwhile, there's a goddammed gif doing the rounds of me pirouetting and worming around the cage floor like a moron. The footage is going viral.'

The gym fell completely silent as she stood over Charlie. Simba whimpered at Luke's feet and nuzzled his head into his thigh, begging for reassurance that his owner's yelling wasn't directed at him. Luke reached down and scratched his ears. 'It's ok, boy.'

Charlie held his palms up. 'It wasn't me, Foxy. I swear I didn't give anyone the CCTV tapes.' He bent over and picked up what remained of the energy drink and looked at the reddening stain with concern. 'You need to calm down,' he said slowly and deliberately, 'then clean that up.'

'Like hell I will,' spluttered Athena, unsure if she was referring to calming down, cleaning up, or both. 'If it wasn't you then who else has access to the cameras?'

She whipped her head around and raised her eyebrows at the lycra clad Luke Mar.

Luke protected his groin with his hands, sending the juniors into fits of giggles. 'It wasn't me, Foxy. I look as much of pillock in that clip as you do.'

Athena growled and stomped up to the nearest punch bag. She eyed it like it was her worst foe and kicked her right shin into it with all the force she could muster. 'When I find out who it was I'll…' She kicked it again, even harder. 'I'll…'

'Easy tiger,' offered Kris. He walked over and placed one tentative hand on her shoulder. 'How about we start with some light sparring and release some of that energy?'

Athena's mouth thinned and her cheeks flushed with rage. 'Fine,' she spat, throwing his arm off of her and turning back to Charlie, who was still eyeing the carpet. 'I mean it, I'm not cleaning that shit up, get one of the kids to do it.'

Magically, all the juniors regained interest in the exercises they were supposed to be drilling and went back to practising their counter-attacks.

Charlie rummaged around in his desk drawer and pulled out some antibacterial spray and a sponge. He began to furiously scrub at the red patch on his carpet. 'And who said you could bring that walking fur ball to training?'

'He always comes training,' said Athena as she removed her shoes.

'He's a hygiene risk.'

Athena stored her shoes against the wall and pulled her shin pads from her kit bag. 'So are half the guys in here.'

Simba stalked a full lap of the cage, sniffed at a line of kit bags and finally made himself comfortable on the mats with his head resting on Luke's spare gloves.

'I just disinfected those mats, Foxy. He'd better not have worms.'

Athena snorted and started to bind her knuckles in a set of blue cotton wraps. 'Worms? If you're worried about worms you need to kick out half the junior squad, not my dog.'

One of the youngsters looked over. His cheeks were a bright shade of pink that almost perfectly matched the distinctive circular patches of ringworm on his legs. He opened his mouth to stutter something but his partner's foot slapped him across his blushing cheek and he was quickly reminded why you shouldn't let anything distract you during sparring drills.

Charlie chuckled at the kid and turned back to Simba. 'And if he pisses or shits in here?'

'Ah, Charlie, let the pooch stay, ya big bald grump,' laughed Luke, patting Simba on his ribs. 'Besides, he wouldn't be the first to shit himself in here. Remember when Big Ahmed choked out Kris last winter?'

Kris threw his arms out in exasperation. 'And remember when we agreed *never* to mention that again?'

'Yeah, yeah, princess,' laughed Luke. 'Shit happens.'

Kris buried his head in the padded corner post of the cage.

'Yeah, speaking of all things toilet related,' started Athena, 'I'll be back in a minute, I've already had a litre of water this morning.'

A quick toilet break later and Athena was padded up and thrown into the cage for ten rounds of sparring. Each round would last five minutes. Fighting for fifty minutes was a hellish feat to go through but her title fight was set for five rounds of five minutes. Being fit enough for ten rounds meant she knew she'd have the gas tank to go the distance. Her first round was against Erin whose long limbs made a perfect substitute for Sissy's. Athena could practice closing the distance whilst evading kicks that felt like they could reach you from ten feet away. It was a decent practice round but Athena knew Erin was holding back, almost scared to hit Athena in case she hit her back harder, and truth be told, Athena always held back against Erin. Just a little. Because, well it was Erin and no one wanted to be the one to hurt the girl who didn't have a bad bone in her body.

Round two was with Jimmy, who also seemed to be holding back. He pawed at her and apologised every time he connected. After Athena failed to take Jimmy down to the mats he landed a clean knee to her ribs and apologised again.

'The next time you say sorry,' gasped Athena through a mouthful of gum shield. 'I'm going to kick you in the nuts.'

For the next three minutes Jimmy kept his mouth shut and his guard low.

One of the juniors stepped in for the third round. This boy had no problem in trying to hit Athena. He was trying to establish himself in the pecking order by proving to his mates that he couldn't be beaten by a woman and as a result was swinging wildly towards Athena's head. His lack of control was his own downfall. Every time the young man went to punch he would throw it from so far out that Athena could have seen it coming from Mars. It only took a few stiff jabs to his jaw and a thunderous kick to his thigh for Athena to send the young lad to the canvas with a thud. Kris pulled him out of the cage once he started to whimper.

In round four Athena took on little Stevie for what seemed like five minutes of nonstop grappling. Stevie got the better of Athena and almost forced her to tap when he had her in a choke hold.

Luke stepped into the cage for round five, the final round before Athena would get a brief break, which was lucky because the pressure in her bladder was beginning to build again. Luke, despite his intimidating size and obvious proficiency in combat, was always controlled with Athena. He would push her hard, but never too hard. Athena never felt like she was in any real physical danger with Luke.

Aside from his prowess at fighting, what made Luke Mar a great champion was his ability to be a grade A windup merchant. He knew exactly how to push his opponent's buttons. He knew what to say, what to do and how to act to make them angry. And angry fighters make mistakes.

'Come on, Barbie doll. You haven't touched me yet.'

Athena tried to close the distance. Tried to work her way around Luke's enormous limbs.

'You should have stuck to ballet class, pretty girl.'

Athena lunged at Luke, who spun on the spot to deliver a perfectly timed spin kick to Athena's face. The tip of his big toe glanced off her squashed little nose and she knew another few inches and she could have been out cold.

Kris sat on the edge of the cage and stared down at the pair. 'Stay focused, Foxy. You know what he's trying to do.'

Athena took a deep breath and tried to get her footwork and head movement back on track. She stretched her kicks as far as they would go but she still couldn't get close enough to land a kick without eating a few punches. Her breathing was starting to become laboured and the sunlight from outside was causing her to squint. Luke threw another spin kick but landed with his feet too close together. Athena saw her opportunity and pounced. She dived at his feet, grabbed his ankles and executed a perfect double leg takedown. The giant toppled and created an almighty thud as his face bounced off the canvas. Luke shook his big, tanned head to clear the fog and he muttered 'Nice one,' as Athena jumped on top of him to rain punches down on his head guard.

A hint of movement in the window caught Athena's attention. A shadowy figure had just ducked behind her car. Athena squinted, wondering if her eyes were playing tricks on her, and then she was airborne. Luke bucked his hips and she flew across the cage like a paper aeroplane. She landed in a crumpled heap, huffed in annoyance and got to her feet.

Sparring Luke was like sparring a ghost. Every time Athena tried to hit him he was gone and out of range again. It was frustrating as hell but she bit down on her gum shield and kept trying. The more frustrated she got the more she started to swing her punches and use sloppy technique.

'Concentrate,' soothed Kris.

There was a flash outside the window to the gym. A camera? Was someone there? Or was it just the sunlight reflecting off a car bonnet? Athena turned to look again and was clipped by a quick hook to her jaw.

'Come on, princess. You gonna hit me or what?'

Athena flushed with rage and charged at Luke despite her better judgement. She was acting like that damn kid, trying to take Luke's head off to prove a point and make herself feel better. Then, Luke poured salt in the wound, 'I bet Sissy would have hit me by now.'

Athena growled, launched herself at him and ran straight into his left fist. Blood began to team from her nose. Bright red lines made their way down her face, over her sports bra and down on to the canvas. Athena yanked her gloves from her hands and spat her gum shield on to the floor. She pinched her nose hard as blood pooled in her hands.

'You can be such a dick, Luke.'

Kris opened the cage door, gagged at the sight of the blood and passed Athena a handful of tissues.

'Luke's not being a dick, Foxy,' he said. 'He's just being… Luke.'

'Same difference,' huffed Athena. She held out one of her bloodstained hands. 'Hand me my water.'

Luke rested against the side of the cage and stretched his arms above his head. 'Don't hate the player, hate the game.'

Kris managed to hand Athena her water bottle without looking at her. She took gulp after huge gulp, never once letting go of her nose.

Charlie barged in the cage - sponge and bucket in hand - and began to scrub the canvas. 'Now, now, Foxy, you know fine well he's just testing you. It's fight week and it's natural for tempers to be—'

'I know it's fight week, Charlie. I own a calendar for God's sake. Why are the damn shutters up?' Athena's voice was muffled through the tissues.

'The shutters?' asked Charlie. He was still bent over, scrubbing at the bloody canvas, his builder's bum showing to the entire gym.

'Yes, the damn shutters,' said Athena, her speech was getting higher and faster with each breath. 'It's fight week and anyone can see in. We already know there's a traitor in here. I mean how else would Sissy get her bony little mitts on the CCTV? And now there's someone out there with a camera.'

Charlie, Kris and Luke turned their heads and peered out of the windows. 'I don't see anyone,' said Charlie.

'That's because you're an incompetent arse,' said Athena as she stomped over to the bin and dumped her blood-soaked tissues into it. 'How else would the CCTV tapes get leaked?'

'You need to watch your mouth young lady,' he fired back. 'Learn some damn manners before I kick your arse out of here for good.'

Charlie returned to his desk, his cheeks red with impatience. He took a seat in the swivel chair. 'Calm her down,' he said, pointing to Kris, 'Or you can help her find a new gym.'

Kris steered Athena away from Charlie and led her over to Simba. He crouched down and tussled the fur behind his ears. 'Good boy,' he said before straightening up to gaze out of the window. 'You need to snap out of this, Foxy. I get it, I really do. This game we play, this path we've chosen to walk, it's a blessing and a curse. Yes, the lows are the worst but the highs, my God Foxy, think of the highs. Focus on how good it's going to feel when you're the champ.'

Athena's mouth twitched but she said nothing.

'We knew Sissy was going to play dirty from the moment you signed the contract,' continued Kris. 'She does this all the time. She calls her opponents unworthy and a waste of her time, she makes fun of them, tries to make them look stupid on social media. We knew this was coming.'

Athena shrugged.

'The difference between you and those other girls is that the public actually *like* you. They're rooting for you, Foxy. Yeah, maybe that has something to do with you flashing a bit of flesh on the internet every now and again but mostly they just like your style. I read the comments when Sissy posted the gif of us all dancing. There're a few trolls obviously but the majority of the comments are positive. Think about it. That Sissy never cracks a smile, never laughs, never does anything that would question her reputation. You, on the other hand, come across as silly and playful and multitalented, and you look like you don't take yourself too seriously. Granted, if the public could see you now, they might change their minds.'

Athena finally turned and looked at Kris. She raised an eyebrow but her pout never wavered.

'Foxy,' Kris sighed, 'this publicity could be great for you. You said MMA Junkie want a statement. You need to own this, embrace it.'

Athena exhaled. She felt as if she hadn't taken a breath in a considerable amount of time. She sank down and cuddled her big fur ball of a dog and when she finally looked back to Kris her eyes were glassy.

'But what if I lose?' she asked in less than a whisper.

There was more movement beyond the window. Both Kris and Athena jumped back to their feet, their hands pressed against the glass as a hooded figure ran behind Kris's blue Golf.

'There *is* someone out there,' shouted Kris.

Luke leapt from the cage and ran out the front door with a herd of junior fighters hot on his heels.

'I knew I wasn't seeing things,' panted Athena. She turned her back to the window and felt her heart begin to race. 'If that's a reporter I'll strangle him with his own camera strap.'

Charlie frowned and got to his feet. He flicked a small switch on the wall and heavy metal shutters began to roll down the front of The Pit.

Athena began to pace. What if it wasn't a reporter? What if it was Owen being a sad pervert and trying to catch a glimpse of her in a sports bra? Could it be someone from Sissy's camp?

'Whoever it was, if they've got half a brain, they'll have legged it half way to The Meadows the moment they saw Luke coming,' said Kris.

Athena continued to pace back and forth. 'First there's us dancing, now there's going to be pictures of me covered in my own blood. If I lose… As far as the media's concerned, I'll be the girl who spent more time dancing than training. Demons won't give me another title shot after that.'

Kris grabbed Athena by the shoulders. It was rough and she froze in shock. 'You. Are. Not. Going. To. Lose,' he barked.

Simba got to his feet and growled at Kris. A thunderous growl with teeth exposed and hackles raised.

Kris's arms dropped to his sides. 'You are not going to lose,' he repeated, gentler this time. 'Go empty your bladder and clean your gum shield, and when you come back, make sure you've got your shit together. You have five more rounds of sparring and reporter or no reporter you need to get your gloves back on. This fight is going ahead whether the people of Twitter like you or not.'

Athena swallowed hard and nodded her head. A hundred thoughts of paranoia and doubt ran through her mind but she clapped her hands together and answered, 'Yes, boss.'

- CHAPTER 24 -

The Laing art gallery had stood in the centre of Newcastle since 1901. Founded by wine trader Alexander Laing, the building was an Edwardian baroque masterpiece. A grand staircase, embellished with a heavy wooden bannister and curved stone balustrades, led the way to the first floor, where the city's collection of eighteenth and nineteenth-century paintings was displayed.

Athena listed her head to the left and squinted at a painting of two young Roman women relaxing by a fountain with a still, topaz sea behind them. Love in Idleness was perhaps her favourite painting in the whole gallery. The women wore soft, floaty dresses of olive and sage green. They wore sandals on their feet and flowers in their hair. They were a stark contrast to Athena who was rather unkempt in baggy grey joggers and an even baggier grey zip hoody. She felt distinctly at odds with the rest of the gallery's visitors, businessmen and women whose smart shoes and heels clacked against the parquet flooring as they sought a few moments of quiet culture on their lunch breaks. Athena enjoyed the tranquility of the Laing art gallery. She'd made a habit of visiting it in the run-up to each of her fights. To Athena, the gallery was an oasis of peacefulness in what seemed like rolling dunes of never-ending pre-fight anxiety.

Kris's footsteps were soft as he approached. Smart jeans and a black polo shirt accentuated his broad shoulders and narrow waist, giving him the triangular appearance of a Greek god. Athena discretely looked him up and down and concluded that he should be cast out of marble and displayed downstairs.

A young couple walked behind Kris and Athena. They left a plume of overpowering perfume in their wake. Kris covered his nose as he read the information plaque to his left. 'Love in Idleness.'

'That's the flowers,' said Athena. 'The ones in her hair. They're a type of pansy said to inspire love. Shakespeare mentions them a few times. See how the girl in green is gazing into the fountain of Cupid? She's deep in thought about the man she loves.'

Kris rubbed his neck. 'How do you know this stuff?'

'We used to come here with Nana and Gramps,' said Athena, staring through the picture rather than at it. 'Molly loved it here. She loved the statues, the plants, she even loved the smell.' A small smile started to curl up from the corner of Athena's mouth as she reminisced. 'I, on the other hand, used to whine and moan and act like the most bored child on the planet. I'd go on like a complete brat until they bribed me to behave with the promise of a trip to the cafe for chocolate cake.'

Kris didn't say a word but he gave her a look that meant he was not surprised in the slightest.

Athena pouted and refocused her attention to the painting. She pointed to the second girl. 'See this girl? She's not gazing into the fountain. She's staring at her friend and she looks so utterly sad. I think she's in love with other girl but she knows she can't be with her because her heart belongs to someone else. That's my theory anyway.'

Kris ground his teeth together. 'Poor thing.'

Athena's phone chimed and several pairs of unimpressed eyes fell on her as the quiet of the gallery was interrupted.

'I'm sure I put this bloody thing on silent.' Athena reached into her bag, took another sip of water, switched her phone to vibrate and discretely read her messages.

Hey Foxy, not long till fight night. Which bikini are you wearing to the weigh-ins? I like your red one.

Athena huffed and rolled her eyes.

'Everything all right?' asked Kris. 'Sissy's not harassing you on Twitter again?'

'No, but speaking of Twitter,' answered Athena. 'I got a sponsorship offer from a tampon company. They saw the clip of us dancing about in the cage and want me to endorse them. Some crap about being able to dance, fight, whatever, even when you've got your period. The usual nonsense. I can't wait to tell Sissy how much money she just made me.'

Kris chuckled. 'That's brilliant,' he said before pausing. 'Hang on, Luke and I are in that video, no one's offering me fat tampon cash.'

'You don't get periods,' laughed Athena.

'And women with your body fat percentage do?'

'Fair point, but I'm still taking their money. I'll give it to The Pit. Tell Charlie to install some showers.'

Kris bowed down to Athena and mouthed, 'thank you.'

'The text was from my ex,' said Athena, not knowing if she should try and claw the words back into her mouth. 'He keeps texting me. I keep seeing him around Shields and Tynemouth.' She took a sip of water and moved on to the next painting. 'He was at the steakhouse for goodness sake,' she continued, feeling her stomach turn over at the thought of him. 'You know at training when someone was outside taking photos? I thought it was a reporter but it could have just as easily been Owen perving on me.'

Kris straightened up and pulled his shoulders back. 'The same guy who was texting you at the cemetery? I told you I can warn him off you.'

'And I told you I don't need you to do that.'

Kris shook his head and ran his fingers through his thick head of auburn hair. 'You hate accepting help, don't you?'

Athena gazed into the painting.

'It sounds like he's stalking you. What if he's here?' Kris turned on the spot and eyed everyone in the gallery.

'I'd bounce his little head off the parquet flooring,' he muttered to himself.

'I can bounce heads off the floor perfectly well on my own, thank you. Besides, this is the last place Owen would be. His idea of culture was a trip to Nando's followed by a marathon of Keeping Up With The Kardashians.'

'Classy,' mused Kris.

'Oh you have no idea,' said Athena, trying not to stare as Kris eyeballed every man in the room and his biceps twitched reflexively. She took a seat in one of two duck egg blue chairs in the centre of the room. One chair faced Love in Idleness and the other faced the opposite wall giving a view of The Bard by John Martin. Athena tapped her hand on the adjacent seat, signalling for Kris to join her, then sighed. 'I have half a mind to tell his wife,' she continued.

Kris jumped back out of the seat. 'He's married?'

An assortment of tuts, hushes, head shakes, and dirty looks flooded over to Kris.

'Yes,' hissed Athena, pulling Kris back down. 'Do you mind not telling the entire city?'

Kris's forehead creased as he raised his eyebrows and shook his head from side to side. He took a purposeful breath and sank back into the duck egg chair, taking in the apocalyptic scene of The Bard. Athena closed her eyes and listened to the soft tip tap of an elderly woman's cane on the flooring as she gradually made her way towards the exit. There was a smell of polish and, if Athena wasn't mistaken, a lingering smell of wax. Above it all was the enticing aroma of Kris's aftershave. It was magnetic. With her eyes still closed Athena's mind conjured up images of sweat on silk sheets, chests heaving, fingernails digging into backs and teeth biting into necks. Before she knew it her mouth was salivating and she was craving a distraction from fight week that would be far more satisfying than a trip to an art gallery.

'So,' whispered Kris, drawing Athena out of her dream world and flushing her face with colour. 'Aside from a psycho stalker of an ex-boyfriend, viral dance videos and a diet of water and eggs, how's fight week treating you?'

'Urgh,' groaned Athena. 'I'm sick to my back teeth of water, well not the water as such, just the constant need to pee.'

'That's good though,' nodded Kris. It means the water loading is working.'

'The real cut starts tomorrow. I only get half a gallon of water. I can have a small steak for lunch, so that's good, then I'm hitting the sauna in the evening.'

The mere mention of steak made Athena salivate so much that a small amount of drool escaped her lips.

Kris shuffled in his chair. 'I hate saunas.'

'We all do,' said Athena, dabbing her mouth on the back of her hand and hoping no one noticed her spittle.

'Luke likes them,' said Kris, getting to his feet and squinting at a vulture perched on a cliff in the painting. 'This must have taken forever to paint.'

Athena got to her feet and joined Kris. 'Luke likes anything that involves being shirtless,' she mused, 'and yeah, artists have the patience of a...' Her voice trailed off and she found herself pulled towards a small painting in the corner of the gallery. The focus of the artwork was an ethereal looking woman who called to Athena as if she were a siren. Athena walked to her, her trainers squeaking as she stepped. When she reached the painting she squatted down to be eye level with the signature of the artist. The signature was a faint brown scrawl of looping cursive above the year it had been painted. 'Eighteen forty-four,' she read allowed.

Athena chewed on her thumbnail as she looked at the date that had been painted in Roman numerals. In an instant, she jumped back to her feet with her mouth hanging open. 'Oh my God,' she said in little more than a whisper, and then, much, much louder, 'Oh my FUCKING GOD!'

An elderly woman in hair curlers and a coat far too bulky for the weather whipped her head around, her face full of irk. 'Shh,' she hissed.

'Kris, Kris,' called Athena, gesturing at him with open arms while her brain whirred at a hundred miles an hour. 'You were right!' her voice was shrill. 'There aren't fifteen symbols. There are only four symbols. Black circles, white circles, circles with bloody dots in them, they're all just fucking circles!'

'Shh, young lady,' repeated the elderly woman, shaking her head so sternly that her curlers bobbed about her head like satellites. 'Or I'll get the security guard.'

Athena wafted her hand towards the woman as if shooing away a wasp. 'Yeah, yeah,' she scoffed. 'It'd be the worst day of his life, trust me.'

Kris gave the woman a placating smile but it met a look of pure contempt. She shoved her frail hands into her coat pockets and shuffled away muttering about the youth of today. Kris cocked his head to the side and savoured being referred to as a youth for the first time in many years. He reached Athena in two strides. Her eyes were like saucers. 'What do you mean *they're all just circles?*'

Athena tapped the corner of the golden picture frame.

'Look!' She pulled his arm until he squatted down to take in the signature and the date painted in fine brush strokes.

'Roman numerals?' Kris asked as he straightened his legs and returned to his full height.

Athena held her head in her hands and mumbled quietly to herself. 'Twenty-six letters of the alphabet. Circles, squares, triangles, crosses. Four symbols in Molly's code. Roman numerals to twenty-six? I, V, X… L, no, you don't need L. Only three Roman numerals. What's the fourth symbol? The fourth symbol?'

Kris looked at Athena with curious caution. She was possessed.

'Erm,' he started, looking around the room for inspiration. People were staring at them. 'Punctuation?' he suggested. 'There was no punctuation on any of the pages.'

Athena lifted her head from her hands, smiled and punched Kris on the arm. 'You're a Goddamned genius,' she said breathlessly.

Kris rubbed his arm and lifted his t-shirt sleeve to reveal four knuckle sized red marks on his skin. 'Thanks,' he said flatly.

Athena began to rummage in her shoulder bag. 'Urgh! I left the diary in my bed.' She buried her head in her hands once more and tried to picture a page from the book. She'd spent so much time fixated on the notepad, she must have committed some of it to memory. Surely.

'Come on brain,' she commanded to herself. 'Work, dammit.'

One by one the shapes from the first page began to fall into place. 'Triangles are Vs,' she said to herself. 'That makes sense. Are crosses Xs? No, that's too obvious. Doesn't work anyway. Doesn't fit. Circles? Three circles together. Have to be Is. Can't have three Vs or three Xs. Squares and crosses. Squares and crosses…'

Kris instinctively moved away from Athena. She was in one of the finest buildings in Newcastle, dressed in scruffy sweats, with unkempt hair, holding her head in her hands and jabbering away to herself like a lunatic.

Athena's eyes popped open. Her pupils were so dilated that only a thin slither of green was visible. She stood on her tiptoes and grabbed Kris by the shoulders. 'Got it!' she gasped. 'Come on.'

Athena took off through the gallery at breakneck speed, almost taking out a pair of nuns who were admiring a painting by Edward Burne-Jones. She was a blur of grey topped with blonde. Athena made for the curving staircase and ran down the stairs two at a time.

'Foxy, wait up!'

Kris quickened his pursuit, vaulting over a toddler who had stopped in his tracks to grab a shiny penny from the gallery floor.

A group of pensioners parted at the sight of the sprinting athletes, pushing their fragile bodies against gift shop exhibits and tutting with resentment.

'Where are you going?' Kris called after her.

'Home!' bellowed Athena over her shoulder as she ran through the streets of Newcastle city centre, dodging pushchairs, shoppers and cars with ease. Water sloshed around her belly and her bladder was dangerously full, but neither of those problems would slow her down.

'I'm going to decode that book once and for all.' *Then maybe I can finally focus on this blasted fight*, she thought.

But instead of zigging right towards Haymarket metro station, she zagged left and ran over a pedestrian bridge that spanned the central motorway.

'Foxy!' panted Kris, still about eight strides behind the little powerhouse.

Kris didn't have to zig zag to get through the crowds. The sight of a six-foot-something, muscular man dressed in black, and running faster than most people could cycle was enough to part the sea of shoppers. 'The metro's the other way,' he bellowed after her.

'The metro's bloody useless,' Athena called back, not breaking her stride. 'Quicker to run back to Shields.'

'But Foxy,' grunted Kris, trying his best to ignore the chaffing feeling of denim on his skin. 'Shields is seven miles away.'

'And?'

Kris took a huge lungful of air. 'And? Seven miles is —' but Athena had already increased her lead to twelve strides.

- CHAPTER 25 -

It took Athena forty-six minutes to run back to North Shields. It took Kris forty-eight. Panting, Athena doubled over and rested one hand on the mighty sycamore that stood in her garden. Kris trotted up to the wooden gates at the entrance to Camp Terrace. He lazed across the top beam for a moment, his head resting on the backs of his arms, before staggering to Athena. He sprawled on the grassy lawn and shook his head at Athena.

'Next time,' he gasped, staring up at a sky full of grey clouds. 'We're getting the metro.'

A leaf of mandarin orange fluttered free from its branch on the sycamore and floated down in a spiral to land on the rise and fall of Kris's chest. A gust of wind took another dozen leaves from the tree and a frenzy of rain droplets began bouncing off the cobbled drive. Autumn was powering in like a cannonball. It knocked down the sweet-scented defences of summer and exposed the good people of North Shields to the full onslaught of the elements.

The fair hairs on Athena's arms stood to attention. She hugged herself, rubbing her upper arms vigorously. Her hair was wet from rain and sweat and it clung unattractively to her rosy face. She hitched her bag higher on to her shoulder, fished out her keys and took a long drink of water from her bottle.

'Come on,' she said, her breathing recovered somewhat, 'you take the first shower. I'll grab the notepad and get start—'

Athena's front door was ajar.

Kris threw out his arm and stopped Athena in her tracks.

'Wait here.'

'Like hell I will,' she said, marching onwards towards the open door.

'Foxy, for once in your damn life will you do what you're told?'

Kris tugged at her wrist and pulled her behind his broad frame. They eased the door further open, cringing as its hinges creaked.

The pair peered down the hallway, aware that whoever had opened the door could still be inside. There were no windows in the hallway and the deep mahogany panelling and walnut flooring meant the entrance was almost entirely dark.

'What's that smell?' asked Kris in a hushed voice as his nose twitched and smelt the air. 'Smells metallic.'

Athena panicked and put all thoughts of her own safety aside. She ducked under Kris's arm and her hands scoured the dark wall until her fingers found the light switch. With a flick, the chandelier came to life and illuminated Simba's mutilated body.

The scream that came from Athena's mouth was like nothing Kris had ever heard before. She buckled to her knees and scrambled across the floorboards. Kris grabbed her around the waist and tried to pull her back.

'Wait, Foxy,' he begged.

Athena's screams were primal and piercing. They tore through Kris like an arrow to the brain. He wrapped his arms tighter around her and flinched as fingernails dragged through his flesh. She struggled against him, kicking her heels back into his shins and butting the back of her head into his chest. It took every ounce of strength she had to break free from his clasp, drop to her knees and dive to Simba's body.

'Simba, please no, Simba. No, no,' sobbed Athena as she tried to scoop the dog into her arms. 'We, we h-, have to get you to the vets.'

Kris tried not to look but his eyes betrayed him. He stole fleeting glances at the river of blood that was flowing out of the lifeless creature. Large patches of Simba's brilliant coat of white were stained pink, indicating a stab wound to his neck and numerous more along his rib cage.

Kris sprinted through the house, searching each room for the culprit.

Athena pulled at Simba's pink and white fur, trying to gain enough leverage to lift his hefty body from where he laid.

'Come on, Simba,' she cried, stroking along the edge of the wound on his neck. 'Stand up boy, I can't carry you.'

Kris retuned with tears in his eyes. 'There's no one here.'

'Help me carry him, Kris. He's too heavy. Help me.'

He knelt next to Athena and a tear rolled down his cheek. 'It's too late, Foxy.'

He pulled her head into his chest and let his t-shirt muffle the sounds of her wailing. The heat of her breath penetrated the fabric and her entire body quivered in bursts of grief. Kris wrapped his other hand under Athena's knees, lifted her up and carried her back to the doorway.

The sound of neighbouring doors opening and closing was followed by gasps and swear words from Athena's neighbours. They had followed their ears to the scene of the commotion. Mr and Mrs Rowe took Athena from Kris. helped her back down the stone steps and sheltered her under the sycamore. Kris supported himself on the railing and wiped his cold, clammy face. He took two unsteady steps back down to the driveway and vomited on the cobblestones.

Men and women, like rats following the Pied Piper, filtered out of the Gunner and huddled at the wooden gates.

'We heard screaming.'

'What's going on?'

'Is everything all right?'

Kris wiped his mouth on the shoulder of his t-shirt and steadied himself. The crowd were craning their necks and jostling for better views. Kris grasped the door handle and pulled the door shut. No one else needed to see the horror that lay inside.

Mr Rowe waved Kris over, he was on his mobile, speaking in hushed tones. Once he'd hung up he placed a hand on Athena's shivering shoulder.

'The police will be here shortly,' he said.

Mr and Mrs Rowe ushered Athena and Kris into their home. Kris whispered something to Mrs Rowe and she disappeared for a few moments, returning with a clean t-shirt for Kris and a knitted sweater for Athena.

'Here you are, dears.'

The shock had frozen Athena's feet to the hallway floor. She cried open mouthed sobs and trails of snot ran from her nose. Athena stared down at the blood stains on her hoodie and with icy hands tried to fumble with her zipper. Her fingers wouldn't work, they were numb and disobeying her. In frustration, she tugged the neck of her hoodie and tried to tear it from her body.

'Hey, hey,' soothed Kris. 'Let me.'

Kris, with slow, calm movements, removed Athena's hoodie and helped her into the borrowed sweater. It was a few sizes too big, but it was soft and warm, and most importantly, it was clean.

Mrs Rowe shepherded Athena on to the sofa, where a crocheted blanket was draped over her shoulders and a mug of tea was placed in her trembling hands.

The passing of time was excruciating and it felt like the police were taking forever to arrive. In reality, it had only been ten minutes. Athena looked up from the cup in her hands when flashing blue lights appeared outside the living room window. Two officers were welcomed by Kris: one male, one female. The woman was pig-faced and wore a sympathetic smile. The man looked stern, with icy eyes, and a hairline that receded half way to London. Kris spoke to them with a low and shaky voice. He gagged three times as he described the scene and covered his mouth for longer each time as he tried to hold back the bile. Athena watched as they introduced themselves but she wasn't really looking at the officers, she was looking through them. Nor did she really listen. Her ears were busy with the sound of her own broken heart.

Kris motioned to the door and the officers followed him. They passed by the living room window, under the shelter of an umbrella, and headed to Athena's home to evaluate the scene. Athena closed her eyes and gripped the cold cup of tea. When her phone vibrated in her bag she jumped and spilt the drink over Mrs Rowe's rug.

'Oh shit. Oh Mrs Rowe, Mrs Rowe, I'm sorry I... Hello?'

'Athena Fox? This is Kaitlin Burton from the Evening Chronicle. Everyone in the newsroom is *super* excited for your fight on Saturday.' Her voice was high pitched and she made *super* last about five seconds. 'We're running a piece on the local fighters and I was hoping to ask you a few questions. Firstly, what attracted you, a promising young ballerina, to the male-dominated world of cage fighting?'

Athena took her phone from her ear and stared at it in her hand. She emptied her lungs in one deep exhalation as Mrs Rowe tended to the rug around her feet. She returned the phone to her ear and said, 'I was too fat for ballet,' before hanging up.

Molly had been good at ballet. Great at it, actually. Athena could see her now, could visualise her ballerina's body moving through the various positions. She could see Molly smiling after her recital in year ten. She had the same grin the day she brought Simba home. Simba, that beautiful, snowy friend who was at this moment lying in a pool of his own blood. Lying in the same hallway where his doting owner had tied a rope around her neck and climbed over the upstairs bannister.

The thought punched a hole in Athena's stomach. She sank back into the sofa, wrapped her arms around herself and buried her head in her knees. Sometime later Kris and the officers passed by the front window. Athena could hear the sound of an umbrella being shaken vigorously and dropped into an umbrella stand. It let out a loud tinny ping that echoed through the old house. In the corridor, hushed voices exchanged words. Athena couldn't make out the conversation but the tone was worrisome and nervous.

Mrs Rowe poked her head back into the living room. Her eyes were red and her complexion peaky. The veins in her temples and forehead glowed a greenish blue through her ghostly skin.

'More tea, dear?' she asked.

Unable to open her lips, Athena simply shook her head and stared back down into her lap.

Kris led the officers back into the living room. He took a seat next to Athena and pulled the blanket tighter around her shoulders.

'Foxy,' started Kris, 'the place has been completely ransacked. Every draw is open, every cupboard's been turned out. There's stuff strewn everywhere. Looks like some piece of shit broke in and Simba took them on.'

Athena raised her head but couldn't meet anyone's eye.

'Ms Fox,' said the female officer. She had a soft Geordie accent. 'I'm Constable Keaton. Is it all right if I call you Athena?'

Athena closed her eyes and nodded. Tears were forming in the pale green. She'd managed to hold them back for a few moments but they were ready to flow once more.

'A crime scene investigator is next door. He's taking photographs and looking for prints and fibres. Once he's finished, we'd like you to accompany Sergeant Myers and myself to ascertain what was stolen.'

Athena opened her eyes, they felt heavy and itchy.

'Simba's claws.'

'Sorry?' asked Keaton. 'I didn't catch that.'

'Simba's claws,' repeated Athena.

'Simba's the dog,' offered Kris. 'He's called Simba,' he said, looking helpless as his hands fidgeted with a crocheted armrest cover. 'Was called,' he added.

'His claws,' repeated Athena. 'And his teeth.' She sighed so deeply she could feel her muscles stretching over her ribs. 'If he got his paws on the burglar he'll have his DNA on him. All that blood, it can't just be Simba's.'

Keaton nodded.

'They'll check him too, Athena,' she said in a calm, gentle voice that Athena hated. How anyone could be calm when Simba was next door with knife wounds up and down his ribs was beyond her.

'And the One Stop,' said Athena, more firmly, looking up to meet Keaton's eyes. 'Across the road. They have a camera above the door.'

She nodded again. 'We have someone speaking to the manager now. We'll be asking to see all the CCTV from the local shops and the pub over the way.'

'What will happen to Simba?'

'Once the CSI has finished his work we can take you to see him if you wish. If not, and I'd understand completely, we can take him before we go back to your house.'

Athena's first instinct was to ask the police to take Simba away. At the age of twenty-six, Athena had seen enough death for a lifetime but she couldn't bring herself to do that.

'I have to say goodbye,' she said as a hot tear rolled down her cheek and settled between her lips. 'He was my only family.'

The officers exchanged a look of pity. Even Myers, with his stern eyes and grumpy posture, clenched his jaw and swallowed hard.

Kris placed a hand on Athena's shoulder and gave it a light squeeze. 'I'm going with the officers to give a statement. I'll come and get you when it's time to head next door.' He placed the lightest of kisses on the top of her head and followed Keaton and Myers out of the room.

×××

Kris had been right. The house at the end of Camp Terrace was completely ransacked. Athena tiptoed around sticky patches of blood on the hallway floor and made her way into the dining room. Drawers had been flung open and their contents strewn across the table and floor.

'I can touch these?' asked Athena, pointing at antique silverware.

Myers nodded. 'Yes, we've taken all the photos and swabs we need.'

Athena began to organise the knives and forks into neat little piles, counting as she went. The top two tiers of the display cabinet had been left untouched, her grandmother's collectors plates still stood on their stands. The same could not be said for the bottom two tiers. Trinkets and heirlooms were knocked over and picture frames had been shattered. Athena picked up the framed photograph of the Fox family. A piece of broken glass had scratched a line over her mother's face and her sister's neck. Athena let out a low, pained sigh. She stood the frame back up and ran her thumb over the image of her grandfather. Books that had been thrown from the bookshelf alcoves littered the floor. Athena crept around them and picked up a porcelain vase that she used to store loose change. There was a chip in its lip that hadn't been there earlier that day. Athena placed the vase back on the shelf, slid some of the coins from the shelf and popped them, one by one, back into the vase. There was a chime and an echo as each coin dropped in.

In the kitchen, the benches were still as gleaming and spotless as Athena had left them. The floor, however, was a jigsaw of broken crockery. Items from drawers and cupboards were scattered over the tiles. Careful not to cut her fingers, Athena picked up two fragments of what had once been a hand painted fruit bowl and laid them on the bench next to her blender.

'This wasn't a robbery,' she said, turning to rest the curve of her lower back against the kitchen bench.

Keaton raised her eyes from the mess on the floor and furrowed her brow. 'Sorry?'

Athena chewed on the inside of her lip until it hurt. 'Nothing's been taken,' she said with a shrug of her shoulders. Athena gestured towards the dining room, 'My Nana's plates are still here, they're Royal Doulton. And there's nothing missing from the silverware.' She pointed to the living room. 'I can see the TV from here. The Blu-ray's still there. They didn't even take the change jar.'

The constable drew out a small moleskin notepad from her back pocket, clicked the top of her pen three times and began to make some notes. Athena stepped away from the bench and pointed at the blender.

'And that blender cost over eight hundred quid. They've just left it.'

In the hallway, Kris let out a little cough. At least it sounded like a cough, it could have been another gag.

'Your blender's worth more than my car.'

He strode into the kitchen, paused next to Simba's water bowl, closed his eyes for a moment and pulled Athena into a bear hug.

'If they didn't steal anything,' he thought out loud. 'Why bother breaking in?'

Keaton's pen made scratching noises as it darted back and forth across the page. 'Would anyone want to intimidate you, Athena?'

Athena pulled away from Kris and looked up into his eyes for a few moments. He looked so much older than he had this morning.

'Sissy,' said Athena.

'Or her team,' added Kris. 'It wouldn't surprise me. That cow fights dirty in and out of the cage. We know someone from The Pit is on her payroll. If they can get her footage from training they can easily give her your address.'

Turning to the constable Athena began to explain her occupation but was interrupted.

'I know who you are Athena. I had tickets for Saturday but I'm working, unfortunately,' said Keaton, making a quick note and clicking her pen top more times than necessary. 'I'm actually a big fan of Superstar Mar,' she blushed. 'I must admit, he's quite popular with the ladies on the force.'

'Oh sweet Jesus,' said Kris. 'Don't tell him. He'll never shut up about it.'

A laugh almost broke from Athena's throat but she couldn't quite manage it and it came out as half a sob.

Keaton's mouth thinned and she straightened her posture.

'We'll send an officer to Ms Clark's hotel. I assume she's already in town?'

Athena nodded.

'Yeah, the other camps started to show up early this week. Everyone's finishing off their weight cuts and honouring their media commitments.'

She pulled her phone from her pocket and twirled it between her fingers. She had another two missed calls. She couldn't ignore The Evening Chronicle forever.

'They're at the Riverside Inn in town,' said Kris. 'Their coach posted on Facebook this morning.'

'Thanks,' said Keaton, making a note.

Kris tapped twice on the kitchen bench, opened his mouth, closed it again, then opened it once more.

'Oh, I'm just going to say it.' He folded his arms. 'This ex of yours. The stalker.' He turned to Keaton. 'Breaking into someone's home? Intimidating them? That's stalker behaviour, right?'

Keaton turned to Athena. 'You have a stalker?' she asked, clicking the top of her pen again.

The noise grated on Athena. She wanted to lunge across the kitchen, wrestle the pen from her chubby fingers and poke her eyes out with it.

'Owen's a coward. He wouldn't do this. He doesn't have the balls.'

And then Athena thought about the last few weeks. How she'd avoided him for years and after bumping into him in bloody Tesco of all places she'd seen him all over. The text messages were too many to count and he'd certainly taken a keen interest in her Twitter feed. When she'd seen him in Jesmond Dene, had that just been a coincidence? What about the steakhouse? He'd cornered her. He'd become angry with her.

Kris pushed himself off the counter. 'I think the police can decide that, don't you?' He left the room, leaving Athena to answer Keaton's questions about Owen and their relationship.

XXX

It had stopped raining when an officer opened the back doors of a police van. A shiny black body bag reflected swirls of orange from the street lamp above, giving the effect of an oil slick on dark waters. The zipper of the body bag was pulled back to reveal Simba's head. Someone had closed the Akita's eyes. He could be sleeping.

Wake up, boy. I'll cook you scrambled eggs if you wake up.

Placing a hand on his head, Athena ran her fingers through his fur. It was the softest thing Athena had ever touched.

You were always there for me, Simba.

She bent over and rested her head on his. Tears rolled into his brilliant white fur. He didn't smell of death like Molly had. He still smelled of dog. Of walks on the beach and rolling in mud.

And when you needed me, I wasn't there. I'm sorry Simba.

'Goodbye, Simba. I'll miss you.'

Athena didn't have to look up. She'd recognise Charlie Fisher's voice anywhere.

'Yeah, we'll miss you boy,' added Kris, stroking Simba's nose.

Athena straightened and dived into Charlie's soft chest. Her eyes clenched shut and she could feel his warmth on her cheek. He wrapped his arms around her and stroked her hair as Athena had done to Simba.

'The guys are on their way, Foxy. No one wanted you to be alone tonight.'

'There's no need,' said Athena. 'I'll be all right.'

'Like hell, you will,' said Charlie, his hand still delicately holding the back of Athena's head. 'Too stubborn for your own good, always have been. We're taking care of you tonight. Not taking no for an answer.' He let go of Athena and held her by the shoulders. 'Luke's neighbour's a locksmith. He'll have your locks changed in no time. Erin's cousin works for a security firm. She gave him a call and he said he'd install cameras and an alarm first thing tomorrow.'

Athena shook her head. There was no need for all this. She didn't want a fuss. She didn't want everyone to take care of her. Hadn't they learned that by now? For the last few years, she'd taken care of herself. She'd gotten used to it being that way. Anything she needed she would get herself. The words of protest came to Athena's lips just as her knees buckled and her legs gave way.

Kris caught her with lightning speed. 'Woah, easy, I've got you.'

Charlie helped him support her weight. 'Let's get you inside.'

'Thank you,' said Athena, watching as the body bag was zipped closed. The doors to the police van were locked and Simba was taken away.

- CHAPTER 26 -

That evening Athena looked at herself in the bathroom mirror. She was unrecognisable. She was dehydrated, having abandoned her water loading after that first cup of tea at Mr and Mrs Rowe's. Her parched skin wrinkled around the corners of her eyes and her cheekbones protruded. Her face was so haggard Athena thought it would look more at home on the body of a zombie.

He was a good dog, she thought, opening the bathroom cabinet and retrieving a box of painkillers. She opened the packet and popped two caplets from their foil casing into her open palm. Her hand shook slightly and the little caplets jiggled like jumping beans. Athena looked at the two blue and white caplets, they gleamed under the halogen lighting. She sighed and then proceeded to pop another two from the foil packet. Then another, then another, until all sixteen caplets balanced in a pyramid in her hand.

Athena bent over the sink and drank straight from the tap. She filled her mouth with water, pushed two caplets between her lips and swallowed. Then she sat on the edge of the bath and stared for a long time at the fourteen remaining painkillers.

A tear trickled down her cheek and dripped off her chin. It was hard for Athena to admit, as capable and as cocksure as she'd forced herself to become, that this was a time when even she wished for a Disney prince to come riding over the hill to whisk her far, far away. Hopefully, he'd be carrying a pack of cigarettes and a bottle of vodka.

Downstairs, Athena could hear the low hum of the television. Charlie and Luke were watching some home DIY show while Luke's neighbour finished tinkering with the locks. Big Ahmed had swung by about four hours ago to deliver his sympathies along with a stack of Domino's pizzas and a 60cm machete. He thought it would be useful, 'in case the bastard comes back.' Lord knows where he'd gotten it from.

Athena had listened from behind her bedroom door as Kris had tried to get Ahmed to take the blade away, stressing that enough blood had been spilt.

'I insist,' was all Ahmed said before forcing the handle into Kris's hand and turning to leave.

Kris had held the machete at arm's length and looked at it as if it harboured the plague. Charlie took it from him and wandered around the house for twenty minutes, looking for a safe place to put it.

'I'm stashing this bad boy somewhere safe. The last thing we need is one of ye lot sleepwalking and getting ya hands on it.'

A couple of hours ago Athena had pulled Molly's diary from behind the panel in the headboard of her bed and had begun to decode the first few pages. A national newspaper had called and pressed Athena for soundbites on being a woman in combat sports. She'd sat in her dressing gown and slippers with Molly's diary open on her lap as the journalist fired off rapid questions without pausing to let Athena answer.

'I, I think I can win. I've trained really h, hard,' was all Athena stuttered before she felt a lump in her throat and tears swimming towards her eyes. She hung up, switched off her phone and hid it in her underwear drawer.

Athena got back into bed and pulled the covers up high around her. She shivered with so many emotions. She ran her hands across the sheets and spotted a few of Simba's long white furs from where he'd been sleeping. Another wave of loud sobs left her body until she heard arguing from downstairs.

Athena crept along the upper landing and leant over the bannister to get a better view of Kris hissing at Luke.

'It's not a good idea. Not now. Not after this.'

'It'll be good for her. It'll keep her distracted,' Luke had replied, leaning against the doorframe to the living room.

'That's not how it works, Luke. The fight won't distract her from *this*. *This* will distract her from the fight. We should postpone.'

'Aye, good luck telling Foxy that,' said Charlie, weighing in from the Chesterfield.

'They can fight on the Dublin card instead,' said Kris. 'I'm sure Demons would allow it given the circumstances.'

Athena continued to watch. Rage building in her stomach. Luke ran his fingers through his curls and shrugged. 'That young lady wouldn't cancel her fight if a bloody nuclear bomb went off.'

Kris shook his head. 'She can't fight like this. She'll get hurt. We're cage fighters, Luke, this isn't fucking tiddlywinks. Sissy could kill her for fuck's sake!'

Athena had stormed down the stairs. Her slippers made swishing noises on the wooden floor and her dressing gown flapped in her wake. She charged at Kris and shoved him hard in the chest.

'Nice to know you have so much faith in me,' she'd shrieked.

'Foxy,' started Kris. 'I'm just looking out for—'

'Don't you get it?' she yelled, pushing him again, this time hard enough to back him up against the wall. 'I don't need you to look out for me. I don't need protecting.'

Kris swallowed. He looked hurt. 'Actually, it kind of seems like you do.' He walked into the kitchen, took a slice of pizza from the fridge and slammed the door.

'The fight goes ahead as planned, Charlie.'

Charlie nodded his head without looking away from the television.

'Sissy did this to freak me out,' spat Athena, turning on the spot and looking at all the mess that was still to clear up. 'She'll pay for it.'

'That's the spirit,' said Luke as he guided her back up the stairs, telling her to get some beauty sleep.

But now, as Athena sat on the edge of her tub with fourteen painkillers balanced in her hand, she was wondering if there was enough sleep in the world to right the way she was feeling now. Perhaps she should just go to sleep forever?

She pushed four more pills into her mouth and swallowed. It'll be so easy. Like falling asleep, she thought as she took two more. She'd see her mother again. And Gramps. Oh, how she missed Gramps on Sunday mornings. Sunday's were for sitting by the radio listening to classical music. Gramps would tell Athena where he was when he'd first listened to the symphony in question. There was a story to go with every tune.

She wished Harry were here. He'd get on with Gramps. Harry, the man who always knew the right thing to say. Harry, the man who had got her through this feeling once before. At the thought of Harry Athena's eyes welled up. Who would take care of him once she'd gone? Who would bring him snacks? And would he even know that she'd gone? No one would think to tell him. He'd think Athena had abandoned him like everyone else in his life.

No. Not yet.

She dived toward the toilet bowl, letting all the other blue and white caplets scatter across the tiled floor in all directions. Athena took a deep breath and forced her index and middle finger deep into her mouth. She closed her eyes and pressed down on the back of her tongue. Her fingernails were short but sharp and they began to dig into her throat. Athena dry heaved twice and finally regurgitated the meagre contents of her stomach into the porcelain. She persisted, with bloodstained bile running down her hand and forearm until she was satisfied that every last morsel had been ejected.

Athena sat back on the cold tiles breathing heavily and staring into space. She wiped her mouth on a clean towel and staggered back to her feet. She slumped over the sink, refusing to look in the mirror until she had brushed her teeth and washed her face.

'Fraud,' she said when she finally had the strength to look at her own reflection. 'You're supposed to be a Goddamned fighter.'

- CHAPTER 27 -

The Gunner had shut its doors at eleven and its last singing drunk had ambled back through Shields a little over forty minutes ago. There was snoring coming from somewhere in the house, presumably, it was Charlie. It was past midnight now, and the rest of the house was quiet. Even the wooden floorboards, that usually creaked and groaned as they heated and cooled over the course of the day, had slipped into a silent stillness.

Athena was sat up in bed, still wrapped in her dressing gown with the bed sheets pulled up high over her chest. She couldn't seem to get warm no matter how many layers she wore.

Decoding Molly's diary was a painstaking process. But the task was keeping Athena busy, and that was important. Once Athena had made the link to Roman numerals she had quite quickly established that squares represented the number ten, that triangles were the number five, and that circles were the number one. It was the crosses that had flummoxed her the most though. It turned out that a single cross indicated a new letter and two crosses indicated a new word.

○╳▩ □╳▲○●○╳△✗ □ ○△✖○╳╳○▩╳ □ ⊙ □╳✖

□ ⊙ □╳ □ □ ○╳○○○✗△○○○✖╳○╳╳○○╳○▩╳ □ ■╳

○○○✖△○●○╳╳

The first line on the page read, *Athena is such a bitch.*

'Charming,' Athena muttered, laying down her pen as a terrible thought crossed her mind. Was she the reason? Had she said something, or done something to push Molly over the edge? And could she handle knowing it if she had?

Memories of their many arguments flashed through Athena's mind. She pulled a pillow to her chest and hugged it tightly as if it were a substitute Simba. If Athena was the reason, if she'd said something awful when she'd been drunk, if she'd hurt Molly and somehow forgotten about it, she'd do the right thing. She hadn't taken her own life earlier that night but she still could, if it were necessary to restore the balance, for justice to be served.

Athena reopened the diary and had got through a number of pages by the time the clock struck one and the sounds of church bells rung out across the borough. Athena's ears pricked as a set of footsteps approached her bedroom door. She pulled her dressing gown tighter around herself and watched as Kris's drained face peered into her room.

'I come in peace,' he said in little more than a whisper, 'and bear gifts of fermented grape.'

Kris held up half a bottle of brandy and smiled sheepishly.

There he was. Her Disney Prince.

Athena's mouth curled and she licked her lips. 'It's not really a gift if you got it from my liquor cabinet,' she started, still seething from their earlier run in, 'besides, Charlie would freak.'

She closed the notepad and hugged it into her chest.

'I think he'll understand.'

Athena shrugged and patted the bed next to her. 'I guess one shot wouldn't hurt.'

Kris perched on the edge of the bed. 'That's my girl,' he smiled, until Athena shot him a look that meant she was not his girl and he was still very much in the dog house.

He poured a good measure of the smokey topaz liquid and handed it to Athena. She took a tentative sip and grimaced as the alcohol hit the cuts on the back of her throat.

'To Simba,' she sighed as she threw her head back and downed the lot.

'To Simba,' echoed Kris, choosing to savour his glass in a more measured approach.

Kris glanced around Athena's bedroom and drummed his hands nervously on the mattress. 'I didn't think you'd be able to sleep,' he said. 'Charlie and Luke are out for the count. Erin came over, she's asleep face down on the dining table if you can believe that. Her face is gonna hurt in the morning.'

Athena snorted.

'Anyway,' continued Kris, 'Apparently the northern lights are putting on quite the show if you want to join me and the brandy for some fresh air.'

×××

Across the Tyne, above the bobbing outline of fishing boats, silhouetted black on black, tiny squares of apricot and tangerine shone through the onyx night, a reassuring nod to Athena that she and Kris weren't the only ones who couldn't sleep on this cold, painful night.

'Pass the brandy,' she said, arm outstretched and palm open.

Athena adjusted her weight on the cold wooden bench that perched on Tyne Street. Kris shook the bottle - it was almost empty - and passed it to her.

'Just one more,' he said.

Athena gave a dismissive hand gesture and gulped the brandy down until the bottle ran dry. The liquor burned her throat and she let her head fall backwards. The star-speckled sky was awash with colour. The northern lights danced delicately above her. They performed in a dress of emerald and amethyst, pirouetting and curtsying to a rhythm of their own. Are they up there? thought Athena, thinking of the fallen Foxes. She blinked back a tear and rested a hand on her heart for Vivian, Nana, Gramps, Molly and Simba.

Kris prised the bottle from Athena's grasp as if he were trying to take a bone from a volatile terrier.

'I'm here for you,' he whispered.

'I know,' she answered.

Athena leant over and rested her head on Kris's shoulder. Her head had never felt heavier. 'What if,' she started, 'what if the break-in wasn't down to Sissy? What if it was Monty?'

'Monty?' Kris asked incredulously. 'Why would Monty want to break in? He's sponsoring us. He wants to help us.'

Athena bit her lip. 'Something's not as it seems, Kris. The guy can't be the philanthropist he comes across as. Think about it. Someone set fire to his house for Christ's sake! I looked up the Pasternaks. They're a Russian gang. Monty has some seriously dodgy connections. And what about the money in the snake tanks? That has tax avoidance written all over it.'

Athena could feel Kris taking a deep breath. 'Hmm. Even so, he doesn't have any reason to do this. Does he?'

'Not that I can think of,' replied Athena, 'I've just had this weird vibe since Saturday night.'

'Have you told the police?'

'Tell them what?' replied Athena, her voice hoarse now. 'That it probably wasn't Sissy, a woman who definitely has something against me, and has a real motivation to do this, and a track record of this sort of behaviour? And that it was probably the guy I think is my sister's dad because he gives me a weird vibe?'

'I still think it was that piece of shit ex of yours.

Athena ground her teeth together and watched as the northern lights swarmed above the black middens reef. Like sirens, they seduced all witnesses to the craggy rocks. The reef had taken many the life of seafarers over the centuries, and after Molly's death, Athena was going to let them take one more. *If it is my fault*, thought Athena, *the middens can take me, and this time I won't let anyone talk me out of it.* The tide would grab her, the icy waters would engulf her and with a single slam into the reef, it would all been over.

The tide would grab her, the icy waters would engulf her and with a single slam into the reef, it would have all been over.

Down on the fish quay, the sounds of fishermen loading up their vessel for another stretch in the unforgiving North Sea carried up to Tyne Street. Athena took Kris's hand in hers and gave it a squeeze. 'Whoever it was, they're going to pay.'

XXX

Back at Camp Terrace, Charlie's phone vibrated as he received a Twitter notification.

Sissy Clark @LittleLionessMMA

That bitch called the coppers on me!

#gonnakillher #firstroundknockout

- CHAPTER 28 -

The Riverside Inn on Newcastle's quayside was the budget accommodation of choice for hen nights and visiting football fans. The hotel was fully booked this weekend with two stag parties, a coach full of Celtic fans and half the roster of Demons Fighting Championship.

Somewhere on the floor above her, Sissy Clark could hear muffled, alcohol-fuelled chants.

'Chug! Chug! Chug!'

She jogged on the spot in her dollhouse sized shower room. The bin liner ensemble she wore instead of a t-shirt crinkled with every movement. Beside her, the shower was running full blast and on the highest heat. Sissy couldn't see herself in the mirror due to a cloud of condensation, if she could, she'd see a skeletal face of protruding cheekbones and sunken eye sockets. Strands of long black hair curled around her temples as they became saturated with humidity. The rest of her ponytail bounced back and forth off the bin liner, making a whipping noise each time it connected.

'Chug! Chug! Chug!'

Sissy switched from jogging to lunges and scowled at the ceiling. 'MORONS!' she yelled at the top of her lungs.

'Relax,' soothed her coach in a thick cockney accent. Eddie Fitzgerald was five-foot-six and fourteen stone of bleached hair and a combover Donald Trump would be proud of.

'Relax?' scoffed Sissy. 'The police all over us and Demons have set us up in stag party central.' She grabbed a towel from the rail and wiped her forehead and under her chin. 'If I don't get a good night's sleep I swear to God I won't renew my contract with them. I'll sign for Cage Vipers! Vipers'll put me up in the Hilton. They'll put me a hotel with a Goddamned sauna. Jogging in bin liners in a shower room? Talk about amateur hour.'

'CHUG! CHUG! CHUG!'

Sissy threw the towel to the ground, where it landed in a puddle of her own sweat. 'That's it!' she growled. 'I'm going to kick them out their fucking window.'

She made a charge for the bathroom door but was blocked by Eddie's barrel of a body.

'Not so fast young lady.' He nodded towards a set of scales. 'Hop on.'

Sissy dropped her arms to her sides and groaned like a moody teenager as she stepped on the scales.

'Hmm,' said Eddie. 'We need to cut another pound tonight, we can cut the rest in the morning.'

Sissy shook her head and stepped off the scales, muttering 'We?' under her breath.

Eddie either didn't hear or chose to ignore his prizefighter. 'Star jumps,' he said.

Sissy pointed to the ceiling as her long bruised legs began to jump in and out and her ponytail whipped once more. 'You bastards'll keep.'

×××

Luke Mar's chest muscles flexed in time to the dance music that was pumping through The Pit. He smiled at his reflection and switched between his favourite bodybuilding poses.

'Two hundred and forty pounds,' he said, jumping off the scales. 'Man, I'm so skinny!' He pointed to one of the juniors, a scrawny boy with acne and wispy blonde hair. 'You there, go buy me a sandwich.'

Luke tossed a fiver at the boy, who looked taken aback. He glanced at his training partner, shrugged and went to put his shoes on.

'Have you been hitting the tanning beds again, Luke?' asked a girl from the junior team who had sweaty mascara sliding down her face. 'You're looking a little more orange than usual.'

'Orange?' Luke checked his reflection and gave himself an approving nod. 'I'm tanned to perfection.'

Athena started to laugh but anger filled her chest instead and she stared at the spot on the mats where Simba used to sleep. She pulled out a set of red hand wraps from her bag and pushed any lightheartedness away. Humour had no place in her psyche.

A police liaison officer had stopped by at Camp Terrace that morning to check on Athena. Athena had sent her away, insisting that she was fine and that she was running late for training. It was half true.

The Pit was a hive of activity. The juniors were buzzing with excitement for Saturday's fights. They'd been given tickets at a huge discount and just the idea of being there had given them a taste for the limelight. Every time Athena eavesdropped she heard them discussing their future fighter nicknames and what they would spend their first fight purse on.

One by one the pro team were arriving to help Athena, Luke and Jimmy with the final practice. Big Ahmed was hitting the heavy bag, its chain rattling and clanging with each punch. Kris was in the cage, holding pads for Erin as she warmed up and prepared herself for three rounds with Athena. Jimmy and Stevie were practising footwork on the mats, their feet moving faster than most people's eyes could keep up with.

At his desk, Charlie was glued to his phone. He was fielding questions from local newspapers, national newspapers, martial arts magazines and MMA websites. Earlier in the day, he'd even promoted the fights live on a local radio station.

'Well you do have a great face for radio,' Luke had told Charlie, earning himself mat cleaning duties for his cheek.

'Foxy,' Charlie called out across the gym with one hand covering the receiver of the telephone. 'It's the BBC. They want you and Sissy live on video chat in five minutes.'

'You're kidding me, right?' said Athena. She had one hand wrapped and was in the process of wrapping the other. 'I'm about to spar Erin.'

Charlie pouted and fluttered his eyelashes at her. It was grotesque. 'Come on kiddo,' he pleaded. 'It's good publicity. The more tickets you sell the more money The Pit makes, and the more money The Pit makes the longer I can keep paying you lot your wages.'

Athena looked around the room. Kris was behind on his rent. Erin didn't say much but Athena got the impression she'd rather be here than at home. In fact, she suspected Erin would rather be anywhere but at home. Jimmy had walked into The Pit this evening grumbling about his lawyer's fees again. Ahmed was worried his mother in law might need to go into a home. Then there were all those kids stretching out at the end of their class. By the law of averages, they should be hanging about outside the corner shop asking strangers to buy them fags and cheap lager. But they'd found the gym, and in that, they'd found purpose.

On the surface, it looked like this mix of people of all shapes, sizes and backgrounds came to The Pit to exercise. But, on closer examination, it was clear that many of them were here to do more exorcizing than exercising. *This isn't a gym*, Athena thought, catching sight of her own sad reflection in the gym mirrors. *It's an island of lost souls.*

Athena could remember an evening last winter when she and Molly had curled up on the old Chesterfield with mugs of hot chocolate and watched a documentary on

Antartica while sleet pounded at the living room window. The documentary had looked at the people who had wound up working on some research base near the south pole. They were all outsiders and weirdos that didn't fit in in their homelands. Athena had pitied them, she figured that they'd been unable to put down roots wherever they'd laid their hats, and without roots, they'd simply slid down the edges of the planet and wound up living at the bottom it. She'd taken a large sip of hot chocolate and smiled to herself. Some outcasts slide down to the frozen wasteland at the bottom of the planet, and some outcasts are drawn to a cage fighting gym in a fishing port off the Tyne.

'Well?' asked Charlie, fluttering his eyelashes again.

'Fine,' said Athena, her eyes on the spot where Simba used to lay. 'But only if you stop making that face. And I promise, if that skinny cow pokes the bear I have no problem telling the whole of the UK that she's a dog killer.' Athena had no idea if Sissy was responsible for Simba's death. Her head told her she was the most likely culprit, but her gut told her Monty was dirty, and Kris was sure it was Owen. She took a deep breath, swallowed down a lump in her throat and continued to wrap her other fist.

'Sergeant Myers warned you not to do anything like that,' called Kris over the hubbub of the gym as Erin kicked his hands with lightning speed. 'Remember? He said something about not using your fame to influence the case.'

Athena busied herself with the wraps. 'Influence the case?' she huffed under her breath. 'I'll influence her *face*. With my fist.'

Charlie sniggered, then he scrunched up his face and worry lines formed across his forehead. 'Please don't lose it on live TV, Foxy.'

Five minutes later and Athena was stood in front of Charlie's computer screen with his webcam tilted toward her. Three windows were open on the screen. The first showed a feed from the interior of a BBC studio. Marcus Lightfoot, a greying man in a purple shirt, was addressing the camera.

'Police are appealing for witnesses. If you witnessed anything unusual around the Jesmond area or saw a man in jeans and a black hoody at around 3 a.m. please call the hotline immediately. And now ladies and gentlemen, forgive me if I appear a little nervous but joining me via video link are two of the scariest ladies on the planet: MMA stars Sissy Clark and Athena Fox.'

Athena took a deep breath and forced a camera-friendly smile on her face. The webcams switched on and live feeds from The Riverside Inn and The Pit were broadcast on a large screen in front of Marcus Lightfoot.

'Good evening ladies, sorry to interrupt your training.'

Sissy's hair was scraped back. She wore a baggy hooded sweatshirt and had a towel draped over her shoulders. Large bags were under her eyes and her skin was dry and flakey.

'The world,' said Sissy, removing the towel from her shoulders and tossing it aside.

'Pardon?' asked Marcus Lightfoot.

'I am not one of the scariest ladies in the country. I'm one of the scariest ladies in the *world*. Actually, let's forget the gender pronouns, I'm one of the scariest humans on the face of the planet. Male or female.'

Athena rolled her eyes.

'I stand corrected,' said Marcus, shuffling his notes in his hands. 'My apologies, Sissy. You'll be defending your belt for the third time on Saturday night. Are you excited?'

'Of course,' said Sissy. She flicked her long ponytail over her shoulder. 'Training has gone smoothly. We've put in many, many hard rounds of sparring. I've mainly been training with men. You see, the women we find to spar me in training never seem to last. I have an excellent strength and conditioning coach. I feel stronger in the run-up to this fight than I've ever felt. I come from the best team in Europe and they—'

'No you don't,' interrupted Athena, not letting her smile falter. She played with a strand of her blonde locks as she continued, 'The Pit has the best team in Europe, Sissy. You really shouldn't lie on television. It makes you look bad.'

To her left, off camera, Luke and Charlie doubled up and covered their mouths.

Sissy bristled and pursed her lips into tiny creases. 'I'll show you who has the best team on Saturday. Mark my words. You're leaving the arena in an ambulance. I promise you that.'

'Fighting words,' said Marcus. 'Sissy, you and Athena are fighting at strawweight. Could you tell our viewers what that is in kilograms?'

'Of course. It's just over fifty-two kilos. My weight cut has been magic. A piece of cake in fact, pardon the expression. The weigh-in's tomorrow morning on Newcastle's quayside. I feel a little sorry for Athena, though. She famously struggles to make the weight. She's a little on the dumpy side you see…'

Luke mouthed, *Oh no she didn't*, at Athena.

'…And it will be oh so disappointing to fail the weigh-in in front of all those loyal, local fans. Not to mention the press,' continued Sissy.

Athena shook her head playfully. 'Oh Sissy, what did I tell you about lying on television?'

Athena tore her vest over her head and stood before the webcam in only her sports bra and hand wraps. Her stomach formed into eight distinct toned muscles and she flexed her biceps either side of her head.

'Do I look *dumpy* to you, Marcus?'

Marcus Lightfoot didn't know where to look. 'Erm, you look… Well you look fighting fit,' he said sheepishly.

Sissy waved her hand dismissively. 'Whatever, posh girl. It's such a shame you won't be able to speak in that sweet private school voice once I knock all your teeth out.'

Marcus looked back and forth between the two video feeds. 'I have in my notes Athena that you're well educated. That you were top of your class at Newcastle

University and could have gone on to a great career in architecture. How did you end up in mixed martial arts?'

'Because she's an attention seeker,' said Sissy before Athena could answer. 'You see it all the time. The posh kids who think it's cool to hang out with the street thugs. Remember that song? *Common People*? She wants to live the street life but she's not prepared for the consequences.

'Or maybe I just like fighting?' said Athena. She was struggling to keep the camera-friendly smile on her face now.

'Nah, you're just playing at this for a while until you get bored and then you'll dig into your trust fund and go travelling around Asia, or marry some other trust fund brat, or get a job as an architect. Marcus, the posh kids never last in MMA. They don't *need* this. It's not a route out of the ghetto for them. I'm from the *streets*. I wasn't born with no silver spoon in my mouth—'

'Careful of those double negatives Sissy, you don't want to sound stupid on television.'

Luke performed a hip-thrusting dance to Athena's left.

'Don't interrupt me,' snapped Sissy. 'Didn't they teach you manners at that posh school? It's OK, I can beat them into you on Saturday.' She pointed into the camera. 'You're just a TOURIST. I grew up on the worst estate in north London. The street makes you tough. It makes you gritty. If the streets didn't break me, you sure as hell can't.'

Marcus turned to Athena. 'Do you think Sissy's background gives her an edge, Athena?'

'Marcus, Marcus, Marcus,' smiled Athena. 'I've been hearing this my entire career. My opponents think that because I come from money I'm an easy target. That having money somehow means I don't train as hard, that I don't want the win as much as they do. Money doesn't solve all problems, Marcus. Money didn't save my grandparents or my mother from dying in a car crash. It didn't stop my sister from killing herself. I'm twenty-six and I have no family left. Is that *street* enough for you, Sissy? Do *you* know who your father is? 'Cause I don't. That's pretty *street*. Any shoplifters or gamblers in your family, Sissy?'

Athena's heart was pounding in her chest. Her smile had slipped and she scowled into the camera.

'Marcus, I've heard it over and over. My opponents always underestimate me because they are too dumb to see the truth. Sissy's right when she says cage fighting isn't a route out of the ghetto for me and that I don't *need* the money. But that's what makes me scarier than any of the other girls in my division, Marcus. I don't fight because I need the money, I fight because I NEED TO FIGHT!'

- CHAPTER 29 -

Sissy Clark Questioned by Police ahead of Demons FC Title Defence

Demons FC Strawweight Champion Sissy Clark (6-0) may have a hurdle to cross that doesn't include a weight cut and a title defence. Clark was questioned by police on Wednesday evening in Newcastle, England in connection with a break-in at the home of her opponent, Athena Fox (4-1).

This isn't the first controversy to concern Clark in the run-up to a title fight. In 2016 former champion Susan Holt (6-3) accused Clark's team of repeatedly triggering the fire alarms in the team hotel to prevent her from sleeping the night before their fight in Wembley. Earlier that year Laura Spears implied on social media that Sissy had seduced her boyfriend two days before the pair fought in Berlin. No other details are available as yet and no one from either fight camp was available for comment.

Clark, a twenty-five-year-old Thai Boxing specialist has been training at Fitzgerald's Fight

Club in North London. She will attempt to defend her Demon's FC title once more against Fox on Saturday evening.

For more on **Demons FC 16** see the **European MMA** section of the site.

'Someone spoke to the press,' said Kris. He slid his phone into the back pocket of a pair of black jogging bottoms and sat crosslegged on Athena's bathroom floor.

Athena, wearing a red Ted Baker bikini, sank lower into the bathtub until the hot water reached her lower lip.

'It was probably Sissy. And she calls me an attention seeker?'

The roll top bath at Athena's had been filled with a mixture of scalding hot water and cups of Epsom salts. The heat and salty water pulled moisture from Athena's body. Dehydration by osmosis was the key to dropping the last few grams of weight. She'd be fifty-two kilos by the morning if it killed her. And if it did kill her, she wouldn't be the first fighter to go that way.

Charlie had been ecstatic with her BBC interview earlier that day. Tickets for Demons FC had sold out within an hour of the news broadcast and rumour had it that touts were reselling ringside seats for twice their original price. The phone in The Pit had been ringing nonstop with women wanting to join the ladies kickboxing class. Every time Charlie hung up the phone he'd rub his hands together and then point to Athena.

'Just sold another three-month pass, Foxy. Thanks to your flat stomach this place is going to be bursting at the seems with chicks wanting to get in shape.'

The heat of the bath water dried Athena's lips. She licked around her mouth to wet them but her tongue felt like a paper towel. Deep in Athena's chest, she felt a tightness that wouldn't subside no matter how slowly she breathed. It could be the physical stress she was subjecting her body to that made her feel this way. More likely, it was the emotional stress: the fear of the fight, her mourning, her temper, and what Molly had kept from her.

How she wished Molly were here. Molly was great before fights. She used to be so upbeat that her positivity couldn't help but rub off on Athena. In all the chaos of cage fighting: the commands from her coaches, the shouts of the referee, the crowd, her own heavy breathing, Molly's cheers would always carry through.

'Come on 'Thena. You've got this!' she would shout.

What if Molly were here? How would she have coped seeing Simba in his mutilated, murdered state? Athena blinked and thought maybe it was best that Molly wasn't here to see that. Maybe it was best that Molly was dead. *What a thought.* The tightness rose into her neck and up her nose where Athena tried to keep it, locking it in place behind her eyes. Visions of Simba filled her mind. It would be his dinnertime now. The giant ball of white fluff would probably be sitting in the bathroom doorway, staring at the pair of them, until Kris lamented and went downstairs to feed him. At that thought, the tightness couldn't be restrained any longer and sobs burst out of her like air from a punctured tyre. Athena was so dehydrated that tears didn't even form in her eyes.

'I don't want to fight tomorrow.'

Her hands flapped under the surface causing splashes of hot water to hit her face. She cried tearless whimpers and her shoulders shuddered. The words *I don't want to fight* stabbed at her ego. The truth of it hurt her heart.

'Jeez, Foxy,' said Kris, wiping a caring hand across her sweaty forehead. 'You always want to fight. Always. What about the interview? You said you need this.'

'I do need it,' answered Athena. 'I need to hurt someone. The pain goes away when I hit people. I know that's sick but it's true. You know it is. You know what it's like but I can't handle it right now. Not right now.'

She spluttered and wiped her nose on the back of her arm, leaving a slug trail of snot. 'You were right. It's all too much, I can't do it, Kris. She's too strong. She's too strong physically and I'm too weak mentally and with Simba gone I jus—'

'Weak mentally? You're not weak mentally!' said Kris, stopping her in her tracks and getting to his knees. 'Think of all you've been through, everything you've coped with.'

'That's just it, Kris. Everything I've coped with.'

Athena covered her eyes and continued to sob. She wept harder but tears would still not come and it made her tear ducts feel as if onions had been rubbed in them.

'

When Mum, Nana and Gramps died Molly wouldn't talk about it, she just went off on her secret mission to find her dad. Then Molly killed herself and I was just left with the blooming dog to talk to. Course he wouldn't talk back. Now Simba's dead too and I've got to fight a bloody psychopath the day after tomorrow and I have no one left. NO ONE.'

'You have me,' whispered Kris, and when Athena took her hands away from her face she could see Kris's beautiful steel grey eyes through the steam, mere inches from hers. Sweat beaded on his forehead and pooled a little above his scar. 'And Charlie,' he continued, 'and Luke, and everyone else who came here as soon as they heard about the break-in.'

Athena tore her eyes away and fixed them on the cold tap at the end of the tub. She eyed it like a child eyes candy, but the cold tap was off limits.

'If I were you,' she said with a parched voice and a hint of cynicism. 'I'd get out of Dodge. If you hadn't noticed, everyone I love winds up dead.'

Kris wiped his hand across Athena's forehead, brushing her wet hair off her face like a windscreen wiper clearing autumn leaves. Athena's heart jumped. Had she just used the L word?

'It's a chance I'm willing to take.'

If she had just used the L word at least Kris was decent enough to ignore it. Still, his decency didn't stop her from squirming petulantly at his hand as he pushed her hair from her eyes. 'Better make sure your last will and testament is up to date then.'

The tall Pole stood up abruptly. 'For God's sake Foxy,' he snapped. 'Stop being so dramatic. Histrionics don't suit you.'

Athena whipped her head around, bloodshot eyes glaring at Kris.

'I mean it,' he added. 'It's not your style. Now as for Sissy being too strong for you that's a load of pony and you know it.'

Athena adjusted her bikini. 'You know I don't speak Southern.'

'Crap. It's a load of crap and you know it. Come on, Foxy. What would Athena do?'

Athena lifted her legs out of the salt bath, they were pink from the heat, and she rested them on the edge of the tub. Little droplets of salty water trickled down to her heels and fell to the tiled floor with a gentle *plop, plop*.

'What do you mean *what would I do?* I've been trying to figure that out for weeks. Sissy's damn near indestructible.'

'Not you,' huffed Kris. He picked up the pack of salt and poured some more into the water. 'The other Athena, the real Athena.'

'EXCUSE ME? *The real Athena?* What am I? The fucking Tooth Fairy?'

That got her attention.

Kris looked to stifle a snigger. 'There she is. That's the Foxy I know.'

Athena folded her arms over her chest. Furious at herself for having been played so easily.

'Anyway,' continued Kris. 'I'd been googling you and a link came up about the other Athena, the Greek Athena, and there was this st—'

'Hold up.' Athena pushed herself up to sitting. 'Why were you googling me?'

Kris looked like a stunned goldfish. 'That's between me and my search history,' he finally mustered.

'Oh Christ, Kris. You'd better not have been looking at that damn pic I put on Twitter,' spluttered Athena. Her face was reddening and it wasn't just because of the hot water.

'Back to the Greek Athena,' said Kris, sidestepping Athena's question. 'You're named after the goddess of wisdom and war. What would she do?'

Athena groaned at the ceiling and slid back down into the tub making a squeaky noise as she did so. Her tongue felt like sandpaper in her mouth. She held out her hand for a bottle of spring water but Kris pulled it away.

'Damn it, Kris. I don't know what she'd do. Should I phone Zeus and ask him to ask her?'

'You're so tetchy when you cut weight. I bet Jimmy's not like this.'

Athena threw her arm out. As she gestured toward the door a spray of hot water fell over Kris's joggers. 'Well if you'd like to go and wipe sweat off Ginger Jimmy Wilson while he sits in a salt bath, be my guest.'

Kris visibly shook the mental image from his mind and leant forward to hand Athena the bottle of water before disappearing back behind a haze of steam. 'Two sips, no more.'

Athena pulled the bottle to her lips. The anticipation of icy spring water would have made her salivate if she'd had enough moisture to do so. It was pure disappointment when the water reached her tongue. The bottled water was lukewarm from having been in the steamy bathroom for so long. It wasn't refreshing in the slightest. It was like drinking a cup of abandoned tea.

'Gross,' she said, handing the bottle back to Kris.

'Anyway, I know what Athena would do,' said Kris. 'I read it. You've heard of Heracles, right? Athena's brother? Well, when Heracles killed the Nemean lion he wanted its pelt. But he couldn't skin it because its fur was impenetrable. So he asked Athena for her help. And because Athena was a damned genius she told him to use the Nemean lion's own claw to skin it, and you know what? It worked. She knew to use the lion's own strength against it.'

Athena sat bolt upright. Sweaty droplets clung to her strong shoulders and chest. She furrowed her brow and stared into Kris's eyes through the haze.

'She used the lion's own strength against it, Foxy. Sissy calls herself a lioness. And since we've been unable to find any weaknesses the cocky bitch might have, maybe you should exploit her strengths instead?'

Now it was Athena whose mouth hung open like a goldfish. For the first time in this cursed training camp, she may actually have a plan.

- CHAPTER 30 -

Athena paced back and forth in a makeshift dressing area. She was thirsty to the point of delirium and nervous to the point of having chewed into her own cheek. The tinny taste no longer spiked her excitement to fight, it only reminded her of finding Simba's disfigured body.

Demons FC had built a stage on Newcastle's famous quayside. The competitors for tomorrow's event would weigh-in before a backdrop of the Millennium and Tyne bridges. The stage was positioned near the law courts and from the dressing area, Athena had spied a crowd of a few hundred people forming in anticipation. Lawyers had descended from their expensive offices and hotel staff left the swanky establishments that lined the north side of the Tyne to see what the fuss was about. Shoppers had stopped by, laden with carrier bags, to take a look. Then there were the hardcore MMA fans who had claimed their stage side spots early this morning. They held posters and pens in the hope of an autograph. One portly, pink-cheeked fan hugged a teddy bear with a heart shaped belly, presumably a gift for his favourite fighter.

Athena looked in the mirror and smoothed down her dress. Most fighters walk out to the weigh-in dressed in sweatpants and hoodies, then strip to their underwear as they step on the scales. But that didn't fit with Athena's image. She had long ago established herself as an Instagram poser and selfie queen. She was known for her designer gear, pretty green eyes and pert behind. It was an image Athena unashamedly used to grow her fan base, and in turn, her sponsorship opportunities. And once you had a rewarding image you had to stick to it. She was Athena 'The Goddess' Fox and she would walk out in an ivory, asymmetric Grecian dress that barely covered her privates.

'Look at the clip of you.'

Athena turned from the mirror and scanned Luke up, down and up again. 'I could say the same to you.' She squinted, then asked, 'Are you wearing makeup?'

Luke perched a pair of aviator style sunglasses on the top of his curly hair. 'No more than you are, Foxy. Equal opportunities and all that bollocks. Anyway, give me a twirl.'

Athena scowled.

'Don't give me that look, princess. You're hot and you know it. I'm the heavyweight champ and I'm gonna be upstaged by a strawweight in heels. Now come on, twirl, you know you want to.'

Athena groaned, shook her head and turned on the spot. 'Happy?'

'Ecstatic,' beamed Luke, peaking out from the dressing area to take in the crowd. 'Monty's out there, looking dapper.'

'Let me see.'

Athena poked her head under Luke's arm. The stage was set, the scales were ready, and a stagehand tapped on the microphone. Another dressing area was on the far end of the stage so that rivals wouldn't have to share the same space. Athena wondered what Sissy was doing right now. Just the thought of that woman made her nostrils flare. Her hands balled into fists, knuckles white and veins protruding. Athena scanned the crowd. The pink-cheeked fan was still at the front, pressed up against the metal railings and bouncing excitedly from one foot to the other. A few rows back stood Monty. The autumnal sun twinkled off his diamond earrings, his braids were pulled back into a small ponytail and he wore a smart striped shirt with jeans. Kris was talking to him, he had one hand over his heart in a sign of gratitude and held a selection of t-shirts in his other. Athena could just about make out the logo of Flamingo Cove, Monty's chain of Caribbean seafood restaurants. Kris pulled one of the t-shirts on over his head. It was awash with bright pastels and seemed a stark contrast to his usual black attire.

''Bout time Kris added some flavour to his wardrobe,' said Luke. 'I'm guessing I'll be wearing one of those to the cage tomorrow.'

'If you want your two grand you will be,' answered Athena, her breathing still laboured and her fists still clenched.

'Is it true Kris paid his rent for the rest of year?'

Athena swallowed. 'Yeah, and he still had some left over for his council tax.'

'Blimey,' said Luke, checking his reflection once more. 'Good Ol' Monty came up trumps. We should go thank him again.'

Athena's mind flooded with emotion as she looked between Monty in the crowd and the other side of the stage where Sissy was hidden behind a curtain. The break-in was still painfully raw. They were both mere meters away from her and one of them was responsible for Simba's murder. It can't have been Owen, it just couldn't have been. He was an aggressive, domineering, asshole but he always loved animals. He adopted a stray cat when they were first years at uni and at Christmas he'd always donate to the animal shelter. It was Monty or Sissy. One of them drained the blood from the only family she had left. One of them forced the last breath from her best friend. Panic started to rise up in Athena's chest. She staggered and grabbed Luke's arm to ready herself. She was barely hanging on. *Breathe*, she told herself, *you can't collapse. Not now, please not now.*

Luke lifted Athena up as if she weighed less than a bag of spuds and sat her down on a table. 'You stay here, young lady. Stay focused. I'll pass on your regards. Besides, I want to find out if they found the mamba,'

Athena closed her eyes. 'Thanks, Luke,' she said.

When Athena opened her eyes again he was gone.

XXX

'Welcome to the weigh-ins!' announced Liam Cooper, the owner and face of Demons FC. 'We have one of the best fight cards of the year for you, ladies and gentlemen. Please welcome to the stage our three, beautiful ring girls for tomorrow evening: Cassandra, Megan and Mercedes.'

There was polite applause punctuated by wolf whistles as three bikini-clad women with silky hair and extremely white teeth joined Liam Cooper on stage. The quayside was a wind tunnel, driving gales from the North Sea inland between the shores of Newcastle and Gateshead. The women shivered, but despite the exposed conditions they preserved their perfect smiles and maintained their hands on hips postures.

Liam's head turned and his eyes followed the women as they walked past him in formation and took their positions at the back of the stage.

'We're going to kick it off with a corker of a flyweight bout between Ginger Jimmy Wilson and Ivan The Terrible Petrov.'

Athena clapped as loudly as she could from the dressing area as her teammate Jimmy jogged on to the stage. He shook hands with Liam Cooper, waved to the crowd and stripped his outer layers of clothing away. Jimmy made a cross over his chest with his right hand and looked to the skies as he stepped on the scales.

'One hundred and twenty-four pounds,' announced Liam.

There was applause from both the crowd and the ring girls as Jimmy successfully made his weight limit. He pulled on his trousers and trainers but stayed topless as he moved away from the scales and watched Ivan Petrov from Kaliningrad bound on to the stage to go through the same routine.

Jimmy's pale white torso shone out against the black backdrop of the stage. He was a full moon on a clear night. Ivan's weight was called, he dressed and marched over to Jimmy for the face off. The two flyweight fighters stood almost nose to nose, fists raised and eyes locked. They held this for a few seconds while the press took all the photographs they needed. When Liam patted them both on their shoulders, his touch magically awakened them from the stare down. They nodded to each other and shook hands.

'Bloody hell,' said Jimmy as he jogged back into the dressing area and pulled his t-shirt and hoody back on. 'Some woman just pulled her top up and asked me to sign her boobs!'

Luke laughed and patted him on the back. 'Into gingers is she? Takes all sorts.'

The Pit fighters jostled for position behind the curtained door as they watched sets of lightweights, middleweights and welterweights weigh-in and face off against each other.

'You're next, Foxy' said Kris, holding the curtain aside for her.

Athena ran her hands over Kris's Flamingo Cove t-shirt, smoothing out the creases.

'Make sure the logo's always visible,' she said into his chest, unable to meet his eyes. 'Sponsors love it when you know your angles.'

'Wow, Foxy. You sure know this game,' said Jimmy, still beaming from adrenaline. 'Time to shine,' he added, punching her lightly on the arm and shepherding her towards the curtain.

Luke winked at her. 'Go get 'em, tiger.'

Liam Cooper brought the microphone to his lips. 'And now, the one you've been waiting for ladies and gents. A strawweight bout between the most talked about women in MMA. Here's your local favourite... Athena The Goddess Fox.'

Oh, Jesus Christ. Athena took a deep breath, plastered a smile worthy of a ring girl on her face and strode confidently into a roar of cheering and hooting. She waved and tried to take in the occasion. Tried to savour the feeling of hearing a hundred voices chanting her name. It made for a pleasant distraction after recent events. She paused for a moment as cameras flashed then slipped the shoulder strap down her arm and slid out of the dress like a python shedding its skin. She slipped off her stilettos and stepped on to the scale in only an ivory bikini. The crowd oohed as Athena flexed her arms. Every hair on her forearms stood on end as she held the position and a lone wolf whistle carried from the rear of the crowd.

'One hundred and fourteen pounds.'

Athena stepped backwards off the scale and slid back into her towering heels.

Charlie and Kris guided Athena to one side of the stage and handed her an isotonic sports drink. It was filled with all the electrolytes she'd lost during the weight cut. Athena chugged eagerly at the bottle, it tasted of heaven.

'And here's her opponent ladies and gentlemen. Please give a warm, northern welcome to Sissy Clark.'

There was a smattering of well-mannered applause as Sissy Clark swaggered across the stage. Dressed in black joggers with a hole in one knee, a baggy gym t-shirt and a trucker cap, she looked every bit the yin to Athena's yang. Sissy locked eyes with Athena as she approached the scales. She slowly drew her thumb across her neck and mouthed, 'Your time has come'.

Cameras flashed again as Sissy disrobed into a navy bikini and stepped on to the scales. She was long and lean with thighs disproportionally big for her frame. They were one hundred per cent pure kicking power.

'One hundred and fifteen pounds,' called Liam.

'Sissy! Sissy, I love you!' The pink-cheeked fan at the front of the crowd tossed his teddy bear on to the stage.

Sissy jumped from the scale and scooped the teddy up in her hands. She held it up in front of her face for a moment before grabbing Liam Copper's hands and shouting into his microphone.

'This flat nosed bear looks familiar,' she said, laughing and pointing to Athena.

Some of the crowd laughed with her. Trash talking being perennially appreciated by sports fans. She let go of the mike and tore the head clean off the bear, screaming maniacally, and pulling the white stuffing from its insides. The actions of an unstable, threatened champion. The actions of a woman capable of harming an innocent animal?

Pink-Cheeks recoiled and looked to the ground. A friend patted him on the back and steered him away.

Sissy dropped the decapitated gift and marched straight over to Athena for the face off. Her coach, Eddie Fitzgerald, held her around her tiny waist in an effort to keep her back. In her heels, Athena could stand eye to eye with Sissy. She raised her fists into a guard and pushed her head forward a few inches. Their noses were so close Athena could smell Sissy's stale breath.

'You called the coppers on me, you evil little bitch. You're gonna pay for that. You're going to suffer.'

Athena bared her teeth and pushed her forehead into Sissy's. 'You killed my dog,' she growled, and unable to hold it back any longer she added, 'and tomorrow night, I'll kill you.'

The air on the quayside changed from excitement to tension. Athena felt Liam's hand on her shoulder, the cue to step back from the stare down. She was going to do no such thing.

'Thank you, ladies,' said Liam with a note of uneasiness in his voice.

Charlie pulled at Athena and Eddie Fitzgerald pulled at Sissy. Neither woman was willing to look away first. Eddie raised a finger and pointed it past Athena in the direction of Charlie.

'Cheap shot, Fisher. Sending the coppers to our hotel.'

'Cheap shot? I'm not the one who hired goons to stage a break in.'

Athena could feel Charlie's beard bristle against her shoulder as he spoke. She watched Sissy's jaw twitch and a vein pulsated in her temple. She wanted to rip Sissy's head from her body and pull her insides out for all to see.

'Your gym's always been dirty,' continued Charlie. 'You're as crooked as my teeth. I heard how you hid half your team in a broom closet when the drug testers came calling. We know your tricks, Eddie.'

Kris pushed himself between Athena and Sissy. Athena still refused to turn her back and was instead, marched backwards across the stage and down the stairs. When she'd eventually lost sight of Sissy, Athena felt safe enough to take a deep breath and turn around, but a hand shot out from the crowd and grabbed her wrist, pulling her off balance.

Struggling to regain her footing, Athena's instinct was to lash out at whoever had a hold of her. She raised her fist and dropped it again, a look of disgust on her face as she recognised Owen.

'The police came to my house,' he said, his grip tightening. 'They said you'd accused me of stalking? How could you, Foxy? Claire was there, she heard everything.'

Athena tried to pull away. She didn't give a crap what Claire had heard. He'd dug his own grave. She only gave a crap about getting his clammy hand off her. Owen's face had an unwashed sheen and new wrinkles had formed under his eyes since she'd last seen him. His stare was less electric now, more deranged.

Kris pounced like a wolf on a fawn, grabbing Owen by his collar. 'Let go of her,' he snarled. 'NOW.'

Owen released Athena's wrist. A red watch strap of friction-burn glowed on her skin.

Kris grabbed Owen around the jaw, squeezing his face in his strong hand. 'I'll only say this once…' Kris towered over Owen, making him look small and feeble. 'Stay away from her, or it'll be the last thing you do.'

Kris pushed Owen back. He was caught by the crowd as camera flashes peppered the air. Charlie pulled Athena towards him and wrapped a hoody over her bare shoulders. He pulled the curtain aside and guided her into the changing area. Athena could feel her entire body shaking and it wasn't because of the cold. She glimpsed herself in the mirror and was horrified at the fear on her face.

Kris stormed in seconds later. His shoulders rounded as he paced back and forth, punching his own palm.

'Foxy,' he started.

'NO!' shouted Athena. 'Don't you dare tell me to pull out of the fight. Don't you dare, Kris Kava.'

Kris met her eyes and put his hands on her shoulders. 'You should fight,' he said. 'You need to end that cow's career.'

Beyond the curtain, Liam Cooper's voice carried, 'The champ weighs in at two hundred and forty-three pounds.'

The wind picked up and blew a small gap in the curtain. Athena pulled the hood up over her head, wrapped the sweater around her bare midriff and watched as Luke Mar's tanned body jumped off the scales and danced around to music only he could hear.

- CHAPTER 31 -

Athena squirmed and writhed in front of a lightbulb encircled mirror. Two buxom ladies were working in tandem to pull her hair into a series of thin cornrows. Molly's shabby diary slid about on Athena's knees as she wriggled and tried to translate the code. The two women were in no way intimidated by Athena's status as a cage fighter and had no problem in repeatedly reprimanding their client for being unable to sit still.

'Do you have ants those lycra pants? Stop wriggling.'

'It bloody hurts.'

'Oh child,' said the taller the two with a sigh. 'How can you handle getting punched in that beautiful face of yours but you can't handle some simple braids?'

Athena bit her tongue and took another sip of her electrolyte drink. She was almost rehydrated now but the nerves of what was to come gave her an insufferably dry mouth. She sipped and sipped but there was no relief.

The shorter woman, whom Athena's inner monologue referred to as *Boobs*, because of her gravity-defying double Gs, yanked at the hair around Athena's temples. 'Petal, my mother, God bless her soul, would always say, if you can't stand the heat you should stay out of the kitchen. I say, if you can't stand the cornrows you should stay out of the cage.'

She pointed at Athena's reflection with a thin comb.

'She has a point,' said Charlie, his eyes peering at Athena from behind a tabloid.

'Don't you start,' she replied, turning to the next page of Molly's diary and translating square, circle, square into the letter S.

'Less talking,' started Charlie, 'and more eating. You've hardly touched your lunch.' He pushed a container of steak and vegetables towards her.

Athena violently stabbed the plastic fork into a chunk of steak and put it in her mouth. Now that the weigh-in was out of the way she could eat as much as she liked. Her new problem was the appetite suppressing nerves that had taken over her belly. Every bite felt like a chore. It was infuriating how her fears could turn even the most delicious of T-bones into a burden. Each mouthful took forever to chew and by the time the plate was empty and her hair was almost finished she was suffering in equal measures from jaw ache and tender scalp.

Charlie had insisted that Athena not be left alone during the morning of the fight and wisely Athena hadn't put up too much resistance. Kris had been busy all morning at the arena, checking the warm-up areas and changing rooms to make sure they would have everything the team could need. Charlie had attempted to get Erin to sit with Athena while her hair was styled but she'd played the gender card.

'Why? Because I'm a girl? I have assignments to finish. Can't you get one of the guys to do it?'

Stevie and Big Ahmed had been next on the list, but they'd proclaimed they'd rather slit their wrists than spend the morning at the hairdressers. So, to Charlie's distaste, the handholding had been left to him.

A bell chimed above the entrance to the hairdressers and an American accent sounded behind Athena.

'Lilly-May, how many times do I have to tell you to tie your shoelaces? Don't come crying to me if you face plant.'

Athena looked at herself in the mirror. Her hair had been braided so tightly that her skin stretched around the edges of her face, giving a wide-eyed, facelift like appearance.

In the gap between Boobs and the other hairdresser, Athena could make out the curves and curls of Elizabeth Wainwright.

'Elizabeth,' she called, turning her head briefly before it was yanked back into position.

'Well, if it isn't Athena Fox?' Elizabeth's Floridian twang sounded exotic and refreshing amongst usual Geordie voices. 'How are you? Lilly-May, get rid of that gum. Take a seat. No, not there... Lilly-May, put that down.'

Elizabeth slid into the seat next to Athena and beamed at her. 'Cornrows suit you,' she said with an appreciative nod. 'The youngest is getting her Bantu buns taken out. She wants box braids. She'll never be able to sit still long enough... Lilly-May! That hairdryer isn't yours, don't touch it... I'm going to have to leave one generous tip when she's finished.'

Athena smiled and tried to adjust her weight without moving too much. 'I can emphasise. This is torture.'

Elizabeth's eyes fell to the diary on Athena's lap. 'You cracked it? Did you find Molly's father?'

Athena's phone vibrated in her back pocket. 'I think so,' she replied. 'Well, I found a man who admits to having known my mother and who looks suspiciously like Molly. But I don't think he was quite what Molly was hoping for.'

'Oh, that's a shame. Alan'll be pleased you had some success though. He was worried about you...Lilly-May! For the tenth time... Excuse me, Athena. I'd better go rescue that hairdresser before my youngest picks up those scissors again. And well done solving that brain teaser,' she said, gesturing to Athena's lap. 'As smart as your sister I see.'

Athena's back pocket vibrated again and she contorted to retrieve her phone without incurring the wrath of her hairdressers as they worked on the final two braids.

'Speak of the devil,' she muttered.

Ms Fox. I'd wish you the best of luck this evening but I know you don't need it. Everyone from Flamingo Cove will be cheering for you and your teammates. I've arranged for Wilkinson to deliver a case of Champagne to the

gym... We know you'll all have plenty to celebrate in a few hours time. M.

A few hours time. In a few hours, she'd be locked in a cage with Sissy Clark. Years of preparation were about to come to a head. One would leave the cage victorious, with a legion of new fans and an extra few grand in their bank account. One would leave defeated: bloodied, bruised, shoulders slumped and head hung low. A tidal wave of anxiety washed over Athena and settled in her stomach. The T-bone turned over and threatened to make another appearance.

'You okay, Foxy? You're looking paler than usual.'

Athena shook her head, only to be quickly chastised and forced back into position by four strong hands. She switched her phone off and tossed it to Charlie.

'Here,' she said. 'Don't let me check my messages or go on social media. Not even if I beg.'

'Aye aye, Captain,' said Charlie, saluting as he tucked Athena's phone into his inside jacket pocket.

A few minutes later and Athena's head was released.

'You're all done,' said Boobs. She folded her arms under her ample chest and admired her work.

The other hairdresser held a mirror up behind Athena. 'You look like a warrior.'

'She is,' said Charlie as he handed over a wad of cash to the hairdressers.

'We'll be rooting for you,' smiled Boobs.

Athena thanked the two ladies and signed a fight poster for them. After they moved on to their next client she turned back to Molly's notepad and took another sip of electrolytes. She quickly worked her way through to the end of the paragraph while Charlie made a phone call to check up on Kris. Athena swallowed hard and realised she was clenching her teeth. *That no good, low life, piece of trash.* With trembling hands, she closed the notepad and placed it back in her bag. She couldn't believe what she'd just read.

- CHAPTER 32 -

Harry Cecil Stafford had long ago grown accustomed to his nickname, Homeless Harry. He'd first heard it in the autumn of 2012 after leaving Christ Church on the crossroads in North Shields. He'd spent the morning drinking tea and putting the world to rights with the vicar and her husband. It had been a blustery day and the streets had been filled with swirling leaves of ruby and gold. As he'd left the church, he'd strode east towards the coast, passing the neighbouring Christ Church Primary School.

It was morning break and the schoolyard was bustling with children in brightly coloured coats. Their excited shrieks carried on the wind as they played on the school's slide and mini climbing wall. Harry smiled as he watched the playground games and reminisced about a happier time, a time when he'd played with his own children. His children were fully grown now, with lives of their own. He hadn't seen either of them in over ten years. He was an embarrassment to his dentist son and army officer daughter, but my God he was proud of them.

'Watch out, Megan,' shouted a chubby boy with rosy cheeks and windswept curls.

He pulled his friend - a tiny blonde, skeleton of a girl - away from the railings.

'That's *Homeless Harry*. Me Ma said to stay away from him.'

Harry never forgot the look of trepidation in the little girl's eyes, and as he looked around himself now, he could see that same look in the men and women who queued next to him. The men shot him warning looks and the women clung to their men. He didn't belong here. He should leave.

Harry dug his hands firmly into his pockets and looked around nervously. He knew this area of Newcastle well. A shelter where he'd be welcomed with a warm beverage and a smile was a short walk away, but it meant walking through the party areas of the city. He'd be pointed at and laughed at by tipsy undergraduates, maybe shoved about a bit by burly rugby players on their tenth pint.

Harry decided he'd take his chances but the queue began to snake forwards and he found himself carried by the crowd. The doors to Newcastle's arena opened and fight fans funnelled in from the cold.

When Harry reached the front of the queue he fumbled in his pocket for the ticket Athena - that little angel - had given him months ago. The steward looked it over and pulled a walkie-talkie to her lips. She mumbled something into the radio and asked Harry to wait at one side while she checked the tickets of the couple behind him.

Harry moved uneasily from one foot to the other and raked one hand through his wild hair. She could tell he didn't belong here. He wouldn't be welcome, not in these clothes. What was he thinking? He should leave now before they escorted him out. He didn't want to cause a fuss.

'Mr Stafford?' asked an extremely large member of the arena's security team. 'Ms Fox asked me to give you this.' He handed Harry an envelope. 'Oh, and she said to tell you *don't argue, just do it.*'

He strode away with long, confident strides, leaving Harry to stare at the manila envelope. He looked around once more and opened it up. Inside he saw a crisp twenty-pound note and a card that read,

> Thanks for coming to support me, Harry. Buy yourself a burger and a pint (or two). Your seat is ringside so I'd better hear you cheering. See you at the pub later for the party.

Harry wiped a tear away on the back of his coat sleeve.

XXX

Sissy Clark was punching the air in quick flurries. Demons had set up two warm-up areas backstage and had kitted them out with everything the fighters and their teams could need. Interlocking mats covered the floor and lockers had been arranged along the far wall.

Strewn across the mats were skipping ropes, kick pads and those rubber bands yogis use for stretching. The room was a makeshift martial arts gym, only without the usual smells and quick-witted banter. A television had been rigged up in the corner showing a live feed from the arena. A crowd of eight or nine people had gathered around the screen to watch as the first fight of the evening got underway.

Sissy gave herself a quick breather from her shadow sparring and sipped from a bottle of electrolytes. Her waist-length black hair had been braided into twelve thick plaits, the ends of which were dyed an electric blue. She wore short shorts and a sports bra in a shade that matched her hair and her hands had been wrapped in white tape.

Eddie Fitzgerald wiped his sweaty forehead on a rag and picked up two kick pads. He held them to either side of his thighs and nodded his ruddy face at Sissy who took her cue to kick him as hard as she could. Her right shin thudded into the pad and the sound reverberated around the room. Eddie's belly jiggled from the impact and he chuckled to himself.

'Poor girl's not gonna be able to walk once you've finished with her.'

Sissy smirked. 'Damn right,' she said, her smirk fading into a scowl as she fired another of her trademark leg kicks into the pad resting on Eddie's thigh.

The group of fighters and coaches who'd been glued to the television turned to stare at Sissy as she fired in another kick. Sissy knew that look. It was a look of wonder. A look that asked how someone her weight could generate so much power. The attention boosted her. It fed her ego and filled her with confidence. Winning tonight would cement her into cage fighting history as one of the best strawweights in the world. The UFC would call and Sissy would swap the cold, grey streets of London for the sunny beaches of California.

There was no way she was returning to that hellhole of a council estate where she'd watched her cousins descend deeper and deeper into gang warfare. Her own mother was too afraid to leave their flat after being mugged at knifepoint twice in a month. Sissy was going to fight her way to a better life and if that posh cow Athena Fox had to be put in the hospital for that to happen then so be it. She'd never liked that blonde piece of work anyway. She'd do whatever it took. There was only room on the world stage for one British female fighter and it was going to be Sissy.

XXX

Across a breeze block corridor, in the other warm-up area, Athena heard an almighty roar from the arena. She turned her eyes to a television mounted on the far wall in time to see Ivan Petrov, the Russian flyweight, running around the cage with his arms raised in victory. Jimmy Wilson lay on his back unconscious.

Erin Summers held her punching mitts behind her head and inhaled so deeply her ribs showed through her t-shirt. A slow-motion replay showed Ivan wrapping his arms around Jimmy's neck and squeezing until he turned purple and passed out. When Erin finally breathed out it was with a grunted, 'balls.'

Athena was briefly distracted from her dark thoughts by the shock of hearing Erin say *balls*. The woman barely spoke and when she did it was almost always a stuttering *sorry* or a *pardon me*. Athena turned away and tucked a set of headphones into her ears. The London Philharmonic blocked the noise of the crowd and the television. She closed her eyes and took ten deep, slow breaths. Inhale to the count of four, hold it to the count of two, exhale to the count of six. It wasn't good to be this on edge. She couldn't use up all her adrenaline just yet. She would need every ounce of it once the cage door locked behind her.

Erin held up her set of pads and said something that Athena couldn't hear but understood all the same. Athena began drilling counter attacks and kicking combinations while Big Ahmed did the same for Luke. Luke was uncharacteristically stoic and serious as they warmed up. He may be the class clown of The Pit but when it came to defending his title he was all business.

After a quarter hour of gentle pad work, skipping and stretching, Charlie and Kris hurried through the door to the warm-up area. Kris's face was flush as he helped a distressed looking Jimmy on to a chair and placed a wet towel over his head.

'The doc'll be with you in a minute, mate' he reassured him.

Charlie ran a hand over his beard. 'Foxy,' he panted. 'It's time.'

Shit. The mats felt like quicksand. Athena swallowed and struggled to move her feet towards her coach and cornerman. She shook her arms but they were like lead, heavy and burdensome.

Kris pulled a headphone out of Athena's ear. 'This is what you trained for. This is what you're born to do.'

Charlie took Athena's hands in his and helped her into a pair of black, fingerless, leather gloves. 'You're a born fighter, kiddo,' he said, engulfing her in a hug and clapping her on the back with his sweaty, frying pan sized palms. 'You know it. I know it. Time to show the world it.'

Athena couldn't speak so she just nodded. She'd been in this situation before. This wasn't her first rodeo. But something felt different now that the title was on the line. The stakes felt higher and the fight felt more personal than it had ever been in the past. No matter how nervous she felt inside, Athena knew she couldn't show it on her face.

Kris picked up a bag that contained everything he and Charlie would need when they accompanied Athena cage side: water, towels, a bag of ice, a bucket. He pulled out a Flamingo Cove t-shirt and assisted Athena in wiggling into it. The shirt was a size too small and the logo stretched over her chest. The two men flanked Athena and each put an arm around her shoulders. They guided her out of the door and into the long, darkened corridor that led to the arena. It was cold amongst the breeze blocks. The hair on Athena's arms stood on end and little goosebumps dotted her thighs. Luke and Ahmed shouted messages after Athena but she couldn't make them out. It felt as if the mute button for the world had been activated. That or her heart was now beating so loud that it drowned out everything else.

Halfway down the corridor, Athena's feet froze. 'Wait!' she gasped, pulling away from Kris and Charlie. Charlie's face flashed with fear. He must have thought she was about to back out. Was that even an option this late in the day? Was there a window she could crawl out of? Athena turned and ran back to the warm-up room. She frantically rummaged around her locker until she found what she was looking for. It was her motivation. Athena turned the photograph in her gloved hands and ran a finger over the faces of her grandparents, her mother and her sister. She kissed the photograph, folded it into a small square and pulling at the neck of her t-shirt, tucked it into her sports bra. She held her hands over her heart for a moment, nodded and ran back to Kris and Charlie who put their arms around her once more.

'They'll be watching,' said Kris.

'Aye,' said Charlie, squeezing her shoulder, 'and they'll be bloody proud of you too.'

- CHAPTER 33 -

Athena placed shaky hands on the door to the arena and held her breath. She stood on a mental precipice, balanced between rising to the challenge or falling into the chasm of her nightmares. A greying steward in a red blazer counted backwards from ten. As much as Athena's mind willed him to slow, for time to stretch on forever, his countdown continued steadily to one. *Heroes* blared from all corners of the arena, impossibly loud with a bass that thundered through her heart. The song triggered a reaction in Athena. A Pavlovian switch had been flicked and all systems were activated.

Six hard hands slammed into the door and the team charged through as one. A spotlight found Athena as she jogged towards the cage. She spread out her arms and let her fingertips brush against those of the countless fans who reached over the railings cheering her name. She ran faster and faster absorbing the energy of the crowd each time her fingers touched someone new.

When she reached the cage Charlie pulled her t-shirt over her head and pushed a gum shield into her mouth. An official checked her gloves and the length of her nails. He wiped his hands along her arms and shins to check for grease and finally motioned to the door of the cage.

Athena exhaled forcefully, raised her head and stepped confidently into the cage. She strutted around, running her fingers over the wire fencing that surrounded her and took in the cheers of the spectators. Her eyes wandered over the first few rows of seats and she found Harry. He held a plastic pint glass between his knees and clapped his hands together with excitement. A few rows further back Athena could see Glen and Nancy White. Dressed in matching shell suits, that would have been all the rage in the late eighties. To their left was Silent Pete who was grinning from ear to ear and bouncing to the music. He looked like a kid on Christmas morning. Athena completed another full circuit of the cage and her gaze settled on the familiar blue eyes and full lips of Owen Daley Phelps. Her stomach gave a quick flutter and she felt bile sting her throat. How dare he. How dare he show his face.

He was sat with a few of his friends, two of whom Athena remembered from high school. One of the men nudged Owen on the arm and he answered with a dirty laugh, a laugh that said, 'Yeah. I've had her.'

Athena's face hardened and she resisted the urge to climb out of the cage and punch that slimeball in his Adam's apple. She shouldn't be worry about Owen now. She had more pressing matters to worry about.

The lights lowered and metal music filled the arena. Athena rested her back against the wire and watched Sissy power walk towards the cage. *Here we go.*

Sissy entered the cage and fixed her eyes on Athena's. The lioness had spotted her prey.

'Ladies and gentlemen, this is a five-round title fight and the penultimate event of the evening.'

A roar of excitement washed through the arena as Liam Cooper, the owner and face of Demons Fighting Championship, raised his microphone to his lips.

'In the blue corner, weighing in at one hundred and fourteen pounds, fighting out of North Shields, England, with a record of four wins and one defeat… Athena The Goddess Fox.'

Athena raised her hands in the air and felt the cage vibrate from the noise of the crowd. Nothing compared to this feeling. It occurred to Athena that right here, right now, she really did feel like a goddess. Powerful and adored.

'In the red corner,' continued Liam as boos and hisses rained down on the cage as if the arena was now hosting a terrible, violent pantomime. 'Weighing in at one hundred and fifteen pounds. Fighting out of London, England. With a record of six wins and no defeats. The reigning, defending, strawweight champion of Demons FC… Sissy The Little Lioness Clark.'

Any cheers from the southern contingent of the crowd were drowned out by the local jeers. Sissy cupped her hand around her ear and egged the crowd on. 'I can't hear you,' she laughed.

As Liam left the cage a hushed tension fell over the room and Athena's ears picked up the quiet chink of the cage door locking. The referee called the two fighters to the centre of the cage. Athena's feet didn't want to move but her mind was strong enough to overrule them. She fixed a fearless look on her face and strode towards her foe.

'Ladies, we've been over the rules in the dressing room. Fight hard, fight clean and obey my commands at all times. If you want to touch gloves do it now.'

As if.

Athena stepped backwards until her shoulders touched the wire fencing. Charlie barked orders and the crowd rumbled like a thunder storm all around her, but all Athena could hear was her ragged breathing as she tried desperately to control it. *This is it.*

The referee clapped his hands together. 'Fight.'

- CHAPTER 34 -

Sissy's right fist clattered into Athena's cheekbone and she dropped to the floor. In a millisecond Sissy was on top of her. Athena pulled her arms around her head to protect herself from a barrage of elbow strikes. Some of the strikes made it through her guard and thudded into her temples and jaw. Even the strikes that didn't reach her face still left marks on Athena's forearms as she tried to cover up.

It was vanity and stubbornness that gave Athena the strength to buck her hips and send Sissy flying over the top of her. She wasn't going to be another statistic. Another first-round finish for Sissy to gloat about. She got back to her feet and took a second to regain composure. Athena's head was spinning but Sissy was already powering back towards her.

'Hands up, Foxy,' shouted Charlie.

Athena obeyed and pulled her guard high. Sissy took advantage of it and fired a hard kick into Athena's left thigh immediately causing it to buckle underneath her. Sissy pounced and Athena hit the canvas with a loud bang. Sissy pinned her to the ground and began to pummel her once more. Athena pulled her legs up high and wrapped them around Sissy's head trying to secure a triangle choke.

'Yes,' she heard Kris shout. 'Shift your hips to the right a little.'

But Athena was too late and Sissy had wiggled free. Athena could hear Charlie swearing in frustration. The two fighters were back on their feet and Athena managed to land a few crisp jabs to Sissy's face. The third punch cut her lip open and bright red blood dribbled down Sissy's chin and splashed on the canvas. Athena grabbed Sissy around her head but Sissy thrust her knee into Athena's stomach, winding her and causing her to wince out loud. Sissy sensed her pain and launched another knee, this time it dropped Athena to the floor. She rolled out of the way and scrambled to her feet just in time to receive another powerful kick to the thigh. Athena wouldn't be able to take many more kicks. Each one slowed her down and made her legs feel heavy. Three claps signalled that only ten seconds were left in the round. Athena hit Sissy in the mouth once more but received one back. She flinched at the pain of her orbital bone fracturing. Athena bit down hard on her gum shield and pushed a kick into Sissy's stomach. It was hard enough to crack Sissy's ribs but the Londoner showed no sign of pain. As the buzzer sounded and the referee called time Sissy snuck in one final kick to Athena's thigh.

'Dirty cow,' grunted Charlie. He placed a stool at the edge of the cage for Athena to sit on. A little droplet of sweat dripped from the end of his nose. 'That kick was after the bell.'

Athena sat and began to massage her leg. It was already swollen and turning purple from internal bleeding. Kris knelt in front of her and held the bag of ice over her thigh.

'Right, Foxy,' said Charlie. 'Take a deep breath and calm down. We're out of the first round. She doesn't normally have to go more than one round so now we'll see how her fitness holds up. We're gonna need some more twinkle toes footwork from you, ballet girl. Make her chase you. You're doing well in the punching exchanges just keep your shoulders loose, OK?'

Athena nodded as Kris pushed a bottle of water into her mouth.

'Sip,' he said. 'Now remember how Athena killed the lion?'

Athena nodded. Her mouth was too dry to speak, and even if it weren't she wasn't sure she could say anything coherent with the pain in her head and the hormones rushing through her body.

'Good,' said Kris, looking Athena in the eyes and causing her stomach to fill with butterflies that she really shouldn't acknowledge right now. 'You've set the trap,' he continued. 'Now make her take the bait.'

The minute between rounds went far too quickly for Athena's liking and before she knew it she was back on her feet and her coaches had been expelled from the cage. The referee gave the signal and the fight resumed. Sissy prowled forwards, closing the distance on Athena until she was backed up to the edge of the cage. As Sissy fired out a hard pair of punches Athena dodged her head out of the way and kicked up high, slamming her foot into Sissy's face and giving her an immediate black eye.

Athena dodged again, this time moving to the other side of the cage. Sissy followed and put even more power into a lightning-fast flurry of punches and kicks. Athena couldn't avoid all of them. She caught a punch right in the mouth and another kick to her already bruised thigh.

She danced around the cage as Charlie instructed her to but she couldn't play *chase me* for too long. The referee would give her a warning for timidity. As Sissy got close once more Athena raised her hands to protect herself from an onslaught of punches. Sissy saw the opening and chopped at the thigh again. This time the bang of shin meeting muscle echoed around the arena and oohs emitted from the spectators in the first few rows.

Athena's leg gave way and the pair grappled on the floor. Both fighters slipped and scrambled trying to getter the better position. Vanity was a wonderful sin. It was the thought of losing in front of Owen that pushed Athena on. She tried manoeuvre after manoeuvre and almost secured an armbar at one point. She rolled on top of Sissy, who pulled her knees in tight and pressed her feet into Athena's stomach. Sissy kicked her legs out and sent Athena staggering backwards giving her time to stand up.

'Hands up,' shouted Charlie.

Sissy kicked as hard as she could towards Athena's leg. Athena lifted her knee and swung her leg outwards. Instead of smashing into Athena's thigh, Sissy's shin collided full force with Athena's knee. An unstoppable force met an immovable object and the immovable object won. Sissy screamed as her tibia shattered. She stood with all her weight on her good leg. Her eyes were wide and filled with an expression Athena had never seen on her before. It wasn't fear. It was inevitability.

'NOW,' boomed Kris.

Athena pounced. The hunter became the hunted as Athena grabbed Sissy around the waist and threw her to the floor. She climbed on top of her and a monsoon of elbows clattered down upon Sissy's face. Blood splatted up as Athena shattered her opponent's nose and turned Athena's face into a scarlet Jackson Pollock painting. It was only when Sissy's body went limp that the referee pulled Athena from her.

It was all over.

Athena held her head in her hands and listened to the roar of thousands of fight fans. She was the champion. She'd conquered the unconquerable. The cage door opened and a pair of paramedics rushed in to tend to Sissy. Athena spat out her gum shield, sprinted as fast as her bruised leg would allow her to and jumped into Kris's open arms. She wrapped her legs tightly around his waist.

'You did it! You did it, Fo—'

Athena's lips pressed into Kris's. She ran her fingers through his hair and held him tightly to her as if holding on for dear life. Eventually, she pulled back to look him in the eyes.

'*We* did it,' whispered Athena.

Four rows back Owen Daley Phelps got to his feet and kicked his pint of lager over. It skidded along the ground to the end of the row leaving a trail of sticky cheap booze. He clenched his jaw, turned his back and stormed out of the arena.

- CHAPTER 35 -

And then the world stood still. All the doubt, all the anger, the tension and fear floated away. Kris lowered Athena's feet to the canvas and she pushed up on to her tiptoes, keeping her face as close to his as she could. He cupped her chin in his hands and bent down to kiss her again. His body felt cool as marble against her burning muscles. They kissed for what felt like an eternity, neither one wanting to break the spell.

'Well, it's about effin' time.'

Charlie Fisher folded his arms over his chest and nodded in approval as a third paramedic pushed past him. 'We had a pool gannin' on you two. Think Erin won.'

Athena pulled away from Kris. She smiled coyly and turned her head as the tiniest of titters broke from her mouth. A diminutive, feminine laugh of pure happiness that stood so at odds with the violent act she'd just committed.

'So, you finally got over your fear of Polish men?' Kris ran his hands over her shoulders and down her arms with a featherlike touch.

'And you finally got over your haemophobia?'

Kris took a step back. Athena had a face full of scarlet freckles. 'Ha! I think you cured me,' he said, his eyes sweeping over Athena's forehead and cheeks.

'You sure? I don't want you vomiting on me.'

Charlie shoved Kris out of the way and wiped Athena's face with a damp towel. 'I'll be the one throwing up if you two keep this cutie-pie shite up all evening.'

The next few minutes passed in a blur. The referee took Athena's hand and lead her away from Kris to the centre of the cage. She ached to return to him. Kris was six foot away but it was six foot too far. Her name was called, her hand was raised and the arena erupted as Athena was declared the new champion and the queen of the cage. Liam Cooper wrapped the belt around her waist and shook her hand.

'You absolute star,' said Charlie, tears forming in his eyes. 'I'm so proud of you, kiddo.'

Athena bowed her head. 'It was Kris's plan. He told me to use Sissy's own strength against her.'

Charlie chuckled and patted Kris on the back. 'Brains and brawn? Foxy'd better watch out. All the lasses will be after our Polish genius.'

Athena removed the championship belt from her waist and slung it over her shoulder. She breathed in the scent of the wide leather strap and felt every curve of every embossed letter on the silver plate.

'Thanks for the heads up, Charlie,' said Athena, 'but if I can handle Sissy Clark, I can handle fangirls.'

'Aye, you're right about that lass.'

XXX

Luke Mar pumped the air with his fist and nodded his head to the beat of LMFAO's *I'm Sexy and I Know It.* His heavyweight champions belt was slung over his shoulder and his face was a mosaic of purple and green bruising and deep fake tan. He held a bottle of Champagne in his other hand and was oblivious to its contents bubbling over on to the floor of Low Lights Tavern. The pub had been commandeered by the local fighters, their family, friends and fans. A set of decks and disco lights had been set up in the corner. Music was blaring, drink was flowing and the celebrations spilt out on to Brewhouse Bank.

Luke had taken eighteen minutes to put 'Dangerous' Danny Davison to sleep. The big Scot had played a clever game for the first two rounds but he was no match for North Shields's man of the hour.

'Oh Christ,' said Kris as he walked into the pub, stooping his head to avoid the low beam above the door. 'Who said Luke could be DJ?'

Luke took a swig from his bottle of Champagne, burped loudly and pointed to Kris. 'I'm taking requests, big boy.'

Kris smiled. 'Something from the nineties,' he called as he pushed through the crowd, making his way to the bar to order a pint of Low Lights Ale.

Luke laughed. 'Now you're talking, Krissy Kava!'

Kris reached the bar just as the sound of The Backstreet Boys filled the room. He shook his head with a laugh and felt a light tap on his shoulder.

'Foxy,' he grinned, 'aren't you a sight for sore eyes?'

Athena wore a Ted Baker dress of deep orange and towering red heels. Her champions belt was over her shoulder, the poor girl hadn't let go of it since it had been handed to her. Kris suspected she'd even took it into the shower with her. The silver plate of the belt caught the disco lights and reflected blue and pink on to Kris's black t-shirt and illuminated his eyebrow scar in a shade of purple. Athena had removed her braids, causing her hair to poof out in crazy blonde curls that bobbed about in all directions. She'd tried to cover her bruised face with makeup but there was no hiding the damage she'd taken. She was a mess, but as far as Kris was concerned she'd never looked better. For the first time Kris could recall, Athena was smiling with genuine happiness.

'Still on cloud nine?' he asked, kissing her as gently as he could on the cheek. 'And heels? Really, Foxy? You get the shit kicked out of your legs and you still won't wear flats.'

Athena curtsied and found a glass of Champagne thrust into her hand by Charlie. He was grinning from ear to ear and swaying unsteadily.

'The queen is dead. All hail the new queen.'

Athena hugged Charlie and he hiccoughed in her ear. She released him, pulling a face half of amusement and half of despair, sipped her drink and patted Charlie on the arm. 'Couldn't have done it without you,' she said.

The Champagne bubbles tickled her tongue. The glass was chilled to perfection and it was all Athena could do not to press the cold glass against her orbital bone.

Charlie ran a hand over his bald head and began to dip his hips left and right. 'You know what this party needs?' he asked. 'A good old-fashioned conga. Who's with me?'

Athena exchanged a look with Kris. 'Thanks, Charlie but I'm too sore to dance. Maybe next time.'

Charlie blinked sleepily and wagged a finger in Athena's face. 'What sort of champion are you?' he said, slurring his words.

'The worst,' said Athena. 'The most terrible champion to ever walk these shores.' She manoeuvred herself next to the bar and rested her body against Kris's. His chest was firm and warm. He wrapped an arm around her shoulders and kissed her head.

'Bah! You lovebirds don't know how to party,' groaned Charlie. He held his pint high above his head, bellowed 'CONGA,' and proceeded to dance out of the bar to the lounge in desperate search of fellow dancers.

As the crowds parted to let Charlie wiggle his way through, Athena caught sight of Ahmed and his wife trying to squeeze their way to the bar. Behind them, she saw someone pass by the window. Athena scowled, it looked just like… No, she was mistaken. They wouldn't have the nerve to be here.

Kris embraced Ahmed in a chest bumping, back-slapping, sort of a hug and his wife, Lana, cooed over

Athena's dress. She asked to hold the belt and couldn't help but stroke Athena's out of control blonde curls.

'Barkeep,' called Ahmed, over the hubbub. 'Two pints of soda water my good man and another glass of bubbly for the champ.'

Athena giggled and pressed her face against Kris's chest. As tough as she was, she adored the safety that she felt in his arms. It was intoxicating. As the merriment continued Athena was bombarded with well wishes and congratulations. Half the boys from the junior ranks had snuck into the pub using fake IDs. They hid behind their pint glasses, drunkenly eyeing up the females from the ladies kickboxing class. Erin popped in to hug Athena and buy her a drink before disappearing back home with a regretful look on her face. Stevie caved to Charlie's pleas and their two-man conga line performed circles around Luke's decks. It felt as if every person in the place had shaken Athena's hand and asked her to pose for a photograph.

'I wish Simba were here,' Athena said when she and Kris had finally been left alone for a moment.

Kris held her and sighed. 'Me too.'

They were quiet for a moment, allowing the feeling of mourning to punctuate the celebration.

'Can you imagine?' asked Kris. 'The big fur ball would be the centre of attention. He'd be bouncing about with Luke and everyone in here would want to give him a stroke.'

'He'd love it,' said Athena, her smile slipping from her face for the first time that evening. 'He'd be in his element.'

Kris drained his pint and placed the glass on the bar. 'Want to get out of here?'

Athena ran her fingers down his t-shirt and tucked her thumb under the waistband of Kris's jeans. She pulled him to her so that they were pressed together from chest to groin.

'I'd like nothing better,' she answered with a deep sigh.

'I'll call us a taxi,' said Kris. 'I'm not having you walk up the bank in your ridiculous heels.'

Athena playfully punched him on the arm. 'If I've told you once, I've told you a thousand times. Don't diss the heels.'

Kris squatted to the floor and a cheeky smile stretched across his face. 'Sorry, heels,' he said to her feet.

'Here, hold this,' said Athena, removing the belt from her shoulder and placing it over Kris's. 'I'll nip to the loo while you call a taxi.'

Kris patted the belt. 'Does it suit me?'

'Nice try. You can get your own.'

Athena pushed her way through to the toilets at the back of Low Lights Tavern. She thought being a mixed martial arts champion would mean that people instinctively got out of your way, but alas they did not. Perhaps that only worked if you were male and over five foot four?

She entered the ladies and took one of the tiny cubicles. It was quieter in the toilets. She could still make out the dreadful bass of whatever nineties power ballad Luke was playing and there was a general level of din from the bar. But back here Athena had room to breathe and a moment to gather her thoughts.

Athena's hands fidgeted in her lap as she relieved herself. She was taking Kris Kava - sweet, handsome Kris Kava - back to her home. Not as a friend as she had done many times before, but as something more. Athena smoothed her dress down as she stood up and it occurred to her that she was actually nervous. She'd had her fair share of nerves when she was waiting for her fight but these nerves were unprecedented. These were the sort of nerves that made great orange and black monarch butterflies perform gymnastics in your stomach. The sort of nerves that made strong, independent women giggle and flutter their eyelashes like lovestruck teenagers.

Athena slapped herself on the forehead and told herself to *keep it together for goodness sake*. She unlocked the door and washed her hands in the little, cracked sink, dried her hands on a paper towel and checked her reflection. Athena's eyes ran over her fat lip, black eye and frizzy hair. She was a mess. A bruised and blushing mess.

A sixth sense honed from years of martial arts registered movement behind her. A distorted shadow moved on the back wall. Someone was lurking in the entrance to the toilets.

- CHAPTER 36 -

Athena spun around. Her hands grasped the edge of the sink and the cool porcelain pressed into her lower back.

'You,' she said. Her voice cracking.

'Me,' replied the Antiques Roadshow watching, quiet church mouse, Alan Sherwood. He took a step out of the shadows. 'I hear congratulations are in order.'

Athena swallowed - it was painful - she must have been punched or elbowed in the throat at some point. 'I solved the code. I can read Molly's diary.'

Alan Sherwood removed his glasses and tucked them into the breast pocket of his shirt. He looked as immaculate as when Athena had first seen him but his posture was more confident: shoulders pulled back, his chin raised. 'Yes,' he said. 'Elizabeth told me.'

Athena's nails started to crack against the sink.

'I'm most intrigued, Athena,' he continued, pushing his fingers into a pyramid beneath his chin. 'Aren't you going to share what young Molly had to say?'

Athena straightened up and slipped out of her heels. The cold, dirty floor barely registered on the soles of her feet.

'It's quite the story.' Her voice quivered as she spoke and goosebumps spread up her forearms.

The corner of Alan's mouth twitched. 'I like stories,' he replied.

'Well then,' started Athena, 'once upon a time, there was a woman called Vivian Fox and a man named Ali Montgomery. Vivian Fox was a great poker player, so great in fact, that she won twenty-six grand in a single night.'

Alan held her gaze and took a step towards Athena.

'Most of that money she won from Montgomery. He was the big man of the casino and Vivian humiliated him.'

Athena's left hand balled into a fist and her short fingernails dug into her palm.

‘But Montgomery was cunning. He was tall and handsome, and charming. Montgomery seduced Vivian and while she slept he emptied her purse of the winnings and disappeared into the night.'

Athena's voice cracked again and she took a moment to steady herself. She wasn't crying but there was a dampness to her eyes.

'Nine months later,' she continued, 'Molly was born. She grew up and tracked down her father. Turns out stealing from Vivian wasn't the only thieving he'd been up to. Montgomery spent nine months in Durham for armed robbery.'

Alan licked his lips. 'Ooh, I like a plot twist. And how did Molly feel about that?'

Athena glanced around the room. A plastic soap dispenser sat atop the sink. A plastic toilet brush stood in the corner of the cubicle. The bin was small and made of wicker. There were no heavy or sharp objects. The only weapon in the room was her body.

'Molly was devastated. She spent her life wondering if her father was a professor, or a sports star, and he turned out to be a criminal. She panicked. Thought stealing was in her DNA, thought she had bad blood or something.'

'Like father, like daughter,' mused Alan. He took another step towards Athena, standing so close she could feel his breath on her forehead.

Athena's body shook as her right hand balled into a fist, mirroring her left. Adrenaline was holding her body hostage. The hormone triggered a fight, flight or freeze instinct, and right now, Athena was frozen.

'Next thing Molly knew, she was in her bed, disorientated, with her knickers on backwards, and with no memory of the previous day.'

A tear burst from Athena's eye. 'She...' She swallowed and winced at the pain. 'She checked her diary and read how she'd been so lost that she'd turned... Turned to the man whom she wished was her father. And you were more than willing to come over and be a shoulder to cry on. Weren't you?'

Alan nodded slowly, deliberately.

Athena unfroze. Quicker than a striking cobra, she slammed her fist into Alan's face. His head ricocheted back and he stumbled for a moment.

'Not many substances can render you immobile and give you that level of amnesia,' spat Athena. She shook her hand, certain she'd just broken a finger. 'But ketamine will. Won't it, Dr Sherwood, esteemed veterinarian?'

Alan's eyes narrowed. He grabbed Athena around the neck and pushed her against the wall.

Athena kicked out as hard as she could. Her instep met Alan's groin full force and he howled in pain, staggering back as Athena fell to the floor. She scrambled back to her feet, her hands rubbing at her neck.

'RAPIST!' she shrieked.

Alan pulled a syringe from his back pocket. He removed the cover with his teeth and spat it on the floor. Athena made a run for the door but Alan grabbed her arm and swung her around, she hit the wall, grunting with pain and felt the tip of the syringe penetrate her neck.

'She knew no one would believe her. The shoplifter, the girl who got kicked out of school.'

Alan went to punch Athena but she was too fast, he missed and hit the wall, the old plasterwork crumbling as he connected. Athena took the chance to thrust the heel of her hand into his face. He lost focus for less than a second, but it was enough time for Athena to grab his arm in both of her hands. She turned her back to him and tried to toss him over her hips in a judo throw. The room was too small and Athena ended up tossing her attacker on to the sink. It cracked and shattered on the ground beneath them. Athena pulled as hard as she could, throwing her weight away from the sink whilst maintaining a grip on Alan's arm. The syringe was only half emptied, she hadn't received a full dose, but she wouldn't let go of Alan until she had the syringe.

Athena stepped barefoot on to the broken porcelain, she squealed and her feet left a bloody trail but she'd created enough space to complete the throw.

Alan hit the floor with a thud and a bellow of rage. Athena landed on top on him, her full weight crashing into his breastbone, winding him and enraging him in one move. She wrestled the syringe from his sweaty hands but couldn't keep a hold of it. It skidded from her grip and spun on the floor until it came to a stop under a toilet.

Athena dropped her elbow on to Alan's brow bone, once, twice, three times. 'SHE KILLED HERSELF!' she shouted as Alan rolled the pair of them over until he was on top.

Alan may have been on top of her but Athena punched upwards over and over while he tried to pin her in place.

Athena could make out the last few lines of a dance tune sounding from the bar. 'Help,' she tried to call as the song came to an end and there was a lull in the volume. 'HELP.'

Alan grabbed Athena's tiny hands in one of his, pinning them against her chest so she couldn't hit him anymore. Using his free hand he pushed Athena's legs apart.

'No,' she spluttered, kicking her legs about but hitting nothing but broken porcelain.

He began to push her dress up above her waist.

'It's all in the book,' she spat. 'But you knew that. That's why you agreed to meet me. You couldn't leave it alone. You had to find out how much I knew. That's why you broke in and turned my house upside down trying to find it. You wanted to destroy the evidence.'

Athena wiggled and bucked her hips but he was too heavy, she'd never shift him. It was now or never. Athena pulled her knees back as high and as fast as she could. She curled one leg around the back of Alan's neck and secured it with the crook of her other knee.

'She turned to you for…' the word escaped her. Her mind started to feel foggy. 'Help. She turned to you for help.'

Alan sensed danger and tried to stand, but it only increased the pressure on his neck and he found himself pulled back down. His eyes began to bulge.

'How does it feel, A—?' *What was his name again?* 'To have someone impose their will on you for a change?'

Alan grunted and hit Athena in the face. Hard. It only deepened Athena's resolve. Fighting was what she did every day. She was used to pain, used to blood. It was a feeling she welcomed as an old friend. Granted, this was a man - not a tall man - but he was heavy and his punch felt like a hammer. There was no referee to step in and save her.

Athena squeezed her legs around Alan's neck with all her might and felt her nose break as another punch thundered down on to her. She squeezed harder but her legs felt as if they no longer belonged to her. The floor was slippery with blood as Athena tried to push her hips to the right. It took a few attempts but finally, she got the angle just right. *Concentrate*, she told herself as the drug started to take effect. Blood was cut off from Alan's brain and without oxygen his eyes closed, his head lolled down and he slipped into unconsciousness.

His body weighed on Athena's. She gritted her teeth and pushed his dead weight off her. Like a possessed predator she stalked to the corner of the room and picked up a shard of porcelain. It was as pointed as a knife. She stood over his sleeping body, her legs wobbling beneath her. She needed to act fast, he would wake up now that oxygen was flowing freely again. The shard dangled over his groin. *Do it*, she thought. *He deserves it.*

Athena knelt in the pool of blood and pushed Alan's floppy legs apart. She rested the pointed edge of the porcelain over the zip of his jeans. *For Molly*, she thought. She pressed down, feeling the point begin to penetrate the denim fabric, thread by thread. *And for Simba.*

There was a knock on the door to the toilets. 'Foxy, are you— Oh my God. Foxy!'

Kris ran towards her and sank to his knees. Ahmed peered in behind him and taking in the blood-soaked scene he bellowed for Luke. Kris's face was white as a sheet as he pried the shard from her hands and tossed it away. He took Athena's hands in his and pulled her to her feet. 'What's going on? Who is that?'

Athena frowned. *Who was that? What was his name, again?* 'Sher—' she whispered. 'Al Sher. He's... he's the reason...' Her mouth couldn't form the words she had in her head. 'Molly. He…Simba. Sick... a sick fucking r...'

Kris's jaw twitched. 'And he came after you?'

'Diary… Worked it out.'

Athena felt numb. It was all too much. She was light headed and the room was starting to spin.

'I shouldn't have left you alone,' Kris said, his hands shaking against Athena's cheeks. 'I'm sorry, I so sorry. What did he give you? Foxy, stay awake. What did he give you? Come on, talk to me.'

Luke squeezed his way into the tiny bathroom. 'What the actual— Foxy? Shit.'

Athena shook her head and wobbled. 'K-Ket,' she stuttered. Her eyes focused on a large chunk of porcelain sticking out of her her thigh. 'Kris. Bleeding.' A dribble of bright red blood was snaking down her leg. She pulled the porcelain from her skin, uncorking the puncture wound.

Blood streamed uncontrollably from the gaping hole and pooled around her feet. Athena's legs gave way and Luke caught her before she could hit the floor. He clamped one of his shovel-like hands over the wound.

Ahmed took out his phone. 'I'll get an ambulance,' he said, 'and the police.'

There was a moan and a stirring from the ground as Alan Sherwood woke up and looked up into the faces of four professional fighters.

- CHAPTER 37 -

The Northumbria Specialist Emergency Care Hospital was a twenty-minute drive north of Shields but Ahmed covered the distance in an impressive thirteen minutes. He had no intention of waiting half an hour for the next available ambulance.

When Athena awoke in the early hours, she didn't have the strength to open her eyes. Her mouth was parched and every part of her body ached. She could hear the rhythmic beeping of a heart monitor, feet pacing back and forth, and roof-raising snores.

'She's stirring.'

'Kris?'

'I'm here,' she heard him answer and there was a reassuring squeeze of her hand as she found the strength to open her eyes.

Athena recoiled at the brightness of the room and pulled a hand over her face.

'I'll dim the lights,' said a blonde woman in scrubs with a Northern Irish accent. 'You'll be sensitive to lights for a while I'm afraid, Athena. A common side effect of ketamine.'

Athena blinked a few times, even with the lights dimmed, she felt like she needed sunglasses. 'It hurts,' she managed to say, her other hand reaching for her chest.

Memories began to filter back to her but they were jumbled. Sherwood. She could remember Sherwood, could remember hitting him over and over, could remember the look on that bastard's face. The heart rate monitor began to beep faster and faster.

The nurse pressed a button and Athena followed her eyes to the morphine drip. Athena winced, leant over and snatched the button from the nurse. She'd pressed it twice more before the nurse could take it from her and place it out of Athena's reach. She scowled but the nurse would not back down. Lying back in the bed she listened to the slowing of her heart rate and began to take in her surroundings. The nurse stood on one side of the bed and Kris stood on the other. Beside the window, three chairs were filled by Charlie, Luke and Ahmed. Charlie had his head in his hands, he appeared to be shaking and a bucket had been placed on the floor next to him. Luke was asleep, his head was tilted back and his snores were earning him disgruntled elbows in the ribs from Charlie.

Ahmed caught Athena's eye. 'Good to see you awake, champ.'

Athena tried to smile but her cheeks were too sore and she could feel a tooth wobble as her tongue pressed against it. 'If fighting doesn't work out,' she said with a grimace, 'you should look at a career in motor racing.'

Ahmed adjusted himself in his seat. 'I think that drug messed with your head, Foxy. I obeyed the speed limit at all times.'

Ahmed's eyes darted to the door where Sergeant Myers and Constable Keaton stood with notepads in hand.

Keaton gave Ahmed a meaningful look. 'I'm certain you did, Mr Bitar.'

Myers moved bedside, his icy eyes showing no emotion. 'May we ask you some questions, Ms Fox?'

The nurse folded her arms over her chest and pursed her lips. 'This should really wait until the morning, Sergeant.'

'We'll only be a few minutes,' answered Myers, his voice stern and monotone.

'Make sure you are,' interrupted Kris. 'She needs her sleep.'

Keaton approached and placed a delicate hand on Athena's shoulder. 'Say the word and we'll be out of your hair,' she said in her soft Geordie accent. 'Alan Sherwood is currently in surgery. We want to assure you that officers are stationed outside his door and at the entrance to the hospital. He won't be paying you a visit, nor will he be in any state to make a run for it.'

'Surgery?' asked Athena. She tried to think back. She'd choked him unconscious, she could remember that much. She'd punched him, and elbowed him too. She'd had the shard of porcelain in her hand. She'd wanted to stab him, but Kris had stopped her, hadn't he?

'Er, yes,' said Ahmed. 'After that sick fucker woke up and Kris dragged you out of there, the bastard, erm, well he stood up too quickly and he must have fainted.'

'Rotten luck,' said Charlie, looking up with bloodshot eyes and speckles of vomit in his beard. 'You should never stand up too quickly after being choked out.'

Keaton tapped her notepad with her pen. 'Yes, rotten luck,' she said dryly, a slight curl to her lips. 'Mr Sherwood appears to have suffered the worst fainting episode I've ever heard of. He seems to have broken his jaw, knocked his own teeth out, broken a few ribs, given himself two black eyes and a broken nose.'

'Terribly bad luck,' echoed Myers, with one grey eyebrow raised. 'He broke one of his ribs so hard he punctured his own lung.'

Athena swallowed and looked at Ahmed and Luke with gratitude. She nodded at Keaton. 'Must have been an awfully awkward fall,' she said innocently.

'Mr Sherwood may remember it differently,' said Keaton. 'But—'

'But nee one's gonna believe a word that sick rapist says,' finished Charlie. 'Trust our Foxy to stop the strawweight champ and catch the Tyneside prowler in a single night.'

'The Prowler?'

Athena tried to sit up but Kris eased her back down on to the bed.

'Sherwood's the Tyneside Prowler?'

Keaton shifted her weight. 'We don't know anything for certain—'

'I knew the second you told me it was ketamine that he'd stabbed you with,' said Kris. 'All the reports said the women had either been injected with something or had had their drinks spiked. And that last woman, the one who spoke out, gave up her anonymity, she was studying veterinary medicine. I'd bet my right arm she'd been on placement at Sherwood's practice.'

'Unbelievable,' snorted Charlie. 'The collective powers of the Northumberland constabulary couldn't track this sicko down. It took young Foxy almost bleeding to death to nab him, and even then it's only 'cause Kris put two and two together. If yee lot had done your jobs properly—'

'That's enough, Mr Fisher,' said Keaton, stopping Charlie in his tracks.

Ahmed patted Charlie on the back. 'She's going to be fine, big man.'

'I was so sure it was Monty,' said Athena, her mind turning back to the night of Simba's death.

Kris handed her a cup of water and supported her shaking hands as she drank. 'Monty called while you were in theatre. He'd turned up at Low Lights about twenty minutes after we left. Wanted to know what the hell was going on and if you were all right. I grilled him but I'm pretty sure that leopard's changed his spots since he was a youngster. Seems squeaky clean. Told me he was audited last year and was actually due a rebate.'

Athena laced her fingers into Kris's. She never wanted to let go again. 'But the Pasternaks?' she asked. 'The fire?'

'Slippery eels, those Pasternaks,' said Myers. 'Running an extortion racket when they're not even meant to be in the country.'

'Yeah and if someone was doing their job—'

'I won't warn you again, Mr Fisher.' Keaton folded her arms and waited for Charlie to slump back into his seat.

'The Black Bull fire? Was that their work?' asked Kris.

Athena's tongue kept returning to her wobbly tooth. 'So… What are you saying? That Monty wouldn't pay protection money so they torched his house?'

'We're still waiting on forensics,' said Keaton, 'but the investigation is ongoing. Now, I don't want to keep you much longer, Athena, but we do need to go over the events of this evening.'

For the next half hour, Athena described Molly's diary and told Keaton where she'd be able to find it and how to solve the code. She cried while she explained what she'd read in there; the horror of reading the details of what happened to her sister was still raw. When she moved on to the break-in and explained how Simba's murder had all been Alan Sherwood's attempt to get the diary back, Athena began to hyperventilate.

'OK that's enough,' said the nurse. She shuffled around the bed, opened the door and extended her arm. 'I really must insist now.'

Myers shut his notepad and nodded. 'OK, fair enough. Constable Keaton will be back in the morning. The rest of you will need to drop by the station and give full statements tomorrow.'

Athena thanked Myers and Keaton as the nurse rounded on Charlie, Ahmed, Luke and Kris.

'That goes for you four as well. Time to leave.'

'Kris stays,' said Athena. She gripped his hand tighter and felt the drip pinch in her vein. 'Non-negotiable.'

The nurse sucked her lips in for a few seconds, she was literally biting her tongue. 'Fine,' she sighed. 'He can stay, but the rest of you need to go. Visiting hours… Well visiting hours had ended before you even got here so—'

'Easy lass, we know when we're not wanted.' Charlie heaved himself to his feet and ran a hand over his bald head and through his beard. 'Urgh. It tastes like something crawled into my mouth and died.'

The nurse wrinkled her nose.

'Come on big lad,' said Charlie, as he and Ahmed pulled Luke to his feet. 'Time for bed.'

Luke spluttered back to consciousness and waved his arms around in protest. 'All right, all right, I'm up OK?' he blinked his chocolate eyes and pointed at Athena. 'You're a badass, champ. Always said you were a little psycho.'

Athena managed half a smile but her eyelids were fighting to stay open. She brought her hand to her forehead and saluted him. 'I learned from the best.'

Luke came bedside and kissed Athena on the forehead. 'You'll be back in the gym next week. Bet ya a tenner.'

Athena took a long blink and felt Ahmed lift her hand and kiss the back of it, just above where her drip was attached. 'Sleep well, champ.'

'I forgot,' sighed Athena sleepily. 'How's Jimmy? Poor guy. Did anyone check on him?'

Charlie huffed. 'Divint gan feeling sorry for that traitor.'

Athena's eyes popped back open and she pushed herself higher up the bed. The simple movement made her head pound. 'What happened?'

'That git's been feeding intel to the southerners all camp,' said Charlie, raking his fingers through the hair on his arms. 'Sold you out to pay for his divorce. 'Fessed up when he was pumped to the eyeballs with painkillers.'

'Filthy ginger snake,' said Ahmed, leaning into the door frame. 'He told them your strengths, your weaknesses, even your bloody run times. He's the one who leaked the CCTV footage.'

'What?' snapped Athena, slamming her palms on the white bed sheets. She pulled the sheets from her body, exposing not only the backless, floral hospital gown she was wearing but also her battered body. 'Judas!' she spat. 'Wait till I get my hands on his treacherous—'

Four firm hands pushed her back down on to the bed.

'Easy,' soothed Charlie. He looked green now. 'Your hands won't be going anywhere near him. None of ours will,' he added in a warning tone. 'No gym's gonna take on a dirty rat bastard like him now that little nugget's out in the open. That'll be punishment enough. Now on a happier note,' he picked up his bucket and handed it to the nurse. 'Take care of that, won't you? What? You look like you've never seen Guinness and Champagne in the same puke bucket. Anyhow, Foxy, I got a call from a scout while I was mid-conga. There's some young lass in the UFC who needs sparring partners for her next fight, Ruby Martinez I think he said. Her camp's looking for strawweight women to fly out to New Mexico next month. Could be a good opportunity.'

It may have been the morphine but a warm feeling was spreading out across Athena's chest.

'Charlie! She's just been attacked for Christ's sake,' said Kris. 'She almost bled out.'

'So she'll probably want to get away from Shields for a while,' answered Charlie.

'It was just a scratch.' Athena smiled, her eyes now closed. 'Isn't that right, nurse?'

Athena heard the nurse's footsteps as she ushered Charlie, Luke and Ahmed from the room and felt a cool draft as the door clicked closed.

'Well, Doctor Moore said the wound to your leg is clean. He's confident it'll heal nicely, you should have a speedy recovery there. Your nose should be fine within a fortnight but you've also sustained fractures to a couple of fingers which will need at least four to six weeks before you can hit anything without gloves.'

As the safe comfort of sleep drew Athena in she managed to pull Kris's face to hers and relished the feeling of his stubble against her cheek. 'I'm going to New Mexico,' she whispered.

Kris swallowed.

'And you're coming with me,' she added. 'Don't even think about saying no.'

- EPILOGUE -

Dearest Harry,

I'm sorry I haven't written sooner. I've been so busy unpacking after we moved. I was ecstatic to hear that the council have found you permanent accommodation. It must be such a relief. I shed a tear when I saw the photos you sent, you look completely different with short hair! Bring back the beard though. Your face looks naked without it. It's great that you made contact with your son again. I hope to hear all about your reunion dinner in your next letter.

Kris and I are loving life here in New Mexico. The training's hard but it's rewarding. It's a little odd having to look out for rattlesnakes when you go for a morning run through the mountains though. The most I had to watch out for when running in Shields was dog mess and hungry seagulls.

I signed my contract yesterday. I can't believe the UFC have booked me for three fights. Things are looking up! Kris is signed to another promotion and he's fighting some Brazilian next week. It'll be streamed on the internet so keep an eye out for it OK? He's really popular at our gym, everyone wants to be his sparring partner. They call him The Polish Assassin.

I miss home and the guys from the gym, but I'm missing Simba the most. I still find it hard to go running without him. Oh, and guess what? I don't know if it's the altitude and this mountain air but I haven't had a smoke or a drink in six weeks. Well, I had a glass of Champagne when Ruby Martinez, won her fight. But Champagne doesn't count, does it?

I had to testify against Alan Sherwood via video link. I'm sure you heard. It's hard to put it all from my mind but it is getting easier now I know he's off the streets. I get the feeling he'll be in for some karma now he's holed up in Durham, or here's hoping. Anyway, I'd best be off, training starts in twenty minutes but I wanted to let you know that I'm thinking of you. Take care, Harry, and stay in touch.

Athena

▩▩✖▲○●○✖△✖✖▲✕□◉△✗◉△✖✕

- MESSAGE FROM THE AUTHOR -

As a debut author I would like to thank you for reading my work. If you have enjoyed The Only Weapon In The Room, I would sincerely appreciate it if you could take the time to leave a review. It would mean a great deal to me.

Thank you to Amanda, your unwavering enthusiasm for this story has been more help than you could know. Ian, thank you for the valuable feedback and suggestions. You helped me get a second wind and make the changes that needed to be made. And thank yous galore to Mum, the reader of the roughest of rough drafts and the finder of typos.

- STAY IN TOUCH -

Stay up to date with future releases by joining Betsy's mailing list.

https://betsybaskerville.wixsite.com/home

Connect with B. Baskerville online:

Web: https://betsybaskerville.wixsite.com/home
Twitter: @B__Baskerville
Facebook: B Baskerville - Author
Instagram: b_baskerville_author

- ABOUT THE AUTHOR -

Betsy was born and raised in Newcastle Upon Tyne. She describes herself as a crime fiction addict and a UFC geek of epic proportions. It was whilst on a morning jog, the day after watching Holly Holm knock out Ronda Rousey, that the character of Athena Fox was born. The idea was filed away until the following year when Betsy finally put pen to paper and began to map out the narrative of a martial arts star with a healthy dose of Geordie spirit.

When not writing, Betsy loves hiking with her boyfriend and their naughty Welsh terrier.